T0163215

RAISING
THE
BATON

RAISING THE BATON

in the lives and times of...
CHRISTOPHER STRAW, ANNA LANE,
and RAJ BHAVNANI

an historical novel by
BRUCE HERSCHENSOHN

**BEAUFORT
BOOKS**

RAISING THE BATON

For inquiries about volume orders, please contact:
Beaufort Books
27 West 20th Street, Suite 1102
New York, NY 10011
sales@beaufortbooks.com

Published in the United States by Beaufort Books
www.beaufortbooks.com

Distributed by Midpoint Trade Books
www.midpointtrade.com

Printed in the United States of America

Hardcover ISBN: 9780825308864
Ebook ISBN: 9780825307744

Book designed by Mark Karis

TABLE OF CONTENTS

NOTES OF THE AUTHOR
TO THE READERS

SOME OF THIS NOVEL IS TRUE, but not all of it. There are fictional and actual characters, dialogues, places, articles and incidents. Much is written with the merger of fictional and actual. In some cases the names of the actual were kept and some have been changed. This book is an interpretive story with importance given to the appropriate sights, sounds, fragrances, tastes and feelings of times passed.

OVERTURE

followed by

THE CURTAINS OPEN

THEME ONE

FIRST THERE WAS NANCY BENFORD

YOUTH COMES TWICE; once as it is lived and again as it is remembered. Although it doesn't seem like it at the time, youth as lived is very brief while youth as remembered can stretch into decades of glancing back at a personal museum invisible to others while it provides a secret foundation to the person's life.

No matter that memories carry the risk of inaccuracy, Christopher Straw was destined to recall his youth with unique precision except for remembering that, at the time, the pre-teen years certainly appeared to be lasting forever.

Summer was having its annual competition with a rising autumn when school started its new semester. Autumn, as usual, would win the rivalry despite any resurgences of a battling summer to retain its presence. There was no question that when the school doors opened it would be the invitation for summer to be strong enough to say goodbye gracefully and stop fighting a losing battle even though summer was likely hiding one more heat wave to come that would have no chance of lasting victory.

Early in that first morning of school's new semester on Monday, September the 11th of 1939, Christopher Straw who had spent seven years on earth, lived through something he had never known in those seven years. It had nothing at all to do with exiting and entering seasons. It had everything to do with Christopher Straw being hurt—over a girl.

It was worse than scraping one knee or his other knee which he seemed to be enduring as habit during his early years of life; maybe once a week or so. This hurt was something different and could not be treated by Mercurochrome or Merthiolate and a Band-Aid. There was no place for him to put those healing products to ease this pain that had no scratch, no wound, no blood, no anything that was easily traceable or treatable.

The hurt came in the voice of a high pitch about the same age as Christopher Straw but not his disposition. She was a girl devoid of hesitancy or subtlety or nuance: "Christopher Straw, you make me sick!"

Nancy Benford said that painful statement with her hands on her hips during the Monday morning playground session of southern Pennsylvania's McConnellsburg Elementary School. As a result of the intensity of her rage along with the increasing intensity of her stomping shoes going up and down in quick succession, her orange freckles seemed to turn darker until they matched the red of her two pig-tailed braids.

While most of the world's attention was riveted on events in Europe since Hitler had invaded Poland ten days earlier, Christopher Straw was oblivious to events beyond his own world and Nancy Benford made it a terrible way for him to begin the semester. Not one person before Nancy Benford had ever said that he made some one sick. In fact from kindergarten all the way through the first grade he had gotten along well with his classmates and this was a girl to whom he had never said one word. He had hardly noticed her.

"Why do I make you sick?" he asked her with genuine curiosity. "I mean I don't know why. I mean I never bothered you or anything. I mean like that. I mean you know."

"That doesn't make any difference! It doesn't make any difference that you don't know why! Oh, you make me so sick!" Then she said a word he had never heard before: "Eewwwch!" The last part of the word was said with a growling in the back of her throat. She twirled around, her petticoats making a snapping crinkly noise beneath her white skirt attached by a thin black belt to her white blouse that had little sewn replicas of blue flying birds on it. Then she withdrew her hands from her hips and with arms swinging in soldier-like exactness under a dictatorship, she walked away from him with head-up determination. As she walked in such triumph and authority he thought he heard her say to no one at all, "Oh, he makes me so sick!"

His hearing was fine. There was no ear error; this was not a hearing problem but a saying problem. But why should such a thing be said or even thought of being said about him of all people?

Christopher Straw was convinced that God was late leaving from His summer vacation or He would have been back to His prime job of fixing things, among them stopping Nancy Benford from being such a jerk.

Although Christopher Straw didn't know the reason for her anger; what he did know was that whether or not he made her sick, she was, for sure, beginning to make *him* sick.

It was going to get worse.

Since this day ushered in the new semester, his entire class was assigned a different classroom than it had last semester. Christopher Straw came into Mrs. Zambroski's second-story classroom a little ahead of most of the others so he could take a seat which would be kept as "his seat" throughout the coming four and one-half months. The seat he selected was not in the front of the room where the smarty-pants sat with their hands signaling in the air so as to be seen and called on by the teacher, and not in the back of the room where the dummies chose those seats to launch spit-balls at whoever may be their target.

The classroom had wooden seats that were each attached to their desks in single-file rows with desks providing the back of the seat of the student in front of that desk, with each row having eight desk-seats from the front of the classroom to the back of the classroom. That meant that students had to slide into and out of their seats because there was no way to move the seats backward or forward for rising and sitting without affecting the entire connected row. Christopher Straw was delighted with his chosen seat in the middle of the class, sitting in a place where he could remain nearly unnoticed. Perfect. Almost.

It was perfect until the emergence into the classroom with a group of others came Nancy Benford and without looking around—or at least Christopher Straw didn't see her looking around—she selected the seat right in front of his desk meaning the back of her head would be in his constant straight line of sight, like it or not, and how could any sane boy like it for a moment to say nothing of a full semester?

Christopher Straw was a well groomed blond-haired boy

and on this day he was wearing knickers and a blue and white horizontally striped polo-shirt. He was the only child of Lewis and Millie Straw in Fort Littleton, Pennsylvania some nine miles north of school. When the United States became a nation, Fort Littleton was a real fort, and now it was a community with little more than one street of residences, with that street surrounded by farms and vacant lots. Fort Littleton was truly a community where everyone knew everyone. That was because no matter where they were in Fort Littleton everyone could see everyone else in a single sweep of eyesight while standing still.

With arrogance, Nancy Benford did not live in Fort Littleton, but right in the cosmopolitan life of McConnellsburg. Why that gave her arrogance was a mystery but probably because she thought McConnellsburg was better than anywhere else her classmates could be living and laughingly better than Fort Littleton.

The bell rang for the class to begin and Mrs. Zambroski called the class to order and then she led them in the Pledge of Allegiance to the flag of the United States and on the word "flag" they extended their right arms with their right hands facing upwards. After the pledge, everyone slid back into their seats and as soon as Nancy Benford was seated she used both hands to adjust her pig-tailed braids to assure they would land right on the desk behind her, and they did exactly that, antagonizing its targeted occupant: Christopher Straw.

Mrs. Zambroski wrote the name "Mrs. Zambroski" in perfect penmanship on the blackboard, pressing unnaturally hard which sent white dust from the chalk all over the place. She then faced the class and said, "My name is Mrs. Zambroski." That made sense since that was what she wrote. What she didn't write was that she was very fat and that she was also built abnormally like an upside down pyramid getting wider as her body progressed upward with her shoulders taking a tremendous amount of width providing a pedestal for an out of proportion amazingly small head.

"And who would like to be blackboard-eraser monitor?" she asked in reference to the person who would beat the erasers out the second story window against the exterior brick wall of the building when class was done. Immediately almost every boy sitting in the front rows raised their right arms with their hands extended, some of them even waving to her to catch her attention. There were repeated quick grunts of one boy who could not hide his enthusiasm for such a prospective prestigious position as blackboard-eraser monitor. And from another boy came a soft "Here!" and then another "Here!" Mrs. Zambroski pointed to one boy who was excitingly waving his hand but hadn't made any noise. She smiled at him and asked him, "And what's your name?"

"Ralph Dorgan, Mrs. Zambroski."

She nodded and then she scanned the class as she said, "Ralph Dorgan is our blackboard-eraser monitor" as though she was announcing the winner of the Nobel Peace Prize. A few of the losers groaned in their defeat.

She nodded and said, "We only need one." It was a justification for making her choice. "And now I would like to know all of your names. Let's start at this row, working up and then down the next row, up the next one, and so on and so on. And one other thing I want to know is what you want to be when you grow up." There were a few "Wwww's!"

Some girls wanted to be a dancer or a singer or a movie actress or a nurse and some boys wanted to be a fireman or a baseball player or a cowboy and one wanted to be an Indian; an ambition which was not too likely for him to achieve.

The row in which Christopher Straw sat was now being called by Mrs. Zambroski at the front of the room pointing at the rear of that row for its start and working its way toward him. When it came to be his turn he said nothing. Mrs. Zambroski squinted her eyes at him. "Young man?"

He nodded. "My name is Christopher Straw and when I grow up I want to be the first man on the moon."

Nancy Benford didn't turn around to watch him give that answer, but she did spurt out a short ridiculing laugh as though that eruption of hers was involuntary and could not have been prevented.

"No, no," Mrs. Zambroski responded to Nancy Benford's laugh and then Mrs. Zambroski looked at Christopher Straw. "That's very admirable, Christopher. Doing what no one has ever done is admirable. But just how do you plan on getting to the moon?"

He answered quickly, proving he had given his ambition serious thought. "With a Chevrolet. A green one."

Nancy blurted out another laugh despite Mrs. Zambroski's having called her down on her previous laugh. This time Mrs. Zambroski gave a smile herself. "A green Chevrolet?"

"Yes." There was a period of silence, and so Christopher Straw nodded and repeated, "A Chevrolet. A green one."

"Why green?"

"Because that's what it should be."

"Is that your common sense at work or your rich imagination?"

"Which one's better, Mrs. Zambroski?"

"In your case, Christopher, I would say your imagination."

"Then I would be on my way to the moon!"

"But, Christopher, you know that the world is round, don't you?"

He nodded. "Christopher Columbus discovered that. He told everyone that."

"But that was Christopher *Columbus* and Christopher *Straw* might have missed the importance of that discovery and what it would mean to any attempt to drive to the moon even if it was his car and was any color and there was a *road* to the moon," Mrs. Zambroski said and she looked very proud of herself. Too bad her quick response was wasted on a bunch of kids who couldn't know how clever she was by comparing the two Christophers. It was such a glorious extemporaneous statement. And then, in a revelation of her magnanimous dismissal of her skillful previous response, she added, "A Chevrolet goes on the surface of the earth—straight ahead. Won't it just go on and over the land until it reaches the sea? How can you take it up to the moon while going around the world and hitting the sea?"

"No. I mean you have to aim at the moon, maybe from the Chevrolet tilted up on a hill and then aimed right at the moon and go real fast."

"Well then," and she couldn't contain herself any longer from dwelling back on her earlier moment of quick-thinking accomplishment. "Christopher *Columbus* and Christopher *Straw*! Well, who knows? Two Christophers!" Then she finally felt obligated to disregard her magnificent cleverness as though she was used to being an ingenious quick-thinker. "But is there anything you want to do here on earth, Christopher?"

"No."

"Alright. Alright. And you, young lady?" She gave a slight

nod to Nancy Benford.

In a move that was unprecedented in these testimonies, rather than talking from her seat, Nancy Benford slid out of it and stood up, facing some of her classmates sitting behind her. "I'm Nancy Benford." Then she turned herself to face Mrs. Zambroski. "And I want to be a great teacher like you, Mrs. Zambroski." Then she smiled and sat back down.

Christopher Straw murmured under his breath, only loud enough for Nancy Benford to hear, "What a kiss-up!"

In response Nancy Benford brushed her pig-tailed braids behind her so they went backwards onto his desk.

Mrs. Zambroski was beaming. "Thank you, Nancy. And I'm sure you will be a great teacher."

Christopher Straw whispered an embellishment to his earlier statement. "A very, very big kiss-up! Like the biggest kiss-up in the whole wide world!"

As other students gave their names and ambitions, Christopher Straw noticed that on the upper right of each desk in this classroom was an inkwell, each one mounted in a hole in the desk, and each inkwell had a shiny near-round metal lid with one flat hinged edge. Each student would be able to open the hinged metal lid to dip the student's pen in the well's ink, and then quickly close the lid so the ink still in the well wouldn't dry.

This presented an opportunity to Christopher Straw: there was the inkwell and there were the pig-tailed braids of Nancy Benford. The pig-tail on the right side of her head was in close range to the ink-well. He opened his inkwell and he very carefully took the end of Nancy Benford's right side pig-tailed braid and the rest of his activity was easy. It was fun. Her pig-tail went in quite far as he stuffed it in further and further little by little.

She didn't know it for a long while but, of course, when the school-bell rang for recess to begin she got up, and as she reached to swish her braids from behind her to be in front of her, the realization came on her right hand. The palm of her hand was covered with a gooey black mess. This automatically set her off as she screamed and cried right in front of everyone as they were leaving class and now the ink from her pig-tail was getting on the front of her frilly white blouse that had those annoying little blue sewn replicas of flying birds on it. She made so much noise that Mrs. Zambroski stormed through the rows of desks straight to the scene of the crime where both victim and likely suspect had yet to leave.

"What's going on here!?" she demanded to know as she looked back and forth from Nancy Benford to Christopher Straw. "What's going on here!? Huh? Huh? Huh? Huh?"

"Looooooook!!" Nancy said. "Looooooook, Mrs. Zambroski!" She motioned her head toward the evidence.

Christopher Straw whispered, "Tattle-tale."

Mrs. Zambroski glared at him. "Did you do that? Answer me, young man, did you do that?"

"No, Mrs. Zambroski," he lied. "Her hair-things are real long and one just must have fallen in the inkwell. It can do that real good." And then he corrected himself. "It can do that real good, Mrs. Zambroski." He thought that adding her name at this moment was a sign of respect, certain to influence her generosity of attitude.

"Are you lying to me?"

"No, Mrs. Zambroski. It just must have fallen in the inkwell. My inkwell is sort of broke because it's hard to close."

Mrs. Zambroski inspected his inkwell by quickly opening

and closing it a number of times. Unfortunately, his lie was not well prepared. The inkwell was not at all hard to close.

After Mrs. Zambroski regained her composure well enough to be a real teacher, she told him the story of George Washington chopping down his father's cherry tree and then admitting his misdeed to his father, saying "Father, I cannot tell a lie."

She told him about this right in front of Nancy Benford who had a look of victory on her face. Even her freckles were looking victorious.

"Now," Mrs. Zambroski asked Christopher Straw, "Are you George Washington or are you a coward?"

"Neither, Mrs. Zambroski."

"What do you mean, 'neither,' young man?"

He thought fast. "I don't know." Good thinking.

"You don't know?"

"I'm not sure, and I want to tell the truth, so I can't say either one." Very good thinking.

She didn't know what he was talking about and neither did he. "Think," she said. "Don't rush to answer. Patience is a virtue." What a quick mind to drag that one up. "Think. Then answer me. Truth, you should know, is stranger than fiction." She had so many great pieces of wisdom packed into her mind.

He hesitated and then said, "I'm more like George Washington."

"Christopher Straw! Christopher Straw! I'll remember that name, young man! And you—" she pointed to Nancy Benford, "Let's you and me go to the Girl's Room and I will wash that mess of ink out of your hair!—you poor thing!"

Through her weeping noises Nancy Benford managed to say, "Thank you, Mrs. Zambroski!"

Finally Christopher Straw was allowed to leave for recess and he was so glad to get out of there without going to prison that he ran out passing the now-open classroom door, down the hall, downstairs and out the school-door to the playground along with the other kids who were screaming in delight and he was yelling the melodious statement, "Schools Out! School's Out! Teacher Let the Monkey's Out!" Then he felt embarrassed because Nancy Benford holding Mrs. Zambroski's hand was out there and they probably saw and heard him and he saw Nancy Benford shake her head in absolute disgust.

As the semester went on and eventually came to its end, and then when more semesters came and went from current to past, what bothered him most about Nancy Benford was that she was beginning to look pretty, and then prettier and prettier. She stopped wearing those pig-tailed braids. Instead she wore her long blazing red hair down to her shoulders and beyond.

And she didn't say he made her sick anymore; she just ignored him which was worse to him than hearing her say that he made her sick. That's when he learned it would be better for a pretty girl to hate him without reason rather than offering him indifference. When she said he made her sick at least he was important to her. This new indifference meant he was not even in her thoughts at all.

He began to like Nancy Benford in a strange kind of way.

A lot.

Pretty girl. Really pretty.

Life takes incredible turns.

But no matter how intoxicating she became, he couldn't help but wish he had put both of her pig-tails in the ink.

THEME TWO

THEN THERE WAS MISS OSBORN

LIKE MOST OF THOSE HIS AGE, Christopher Straw ran with his arms flailing beside him while older people were satisfied walking at a reasonable pace; even a stroll and some even slower than a stroll and with little arm movement. But Christopher Straw was much too new to the world for all of that slow stuff. He would soon be in such a hurry that it could appear that a band of armed assailants were chasing him. But since no one was chasing him, Christopher Straw's youth was often a goldmine of adventure. Unlike new things that hurt, like that terrible day when Nancy Benford had told him she hated him, he ran for the same reason that most of his age ran; to see all those things that could be seen while the sun was up—and that was because everything was so brand new. The regular taller humans had probably seen those things hundreds of times, maybe thousands of times, but Christopher Straw could see new things with almost every glance, and beyond that he could also smell new things and hear new things and taste new things and touch new things with little if any difficulty.

There was the thrill of walking in a small vacant lot which was perceived at the time to be a giant field or maybe it even looked like a forest that could be explored like a pioneer, and above it a deep blue sky with the emerging heaviness of gray on the horizon and the scent of a coming rain and the thrill of seeing birds who knew for sure that the rain was coming and so they would fly in magnificent formations and there was the chirping of a foreign-sounding melody being sung to other birds to tell them about something probably other than weather.

And there were the inventions of Man that seemed to have passed by the attention of taller generations. There was the taste of the small candy confections that were called Sen-Sen; tiny black licorice squares that came to the extended hand through a hole in a match-box-sized red cardboard box. Those miniature boxes were easy to hide because of their Lilliputian size. The Sen-Sen's from within them were intriguingly spicy-hot which appeared to be made for older people but he, somehow, had been granted a preview of what he would be able to taste in years to come.

And there was learning about competition because without such a small box and without the name of Sen-Sen's, here were small round and red cinnamon candies that were not real Sen-Sen's but gave a somewhat similar taste—not really the same and not as easy to hide but were eatable.

And there was the feel of the back of a frog that was hoped would become a friend, but no luck because it would quickly jump away out of fear of Christopher Straw's exploring hand. Frogs did not have the same appreciation of newness as did small human beings.

When winter came there was the excitement of snowflakes falling all over the ground and making a thin white blanket on every parallel horizontal tree-branch and there was the ability to make and throw snowballs. How could anyone be content with staying inside with outside having such a variety of sight and feel?

Seasons known before then came back, one after the other just like last year. There was an unexpected rhythm to most of this. Disinterest in repetition was not yet an issue in life because at that age there was so little of it. The few repeats encountered were welcome to Christopher Straw because he was proud that he had now lived long enough to be aware of reappearance.

One of the particularly pleasant additions to his life came two years later when he entered the grade of 4-B. It was his teacher, Miss Osborn, in 4-B's September and she was, to him, newer than anything else so far this semester. She touched something inside of him similar to, but even better than how he felt when he first noticed that Nancy Benford was getting pretty. How many more incidents would be there to bring about more of that feeling inside of him? Does each incident get better than the preceding one? When do you just blow up, and is that the end of you?

He stared at his new teacher throughout September and October and by November he was ready to ask her to marry him. Significantly that was when the leaves of Pennsylvania were golden while others were red, and some of the branches of trees were already barren with mounds of fallen leaves on the sidewalks and yards. Christopher Straw was now nine years old and his Miss Osborn was not anything at all like Mrs. Zambroski. Miss Osborn, he assumed, was some one-hundred-fifty years younger than Mrs. Zambroski (give or take one or two years) and looked something like the movie star, Betty Grable, who he had seen in a movie called "Million Dollar Legs."

Like all teachers, Miss Osborn had no first name. That never bothered Christopher Straw before but now it bothered him a lot. What if she asks him to call her by a first name? Maybe she would make up the name, Beautiful Betty. Then what?

In this new semester and new classroom Nancy Benford did not make the mistake she had made only once before when she had sat in front of Christopher Straw. This time she sat one row to the right of him where her pig-tails were safe. Not that he cared anymore. His interest was neither anger nor lust of Nancy Benford, but instead he was fastened on the dazzling good looks of Miss Osborn.

Beyond her extraordinary prettiness, what added to the delight of having her as his teacher was that she talked with enthusiasm about astronomy and told the class that the next complete solar eclipse would occur in about a year and a half on February the 4th of 1943 and she hoped to go to Japan to witness it because the view there should be excellent. When he rose from his seat and said he would like to go there with her, she laughed and then said she would like to have the entire class go there with her. (As it worked out, of course, neither Miss Osborn nor anyone in her class would make the trip to Japan in 1943 unless one of them would be part of a bombing mission.)

"Christopher, you'll have plenty of opportunities to see solar eclipses in the future! There will be one you can see in Canada in 1945, and since you'll still be in school in 1945, you should probably wait even longer; because even better, you can see one from right here in McConnellsburg in 1954."

"1954!?" he asked with disappointment. Wasn't that number too far ahead to even think about it ever being a real year?

Miss Osborn sensed his depression. "Is that too long for you to wait?" she asked.

"That's forever! How old will I be then?"

"You tell me. How old are you now, Christopher? Eight or nine?"

"Nine! Not eight! Eight was a long time ago! I'm nine!" And then louder he said, "I'm nine!" Of course he repeated it with volume because he wanted her to be sure to know that he had left behind any remnant of his childhood. He was probably close enough in age now for the two of them to get married. "How old are you?"

For a while she was speechless, and then she smiled widely and said, "Christopher, you and every other boy in the room should know that you never ask a lady her age. But that doesn't mean a lady can't ask a boy or a young man his age! Now, you figure out how many years will pass until the year is 1954?"

"Thirteen years!" Miss Know it All, Nancy Benford, the giant of all information and calculations and smartness and authority and pomposity said quickly.

"Very good, Nancy! Now, Christopher, from you: how old will you be in 1954? I don't know the date when the eclipse will be in 1954 but let's assume it will be exactly thirteen years from today. How old will you be then?"

He started counting on his fingers by spreading out his hands on his desk, whispering each number as he progressed from his right to his left hand, but not fast enough to shut up Nancy, who said in a soft voice but loud enough to be heard, "Twenty-two."

"Shhh!" Miss Osborn said. "No, Nancy. I want Christopher to do it."

He continued to look down at his spread-out hands and nodded. "I was just going to say 'twenty-two,' Miss Osborn. Twenty-two. It's twenty-two."

Miss Osborn nodded. "See?" she asked without looking at anyone in particular. "He could do that without anyone's help!"

Christopher smiled with a shy expression as he looked away from Miss Osborn, moving his hands from in front of him and he stared at his vacant wooden desk.

Then Miss Osborn asked, "Christopher? You did do that without any help, didn't you?"

He nodded but he didn't say anything.

"Is that right?" She wanted affirmation said by voice.

He nodded again.

"Then that's very good."

But it wasn't very good. Even he knew that.

"Now," Miss Osborn said, "for just a moment let's go on to look at the sky as though we had a giant telescope like the ones they have at observatories. And pretend that we can see every planet in our solar system. And do you know what it would look like if we could—"

"Miss Osborn?" Christopher interrupted.

"Yes, Christopher?"

He hesitated and then said, "Nothing."

She looked at him with her head tilted, a characteristic that came from her inborn femininity, and she gave a mystified look along with her tilted head. "What?"

"Nothing."

Now she tilted her head to the other side. "Oh, I think there was something. Wasn't there something, Christopher?"

This time his hesitation was very long and Miss Osborn let

it go on as long as he wanted.

But when the silence got to the point that it was overbearing to him, he said, "Yes, Miss Osborn. There was—something." He hesitated again but not for long this time. "I lost count on how old I would be in 1954, but I heard Nancy say it. That's how I knew I would be twenty-two."

That surprised Miss Osborn and, even more, it surprised Nancy Benford, and most of all it surprised Christopher himself who had learned much more about honesty from Mrs. Zambroski in semesters back in time than he ever thought he had learned.

"You have a marvelous sense of values, Christopher," Miss Osborn said. "That means far more than any test you need to pass in this class."

Nancy Benford was looking at him not with indifference which was good enough—but with admiration, and even flirtation. Her look was so flirtatious that she quickly brushed aside long locks of her red wavy hair from in front of her right eye just like the movie star, Veronica Lake, so he would be sure to see her blink a couple times.

And he just looked away from her without any expression at all on his face.

He was the indifferent Christopher Straw.

He was getting smart on all fronts.

Not bad for progress in growing up early.

THEME THREE

THE HOLIDAY

HONESTY, for which he was so richly complimented in public praise, made a great change in him. Because of the words of Miss Osborn and the quick blinking flirtation of Nancy Benford, for Christopher Straw the consistency of honor became an ambition. That was not to minimize but to maximize the earlier things in which he wanted to excel. After all, he thought, George Washington's reputation of honesty was not the only virtue of his life or he wouldn't have stood up in a rowboat rocked by heavy waves in the Potomac River and then he became Father of his Country. Those things didn't happen because of honesty as much as other qualities of his character. And so Christopher Straw reached further into those things in which he wanted to excel.

"Learn everything you can," his father told him. "Know things. Many things. But keep in mind that a lot of people know many things. As good as that is, know one thing—one thing better than anyone else knows it. Better than anyone else in the world."

"What should it be?"

"Your choice. If you don't know yet what it is, then let your passion lead you to it."

"Going to the moon?"

Without any hesitation his father nodded and said, "Do it. Follow it. Daydream about it. Dreams make things happen. And don't be afraid even if you make mistakes on your way—to the moon. You can avoid most mistakes if you find those who failed at things in their days that you do successfully in your dreams. Find out why they failed and then you don't duplicate their failures. Can't beat it. And—oh, yes—be good. Be good in all things—in big things—in little things. No, no. I take it back. There are no little things. If you think you have been good in nothing more than a little thing—then *you* are the little thing."

The weeks ahead held a lot of *big* things.

Christopher's weekends had Saturdays reserved for playing outside with other kids from the neighborhood even if it was very hot or very cold. Then the streetlights would turn on and so he and the other kids would all quickly run home except for Raymond Gerabaldi who would wait for his mother to yell his name with a threat of no dinner if he didn't get home "in exactly thirty seconds! I'm counting! 1-2-3!" She never seemed to get beyond eleven before seeing his running frame come from over the horizon.

Christopher's Sunday mornings were spent reading the Sunday newspaper's comics while still in bed, then the walk to the Fort Littleton United Methodist Church in "your Sunday best" of dark suit and tie with his parents and then, depending on the weather, his mother and father would go to the movies and Christopher would go with them. After that would come the dinner at home that was always followed by the hushed fifteen minutes as nothing could be said while Walter Winchell was on the radio giving the news followed by Jimmie Fidler telling what was going on in Hollywood. It was permissible to speak while Jimmie Fidler was on but it was still a big thing because Chris' father would say, "People need some entertainment. Fifteen minutes is not too much for a Fidler show. The world is serious enough and diversion is important. Fifteen minutes is fine for Fidler as long as it isn't any longer."

The following Thursday was going to be a very big day as it was going to be the holiday of Thanksgiving. Although Christopher would miss not seeing Miss Osborn for four days since school would be out for Thursday and Friday and then the weekend; for both public and private reasons this was not going to be a normal Thanksgiving. The public reason was that two years earlier President Franklin Delano Roosevelt declared that Thanksgiving would be the fourth Thursday of November rather than always have it be the last Thursday of November. That would affect some years but not most of them since in most cases the fourth Thursday of November would already be the last Thursday of November. Christopher Straw's parents clung to the old simplicity and called the new rule designated by President Franklin Delano Roosevelt as Franksgiving. The private reason for this being unusual was that this year Christopher's parents were torn between Thanksgiving and Franksgiving even tough this year both the fourth and last Thursday were one and the same. As penalty to FDR his mother was not going to prepare a turkey or the stuffing or sweet potatoes or cranberries or a pumpkin pie as she had in the Thanksgivings that Christopher had known from previous years before FDR messed it all up. This time his mother and father decided to get away from giving thanks or franks, and instead they would take a trip from Thursday through Sunday, going all the way to Lancaster and back, and take Christopher with them.

Christopher would then have to miss the movies on Sunday where the theater had a succession of Lone Ranger serials that continued each week, and last Sunday the serial ended with the Lone Ranger getting stuck in quicksand and worse than stuck when the quicksand covered him all the way up to near his shoulders. That's when the serial ended with the wording on the screen that spelled "Continued Next Week!"

His four-day holiday weekend started very early Thanksgiving morning with Christopher's father taking out a wide Conoco Oil Company's book of maps that had the trip outlined for him by someone at Conoco. It was outlined as a one hundred mile sight-seeing ride to Lancaster.

Much of the fun and newness began in simply getting there with his father driving his old Model A Ford and Christopher's mother sitting beside his dad in the interior seat while Christopher was allowed to sit in the rumble-seat that was like a trunk of the car that opened from the bottom just above the bumper with nothing but the sky above and the earth's scenery on both sides. His mother took one picture after another with her square black box-shaped Target Six-16 Brownie Camera with its leather-like aroma.

It was a magnificent adventure. They passed through Gettysburg and had breakfast there and then saw a lot of cannons on hills and went to Cemetery Hill to the spot where President Lincoln gave the Gettysburg Address and Christopher was thrilled particularly because his class had that speech read to them earlier by the beautiful Miss Osborn with her wonderful voice. Then the Model A was driven off to the east where Burma-Shave brushless shaving- cream signs dotted the sides of the highway with their quick-spaced sentences in rhymes that made Christopher laugh:

"Don't stick
"Your elbow
"Out too far.
"It might go home
"In another car.
"Burma-Shave"

The most surprising sights of Lancaster to Chris were the Amish people in their traditional clothes; women in their long deep blue dresses with full-sleeves covering their arms along with the black-suited men with beards and top hats riding their horse-drawn black and gray wagons. It was like a movie at school without need of a big kid bringing a projector into the classroom and setting up a beaded screen that smelled so good.

This was the furthest Christopher had been from home and the furthest from life as he had lived it at this time, and the great adventure was capped off by stopping at a Gulf gasoline station that his father preferred to others because Gulf's headquarters were in Pennsylvania. At the station they all got out of the car to go to the rest rooms and to get drinks of water, then just stand around while the station attendant filled their car's gasoline tank; wiped the windshield and the side and back windows; checked the oil with a long rod and then checked the water in the radiator and, finally, checked the pressure in each of the car's tires. This was living and exciting. "Highway 30!" his father said. "Good straight Highway 30—It's the old Lincoln Highway you know. Son, while you're learning about going to the moon but before going there, see this magnificent country; all of it, and then after you've seen this magnificent country, see the magnificent world! All of it. Then you can go to the moon. It's a good schedule. You need to know first of all what there is here in the United States. All of this country first and you'll learn a lot."

Christopher then saw a marvelous sight as the car was leaving the Gulf gasoline station. It was a pretty girl probably in her late teens leaning against a gasoline pump drinking from a Coca-Cola bottle. No one was with her. There was a slight breeze and her clothing gave evidences of that slight breeze just very little above one knee. It would not be forgotten throughout all his years to come, although the sight lasted only seconds.

The family spent Thanksgiving night in Lancaster at a motel his father chose because they could park right outside the room and there was an American Automobile Association symbol on the sign outside the motel that wrote it as being an AAA endorsed hotel which was considered to be the evidence that it was clean and good. They spent Friday and Saturday driving around and back to the motel each night.

Even with such a marvelous four days and nights of new adventure, there was to come the even more marvelous welcome not of newness but of familiarity that was felt Sunday night when they arrived back home in Fort Littleton; a return to the security of the known. There were now the familiar sights of the tree in front of the house; the porch made of wood with the rocking bench built by Christopher's father and where his father normally sat smoking his pipe once a day and twice at night, and there was the scent of all those things. And inside the home there was the soft brown couch with the gray throw-pillow resting on top of the unseen place where the upholstery was slightly ripped. And there was the davenport where guests could sit in a row, and wooden chairs with big backs in the dining area, and there was the tall brown Zenith radio, even taller than Christopher, and it had two knobs and a green gauge that was a station-index that lighted up when the radio was on, and there were shades over the windows with a little rope on the bottom of each shade with a doughnut-shaped wire covered by yellow cloth so you could put your index finger in the center of each rounded cloth to raise or lower the shades, and there was the goodness of all those things. As unique and memorable that trip was that went to far away and then back home, there was the unexpected kind of protective warmth given by so many things—all those things waiting for him.

"Home Sweet Home!" his mother said as he so often heard her say, but this time Christopher understood what she meant.

That night was spent with nothing different scheduled other than the normal with which he was so familiar and comfort-able and what he now discovered was what he liked best of all. Everything had its independent importance. Even Jimmie Fidler on radio. On this particular Sunday night Christopher and his parents would not talk over Jimmie Fidler's entertainment news. None of his show was very important to them other than that it was Fidler's voice that was familiar and harmless and so that was enough to be good to hear on this Sunday night.

counterpoint

THEME FOUR

NEXT CAME MALAHIA KAHALA

ONE WEEK AFTER the coming home from that trip to Lancaster and back to Fort Littleton, there came a Sunday that was even more abnormal. It began as expected with the reading of comics in bed and Church and going to the movies with his parents.

Outside the theater there was a poster with a big picture of Greta Garbo and Melvin Douglas in *Two-Faced Woman* and next to it a sign that read, *The New Garbo!* Then inside the theater came the parting of the curtains revealing a screen while Christopher ate Milk Duds his father bought for him at the concession stand. The fun of the hand-sized yellow-boxed Milk Duds increased, as usual, when he thought all of the Milk Duds were gone and, happily, there was invariably one or two or maybe more stuck to the wax paper at the bottom of the box. Those last ones tasted best of all since they were like a secretly added gift; the amount unrevealed to the world until his fingers found them. Then there was a Walt Disney cartoon with Donald Duck and his three nephews, Huey, Dewey and Louie. This was followed by a Coming Attraction for *Hold Back the Dawn* with Charles Boyer and Paulette Goddard, and then there was a Short Subject called *We Must Have Music* with Judy Garland and it ended with Rise Stevens singing "America the Beautiful" and it was very good. The supplements before the major films were not done yet as there was the continuation of the Lone Ranger serial and Christopher could not figure out how the Lone Ranger got out of the quicksand two weeks back while he was on the trip with his parents. All of this was followed by a "B" feature-film called *Marry the Boss's Daughter* with Brenda Joyce. It was okay but it was a little long. Then came the "A" feature, *Two-Faced Woman*. There was a sequence in it that was filmed in the snows of the High Sierras, and it was good until something unexpected happened in the theater:

That was when life changed.

Not a change in the lives portrayed in the film but a change in the lives of everyone in the theater and in the United States and in much of the world.

Two-Faced Woman was interrupted by a notice that came on the screen that read: "FLASH: ALL U.S. SERVICEMEN REPORT TO THEIR BASES AT ONCE. BY AUTHORITY OF THE FEDRAL COMMUNICATIONS COMMISSION ALL SERVICE PERSONNEL ARE TO REPORT TO THEIR BASES AT ONCE." Christopher's mother and dad looked at each other. There were some murmurs between them and throughout the theater. The movie continued and then the notice came on again. And again. And again.

When the movie was done and the audience left the theater there were Newsies on the sidewalks selling newspapers whose headlines read, "WAR! JAPS BOMB U.S. BASES!" And the Newsies were boys little more than Christopher's age and they were holding a stack of newspapers under one arm and with their free hand waving one of the newspapers while yelling, "Japs bomb Pearl Harbor! Read all about it! Japs bomb Pearl Harbor!" Christopher had never heard of Pearl Harbor. Probably the Newsies never heard of Pearl Harbor before today either. But it didn't take long for everyone to learn its importance.

The rest of the afternoon and night were spent in the living room with his parents and their next-door neighbors, the Frackers; Mr. Fracker and a very pregnant Mrs. Fracker, who Christopher's parents had invited over to have company on this strange night. All four sat on the davenport so they could stare at the large brown Zenith radio with the green lighted dial that stood center-stage that night. The constantly repeated message coming from its brown-clothed speaker was only a slight change from the notice that had been seen on the screen at the theater: "By authority of the Federal Communication Commission all service personnel are to report to their bases at once! Do not call your radio station. By authority of the Federal Communication Commission all service personnel are to report to their bases at once! Do not call your radio station." Between the repetitions of that announcement was a very deep voice saying that the Japanese Empire had attacked Hawaii in a sneak attack with an uncounted amount of sailors of the United States killed and U.S. ships destroyed.

Then it was time for Walter Winchell who did not speak as fast as he usually did. He was solemn. Jimmie Fidler was not on at all.

The next morning at school, Miss Osborn brought in her own radio. She brought it in because the school didn't have a radio. The one she brought was unlike the big Zenith Christopher knew at home. This one was a small Philco with a handle on top and the radio was almost as blonde as Miss Osborn except it seemed to be a blonde-tweed-fabric and she wasn't. The class was excused for lunch earlier than normal so the children in her class could all be in their seats by 12:30 to hear President Roosevelt speak to the nation in a Joint Session of the 77th Congress.

All the children were back in the classroom in time and Miss Osborn said a loud "Shhhhh!" and she and everyone in the class stared at the radio. Then came the authoritative voice of President Roosevelt as he said, "Mister Vice President, Mister Speaker, members of the Senate and the House of Representatives: Yesterday, December the 7th, 1941, a date which will live in infamy, the United States of America was suddenly and deliberately attacked by naval and air forces of the Empire of Japan."

And he announced that the Japanese Empire had also attacked Malaya, Hong Kong, Guam, the Philippine Islands, Wake Island, and Midway Island. He concluded by saying, "As Commander in Chief of the Army and Navy, I have directed that all measures be taken for our defense. Always will we remember the character of the onslaught against us. No matter how long it will take us to overcome this premeditated invasion, the American people, in their righteous might will win through to absolute victory...With confidence in our armed forces, with the unbounded determination of our people, we will gain the inevitable triumph, so help us God.

"I ask that the Congress declare that since the unprovoked and dastardly attack by Japan on Sunday, December the 7th, 1941, a state of war has existed between the United States and the Japanese Empire."

He appropriately and accurately said that a "state of war *has existed*" since the attack on Pearl Harbor. He wanted a formal vote for a declaration but, regardless of the vote, "a state of war has existed."

After the speech was done and Miss Osborne turned off the radio, she forced a closed-mouth smile and said, "Children, you are living through something you will remember the rest of your lives." There was absolute quiet. She knew she had to say something more: "And you will see that we will win. President Roosevelt said 'Victory'. It will *be* victory. And that, too, you will remember for the rest of your lives."

What Christopher didn't know was that he and his classmates were to be some of the youngest members of what in years ahead would be called the Greatest Generation (as Tom Brokaw would later coin that phrase to define those World War II Americans and allies.) Even the youngest would be part of it because all citizens of the United States, no matter their age, were to be involved in the every-day events of the War Effort to ensure the United States would win the ultimate victory. For the children of the time, of which Christopher was a member, there was the frequent putting together of stacks of old newspapers along with waste paper and the stacks brought to the playground of school for Paper Drives; and there was the gathering of metal junk to bring onto that playground for Scrap Drives; there was the finding of old tires for Rubber Drives; Christopher's parents would often give him a dime to bring to class for a War Savings Stamp; his mother would give him grease from something she prepared on the stove, the grease to be brought to school for putting in large containers along with other portions of grease from other students; there was the peeling of tin-foil that had been loosely sealed on paper from within the inside of cigarette packs then the rolling of the tin-foil into a ball until it got large and then having the final layer be a piece of gold-colored tin-foil from a pack of Old Gold Cigarettes and then bringing the ball to school. It was another participation in the War Effort of all the students.

That was when he learned that those events happening in the world could be so massive that not even his parents could control them in their entirety. Only in pieces. His father was soon to be in the U.S. Navy and his mother would be working at a machine shop in Harrisonville that was under contract to the U.S. Department of War.

The every-day vocabulary of the time became the word "Victory" repeatedly said by President Roosevelt and Great Britain's Prime Minister Winston Churchill. Christopher sent letters to his father and received letters from him, always on V-Mail; a thin, almost wispy but crisp piece of paper that folded together in such a way for it to be both a letter and its own envelope. And his mother sent away for a badge for Christopher from Red Ryder's Victory Patrol of the Red Ryder Radio Show; the badge with a big "V" that, along with the printed words and a picture of Red Ryder on his horse, shined with a blue-white glow in the dark from its luminous paint. Each night, before going to bed Christopher would hold the badge up to a table-lamp's brilliant light-bulb so the luminous items on his badge would absorb plenty of light and would shine strong and long in the black of the room at night once the lamp was turned off. Importantly, it had arrived in a brown envelope sent all the way from Red Ryder at P.O. Box 2250 in San Francisco with a notification to the Postmaster that the parcel could be opened for postal inspection if necessary. Who could ask for more?

The night before his father left to report to duty and before his bedroom lights were turned off, Christopher's parents came to his room to assure him things would be alright. To make his eyes brighten and to make him forget about the news of war, they both talked to him about space exploration and how important Christopher would become in its future.

"I'll miss you, Dad." Christopher wasn't talking about space exploration. He was talking about his dad and the war.

It took a while before there was a response because his father wanted the response to be with a smile and without choking up and without any glimpse of sadness. "I'm glad you have some good friends, Chris. Tommy, that little fat boy. Good boy. I like him. And Freddie. Isn't that what you call him? Freddie? And that little guy. I don't remember his name. He's a little fella."

Chris smiled. "Henry."

"That's it. That it! He'll probably surprise us all and be a prize fighter or something! Maybe little Henry will surprise everyone and be another Gene Tunney!"

"I don't think so, Dad. Not Henry."

"But he is your friend, isn't he?"

Now, more confident, Chris said, "He isn't just a friend. He's important. He's real important because he knows the names of every President."

His father nodded. "That's good! Of course he's important. You remember that you will never know an unimportant person. I'm proud of you, Son, having such good friends. Friendship is something that is even more important than—than a rank or a title. Do you know what I mean? You won't have many real friends. Not like Tommy and Freddie and—and—"

"Henry, Dad."

"That's right."

For those few moments during that night, war was not now being discussed. But those few moments did not last long and the one to bring it up again was Christopher who said without transition of subject. "Do you know when you'll be home, Dad?"

"Oh, yes. I know when."

"When?"

"When we win."

"When will that be?"

"I can't predict a date. But I can say with certainty that wars are either won or lost. And we are going to win. This family is going to be a part of that victory. Your mother will be part of it. You too. Don't circle a date. But it will come."

Not yet.

February of 1942 meant another new semester and that, in turn, meant that Miss Osborn was no longer his teacher and instead he was in the class of Miss Gunderson. She was neither beautiful nor awful. She was Miss Gunderson. This was when Christopher learned there were three different kinds of teachers: beautiful, awful and Gundersons. With all of the terrible events in the world, when this 4-A semester started in February there was a surprising single glow of brightness. There was a new girl in his class. And of all things, it was because of the war.

She came "to be here in the mainland for a while" as she said and Miss Gunderson repeated that.

She was gorgeous in a dress with a design of small white and brown flowers against a lighter brown background. She made him glad that he never had asked Miss Osborn to marry him. What if Miss Osborne had accepted his proposal? Then what would he do about this girl who was from Hawaii of all places?

Her name said everything there was to say. Her name was unbelievable. Her name was Malahia Kahale. What? Who gave her that name? Her parents? Her father? Her mother? God? And then to emphasize her beautiful name—she was very tan and she had long black hair and she had uniquely almond-shaped eyes. Oh, my God! What a face. She was an Asian Vivian Leigh except even prettier because of those almond-shaped eyes and everything.

And so, predictably, Christopher made a terrible mistake. He couldn't stop staring at her as she sat at her desk and when she saw him do that, he smiled at her and she looked away. Then later, so much worse, he walked down the aisle of desks in the classroom and he stopped by her desk and he said to her, "Did you get hurt at Pearl Harbor?" Those were his first words to her. No, he couldn't possibly have done that. Could he? Why on earth did he do that? But he did.

She just shook her head in a silent "no" and then she looked away.

But he couldn't just leave it alone. "I mean the war." Why explain? That just made it worse. She undoubtedly knew what he meant and why could this make his initial question any more sensible than without his clarification?

She nodded politely and then she started drawing.

That's when Christopher learned that he could say the stupidest things when he could least afford them. Why didn't he just leave things alone? Because he couldn't. She could not be ignored. She was a Hawaiian angel. They must have angels in Hawaii and the Japanese were jealous and so they bombed it.

He couldn't let it end at his dumbness. But this time he had to plan the next move rather than just let his voice take over the moment. He could not afford to lose again. This must not be another day of infamy. Malahia Kahale? A Saint. There can be no defeat. Win. Victory. Marriage was not far away. This was too big and even though women who saw *Gone with the Wind* seemed to be captivated by the self-confident Clark Gable, Vivian Leigh preferred Leslie Howard who was soft-spoken and not pushy. Christopher decided he must be more like Leslie Howard. Besides, Clark Gable had black hair and a mustache. Leslie Howard was a blond and no mustache so Christopher had a visible advantage as Leslie Howard. That was to be Part One of his plan now that he was concerned with the Vivian Leigh lesson. His whole being was clouded with Part Two which was presented not by physical ease but by supernatural fate:

At the time there was a fad of kids collecting playing-cards. Although the faces of the cards were all similar in clubs, spades, hearts, and diamonds, each card in a collection came from different decks of cards with different designs or pictures on the back of each of the collected cards. Christopher noticed that Malahia Kahale had maybe ten of them in a single stack on her desk and every once in a while she would flip the horizontal edges up to catch a look at them. There was something so appealing in the attention she gave to those cards and the obvious joy she displayed in having them, not knowing that her joy was seen by Christopher or by anyone. Then he noticed that the homely girl across the aisle from Malahia Kahale had a bigger stack of cards than the stack possessed by that Hawaiian Goddess. The homely girl must have had twenty or more of them. Probably more than twenty. Tramp.

Then he saw the beautiful Hawaiian rare jewel trading two of her cards for one of the cards of Miss Awful across the aisle. Not only did he see that but the teacher, Miss Gunderson, saw it, and she said in a very loud voice, "Children, there will be no more trading of cards in class. You may wait until recess or lunch! Trading cards is not an activity for the school room!"

Now Christopher knew what to do. The plan was being written by fate itself: Christopher's mother had a number of decks of cards since she played the game of Bridge with Mrs. Fracker and some other friends every Tuesday night and Christopher's father had bought her decks of cards to have on hand. One of those decks had a very colorful picture of pelicans on the back of each card. So Christopher told his mother about Malahia Kahale who was very close to Pearl Harbor when the Japanese attacked and she was somehow rescued and was sent to Pennsylvania and now she receives pleasure by collecting cards, and out of sympathy he wanted to give her some cards. Christopher's mother understood even more than he thought she would understand, and she not only gave him that deck of cards but another deck as well and the second deck hadn't even been opened yet but was still wrapped in cellophane. The picture that was on the cards in that deck was of a waterfall. His mother told him that each deck had 52 regular cards plus a joker.

He didn't know much about cards nor much about mathematics and it took him a long time to count to 52 plus 52 plus 2 on his fingers but that told him that he needed to find 106 kids who were engaged in the trading-fad who would trade with him, and because he suddenly became an expert in mathematics he was certain that he needed no more than 53 kids who would trade two different ones of theirs in trade for one from each of his decks. And that's what he set out to do as he pretended that, like them, he was a collector. And in five days from a Monday to a Friday that's what he succeeded in doing. Even better, he succeeded in getting more cards than he had planned since he soon learned that particularly the waterfall deck was so good that he could offer just one of his cards for at least a few of theirs.

He now had 218 cards. Should he give them to her now? At first he felt he couldn't wait—but he did. "Patience is a virtue," his long-ago teacher, Mrs. Zambroski had told him, and his delay of asking Miss Osborne to marry him had proven the validity of that statement.

His trading included receiving some duplicates and starting the following Friday at school he planned to trade any duplicates away so by the time he would give the stack of cards to the Hawaiian Deity, they would all be different.

The weekend was terribly long and the only bright spot was listening to Lucky Strike's "Your Hit Parade" on the radio Saturday night. "Your Hit Parade" was a show that told what song had sold the most copies of sheet-music and single records during the preceding week with some Lucky Strike extras added. A song he liked called "Mr. Five by Five" made its debut on that program not as an extra but as number six, and even better news; a romantic song that reminded him of Malahia Kahale was starting in tenth spot: "There Will Never Be Another You." The title was right. There would never be another Malahia Kahale. In addition, how could there be another one with that magnificent name?

And now, of all strange things, the announcer of "Your Hit Parade" said in a loud, booming voice that "Lucky Strike Green Has Gone to War!" The loud booming voice explained that the color of the pack of Lucky Strike cigarettes would now be white instead of green but he didn't explain why the color would make any difference in the war. Not even President Roosevelt explained it. Would the Nazis and the Japs win if Lucky Strikes still had a green pack? It was like the mystery of why it was important for grease to be brought to school for the War Effort. It almost seemed to be a sacrilege to ever ask what these things had to do with fighting a war, so no one asked. Did our servicemen and our allies throw grease at the axis powers? What for? Couldn't the Nazis and the Japs just duck? And now what is this about the color of green?

By Sunday night Chris had counted the collected cards three times. The total amount was 214 cards. There were two duplicates so he took them out, making 212 total. Then he divided them into four stacks with a rubber-band encircling each stack.

Christopher woke up two hours earlier than normal on Monday morning because even in his sleep, and even though patience was a virtue, he was in a hurry for the big day to begin.

He took off the rubber-bands and recounted the cards before leaving home and, sure enough, there were 212 of them. None had escaped during the evening when the lights were out. His luminous Red Ryder Victory Patrol Badge must have been keeping watch for him. He put the rubber-bands back around the stacks. Then he put the stacks in a brown paper bag.

To Christopher, seeing McConnellsburg Elementary School on the horizon looked like the yellow brick road to Oz. His impatience was near its end. But he didn't run to the door of the school as he felt the urge to do. He sauntered. He was a very nonchalant guy. Casual. Just another day for a casual kind of guy.

Despite his nonchalance he couldn't help but be the first one in the classroom. He sat at his desk with the bag by his side. The clock seemed to be having a tough time in its move to get to nine o'clock. "Come on," he whispered to it. "Come on! Come on! Come on!" It must have started going at a slower pace and needed to be fixed. Then something wonderful happened with minutes to go before the bell rang to start class: the Hawaiian Wonder Woman came in the classroom and sat down at her desk. The casual kind of guy got up slowly and ambled over to her while he held the bag that enclosed the four stacks of cards. With care he placed the bag on her desk while he retained his new-found easygoing attitude. She looked up at him and he held to a minimum of words so he wouldn't make another mistake and start blurting out something about Pearl Harbor. He said, "Here."

But he did stay next to her so he could watch her reaction when she would see what was in the bag. She carefully opened it and took out one stack of cards with her almond eyes becoming almost as big as her desk. Then she picked out the second stack and her eyes got so large and joyfully tearful this time that it seemed as though her eyes would collide with the ceiling and start a rainstorm. Then the third and fourth stacks. Mount Vesuvius.

"Christopher!" she said.

He opened his mouth and said nothing. Then he corrected her by saying, "Chris," which was an abbreviation he never gave to anyone other than his parents.

"Chris! Oh! Oh! Thank you. Thank you, Chris!" And she started looking through the cards by flipping them without yet entirely taking off the rubber-bands. She was probably checking to see that they were all different. "Oh! Oh!"

The bell saved Christopher from himself by ringing in the signal that meant the beginning of class. He only had time to say, "You're welcome." It was exactly the right thing to say. Not too much. If it wasn't for the bell there is no telling what rambling of words he would have produced in his state. He walked back to his desk captured in pride and self-congratulation by his brevity of words. "You're welcome," he whispered to himself to relive his moment. "You're welcome. That was right."

It was intolerable to wait for recess but he waited. He walked out of class without even glancing at her. He knew that was the thing to do. But he stayed very close to the school-door during recess. When Malahia Kahale came out she looked at him and smiled broadly which was rare for her to do and she said very softly, "Thank you, Chris."

"You're welcome again," he said and quickly knew he shouldn't have added the word "again" but it was done. He looked down at her brown and white saddle shoes and then she walked away. Christopher noticed her shoes had some scuff marks on the sides of the white parts of their backs above the rubber heel, and he liked that. After all, they were her shoes. Somehow she got them scuffed. It occurred to him that her shoes saved her from probably hurting her feet. And so they were good shoes.

He learned so much in those days. Most of all he learned that he was crazy, and that's what love could do. Love could do that to him even in a time of war in which he was engaged in the War Effort and most of all with his father in the fight. Those varied events of his life were simultaneous and were dominating his mind. How could he feel horror at world events and fear for his father's current days and nights and still feel ecstasy knowing a new girl in his classroom, and all connected in their outrageous coupling?

His insanity lasted only four years. Not bad.

THEME FIVE

OF ALL THINGS

NOW CHRISTOPHER STRAW was thirteen years old and in Grade B-8. (When he was in Junior High School as a Seventh Grader, in many states the designation of A and B for semesters were put behind the year of semester rather than following the year of semester.) But the B-8 was a minor fact of his times as his major factor was that his father was alive and wrote that he was unwounded and uncaptured. The United States and its allies in Europe achieved one victory after another. Yet immense sadness came with the death of President Roosevelt on April the 12th of 1945. Christopher's mother cried at that although earlier she had voted against him for a third term, voting for Wendell Willkie shortly after he had smiled and winked at her when he was in a "We Want Willkie" parade in an open-roofed car while she was among a huge crowd on the sidewalk waving at him. Mr. Straw did not seem pleased at that 1940 incident. Christopher then assumed that his father probably voted for FDR while his mother voted for Wendell Willkie. To Christopher's knowledge Mrs. Straw didn't tell for whom she voted in the newer, 1944 election between Roosevelt's fourth term and Tom Dewey. With so many big things taking place in such short time, was there room to allow for even more big things?

Yes. The Nazis surrendered and there was victory throughout the European Theater with the proclamation of V-E Day on May the 8th. Less than five months later came the revelation of the secret weapon called the Atom Bomb. President Truman ordered it to be used on Hiroshima and Nagasaki and that brought victory over the Empire of Japan. With the proclamation of V-J Day, the war was won and over.

With hugs and kisses and tears of happiness in the personal world of Fort Littleton highlighted by the home of the Straws, Christopher's mother and Christopher greeted his father back home from the Pacific Theater of the war. Now he had a limp and a cane. He never explained why he was limping; why he had a cane. After all, he had written that he was unwounded.

With all the good news there was an event that in Christopher's world there was a sadness coming from the victory in the terrible news that Malahia Kahale would soon be going back to Hawaii to be home with her parents.

With the passing of four years since they first met, now she was in every way even more gorgeous than she was before and it was obvious that of all things the full bloom of womanly beauty was not yet achieved but was still ahead.

But when he confided in Minister McAllister at church, telling him the wrenching he felt at the news that Malahia was going home, Minister McAllister told Christopher that in the Old Testament according to Ecclesiastes, "there is a time for everything." And he added, "In this case, Christopher, there is a time for Malahia to be here and a time for Malahia to return to her parents, to all of her family, and to home. The war is over and be glad for her that she is now able to do that safely. Your attitude will tell her that and even tell *you* that—if you love her. Love her, Christopher! Do not try to possess her. Possession is not love."

According to Christopher's testament about Malahia unknown by any Biblical scholars, she probably would take her playing-cards with her. Or maybe she would give them to someone else. Maybe she would give them to some boy at school who wasn't Christopher; maybe to that wretched baseball-playing kid who Christopher had seen walking with Malahia. Twice. His name was Malcolm and he always had a dumb smirk on his face. Jerk.

Christopher knew his sanity had been restored during his next meeting with the Hawiian Empress, Malahia Kahale. But sanity's restoration was replaced with the unexpected resurgence of severe pain that he once felt from the years-ago statements of Nancy Benford. Why did women give pain in one way or another? Nancy Benford was one way and Malahia Kahale was another. Or was it the same?

The setting for this meeting could have been drawn and painted by a Hollywood Art Director. Christopher and Malahia were sitting together side by side on the railing of the school's playground with no one else around since all the classes for the day were done. There was an October breeze just beginning to sway the branches of trees behind them. The sky was glorious in its deepest blue and there were such white thick clouds that they looked as though they belonged above Florida or maybe somewhere over the African Continent but not Pennsylvania. And beyond the visual there was the marvelous aroma of autumn that was returning to Pennsylvania.

"When are you going home, Malahia? Do you know when?" He had to ask because the unknown was lurking continually and causing him pain. He had to know if their closeness would last weeks or months or years or forever.

She was looking down and kept looking down. "Friday."

The hurt was sharper and more intense than he had feared. For a while there was no audible response.

Then there was a short "Oh" followed by a long silence before he asked, "For forever? I mean will you stay in Hawaii forever? All the time?"

She shook her head, still looking down. "I don't know."

"Are you happy? I mean about going?"

She took a while to answer. "I miss my mother and my father and my brothers and my sister and I miss my home. I mean where I live; Hawaii. I didn't want to come here to the mainland. But then—I don't know—I got to—I don't know, Chris." And she looked very briefly at him and then she looked away again. "But then I met you."

There was a rush inside him. "Well," he barely got it out. "Well, I mean—I'll miss you, Malahia."

Suddenly she looked at him directly, now not at all ignoring his eyes and she talked as though she was already a young woman and not a little girl. "Oh, Chris! I will miss you so much!"

Then knowing that any sign of jealousy would do him no good, he suppressed his instinct to ask her if she would miss other guys—like Malcolm. But the suppression was not total. "Will you miss other things, too?"

"No," she said in a loud and certain voice. "I won't miss anything else but you."

Now it was Christopher who looked down. His eyes fastened on those brown and white saddle shoes that were so distinctive as being hers. Somehow the toes of her shoes faced each other. How could she do that? How could that be comfortable for her? When he sat there his shoes pointed outward. "What if I came to see you?"

"In Hawaii?"

"Yes."

"Oh, Chris. Could you? Would you?"

Realism took over. "I don't think so."

Again there was silence. Then she added, "Do you think that after you get out of school maybe you could?"

"Will you wait for me?" He asked her as though he was either going to prison or to fight the enemy. But no one was threatening him with prison and the war was over.

"Oh, yes!"

"Then I'll come to Hawaii."

"Will you? Promise?"

Suddenly remembering who he was and who he wanted to be, he added, "Will you wait if first I have to go to the moon?"

As soon as he said those words something happened that seemed unbelievable to him. She put her hand on his arm. Her hand was so small. He quickly jarred his head toward her and just as quickly she started looking straight in his eyes. "That's what I love about you, Chris. I want you to go to the moon first. Even if I have to wait."

"You do?"

"When everyone finds out you're on the moon I will tell all my friends that first you told me you will go to the moon and then you will come to Hawaii to be with me."

"Yes," he said and quickly thought to himself to make any statement to her to be brief. He thought, 'Leave things good between us. I can't do any better than what just happened including what she said to me. Don't mess it up.'

But of course he did mess it up. He asked, "May I—I mean do you feel—it's you know. Do you—would it be okay if—I mean what I mean."

She somehow understood the totally incomprehensible. "Christopher, I have never kissed a boy before so I don't know how."

"Oh."

She was unprepared for the brevity of his response of "oh" so there was an uneasy silence and then she asked what came naturally to her: "Have you kissed a girl before?"

"Yes."

"How many?"

"About 200." He didn't know from where in his head that answer came but he quickly remembered he shouldn't lie. "Maybe not exactly that many but—" and then he stopped talking because an end of sentence was not coming into his head. He just let it lay there without completion. They sat there on the railing for at least three minutes more lingering in silence. No kiss. Not right after that dialogue. But she knew how to talk without saying anything at all by leaving her hand on his arm and occasionally moving her hand very lightly above and below his elbow.

With that, like a breaker in the sea, something came over him that he had never felt before. Could her hand on his arm do this to him? It was something inside his entire being that was telling him he was not through with newness, and this was a newness of a never-felt-before internal paradise fighting and pushing to envelope him.

She stood up and they stared at each other and she took a piece of folded paper from under the cuff of her blouse and she handed it to him and she started to walk away. Now he could see the back of her shoes and those wonderful scuff marks were still there and he felt 'they better not be cleaned when she gets home.'

He watched her walk from him. This time, no psychology. He called her back.

She came back—almost ran back.

They kissed. They had to. And it was beyond anything either of them hoped it would be.

She walked away again and he knew to leave her alone. He looked down at the piece of paper she gave him and he unfolded it. It was a letter to him written in ink in her slanted handwriting:

'Dear Chris. I will think of you every time I look at my cards. They will be with me, a few always near my heart. In that way you will always be so close to my heart. Love, Mala.'

Near her heart? Yes. Love? Love, Mala she wrote. Love, Mala. That is what she wrote. Is that what she meant? It was what he meant and hadn't said. It is what he felt.

God—is life ever wonderful!

So much of it anyway.

THEME SIX

THE NEW LOOK

CHRISTOPHER MISSED MALAHIA KAHALA so much that he felt that faithfulness was his new and permanent trait. As more years passed and letters continued between them, he continued to long for her.

Because of that he ignored a unique visual trend. With the war done, girls and women adopted the wearing of a new wardrobe: "The New Look" with full-length dresses that looked like they were ready to go to a formal event every day and night even though they were just going to school or to work or to a snack-counter for a chocolate malt.

But "The New Look" of the post-war years would soon have severe competition that would even receive the attention of Christopher Straw no matter that it had nothing to do with Malahia Kahala:

Cars. New cars that like their competition, also had a New Look.

There were automakers who were busy designing and then building what would be the 1949-model cars. During the war years most car manufacturers were making vehicles and other items for the War Effort and after the war ended it took the automobile-makers some time to retool. While they were retooling they temporality put out little for sale more than dull re-dos of pre-war cars with some incidentals to make them look a little different but they did not cause great interest with one exception: a car called the Tucker 48. It seemed as though everyone wanted to see this car with three headlights; the middle headlight turning with the movement of the steering wheel; a driver's seat in the middle of the width of the car; no running boards; no traditional fenders, and magnificent innovations of creativity throughout both its exterior and interior. Christopher hoped for a day he would own one, or more realistically at least be able to see one other than in a newspaper photograph. But even if he had the $3,000 or so to own one, and he didn't, few could own them and few could even see them because there were less than 100 Tuckers that had been manufactured.

During the last months of 1948 came the introduction of the 1949 models that had been completed by automakers other than Preston Tucker. Those '49 model cars each had one or more innovations distinct from one another. Along with all of their admitted Tucker-like rejection of running boards and no more traditional fenders, they were each making their mark in the post-World War II world when cars could not only be built again but would look better than cars looked before (or ever again in the 20th Century) and took center-stage in visually stating that the war was over.

Studebakers that were being driven, for instance, south or east looked like they could well be heading north or west because the front and back of Studebakers were of similar shape with observers not always knowing which way Studebakers were facing.

You didn't have to raise your feet to get into every new car as the new Hudson was made in such a way that when getting into a Hudson you had to step down. No one seemed to understand how this could possibly be true, but it was.

Fords had big chrome-covered circles on the front of their grills somewhat looking like a non-lighting and non-moving Tucker middle headlight while the rest of the car was just as un-Ford, giving the illusion that it was driving right out of a Plastic Man comic book.

Depending on the model, Buicks had three or four small port-hole circles on their sides close to being above their front tires, and they had one large, heavy metal circular object standing upright on the front of the hood with that object being able (although not easy) to be removed by a boy and given to a girlfriend as a bracelet.

There were fins on the back of Cadillac Eldorado's as though they were metal encasements hiding a giant shark.

Henry J. Kaiser and Joseph Frazer were two men who joined their talents to manufacture deluxe looking cars named the Kaiser and the Frazer and also the Henry J. (which was the first name and middle initial of Kaiser) and other models. After building war-ships for the government, now the two were making cars with their own New Look. But with the unexpected luxurious post-war models from more well-known automobile manufacturers enticing customers, the Kaisers and Frazers were not selling at the pace they wanted to stay in business.

The Crosley automobile (built by Powel Crosley Jr.'s company that had made pre-war automobiles as well as more

well-known radios and refrigerators and other appliances) were
so small and light that four high-school boys could lift a new
Crosley from its parking place by a curb and put it on someone's
front lawn or anywhere so that some pre-spotted girl coming
out of school, had to look all over the neighborhood to find it.

A pretty American-Indian girl who was a couple grades
below Christopher had a Crosley and therefore had to look for
her Crosley every late afternoon after the school-day was done.
Christopher Straw was not considered by anyone to be a par-
ticipant in such a car-moving-scheme. But he was. After all, she
was pretty and now he noticed that she wore a New Look dress.
Chris had spent most of his life thinking that Indians were like
those he had seen in the movies; some with headdresses adorned
with feathers; some giving chants while moving one of their
hands back and forth in front of their lips while while making
a strange noise from the back of their throats; and some Indians
who were either fighting the white man or were assistants to
comic book and movie-serial characters. But this girl was pretty.
Not as pretty as Malahia, but not bad at all, so she was an ideal
candidate to have her car moved on a daily basis. And it was
mind-engrossing and an ideal time-passer for Christopher who
had no Malahia and no car. At least he could help lift a new '49
Crosley and see the reaction of a pretty American-Indian girl,
with both the car and the girl each having a post-war New Look.

During the first few years following the war, the world was
full of all kinds of New Looks beyond cars and girls. The major
one was seeing the war from a vantage point unknown when
the war was current. Christopher's World History teacher in
B-11 of McConnellsburg's high school, Mr. Pratt, described

the Post-War world as being "like a movie full of tragedies and triumphs that has ended with our victory and now the theater's lights are on and it's time to walk up the aisle and go home. In great relief, we won.

"But," Mr. Pratt continued, "You were probably told from your parents and your teacher—very accurately—from the moment of Pearl Harbor—that we were going to win the war."

There was a chorus of "yes's" from the classroom.

"At the outset they probably knew we were losing," Mr. Pratt continued, "and losing throughout most of 1942. I knew and yet I, too, told my students at the time that 'we will win!' I believed it when I said it and it was also meant to keep spirits high and not to worry about what could be—what could be losing. What could be no more United States. And no matter what we knew at the time, in the end we *did* win. And do you know how?"

There was absolute silence. "Because of you—and everyone in the country who would not accept—or even talk about this nation's potential of facing our defeat." And Mr. Pratt gave a back-of-right-hand signal of a "V" facing the students, using the visual pursuit of Victory as Winston Churchill initiated it. "There was no other cause but Victory. No other international pursuit of us and our allies other than victory. That's how we won. That's how you won. Thank you for what you did during those years, boys and girls."

Christopher raised his hand and Mr. Pratt called on him. "Mr. Pratt, why were we asked by President Roosevelt to bring grease to school for the War Effort? Why did that help win the war?"

Mr. Pratt looked confused. "You know," he said with a slight smile. "I don't really know. I never gave that thought.

I'm sure there was a good reason."

Christopher went on. "What reason could that be?"

"I think I remember knowing at the time. I think so. But I don't remember the reason. I don't know." Then he paused, "What do you think? What do you think was the reason?"

"Mr. Pratt, I think President Roosevelt wanted to make sure we never forgot the War Effort so he made things up for us to do, and then companies reminded us to work for the War Effort all the time."

Mr. Pratt with his now continuing smile, added a nod to the smile. "Maybe you're right! If so, do you think that was good or bad?"

Without even a pause Christopher answered, "It was necessary."

Now Mr. Pratt said nothing. He stared at Christopher. One of the other students started to say something and Mr. Pratt stopped him by stretching out his two open hands. "No. Not yet. Absorb that. Absorb what Cristopher just said. You all just heard wisdom said by a classmate."

And Mr. Pratt held to the silence as though it was a long paragraph of dialogue. Then he added in a much softer voice than before, "Starting from so far from behind, our winning was exceptional. Everyone thought of the War Effort every day and night. That's how we won. In addition, boys and girls, I hope you noticed what just happened this year that was beyond exceptional: most victors in war ignore or punish the people who have been governed by the losers. We could have charged those countries who fought us so that our citizens would not have to pay taxes far into the future as the losers in the war would pay our taxes. That was common for other victors at other times in other wars. Instead, just this April our nation revealed a plan not only to dismiss all that and, instead, have our own citizens give their funds—not our former enemies to give funds but ourselves to give *our* funds to both our friends and to our former enemies so they can rebuild their cities and particularly for our former enemies to construct democracies where they had previously built governments of horror." Then his voice raised in tone. "Think of it! Ever hear of a victor like that? Exceptional. I have never seen anything like that human kindness extended from victors. To me—to your teacher—I believe it was a new height achieved by the human race after attaining victory. Do you think such policies would have come from our enemies had they won?"

Mr. Pratt had an unusual habit of changing the subject in a radical way, simply yelling the name of a new subject, therefore scaring any students of drifting minds to jump from their seats to accept whatever Mr. Pratt may want to now discuss:

"Mahatma Gandhi!" Mr. Pratt yelled in rejection of seeking any frame of continuity from his previous subject. His tone would have been just as appropriate of yelling the disconnected name of Perry Como or Joe Louis.

"Did you hear me?! Mahatma Gandhi! He wanted independence for his nation of India from Great Britain and he got it. Do you know when? Do you know when that simple man achieved independence for his nation of India? August the 15th of just last year! Do you know who Indians are? And I don't mean Hiawatha and Geronimo and Sitting Bull and I certainly don't mean Tonto and Little Beaver!"

There was no reason for him to suddenly become angry but he appeared angry. Then with a quick smile he looked at

Christopher Straw, "Nor do I mean the American-Indian girl who is the owner of the new Crosley that seems to find its way to a different home's lawn across the street from school to her surprise every afternoon!"

He went on to explain that when India claimed independence from Great Britain, so many of Great Britain's colonial territories chose and received independence *from* Great Britain. "They chose it and they got it! Great Britain gave it to them! So there!"

By coincidence, while Mr. Pratt was introducing India to his B-11 class, this was also the time when a little boy who lived in India was creating his importance-to-come and who, in time, would make an indelible effect on many people in the world, for sure including Christopher Straw and unknown by Savannah Lane who was yet unknown by Christopher Straw.

And the little boy in India was not like any other.

THEME SEVEN

"THE FAR AWAY BIRTH AND THE GROWING UP OF RAJ BHAVNANI"

RAJ BHAVNANI was probably born in Sholapur, India, or in some Indian village close to Sholapur, and probably he was born sometime in the mid-1930s. The imprecision of such important data was due to Raj Bhavnani never having been told anything about his parents; not even their names, or the date of his birth, nor precisely where his birth took place. He retained the name of Raj Bhavnani because as he grew older he remembered that others called him that and best of all he thought his name had a rhythm to it and people seemed to like saying it in its entirety as though it was one word. Without a home he wandered between village to village and when in cities, from squatter settlement to squatter settlement usually between the cities of Sholapur and Hyderabad. He had been told by a few Sadhus who admittedly were not present at his birth and they had no evidence when and where he was born, said he was born in the period of time in which Mahatma Gandhi was trying to end the jurisdiction of Great Britain over India, calling for Great Britain to "Quit India" and with or without Great Britain, calling for the end of the struggles and the killings between Hindus and Moslems. That covered a lot of time and Raj Bhavnani proclaimed his birthday as August the 15th of 1947 because that was India's Independence Day and, in that way, he could be part of the national celebrations throughout his life regardless of the outrageous attempt to erase some obvious years from his age.

That fictitious birthday was, of course, when the British officially left India as its dependency and there was established the partition of India into two countries; India and the new country of Pakistan with more than one million estimated to have been killed in that struggle of separation and in the lines drawn in the making of West and East Pakistan with one thousand miles of Northern India between them.

From that history, Raj Bhavnani was able to either know or, more likely, develop a story about the mystery of his identity. He would tell others that he was "caught in the war. My parents were Hindus and they were killed in the war by Muslims. They left their baby—me—in the vacant place in which they had lived."

Maybe. But he told the story for its drama and not for the sake of documented accuracy. When some looked at him suspiciously and asked if he was sure those who told him the date of his birth were accurate he would simply answer, "Ah-Chah. Yes, yes" and go on about his business with little interest displayed in what he was asked.

In early 1957 he hitched a ride on a Bullock Cart as villagers offered him a trip to Bombay with their major cargo of cow-dung for delivery along the way to villages where the dung would be used to make walls of shelters and also to be used as fuel in the more urban places through which they passed for either payment of funds or food or shelter or for nothing at all.

Once he arrived in Bombay he went straight to the place he had always wanted to see since he had first heard of it: the water's edge where Bombay touched the Arabian Sea.

What he saw in that great body of water that had no visible ending was surely spectacular enough, but by its edge on the continent was a rival spectacle: a mammoth architectural wonder called the Gateway of India. It was a concrete archway close to 100 feet tall and even wider in width; its main archway bordered by smaller archways with the entire building standing on a small peninsula jutting out into the sea and providing the welcome to India for those who entered in a kind of similarity to the way that the Statue of Liberty provided entrance to the United States. Across the road was even more rivalry to the spectacles of the scene and this one was the Taj Mahal Hotel (not anywhere near the Taj Mahal in Agra, India) whose massive façade looked like it was trying to over-match not only the close sites of Bombay but the exterior of far-away Buckingham Palace in London.

Raj found home with dozens and dozens of street-people under the main archway of the Gateway of India and like them, at night he slept on the cold stone under the protection of that arch. And he stayed there not just for a short while, but for three years. And like so many others under the archway, it became not only his place for shelter but his place for all things including his place of work and its corners for things otherwise done in a bathroom. And there were some hundreds of thousands more street people living close to the Gateway and on the streets of Bombay using those streets as their homes for all of those purposes.

Raj Bhavnani's occupation was the primitive profession of holding his hand outright while saying to strangers, "Baksheesh?" He became an expert in begging, targeting British and Americans and other foreign tourists who stayed across the road at the Taj Mahal Hotel and who came to the Gateway to take pictures with their Kodak Brownies loaded with rolls of 127 film taken from yellow-boxed small cardboard cartons left all over the place.

Raj Bhavnani soon realized that his begging abilities were proportionate to his skill in speaking English which was already quite good while he coaxed British and American tourists to repeat and define every English word he could not understand. Soon his "Baksheesh" fees increased with his English skills that were giving him the confidence to offer to take guests who came from the hotel on a tour around the Gateway, telling them all what he described as the Gateway's history, most of which had no basis in fact but came from his imagination. He came to speak English as well as the United Kingdom's Prime Minister Harold Macmillan spoke English and he felt he lied as well as (what he assumed with absolutely no confirmation) Pakistan's President Iskander Mirza. He was, however, even-handed since he did not hesitate to criticize his own nation's Prime Minister, Jawaharlal Nehru, who he also accused of lying and added to Raj Bhavnani's accusation that he didn't like Nehru's wardrobe. He would say, "Nehru's buttoned up tight necked closed-collared jacket is almost as bad as his hat."

He ended his three years of enterprise in the Gateway of India because near the end of 1959 a young man (but not as young as Raj) named Venu Ramachandra, who worked as an office manager for the Taj Mahal Hotel, walked across the road at noon to the Gateway to see for himself the boy who had captivated so many of his guests at the hotel; some calling him a genius, some calling him an historian, some saying he was unnaturally mature for his age, and some saying he was a treasure who made them love India.

Venu Ramachandra found him easy to spot from the descriptions given him by the hotel's guests: the tall, thin, heavy-haired Indian boy who always wore a white kurta which was the Indian shirt that went all the way down to his knees, and sheer white dhoti trousers. Venu Ramachandra introduced himself to Raj and told him about the compliments of hotel guests that he received about Raj.

"Thank you, Sahib" Raj said with forced but appreciated humility.

"Do you live here?"

"Yes, Sahib."

"You beg for a living?"

"No, Sahib. Begging is for the poor. I was poor when I came to Bombay from Sholapur, but that's when I was very young and so I begged then. But I didn't like it. And so I became a great historian. I know everything there is to know about this Archway and about the Arabian Sea and when I tell the history to the tourists from your hotel who come here, they give me what I have earned. Your guests are very kind and grateful to me."

"How much do you normally make in a day?"

"A great deal. May I take you out to lunch, Sahib?"

Venu Ramachandra laughed. "Oh no. I appreciate that invitation and I would ask you to have lunch with me at the Taj dining room but I ate already. Tell me, Raj—your clothes. Do you have any other clothes?"

"Of course. They are presently at the cleaners."

Venu Ramachandra smiled. "I see. At the cleaners."

"Yes, Sahib."

"Do you mean your clothes are presently with the Dhobis?" He was referring to those called Untouchables who make a living by beating clothes on rocks in the sea and rivers and creeks to remove any dirt from the clothes.

"No, Sahib. I bring them to western style cleaners. Big machines."

Venu Ramachandra tried his best to hide his smile. "What else do you tell the tourists?"

"If they are British I thank them for all they have done for India and that we all appreciate the railroads and bridges and tunnels they built for us when we were a colony of theirs. My name, Raj, is in honor of the British Monarchy since Raj was the term for their rule—their fine rule. If they are Italian I tell them I lived with an Italian family in Hyderabad and although I don't remember the names of all the pasta the woman of the family used to make I do remember that she turned half of the neighborhood into lovers of Italian food including me. If they are French I tell them that all of India knows that it was their Underground that won the war. Now we are finally getting some Americans in India and I tell them how much I love Eisenhower. There are also even more people now coming down to India from the Soviet Union; some Uzbekistanis and Kazakhs and Russians, and I tell them I always carry a picture of Khrushchev with me."

"Do you really?"

"Do I really what?"

"Do you really carry a picture of Khrushchev?"

RAISING THE BATON

"Of course."

"May I see it?"

"No, Sahib. It is sacred to me. I do not carry it to impress others; only to look at myself when I am alone. It is sacred to me."

Venu Ramachandra laughed as he simply couldn't control himself although Raj retained a serious face. "Raj, let me ask you something."

"Yes, Sahib."

"I have an idea for you. Just an experiment. And I have to check it out with others. But you do have a talent! What would you think of an offer for two weeks of work at the Taj for you to greet tourists and carry their bags and help with their itinerary and things like that?"

"For two weeks?"

"Just to see if you like the job, and for us to see if we like having you with us."

"It would take *three* weeks for me to tell if I like the job, Sahib."

Venu Ramachandra was somewhat unprepared for that answer but he nodded with an unhidden smile. "I'll ask. I'll find out."

"How many rupees?"

"Well, I haven't thought of that. How many rupees do you need?"

"I haven't thought of that either, Sahib. These people who beg here are my friends and they are very poor and they know that I have great wealth and it gives them hope. So I am important to them. I am not sure I want to leave them even for three weeks. You must make me an offer, Sahib."

Venu Ramachandra tried not to laugh and not even to smile. He was almost successful. "I need to talk to my superiors at the Taj to find out what they're willing to pay and—and I will probably be here tomorrow at around noon again to tell you what we can offer—if anything. Will you be here then?"

"No, Sahib. At noon tomorrow I have to pick up my clothes at the cleaners. I like to be prompt when I give my word. Can you make it an hour earlier, closer to 11 o'clock so I can be at the cleaners at noon?"

Venu Ramachandra nodded. "Good. Then tomorrow I will be here at around 11 o'clock with what I hope will be an offer."

Venu Ramachandra was there ten minutes before the designated time and Raj Bhavnani was waiting for him—and by 11:03 in the morning the deal was done.

Raj Bhavnani would make 150 rupees each of the three weeks, which was about $31.50 a week at the exchange rate of the time (with a rupee worth U.S. 21 cents) and his major duty was to be himself in helping and dealing with hotel guests—but with the difficult provision that he "tells no lies." In addition he would be living in a small room at the far end of a magnificent hallway in the hotel atrium with his room having a revolving fan in the ceiling. There would be a closet that would hold two hotel uniforms on hangers, a pair of black shoes on the floor, and even five pairs of black socks and underwear on a shelf. The bathroom would be down the hall and he would be allowed three meals a day to be eaten in the kitchen down the hall from the dining room.

On the first night of Raj Bhavnani's occupancy, the fan in the ceiling turned at low speed through eight revolutions before it stopped, never being able to start again. Raj didn't care and was so glad about his new riches that he would not complain about anything; certainly not a malfunctioning fan.

Before the second of his three weeks was done he realized that he had attained a tremendous success already by, without being directed to do it, he memorized the history of the hotel and he already knew practically every building within blocks including every shop. During these weeks he shared all his knowledge with guests of the hotel.

He received one compliment after another from his employer; Venu Ramachandra. By the end of the third week he was offered and he accepted a full-time job.

All of this gave Raj a dream that he knew he could achieve: A place where dreams come true: Get to America.

With self-imposed silence he waited before presenting some schedule for his plan to Venu Ramachandra. He was wise in waiting because a scheme presented itself without effort as he was told by a guest from the United States that he ought to go to Cornell University's School of Hotel Administration near Rochester, New York. That meant Raj's research was done. His announced destination would be Cornell University. He would ask for a paid vacation from the hotel so he could learn more in his chosen ambition of hotel administration here at the Taj. That would likely not be true but by his calculation, 'only one lie in all this time is pretty good' and probably a new record for him. He would stress that his American education would then be of "priceless value to the Taj Mahal Hotel in Bombay. Therefore I would need a coach-fare round-trip ticket to New York. Coach is all I need."

Venu Ramachandra nodded, expecting something like that from Raj Bhavnani. "Your vacation will likely be granted but it won't be paid. You haven't been here that long. And the fare to America is your business, not ours."

"Yes, Sa'ab," Raj said with a magnified tone of sadness.

"Now just keep working as you have been, and make enough rupees to earn your trip to America. And then unless I tell you otherwise we will discuss such a schedule depending on its length. Do you know how long the course at Cornell lasts?" And before receiving an answer he added, "The most important item you told me about such a trip is its value to this hotel. I'm quite sure that we can let you go and maybe we can work out some payment or courtesies but no airline fare and we will expect you back here at the Taj with your new knowledge as soon as the course is done. Now, how long is the course?"

"Three and one-half months," he said with arbitrary but exact-sounding length, 'One more lie but not immense,' Raj thought. 'Surely still permissible by any competent judge.'

"Do you have a passport?"

Raj looked confused and didn't answer.

"A passport, Raj! A passport from the Republic of India!"

"No, Sa'ab. I do not have anything," he said in his most pathetic-sounding voice.

"You'll need one."

"Yes, Sa'ab."

"That's through our government. That's for the govern-ment of India to give you. That should be easy enough. Then you'll need a visa to the United States. You have to do that at the American Consulate. We know people there so we can be of help. I can write a letter of introduction for you to a friend there who has been very good to the hotel."

"Yes, Sa'ab" he said with the continued weepiness in his voice.

"You tell me when you are in a position to make the trip. There isn't any rush on the paper work and all the formalities because it will be some time for you to have enough earnings saved for the funds it will take. Alright?"

Raj nodded.

It took him little more than one year to accumulate near seven thousand rupees by spending very little of his salary, (mostly for western clothes with the help of the tailor at the hotel) with seven thousand rupees giving him enough money for a British Overseas Airline Corporation one-way flight to Heathrow Airport in London and from there a transfer to a Pan American Airlines flight to New York City with $720 in U.S. currency to have in his pocket when travel would have then have been accomplished and New York would begin. Not Rochester but that could come later from New York City—if he really wanted it.

He was too young for years to go too fast and like most years when young, this one went too slow, but it was finally time to tell Venu Ramachandra that the required period had passed and the money was saved and his trip could be imminent and America could soon be streets and buildings instead of wide-awake dreams if Venu Ramachandra could now let him go from the Taj Mahal Hotel.

There was now some sadness in the voice of Venu Ramachandra with his words spoken slowly: "Congratulations, Raj. You have done what is unlikely and difficult. You have adhered to schedule when so many people do not adhere to schedules. You have saved the money needed. And your enthusiasm has not waned. Congratulations. All of us will miss you here. Now, do you have the necessary documents?"

Raj no longer used his pathetic tone. "No. I know you told me but I don't remember what documents are needed."

"You know, at this moment I don't remember everything you'll need. The expert on this is Arthur Mansfield at the U.S. Consulate. He knows both ends; ours and what you'll need in America. He's an expert. He's been here since Truman was the U.S. President. I think I told you he would be important to see. I'll line up an appointment. Now, it is important to answer every question of his honestly. Tell the truth. I know that will be very difficult for you—but do it. The truth will come out one way or another anyway."

"Yes, Sa'ab."

"One thing I do remember is that the U.S. Consulate is at 78 Bhulabhai Road. We go there quite often for one thing or another. I'll write it out for you. You'll need to give it to the taxi-driver. It's a ways from here. It's across town. They call it Lincoln House after Abraham Lincoln. You know who that was?"

"Yes, Sa'ab. He freed the slaves."

"Very good! Mr. Mansfield is in the little one-story building to the left as you enter the compound of the Consulate. I'll write that, too."

It looked like the Consulate had surely been there during the war. Every war. And it looked like Arthur Mansfield had been sitting behind his desk in the same position during all wars that had ever been waged. "Where do your parents live, Mr. Bhavnani?"

"Neither of my parents are living, sir."

"I'm sorry. That is a shame. If I may, what was your father's name?"

"Bharat! He was named after the real name of India: Bharat!"

"Bharat Bhavnani?"

"Yes, yes, of course."

"Good. And your mother?"

"Yes."

"What do you mean; yes?"

"I had a father and a mother."

"Good. Yes, of course. I thought so. What was her name?"

"Mary Lincoln."

"Mary Lincoln?"

"Yes. She was named after President Abraham Lincoln's wife."

He nodded. "That's unusual. That's quite thoughtful."

"Named after a fine woman," Raj offered.

"That's just odd; that's all. I mean that very few are named after her."

"My mother was an American, and so she was named after a fine American woman whose husband freed the slaves, you know." After all, that particular piece of his knowledge was praised by tourists he met at the Taj, and maybe it would work as well on Arthur Mansfield, particularly because he worked in the Lincoln House of the Consulate.

"That's very good. So that was her maiden name and then she became Mary Lincoln Bhavnani?"

"After she married my father; yes. That's what I was told that happened. She got that last part of her name on the day she married him."

"Well, that's what generally happens. Now, when were you born?"

"Independence Day. August the 15th of 1947."

Consulate Officer Arthur Mansfield looked suspicious but he didn't care to enter an argumentative discussion with someone who was sent by Venu Ramachandra. "Wonderful!"

"On Independence Day!"

"In what city were you born?"

"Just south of Sholapur. Maybe you've heard of it: Vadigenahalli."

"At the old general hospital there?"

"Then you have heard of it!"

"Oh, yes. At the old general hospital there?"

"No. At the old general railroad station there."

"She gave birth to you in the old general railroad station?"

"Yes, yes."

"Is there a record of that?"

"Oh, no, no. She died there giving birth to me."

"Oh, I'm sorry."

"I was told that both my mother and father fought for independence. So I have a heritage of courage."

"There is no record? I mean of your birth."

"Maybe some old passengers waiting for the train remember. I don't know. There was a doctor who was waiting for the train at the time but he's dead now."

"Maybe some old newspaper write-ups about it?"

"Maybe. Perhaps. I understand that allows me to be President of the United States. Is that true?"

"What do you mean?"

"If my mother was an American."

"President?"

"There must be something I could do to become President since my mother was American."

Arthur Mansfield had heard enough. "I don't know. That isn't what we take care of here. We don't deal with the rules on presidential candidates."

"Yes, yes. That's what I understand. Then do you know what I will do if I become President there?"

"No, I don't know. What?"

"I will change the official language of the States from English to Hindi."

"That would certainly be an unusual campaign pledge for a nominee for the U.S. Presidency to promise."

"Can Presidents do that?"

"That's way outside our sphere of business here at the Consulate."

"I suppose if I changed the language to Hindi that some Americans might be angry."

"That could be."

They stared at each other for quite a while until Raj asked, "Is that all, sir?"

"Mr. Bhavnani, you will need some papers."

Raj Bhavnani nodded. "Can you write down the papers I will need?"

Arthur Mansfield nodded and took some Consulate stationary from his top desk drawer and a Paper-Mate ball-point pen from his shirt pocket and started writing the requirements needed. "If you don't first have a Birth Certificate this is going to be a time-consuming procedure. You're going to be spending time going all over Bombay dealing with this nation's bureaucracy. You might even have to go to Delhi for some of them. I don't know all the addresses of the places but I know the bureaus with which you'll need to deal."

Raj didn't like that idea and so he found a single source from which he would receive all of his required papers including a Birth Certificate with his specified place and date of birth that he told them was as accurate as could be, and the names of his parents, Bharat and Mary Lincoln Bhavnani, as he had spelled it out and there was even a U.S. Social Security card with a number in case he should ever need it and a load of other papers stamped and pinned in batches, all of this from the beginning paper to the final pin having been attached by an old friend; a bearded "wise man"; probably a fake Sadhu, named G.K. Tarkunde who lived across the street from the Taj Mahal Hotel protected by the most north-eastern archway in the Gateway of India.

It only took Mr. Tarkunde three days to create the papers or have them made, and they only cost Raj one pair of shoes, a thin cotton blue jacket, and what appeared to be a baseball cap. That payment of goods then induced Mr. Tarkunde to add two small cloth-sided suitcases for Raj to take on his international travel.

By trading goods rather than buying his documents, Raj still had $706 of the $720 in American currency left in his pocket on his arrival at New York's Idlewild International Airport during the late and cold and overcast Thursday afternoon of January the 19th of 1961.

For a man who had no long-time career, no savings account and no current income, he was a very wealthy man.

THEME EIGHT

ANOTHER WORLD

RAJ BHAVNANI TOOK THE AIRPORT BUS to Midtown Station in Manhattan and it was the first time in his life that he took a public transport vehicle without passengers hanging out the doors because of lack of space inside, and holding on to posts and on to one another on its roof, and on the road there were no bullock carts slowing vehicles behind them, no red-stains of betel-nut juice that had been spit out on the floor or back of seats, and for good or ill, no sacred cows that would, without exception, be granted all rights of way.

He strained to see what there was to see of the New York skyline but there was too much overcast and a disappearing late afternoon sun behind the overcast and snow falling and the aisle seat on the bus all allowing him to only see little more than dots of lights at all elevations. He was not fascinated by snow as he saw pictures of the Himalayan Mountains throughout his life and others had boasted to him that India was where snow was born.

When he reached the Midtown Station he walked from there while holding the straps of one piece of luggage in each hand then changing each hand to the other strap, in route to the easily found Algonquin Hotel on 44th Street between 5th and 6th where Venu Ramachandra, back in Bombay at the Taj Mahal Hotel, had lined up an accommodation for him prior to going to Rochester.

Compared to the Taj back home, this was a small hotel—but one with a very prestigious history and traditions including only one small elevator with barely enough room for two passengers and the elevator operator to ride together. Raj's room (the lowest-cost room in the hotel) was so narrow that he needed to walk sideways around the bed to get from one side of the room to the other. He looked through the window at what he hoped would be a view of the Manhattan skyline when weather would permit but, instead, there was a view of the windows of the building next door a few feet away. And even though there was still some daylight, the view of the neighboring building was very dark with little if any brightness seeping through the shade from the adjoining buildings. Next, he tried to control the gurgling and whistling noise coming from the heater and he couldn't control it. But all that was part of the tradition that had been born in the earliest days of the Algonquin. Any modernization by management brought protests from regular guests, leaving the management no choice but to renovate the hotel back into its eccentricities of the past.

That Thursday night at the Algonquin Raj Bhavnani sat at a small white-clothed table in the lobby with an iced Coca-Cola and a plate of cheeses with his chair very close to the Algonquin's large oak grandfather clock that was near one of the great old and dark mahogany-lined walls. On the small table that held his Coca Cola and cheeses was a copy of "The Playgoer—The Magazine in the Theater—Camelot—Majestic Theater." It was filled with advertisements of New York stores, restaurants, and products as well as the program, cast, scenes, acts, and staff of "Camelot." Raj was looking at the magazine's advertisement of the restaurant, "Top of the Sixes" with a photograph of its nighttime diners on what was written in the advertisement to be the 41st floor of a building when Raj's solitude was interrupted by a deep voice: "Mr. Bhavnani?"

Raj Bhavnani quickly threw down the magazine as though he was guilty of reading something that was criminal, and he stood up. "Yes, sir."

The voice who had interrupted him belonged to a gray-haired man with a friendly smile who gave a short nod. "Good! I thought it was you. May I sit with you for a moment? I'm Paul Hafetz, the general manager's executive assistant for the Algonquin. Ben Bodne, the owner and president of the hotel, wanted to make sure you are comfortable in your room. He heard about your arrival from our friend, Venu Ramachandra at the Taj Mahal Hotel in Bombay. Mr. Bodne told us to give you a discount and he wants to make sure your stay is a pleasant one."

"Please. Please sit down with me, sir. Do you mean that Venu Ramachandra told the owner about my arrival? The owner of this hotel is the one who gave me the discount?"

Paul Hafetz nodded as he sat, "He did. And Mr. Bodne demanded that we be nice to you!"

"Otherwise you wouldn't be?" Raj said lightly as he sat back in his chair.

"I'm sure we would have been! Mr. Bodne is a self-made man like you. He started out in business as a newsboy when he was fourteen years old. From what Mr. Ramachandra told him, Mr. Bodne feels that you're following in his pattern. So, you worked at the Taj Mahal Hotel! That is truly a grand hotel."

"Yes, it is. I miss it already."

"Of course you do. It's your home, isn't it?"

He nodded and his voice softened. "It is." And then he repeated, "It is."

Paul Hafetz looked ill at ease at what could be Raj's emotion and he changed the conversation to something he hoped would get him out of thinking of what he left behind. "Did you see our cat?"

"Please?"

"Our cat. See him over there?" He pointed to a cat lying on a chair on the other side of the grandfather clock.

"Is it alive?"

"Of course he's alive. He's Hamlet. It's a tradition here. When John Barrymore was first here he named the cat who was here at the time—Hamlet. That was back in the 1930s and we have had more Hamlets since. When we have a male it's Hamlet and when it's a female it's Matilda. You are here while we are graced with another Hamlet! He is a good fellow!"

Raj smiled. "We love cats in India. You know, they're sacred!"

"They are, aren't they? And you have some pretty big ones, don't you?"

"Tigers. We have tigers."

"Of course. Well, we don't have tigers. But we do have Hamlets and Matildas. And we do have a lot of guests that come here just to pet the Algonquin's cat. You know, our lobby is generally packed with our guests at this time—writers, artists, dancers, musicians and actors and actresses—but a lot of them have taken leave to be in D.C."

"To be where?"

"D.C. Washington, D.C. The District of Columbia for the inauguration of our new president tomorrow: John Kennedy. John F. Kennedy. Fitzgerald. It should be quite a day. Let's pray for some sunshine or at least no snow there."

"Ahh, yes, yes. Kennedy! That would be worth seeing, wouldn't it?"

"Of course!"

"I crave to see his inaugural. It's why I made sure I would land on the 19th, so I would be in the United States if I could just get to—to D.C.," he lied. Raj was back to normal.

It only took a short while for an invitation from Paul Hafetz to invite Raj, not to D.C., but to the New York Athletic Club on 59th Street the following morning to watch the new President's inauguration on the television set the Club had recently acquired. It was a marvelous invitation for Raj for two reasons: he would see an inauguration of a U.S. President as it would take place, and for the first time he would see a television set. After all, any American could get to D.C. to stand in the cold outside the U.S. Capitol Building because, Raj thought, Americans are all rich and would have warm clothes and hats, but to actually see it on an operating television set would be special.

The morning of January the 20th greeted Raj with both snow and a bright sun and his first immersion in Manhattan. He didn't walk; he promenaded up Fifth Avenue for the major part of his morning journey to the New York Athletic Club with his sight-seeing stroll continually interrupted by his own frequent motionlessness, standing still while he stared upward at the top of buildings the likes of which he had never seen before. Some of the herd of many fast-walking pedestrians went right into him because New Yorkers believe that standing still is against the law with "standers" to be turned over to the police for quickly determined life sentences or extradition to New Jersey.

None of that bothered him. It was different from anything he had known before and everything was a gift of sight. "What clothes they wear! What coats! What things in the windows of stores! What colors! What buildings! Another world! Where's the Empire State Building?" He slowly turned around. "There! There! It is down there! It goes into the sky! What a building! It's there!"

"Hey, Mac! Don't we have a sidewalk where you can move in one direction at a time?"

When Raj reached 59th street across from Central Park he started asking others where he could find the New York Athletic Club. Everyone he asked gave him directions, all of whom were wrong, but the New York City tradition is to always give directions to a stranger, with truth being an unnecessary triviality.

He ended up finding it by himself after strolling in and out of countless buildings on 59th Street.

The sign in the reception room told that "The Presidential Inauguration Event on Television for Members and Invited Guests Only" was being held in the Ninth Story Lounge. Uniquely, that was accurate as that was where it really was taking place.

The crowd of men was huge with little if any free space. There were no chairs and so everyone in the Athletic Club Lounge was standing except three men who were seated and that's because they were in wheelchairs.

The most prominent space in the room was held by the star: the RCA television set resting on top of a high podium with a magnifying lens mounted in front of the television screen.

Although Raj could barely see the black-and-white images between the rounded corners of the magnifying lens, and although there was no snow falling in D.C., there appeared to be snow falling on the television image. Worst of all, however, was that Raj couldn't hear the voice of the new President very well since Raj had come in breathlessly late from his exploratory slow walk, and his tardiness guaranteed a position far from the loud- speakers of the television set and not far from the door in which he entered the room.

Somehow Raj did hear President Kennedy saying that "… the rights of man come not from the generosity of the state, but from the hand of God." Raj said in a very loud voice not to anyone in particular, "Yes! Yes! He is better than Jawaharlal Nehru and Vinoba Bhave put together!"

And when President Kennedy said something about "those peoples in the huts and villages across the globe struggling to break the bonds of mass misery," Raj cheered and yelled to no one other than an invisible Chairman of the Soviet Union; invisible because he was not there. "Are you listening, Mr. Khrushchev?"

Then President Kennedy concluded with "God's work must truly be our own." And the people outside the Capitol Building in D.C. and the men in the New York Athletic Club in New

York City applauded and cheered and Raj gave a short vocal phrase of esteem in Hindi: "Kennedy-ji!" Only a few heard him because the applause and cheering for the President was too loud and they probably wouldn't have understood Raj Bhavnani even if they did hear him.

There was one exception to that who heard and did understand what Raj said. The exception, by chance, was standing in front of him and, with a big smile, that exception quickly turned around for the two to be face to face.

"Namaste!" the man said to Raj with his two hands straight up and pressed together at the tips of his fingers, and he made a slight and bowed nod of his head.

"Namaste!" Raj answered him with the same audible and visual gestures of his new acquaintance and with beaming eyes and a large smile. "You are from India?"

"No. I have been there on travels. I heard you."

"Yes. Yes. You have been to India?"

"Calcutta, Madras, Bombay, Delhi, Jaipur, Agra, up to Hill Stations. A lot of places."

Raj extended his hand. "My name is Raj Bhavnani. You have seen more of my home country than I have!"

They shook hands while Raj's new acquaintance said, "It is good to meet you, Mister Bhavnani. My name is Christopher Straw."

"It is good to meet you, Mister Straw! A British name, isn't it?"

"Yes; a couple generations back."

"But now an American through and through?"

Christopher smiled. "Through and through."

"Then the Brits lost—" and he paused for a moment. "Then

the Brits lost four times, didn't they?"

"What do you mean?"

"They lost to America's Revolution. Yes, yes. Then they lost you. Then they lost what they thought was their colony forever—of my country—India—when we won our independence. Then they lost me! Four losses! Which one do you suppose they regret the most?"

Christopher laughed. "Losing you, Mr. Bhavnani. That is for sure. Queen Elizabeth has told me that many times."

Raj Bhavnani gave a wide smile. Then he nodded. "I like your pretending. You, Sa'ab, are American through and through!"

THEME NINE

TOO MANY TIGERS

"IMMENSE! IMMENSE!" RAJ SAID as he sat across from Christopher at a dinner table in the very crowded Mamma Leone's West 48th Street restaurant. Absorbed by the fact that this morning he had already seen another world, he now said, "Another another world!" That was because in front of both of them were the usual Mamma Leone's massive portions of welcome appetizers: Salade Leone including separate clusters of celery and olives and tomatoes and scallions and pastas and cheeses and Italian breads with no room on the table left; not even for an elbow or additional silverware. All of this for no reason except that Christopher Straw and Raj Bahvnani walked in and got a table, ordering nothing yet.

"Mama Leone's portions here are a lot bigger than you ever found in Old Delhi's Mati Mahal, aren't they?" Christopher asked his companion in a clear New York vs. Delhi unfair but proud competition.

"I have never been to Mati Mahal," Raj proudly admitted as though not having ever been there was a medal of honor.

"Tourists. It's for tourists in Delhi. But this has more food for customers than any restaurant anywhere in the world! Do we have to eat all of this?"

"All of it. If you don't—then Mama Leone shoots you."

"She does?"

"Oh, yes. She sweeps the bodies into the alley before they close up for the night here."

"That is not good, Sa'ab."

"No it isn't. It's why people come here only if they are very hungry."

"In my country people are starving. There is no place like this where people can go if they are poor and very hungry."

"Oh I know! I know that. I just said that as a joke. I'm sorry. I have seen people starving in India. I saw them every day and every night I was there. I'm sorry. It was meant as a joke about this place. It was thoughtless."

Now it was a competition in thoughtfulness of all things. "No apologies, Sa'ab, my friend. I know American humor. I know India and I know *of* America."

"And never the twain shall meet."

"I do not know what 'twain' means."

"Neither do I," Christopher admitted.

"What took you to India, Sa'ab?"

"I was on a long around-the-world trip for Western Electric here in New York where I work on their contract with NASA; the National Aeronautics and Space Administration so it's called NASA; an abbreviation. When we start orbital flights with Astronauts we have to track them. So, in preparation I go to different areas of the world in which we're going to build satellite tracking stations in our network for Project Mercury. I make sure that everything in those sites work so that every piece of information and data are in sync between the Project Mercury Astronaut in flight or in orbit and the Capsule Communicator on earth at Cape Canaveral and all the ground crews around the world. Do you know what Project Mercury is?"

"No, Sa'ab" he said softly with some boredom in hope Christopher would not explain it to him. He already heard enough.

"Seven Astronauts—people—men. They're going to go into space from Florida—from Cape Canaveral there. That's what I crave to do—go into space."

"Yes, Sa'ab. That's good. Then you go into space. Why wait? Go now, Sa'ab!"

"I can't go now. I'm too hungry."

"Too hungry! Let us eat!"

"Although India probably won't be in our tracking network, I had to go from Zanzibar to our next tracking sites planned in Australia. It's a long distance between Zanzibar and Australia so I wanted to stop in some logical but good and interesting place between them. That worked out to be India since there's likely to be a tracking ship in the Indian Ocean."

Raj still had absolutely no idea what Christopher was talking about.

"I had the time to stay in India for a while and I did it because I always wanted to see it for myself."

"Yes, yes. A good choice. Yes, yes. That was very good." "Very good, very good," Raj repeated.

"Absorbing. That's what I did in India. I wanted to absorb it. Now, you were born there; you lived there; you grew up there; you worked there so you know more about it than I'll ever know.

What was your career in India, Raj?"

"Philosophy. I am a philosopher, Sa'ab."

"A philosopher? That's what you did in India?"

"Yes, Sa'ab."

"Where?"

"The University of India."

"Is that in Delhi?"

"No, no. Close by. Close by."

"And that's what you did?"

"Philosophizing."

"You made money at it?"

"Many rupees."

"What do you do here in the States?"

"Philosophizing."

"Does that—are you doing well here?"

"Oh, yes. Now, tell me, where else did you go on this space-man's trip? Cities around the word?"

"A lot of places. All over. My father once told me I should travel the United States to learn—and then to travel the world to learn. In the U.S. I've traveled to every state except North Dakota. I don't know how, but I missed it. Just not ever got there. But for me the best was Hawaii. There's going to be a Mercury Tracking Site in Kauai and I spent some vacation time in Honolulu. I was looking for a girl—a beautiful girl I met many years ago. A wonderful girl. Beautiful. It's a long time ago. Gorgeous. Hawaiian."

"Ahhh. Did you find her?"

"No."

"Good."

"Good? Why is that good? I said I didn't find her."

"That's very good. You had a good time with her many years back. Is that not accurate?"

"Yes. Wonderful memories."

"That's enough then. Don't try to recreate memories, Sa'ab. You will only destroy the memory because it will be confused with the new visit. It won't work. She's probably married by now anyway. Leave good memories alone. Appreciate them and let them be. Each memory is not only a person and a place; it is a time so you cannot have it again, Sa'ab. It's gone. Appreciate what it was."

"I don't think she's married."

"Of course you don't. She's married. Maybe divorced but maybe not yet. Now, let us get to your new President Kennedy," he said in an obvious move to be done with Christopher's incoherent biography and obsessions. "Your Kennedy seems like a fine man. Did you hear him when he said that those who foolishly sought power by riding the back of the tiger ended up inside the tiger? He was right. Don't sit on a tiger. You have too many tigers, Mr. Straw. He was so right. I see that in you. I have seen tigers eat those who sat on their backs."

"You have? In India?"

"Oh, yes. They don't eat the whole thing. They kill the man, eat some of him and the rest of him is eaten by vultures."

"My God."

"So Mr. Kennedy said not to sit on a tiger. I never have. And what did you like hearing from your new President?"

"From John Kennedy, you mean. He's now President John Kennedy."

"Yes, yes."

"He said, 'Together let us explore the stars.'"

"Rhe-*tore*-ic. That's all it is. Rhe-*tore*-ic."

"You mean rhetoric."

"Rhetoric. Rhetoric. Thank you, Sa'ab."

"And 'no.' It was more than rhetoric. He meant it—I hope."

"I missed that."

Christopher ate for a while since his dinner companion was taking issue with the subjects. "Good food, huh?" Christopher asked.

"Yes, yes!"

"Do you live here in New York now?"

"At the Algonquin Hotel. In Bombay I lived at the Taj Mahal Hotel. Hotel living is the only way. They make your bed for you every morning. There is always food at the restaurant. All things are done for you. And at the Taj, we who used to live there met very important people."

"Of course you did. But not just those in a hotel. All people are important."

"Really?"

"Really. Who did you meet?"

"Churchill."

"You met him?"

"Oh, yes. A fine man."

"That's wonderful."

"He's British, you know."

"Yes, I know."

"He told me about Taylor Woodrow."

"Who?"

"Taylor Woodrow."

"Who's that?"

"It's an organization. They build things. Taylor Woodrow

built Heathrow Airport. Taylor Woodrow builds everything."

"Churchill told you that?"

Raj nodded. "Yes, yes. I am going to ask Taylor Woodrow to do some renovations at the Algonquin."

Christopher nodded. There was something about what Raj had said that Christopher couldn't quite lock down but the name of Taylor Woodrow was familiar to him. "Tell me more about Mr. Woodrow or his organization."

"He builds everything! Everything, Sa'ab! Churchill told me he and his company builds everything. Heathrow. Everything."

Christopher's attention was being diverted by someone who probably never met Churchill or Taylor Woodrow. The diversion was a very pretty young woman with a group of people at a table just across from Christopher and Raj, and there was no question but that she had cast a glance at Christopher and he spotted that glance; the glance probably less than a few seconds but what a wonderful less-than-a-few seconds that Christopher saw. He had actually taken some of her time. That, in itself was a victory. "Look at that girl. She is something, isn't she?"

"Where?"

"There. There at that table" and he gestured with his head toward her. "The one eating spaghetti and cutting it up into small pieces so it doesn't slurp from her lips."

Raj looked over at the table and then back at Christopher and then Raj rolled his head in the Hindu motion that meant a somewhat "yes" but without enthusiasm.

Christopher said, "She is something!" He wasn't giving up.

"Don't go over there, Sa'ab. She is nothing."

"I'm not going over there. What do you mean she is nothing?"

"Nothing. She is nothing. Leave her be. She is trouble. And

I know you are planning to go over there because you moved your chair back with enough room for you to leave the table."

"Did I?"

"What for? She is ugly."

"Ugly!? She isn't ugly. She's gorgeous."

"Believe me, Sa'ab. She is ugly. Look at her. Ugly."

Christopher laughed. "In that case I have just become the world's greatest advocate of ugliness."

This time it was Raj who gave a smile and then he gave another roll of his head. "She, Mr. Straw, is no good for you."

"Why do you say that? What do you mean?"

"Do you mind if I discourage you from ruining your life? Mr. Straw, do you mind if I philosophize to prevent you from making a serious error?"

"An error from what?"

Raj gave a quick look at the young woman at the table and gave a nod; this time an American nod. No rolling of the head. "In the beginning God created two sexes. And He called them Men and Critics. And for some, God made the Critics so alluring, so tempting, so desirable, so intoxicating that Men ignored all the criticism longing to get out of that pretty thing. But God gave the Critics nearly infinite patience that He took from Men, leaving Men with practically none."

"What are you talking about?"

"My friend, I will save you from her." And with that Raj pulled back his chair and headed over to the table with the young woman sitting there eating spaghetti after she cut it into small pieces.

And that was the beginning of Christopher Straw's twenty minute stomach problem as it got twisted into knots no surgeon could untie. His stomach problem came from his brain problem that came from his jealousy problem that came from his Raj Bhavnani problem.

The twenty minutes problem was finally done when Christopher saw her glance at him with a longing expression as though she was trying to silently tell him she wanted to be with him and not with this Raj-guy who came over to her. But then the pain came back in Christopher's stomach when Raj grabbed her hand, kissed the back of it, and her face turned red and she laughed. Was this the ultimate of fickleness? She did this act of incivility just seconds after she flirted with Christopher with her making eyes at him. Was there not an iota of faithfulness in the moral code of this thoughtless woman? Was his philosophizing dinner companion right about her? That incident at the neighboring table was followed by conversation between Raj and the young woman and some laughter and then Raj started writing something on the yellow edge of the menu of Mamma Leone's while the young woman dictated something to him. He then ripped that piece off the menu, folded it and put it tightly in his left hand. He took his right hand and once again took her closest hand to him, the left one, and kissed the back of it and the thoughtless wench appeared to be delighted. Christopher Straw's statement of that young woman being gorgeous was not an exaggeration but an understatement. Her blonde hair was full and went below her shoulders in waves as if God was her hairdresser. She was near to looking angelic except that angels don't have glimmers of mischief in their eyes and she had even more than such glimmers.

Then Raj almost ran from that table back to the table where Christopher had been sitting alone since Raj's earlier sudden departure in the pursuit of saving Christopher from making an error with such a woman.

"You must come with Savannah and me, Christopher! Savannah told me about a wonderful place she believes that I would love too. From what she said I would love it because there is real Indian dancing there. It is just blocks away. You would love it too! I know you will! You know India! You must come with us!"

Now there was practically no part of Christopher's anatomy that was free of pain.

"Christopher? Christopher, are you listening to me?"

As though in a hurry, Christopher asked, "What? What? What?"

"You must join us! You must join us! It is called Ceylon India Inn." And he unfolded the piece of paper he had been holding in his left hand. "Savannah told me the directions. I wrote them down. It is one block up to 49th and then across Seventh Avenue. It will be on the north side of 49th. She told me. You will be there?"

Christopher stared at Raj until it became very uncomfortable for Raj. Then, totally unhurried but with soft and measured words Christopher said, "I know how you heard of Taylor Woodrow."

Raj was confused. For a while he said nothing and then he said, "Taylor Woodrow?"

Christopher's soft, measured words were now said even more softly and they were said with increased measurement. "Taylor Woodrow. You didn't hear about him from Churchill.

And you didn't know him."

Now Raj smiled but his smile was a nervous one with his closed-mouth grin giving some twitches. "What do you mean?"

This time Christopher had an added almost maniacal rhythm to his words accented by a new device: whispering: "At Heathrow I saw what you saw there. Walking from the plane that just landed and walking to customs and the transit lounge— during that walk there was a sign that read, 'Taylor Woodrow Built This Airport. Taylor Woodrow Builds Everything.' That's where you got it."

Raj nodded. He was caught. He nodded again. Usually those who lie attempt to protect the lie told by telling a second lie in support of the first one. Not Raj. No attempt. Instead he reverted to his habit of accepting the fact that he was found out before digging deeper. And so with Raj's nod having acted as a surrender, he chose to go on with life as though being caught was done and forgotten and the capture was of no consequence.

Raj shrugged and asked Christopher again, "Will you go with Savannah and me to the Ceylon India Inn?" And he added, "You know; it is named after the country, Ceylon, that is just south of India. Savannah told me there is real Indian dancing there."

Christopher shook his head from side to side and in case the visual response was not enough he softly answered. "No. I will not go with you" and he hesitantly added, "—and Savannah."

"Savanah Lane; that's her name. It describes her perfectly. Unique! It's Savanah Lane," he said as he injected an added insult to Christopher's lack of knowledge about her.

Rejection of Raj's invitation proved to be a stroke of prophetic wisdom because had Christopher accepted the invitation he would then have severely injured his self-confidence in the evening's unexpected rivalry with Raj Bhavnani. Although Raj left the bill at Mamma Leone's to be paid by Christopher, at least Christopher Straw saying "no" to the new invitation saved him from being a witness to the small dance-floor of the Ceylon India Inn that would be vacated by others when Raj would take its center.

The dance floor was left to no one else; not man or woman or couple could compete with Raj Bahvnani's ability to perform Indian dancing. And all others would not allow him to leave the floor. They applauded and cheered and Savannah Lane was the most demonstrative and led the chant of "More! More!" and someone yelled "Bravo!" and someone else yelled something that sounded like "Shah- bash!" Whatever it meant, in the way it was said it had to be a compliment.

Such dancing was not seen before in Manhattan; at least not in the way he did it: his feet moved as though they were not in New York or even in Bombay but in Moscow's Bolshoi Ballet Theater; his legs running and jumping with movements above his knees different from those below his knees; his arms twisting and turning with flexibility as though each section of his arms were not connected to the next section of his arms; his hips revolving as though they were in London's Soho District's maze of clubs for the young to rock and roll; his neck went side to side and front to back as though he was a headhunter in the Ivory Coast; his fingers behaving as though they were performing in a Bangkok wedding celebration. That exhibition of Raj created the epitome of Indian dancing that had no challenger but had only surrender as the applause and cheers kept any dancing rival away from competition.

But it had to stop sometime and Raj volunteered to stop himself by ignoring the crowd who wanted even more from him. The applause and cheers escorted him from the floor.

In a heap of perspiration and exhaustion he headed toward the small table and its empty chair he had left beside Savannah Lane, and he almost fell on the chair. He took a folded handkerchief from his back pocket and he wiped his forehead.

"You are unbelievable!" Savannah Lane said with a soft southern accent. "You are a danc-uh! A real danc-uh!"

In a display of modesty which was something previously unknown in all his years on earth, he said with breathlessness, "I don't know how to dance."

"What!?"

"No. I never danced before."

"How on earth is that possible!?"

While attempting quick breaths, he rolled his head in that native Indian style that seems to be inborn and so automatically that no non-Indian find it easy to accomplish. "I watched the movies. All Indian movies have dancing in them. All of them: dramas, comedies, tragedies, history; every movie has Indian music and dance." He took deep breaths and then continued: "I watched movies in the theaters of our cities and on the stretched out white sheets between two trees in our villages that were carried to the village by someone who brought a projector and a sheet and wanted some food from the villagers or wanted a sleeping place from us or wanted something else, but wanted something. I didn't know I could do what I saw in movies—I didn't know I could dance—and then I added my own meaning of dance with my own steps and motions I never knew I had."

Then he wiped his forehead again and this time he added

some wipes of the handkerchief on his cheeks and that did it: he was able to wipe away more than his perspiration. This time he was able to wipe away his recently found modesty that was so difficult for him to find and now his old habits came back as he congratulated himself. "Did you like the way I glided—skated—rolled—lifted this audience across all dimensions?"

"Oh yes!" she foolishly agreed. "No one here ever saw anything like you!"

He nodded. He knew she was observant and smart. But then she said something that was not observant or smart. "That man at your table at Mama Leone's. He is a friend of yaws?"

Raj laughed. "Oh no, M'em Sa'ab! No friend. No friend. Hungry. He wanted a good dinner. He has no money."

"So you took him to eat?"

"I always do that for the poor."

"Oh."

"Why do you ask, M'em Sa'ab?"

"I was just wondering."

"Nothing to wonder. He is a dreamer. That is why he is always in trouble—why he has no money—no talent. He dreams of flying through space," and he pointed upward. "He dreams of heading toward Mars or Saturn or Nirvana or somewhere—from Florida or somewhere—from somewhere." And Raj laughed, then spread his arms and moved one of his arms up as he moved the other down as though he was flying through clouds.

"He plans to go into space?"

"To hear him, he is going to go everywhere. But he has been nowhere. No money. No nothing. I take him to eat. He was hungry. Now, shall we go somewhere else—for a drink? Not into space. Unlike our friend, we will stay in the United States tonight, M'em Sa'ab!"

"I am not M'em Sa'ab." There was the certain tone of annoyance in the rhythm of her words as only a woman's cadence can perform as it becomes somewhat of a warning. Any man would either have ignored the designation of M'em Sa'ab or laugh at it or say "Hey Buddy, I ain't no M'em Sa'ab!" She, however, was very much a woman. "I am Savannah Lane. That is my name: Savannah Lane."

"Of course. I said 'M'em Sa'ab' because I am taken back home, so very comfortable with you that I go back to—to habits of respect at home. Now, should we go somewhere else?"

"Somewhere else? Why?"

"Because there are more places to go!"

"Where?"

"Ahhh. Top of the Sixes."

"Top of the Sixes? What is Top of the Sixes?"

"It is the Top of the Sixes."

"I don't know what you mean. The top of what sixes?"

"666 Fifth Avenue. That's the address because there are three big 6's that are lit up on top of the building and there's a restaurant on top of the 666's. I know it well. Fine people. Fine People. There's a bar there, too. The people who own the Sixes are all close friends of mine. Yes, yes—good people." What he didn't tell her is that he knew of it because he read about it while sitting in the Algonquin. "They are my friends."

"I'm sure they are—but not tonight. Some other time. It's been a long day and I better get home. Alright if we get our coats?"

Raj gave a very quick expression of squeezing his lips together while nodding in agreement. Like being caught by Chris in the telling of his Taylor Woodrow story, this was just another time for him to accept defeat as gracefully as he would accept victory. "I'll get your coat. I won't get mine because I didn't bring mine," and he laughed with a new twinkle in his eyes.

In contrast to Raj Bhavnani, defeat was not an accepted trait of Christopher Straw. And so Christopher Straw would not allow the evening to end where it had been headed for him and, instead, he wanted to insure that the hours that had passed so miserably for him would be no more than a misplaced prologue to the more important exaltation ahead for both Christopher Straw and Savannah Lane in the later hours within that January evening.

d u e t

THEME TEN

A GOOD NIGHT AT ANGELO'S

RAJ AND SAVANNAH WALKED toward the exit area of the front parlor of the Ceylon India Inn. The parlor housed the coat-racks and desk with the coat-checker behind it, and a telephone booth near the revolving doors of the Inn. Through the picture-window Savannah caught a glimpse of a man outside on the sidewalk with hands in the pockets of his black overcoat and he was pacing in the cold. Savannah recognized him as the one who had been at the table with Raj Bahvnani at Mama Leone's and who had exchanged a quick but intense glance between the two of them. He was bold enough to be making himself noticeable to her by waiting for her exit from The Ceylon India Inn with or without Raj Bhavnani.

Savannah did not want to find out what he would say or do if she and Raj were to walk out together. As Raj helped her put on her coat, Savannah asked, "Raj, you live in Midtown don't you?"

"Yes. That's right. I live at the Algonquin Hotel. Would you like to have a drink there? Do you like cats? We always have a cat in the lobby—a friendly one. Do you want to have a drink there? Just some—I don't know—it's just some five blocks away; the short ones."

"Oh, no. I can't do that. I have to get home. You go ahead. I live in the Village and I'm going to take the subway home. I always do. I live right across the street from the station. I told the girls who live there—we live together—that I'd be home before 10 o'clock. I'm going to phone to tell them I'm on my way so they won't worry. You go ahead."

Although Raj Bhavnani won the attention of the pretty young woman at the Ceylon India Inn by his dancing abilities, she now had given him increased signals that he fell short of winning her affection. He again handled her gentle rejection by using his frequent facade of disinterest. No anger. No hostility. No victimization. By this time he knew what to do because he had already known so many disappointments in life. Even when he was a child no one ever saw tears from his eyes. He wanted to give evidence that he could handle life. And he could.

So even with that quick direction of hers for him to "go ahead," he at least gave the impression that it was of no consequence whether she stayed with him or if their night together was done. Without protest he watched her as she walked toward the phone booth in unchallenged obedience to the wishes given him by the pretty Savannah Lane. He walked out the door to the street.

All of this while the uninvited wanderer outside turned the other way, his face remaining invisible to Raj who was signaling for a cab. One came in short time, whisking Raj away.

It was close to five minutes before Savannah walked out of the Ceylon India Inn after feeling that enough time had passed to pretend to have made a telephone call, just in case Raj would be waiting for her. She could see he wasn't waiting but the wanderer was.

She buttoned her coat, walked out through the revolving door and this time the pacing man in the black overcoat made no turn-away for face invisibility. And for the first time he saw her full-length. Even though her coat had a fur collar and there was fur around the bottom of her sleeves and looked warm, its short length didn't care about the temperature. It was short enough for him to see her legs clearly for the first time by her keeping up with then-current fashion. She looked gorgeous. "Savannah?"

She turned her head toward him. She made no effort to hide her smile. Nor did she keep distance. "Yes. I'm Savannah Lane. You ahh persistent, ahen't you? Should I pretend that I have no interest?"

He gave a wider smile than hers. "If you want. Sometimes persistence doesn't pay off at all for me. Tonight it did. Seeing you smile just now—and smile while so close to me—and hear that southern accent of yours—is worth all the failures in persistence that I've endured in my life."

"Oh, my! I am complimented by what you just said but all I asked was 'should I pretend I have no interest?' I didn't say how much or how little or what kind of interest. I noticed you were staring at me at Mama Leone's and then I saw your angry look at Raj Bhavnani when he came to where I was sitting with mah friends."

"Of course I was angry! He ate too much and he left the

check for me to pay. And that's what made me angry."

She smiled. "And you expect me to believe that?"

"No." He gave a slight smile and it quickly disappeared. So did hers. Their smiles had been exchanged for studies of each other's face. For a while neither said another word.

She broke the silence. "What's your name?"

"Chris. Christopher Straw."

"Now, Christopher Straw, tell me the real reason you were angry at your friend."

Christopher nodded with his lower and upper lips pressed together. "I wanted to be with you and he was with you. I normally do not stand outside in the freezing cold waiting for one more glance at a girl. But I'm not complaining now and I'm not angry at him or angry at anyone. Not now. Look. It is very cold and I can't compete with Mama Leone so I won't ask you if you want to go somewhere for a second dinner, and I don't know where to ask you to go with me to hear good music, but do you want a drink, or a Coke, or a dessert, or maybe an aspirin?"

Her smile was back. "An aspirin sounds good!"

"Good. Then I'll have an aspirin too. I never take aspirin alone. I just generally need a cup of coffee to get it down. I'm glad you want an aspirin, too."

"Yes! That's the best way-uh to get it down, Christopher Straw." She said his name for the second time, this time playfully and in the playfulness she was proving she had put his name solidly in her mind.

"Right! Now, just stay next to me," he gently directed. "I know a place that's pretty good that's straight ahead. Angelo's. It's not even a half block away. They have great aspirins there. Bayer. Besides that, it gives us a place to get out of the cold—and gives me more time to be with you." He took her hand and, surprisingly, she held it tightly.

"We don't need gloves" she said as they walked briskly down 49th Street. And as they got closer to the destination he then changed their pace into slow steps and she accommodated, and after that her head found its way to rest on his close shoulder as the slow steps became even slower. What a marvelous interlude no matter its brevity.

Too bad, but entering the restaurant meant her head went into an upright position. Too bad since there was now too much brevity after all.

He placed their coats on the hooked coat-stand next to their table and as soon as he did that they were greeted by someone who Savannah thought was obviously the owner or the maitre d' or at least someone in authority at Angelo's. "Christopher Straw! For the seventh time this week you are back! Each time a different girl!"

Christopher laughed and said to Savannah, "He kids around. He just kids around. That's Angelo and he will say anything he can think to make his customers uncomfortable. That's what he does." Then he looked back at Angelo. "It is not! The seventh night this week! What are you talking about? That's outrageous!"

"Then it was the eighth night this week; so what?" He looked at Savannah. "Mister Straw comes here every night with a different girl."

Christopher shook his head but it was combined with a smile. "What are you doing to me, Angelo?!" Then he twisted his head to look away from Angelo to look at Savannah. "The owner here is trying to ruin my evening."

Angelo nodded. "Alright; I didn't count the times. But all so young. Yes, a different girl every night, barely out of their teens." Then he bent down to whisper in Savannah's ear, "He's a pervert, you know. Be careful."

"Oh, I know," Savannah said attempting to hide a smile or any other sign of lightness, and suddenly her southern accent disappeared. "I'm a policewoman and I read his entire folder—his record before leaving the station tonight. That's why I'm with him! He should never be left by himself. Angelo—you're Angelo, right?" Angelo gave a quick nod. "Angelo, just insist on cash tonight. I think he still carries stolen traveler checks and a stolen Diners Club card. It's why we first arrested him."

Christopher could not help himself from laughing because she was the only one he ever knew who topped Angelo's urge to insult with such matter-of-fact ease.

Then she turned to Christopher and asked, "Do you mind, Chris, if I give our order to him?"

"Sure. Go ahead."

"Two pieces of buttered white toast for each of us. So in other words four pieces in all; two for him and two for me. Butter them for us so the butter melts way into the middle of the depth of the toast while the toast is hot. And a cup of coffee for each of us—regular coffees—and two aspirins for each of us. In other words, add to the four pieces of buttered toast two regular coffees and four aspirins: Bayer, please. Got it?"

"Yes, Ma'am." He looked away from her and nodded at Christopher. "I like her, Mister Straw. She doesn't kid around. She isn't a child like all the rest you've brought here. I think this one might even have passed her 20th birthday. Maybe. Just maybe. Admittedly, she doesn't look it—but she acts it. And she knows exactly what she wants."

Savannah gave one of her most feminine smiles with slightly squinted distrustful eyes and then a quick wink at Angelo. Then she tilted her head just like Miss Osborn did when Christopher was in 4-B. "Thank you, Angelo."

Angelo nodded, then walked into the maze of tables and stopped to talk to some other customers.

Savannah was glowing. "I love Angelo! I'm so glad you brought me here! I never knew this place existed! Does it have a good reputation?"

"No. Terrible."

"Then how come they have so many customers?"

"To be insulted. They come here to be insulted. Angelo hates all his customers. What do you think? Do you think this place lives down to its reputation?"

"Oh, yes. It's appalling. I love it."

"Savannah, where did you get that name: Savannah?"

Suddenly her southern accent became hauntingly re-pro-nounced. "The same place you received yaw name: Christo-fuh." How did her accent re-appear in one flash?

"The same place? What do you mean, the same place I received my name?"

"Muh parents. Muh parents named me Savannah just like yaw parents named you Christo-fuh." Perhaps her accent wasn't put on, he thought, and maybe it was that hearing nothing but a Yankee talking made the southern accent predominate with automatic ease and quick command, totally beyond her control with something inside of her telling her how to talk to whomever she was with much in the way a person who speaks two or more languages almost unconsciously is able to use them interchangeably without more than an involuntary click going on inside the person's mind. But of course he was giving her an excuse to what could well be a put-on accent.

"Oh! Okay! Gotcha! I mean did your parents name you Savannah because you were born there?"

"I wasn't bawn theyuh. Ah was born in Chahleston. Savannah's in Gee-aww-juh. Chahleston's in South Carolina, y'know." Nothing is worse than a geography lesson taught by a southerner with a time-increasing accent.

"Yes, I know." He never really gave it much thought.

There was a long silence that was finally broken when Savannah said, "So ah wasn't bawn theyuh."

"Okay. That's okay. I get it. Good. Sure. I get it." He didn't get it at all. He just didn't want to go on and on about something so petty. With tremendous relief the very small dinners arrived for them brought by a tall thin waiter with a black bow-tie who looked at the diners and their dinners with the displeasure born of certainty that there would not be a large tip to come. He quickly walked away after the placement of the two dinners.

She ignored their arrival. "So they didn't want my name to be Chahleston. After all, they thought that when I would get old-uh, people might call me Chahles fow sho-awt and they didn't want that."

"That was good thinking. Sure."

"Shoe-uh," she said. But she wouldn't stop. "Ah was supposed to be bawn in Savannah which was home but they were in Chahleston when I arrived. It's only 98 miles up U.S. Highway Numbuh 17 you know." One hundred miles would probably have been close enough.

"Huh! That's a good sized ride."

"It's a wonduhfuhl old road, y'know. Lined with big old oak trees with Spanish Moss hangin' from every branch, even right ovah the road!"

"Is that right? That's great." Well, maybe not great. But it was just fine.

"Do yuh know how we got all that gawjus ol' Spanish Moss throughout all of Dixieland?"

"I suppose I learned, I guess. But I don't remember that too well." He never learned.

"The Timacua Indians."

"The what?"

"The Timacua. And they were real Indians. Not like Raj Bhavnani. The Timacua were the real ones. Ah means Raj Bhavnani wasn't a real one." She probably got her facts reversed but that didn't make any difference. What a face. What an accent. What legs even though he couldn't see them now because they were under the table. Just knowing they were there was good enough. Christopher didn't care about the Timacua Indians under the conditions. But, somehow, she cared. "There was a Timacuan Indian girl who lived off the Okefenokee Swamp and she fell in love with a young white man who was not a Timacua. He was white. Real white. The two of them would meet every night under the branches of an old oak tree and they called it their own oak tree and the Timacua elders found out about it—every night those two lovers were there—and that's what they were—two lovers who would go to that tree—and so the elders killed him. Knives. They killed him. They brought his body to the Okefenokee—they put it in the Okefenokee—somewhere deep in the swamp. Alligators there, you know. They told her what they did. She cried and screamed and cried and screamed, and then at that day's sunset she went back to their tree and waited there until it got hours after dark. And because her lover always had told her how much he loved her long black hair—when it got so very late she cut off a lock of her hair and placed it on a lower branch of their old oak tree.

"In the years ahead the lock of hair spread from the lower branch to the one above it and then spread throughout all the branches of that tree and then to the neighboring tree and the neighboring one to that one and on and on until her hair spread throughout the south—throughout Dixie."

"Really? That's a beautiful story. Absolutely beautiful. I won't forget it. Who could? Was her hair gray?"

"Not when they used to meet there. But after she put her lock of hair on their tree and after it spread and then after many years passed, she got older and her hair became gray—and so did her hair that rested on the branches of trees in Dixie. All those strands on the branches turned gray."

"I'll never look at Spanish Moss again without thinking of what you just told me."

"People who didn't know what they were talking about named it Spanish Moss. It wasn't Spanish. It was Timacua hair that spread all over from Georgia—Gee-aww-juh,"—she corrected herself back into a prominent accent that had dropped while she became so engrossed in telling her story of the Timacua hair—"it spread to Louisiana to Mississippi to Alabama down to Flaw-ida up to South Carolina."

"That's a sad story—really sad—but it's beautiful even with its sadness, Savannah."

"It's true."

"I'm sure it is."

"Yes, it is. At least I was told the story by those who heard it from generations that are now gone."

"What was the Indian girl's name?"

"Savannah."

He stared at her with a quick glance from her eyes to her hair and back to her eyes. "But your hair is blonde."

"She wasn't me. No relation. I'm not Timacua. And I'm not old yet."

"I know you aren't old but—"

"She was the best of the tribe."

"Are there still Timacuas?"

"Of course."

With each quick back and forth statement between the two of them the distance between their faces diminished because it seemed the distance had to do that until there was no distance at all. None. It was not planned by either of them. But when there was no distance at all between their faces there was an invisible avalanche that both of them felt simultaneously without doing anything except to look into each other's eyes.

For some time neither of them could calibrate the passage of time; they didn't speak nor could they hear anything; not Angelo; not silverware clicking; not conversation from neighboring tables; nothing. Silence. There was a magnificent silence.

The avalanche seemed to have staying power.

Then a memory somewhere in Christopher's head came into the foreground of his thoughts; not Miss Osborn this time but the memory of sitting on the railing of the playground at school with Malahia Kahala, and the memory of her asking him how many girls he had kissed and he lied by greatly exaggerating the amount since at that time he knew well that the accurate count was zero.

The memory brought him to ask Savannah, "Have you kissed many men before?"

She shook her head. "Not many. I make sure I find out in advance how many cups of coffee, toast and aspirins I can get out of a date first."

He gave a wide smile. "You want some more?"

"Not yet." She put her hand over his hand. "Your friend, Raj Bhavnani told me about your interest in space—I mean the big space; way up through the stars. I don't know if it's true because I don't trust that man. There is something about him that calls for distrust." She knew that would please Christopher. But then she thought she might have given the impression she was ridiculing space flight. She quickly corrected that possibility. "Is the big space something you're interested in? That's wonderful if it is. Do you want to go to the moon? That's what Raj Bhavnani told me about you."

"He did, indeed, tell you the truth if he said I care about—about—about the big space—about space exploration. I work on its exploration. And I do want to go to the moon. I realize it's dreaming but I believe in dreaming. He was not lying. We are not friends—but he was not lying about those things."

"You aren't friends?"

"No. I mean yes, we aren't friends."

"I can see why."

"The 'why' has everything to do with his interest in you."

"Maybe, but he seemed to be in love with himself. He's a show-off. He acts like he is so, so important. Is Raj Bhavnani an important person?"

"Yes."

"Really?"

"Really. Savannah, I have never known an unimportant person. And neither have you. There aren't any."

She stared at him with affection. "You are something, Christopher Straw."

He shook his head. "No. I didn't know everyone was important until my Dad told me that. Then I noticed every person I met, and he was right."

She stared at him again, and then softly said, "Is your father gone, Chris?"

He took a while before answering. "Oh, no. No one is gone."

She gave a slight smile and a slow nod. "He taught you quite a bit didn't he?"

"My Mother taught me that one."

"You had good parents?"

"Yes, they are," he corrected the grammar without fanfare. "Past-tense doesn't exist. That's one marvelous thing about the—the big space. Everything is present-tense. That will be proven when we go fast enough and long enough. Everyone is in the present."

Savannah would not tread on that. She felt as though she would be sacrilegious to ask him what he meant. At least, not now.

He rescued her by changing the subject. "Savannah, I don't want to delve into something that is none of my business but although I am so fond of what I see of you and hear from you, I know nothing about who you are. If you feel easy about it, please tell me about yourself. I don't mean private things. Are you a student? N.Y.U.? What do you study? Or do you work? If you do, where? Do you still live in Georgia or do you live here in New York now? Tell me anything. I want to know about you. I don't mean secrets. I just mean that I want to know anything you want to tell me about you."

"Not now. I'm a very private person. Let me leave it that way for now. You're leaving out some things about you, I'm sure. So am I. Is that alright with you? I want to talk about you—not me. I already know all about me." She gave a big smile.

Christopher nodded. "Of course." He gave another nod and said, "Savannah, will you excuse me for a moment?"

She nodded, assuming he was going to the Men's Room because men never tell women they are going to the Men's Room. It is quite acceptable for a woman to tell a man she is going to the Ladies Room. After all, a woman could be fixing her lipstick or putting on a touch of perfume or adjusting her earrings or straightening her dress or other things like that. There are no such things like that for a man. He goes to a Men's Room to go to a Men's Room without something to talk about.

In this case he was not going to the Men's Room. He went to borrow something from Angelo and he produced it at the table as he put it in Savannah's hand. It was a small scissors. "Please, Savannah—Will you cut off a lock of your hair and give it to me?"

She gave a wide smile and nodded. "Of course. What are you going to do with it, Chris?"

"I am going to climb a tree in Central Park. A high one. And I'm going to put your hair on a branch so high that no one will knock it off or take it off, and other branches will cloak it from the wind."

"Are you really?"

"Really."

"Do you think some day it will turn gray?"

"Yes. Given enough time, yes."

"Will we see it when it's gray?"

"Yes."

"Christo-fuh?"

"Yes?"

"Let me tell you one thing about myself. Call me Anna."

"After all that explanation of Savannah? The Indians and all that?""

"Shoe-uh. Yes. As soon as my parents named me Savannah they started calling me Anna for short. Since then only my parents and my closest friends—only the closest people to me called me Anna. Just the closest."

"And you want me to call you that, too? Anna?"

"Yes."

"Anna Lane. I like that. And I will be one of the honored few."

"Even if you don't call me Anna, at least—call me."

Christopher nodded very slowly and while nodding he said, "I will."

Then the magnificent long silence came again and there was no distance between their faces again. Neither one of them took the aspirin. Bayers. In total it was the kind of New York City night that would have a difficult time duplicating itself just about anywhere else. Of course other places have good nights but not exactly like that one at Angelo's.

THEME ELEVEN

COMMON AND UNIQUE DESTINATIONS

DURING THE NEXT THREE MONTHS Christopher Straw and Anna Lane walked together down the crowded streets south of Midtown and walked together up the empty streets north of Midtown and they stood together in lines of people at night outside a Times Square theater and they sat together on a horse-drawn carriage in Central Park, and in all but one case they were either holding hands or with an arm around the waist of the other one or there was some different visual sign of affection. One night when Chris looked around to insure there was no policeman watching, he climbed a tree in Central Park and put her lock of hair on a high branch. The promise made at Angelo's was kept.

The morning of Midtown's Friday, May the 5th, was cool and cloudy and crowded. At 9:00 A.M. Christopher and Anna joined the mass of people outside the tall, wide windows of a Seventh Avenue store that appeared to have no name because there was no room for a sign but, rather, dozens of watches and jewelry and gadgets and radios and even, of all things, two television sets. That is what the crowds were there to watch because this was the morning scheduled for the first U.S. Astronaut's ride in the nose-cone on a rocket, depending on the progress made at Cape Canaveral in Florida and dependent on the weather over which the greatest scientists in the country had no control—and then dependent on television transmission from the Cape.

In a public sense it was Alan Shepard in a capsule he had named Freedom Seven and in a private sense it was Anna sharing in Christopher's passion for space exploration. If it should be a big moment for him to be a viewer, she wanted to be standing by him during that moment.

She did not need to pretend the thrill of seeing the rocket's lift-off. No pretense needed. At 9:34 A.M. with the Redstone launch vehicle's lifting above the flames coming from its thrust section on Cape Canaveral's Pad LC-5 and its simultaneous audible blast, and like everyone else watching on the New York sidewalk she showed shock and gave the sincerest of yells of joy and she even surrendered her hand-holding with Chris so as to join the piercing applause of the expanded crowd of strangers with her eyes and Chris's eyes and all eyes outside the Seventh Avenue window glued to the black-and-white images on the two television sets with their rounded-edged glass screens encasing a visual miracle: man off toward space.

The image stayed with the rocket until the glow from its thrust section became nothing more than a bright dot in the sky.

"Where is he going?" she asked Christopher.

He shook his head and wiped his eyes. "Up and down. Just up and down for this one, that is if everything goes well."

"How long until he comes back down?"

"If all goes well, about fifteen minutes. It's scheduled for that."

"Is that what the Soviet Union did?"

"No. They did much more—so much more. Last month they sent an Astronaut—or a Cosmonaut as they call him—Yuri Gagarin—he went into *orbit* around the world! Yuri Gagarin. We are behind but we're on the way now. But Gagarin went into *orbit*. Around the world! He went around the world in a little less than two hours. Can you imagine that? That's what it probably takes you to—must have taken you to drive from Savannah to Charleston!"

Like everyone else, they stayed in front of the store until the image was nothing more than sky and the television cut to a close-up of the NASA communicator, a jubilant Shorty Powers giving a narrative to the television audience which was his summation of what had just occurred.

What, of course, Shorty Powers missed in his summary was that Anna Lane was interested enough in Christopher Straw that she had actually agreed to have met him in Times Square in the morning to watch a rocket go off on television through a store window. And in the doing of it, although she was thrilled and showed it, she was simultaneously trying not to exhibit evidence of her anger that was best kept inside her. She was, after all, a woman who was with a man who seemed to be more interested in something other than her. Shorty Powers at Cape Canaveral didn't know it. Neither did Alan Shepard know it. And neither did Christopher Straw know that Anna Lane was jealous of her morning's rival named Freedom Seven. Men can only do one thing at a time. Women can do many things at one time.

At this time, with that feminine ability, she couldn't help but give a risk of honesty with a symphony of a southern accent by softly—very softly—saying, "You, Mistah Straw ahh not aboard Freedom Seven. You ahh aboard Enslaved Eight!"

As the enslaver, she knew she had made a point he did not understand but enjoyed.

THEME TWELVE

IN DOLLEY MADISON'S HOUSE 112

YEARS AFTER SHE LIVED THERE

IT WAS THE MOST UNCONVENTIONAL airplane travel service in the history of commercial airlines. Eastern Airlines did it. It was called "The Shuttle" meaning that at LaGuardia Airport in New York, every two hours from 8:00am through 10:00pm an airliner would leave LaGuardia headed toward Washington National Airport without reservations needed. (The same was true in reverse from Washington National to LaGuardia.) No tickets sold in advance. If even one more passenger than capacity showed up at the gate to be on the airliner, another plane would be provided for that person. Once on the plane, and once in flight, all passengers would buy a ticket from the stewardess who walked through the aisle of the plane wheeling her metal cart while passengers paid her $12.75 in cash or paid that amount by a personal check or a traveler's check or a Diners Club Card or a Carte Blanche Card.

In the chronology of flight-technology, this bus-like

service was started just five days before Alan Shepard went into space. Not coincidentally, 20 days after Alan Shepard's flight Christopher Straw took the Shuttle for two reasons: to try it out, and to get to the newest bureaucracy operating in D.C.

Government agencies are not regularly headquartered in old homes but no previous agency was like the current one and no preceding occupant of the home was like the wife of the fourth President of the United States.

The address was 1520 "H" Street N.W. just two and one-half blocks from the White House, a house located on a block of somewhat similar looking row-houses across from Lafayette Square. It had been the home of Dolley Madison during the last uninterrupted six years of her life and thirteen years after the death of her husband, James Madison. Thirty Presidents later, after Dwight Eisenhower became President, Dolley Madison's home became the headquarters of the new government agency, the National Aeronautics and Space Administration that was fast becoming known by its acronym; NASA.

On May the 25th of 1961, Christopher Straw went through Dolley Madison's old doorway into the current headquarters of NASA that had the same pleasant mustiness that had entered his home in Fort Littleton when he was a boy. Good. Was that mustiness of Dolley Madison's old home noticed just when entering or was it musty all the time? It was hard to tell until he could know it better.

What was even more important than the fragrance and feel of the place was that the bureaucracy there was so small that all its members could fit in Dolley Madison's house. It proved to be the D.C. evidence that the smaller the government bureaucracy, the more it accomplishes. NASA was quick to be a tremendous success.

Christopher introduced himself to the woman at the most prominent desk of what had been said to have been Dolley Madison's parlor but was now the reception room shared with three women and one man and four desks.

"Hi. I'm Christopher Straw from Western Electric in New York. I have an appointment at 2:30 here with Dr. Hagen. I just came in from New York on the Eastern Shuttle" he added as though such a heroic feat was worthy of having a White House banquet in his honor.

Too bad this woman was not about to at least pin a medal on his lapel. Instead she gave a smile and introduced herself as Dolly.

"Dolly?" Christopher asked.

"Yes, but not Dolley Madison! She spelled it different than me. I spell it right!" Obviously that was something she had said many times before in total disrespect of the original Dolley who, it seemed, was not considered to be as smart as the current Dolly.

The new Dolly nodded. "Before I get him, the Administrator was told about your appointment with Dr. Hagen and the Deputy Administrator would like to see you."

"The Deputy Administrator of what?"

"Of NASA."

"He does? He wants to see me? What for?"

"Well, I don't know. That's up to him. All I know is that he asked me to buzz him when you come in."

"Are you talking about James Webb's deputy?"

"Yes. Deputy Administrator Carl Sanford." She pressed a button on her intercom and announced to whomever was listening to her that Christopher Straw had arrived.

"Yes, by all means," the voice on the other end said, "Have him come in, if you would, Dolly."

The Deputy Administrator's office was comparatively small for a high-ranking officer of such an important Agency, but Dolley Madison apparently thought it was roomy enough. He stood up from behind his desk and there was a big smile on his face. He extended his hand and there was a firm handshake and Deputy Administrator Sanford gestured toward a chair to the side of his desk. "Sit down, Mr. Straw. You probably know why I asked to see you!"

Christopher looked mystified. "No, sir, I don't."

"You don't?" And Carl Sanford sat back down behind his desk.

"No, sir. I came to see Dr. Hagen but I am so delighted to meet with you, sir. This is totally unexpected!"

"Well, I'm delighted to meet with you. Oh, I know that you didn't ask for this meeting but—but I received a phone call telling me you would be in this building today!" And his smile became wider. "An old guy like me got a phone call about you coming here—a phone call from Savannah Lane!"

That startled Chris and there was no hiding his surprise. "You know Anna—Savannah Lane?"

"No. That's the point. But we certainly knew who she was on the phone. You can imagine our surprise: every Saturday night Irene and I—my wife, Irene and I watch *Gemstone* on television faithfully—unless Administrator Webb or the President calls!" And he laughed. "Or unless other work here interferes. Since they put her on the show just a short while back—we have liked that girl! Great little actress! You know, the whole family on that series. She's a real star. Great series. The real west."

"No, sir, I didn't know she was on it and I don't know about the television series."

Through the good luck of Chris, it was as though Carl Sanford didn't even hear Christopher Straw. "So when she phoned the office for me I was delighted to take the call. She told me about you and your dedication to NASA's space exploration efforts; that you work for our contractor, Western Electric. That's good. Great organization. A couple days ago she called to tell me you would be here on the 25th to see Dr. Hagen on what she said you termed as a courtesy call before going around the world to all the planned tracking sites for when we make an orbital flight in our Mercury program. Good. That's good. We will be glad to have you at our sites. She said you were coming to NASA today—the 25th—and I might want to meet you. I told Irene—my wife, Irene—about it and she was as thrilled as I was that I heard from Savanah Lane of all people!"

"I didn't know she was on television."

"Savannah Lane?"

"Yes."

"You didn't know?"

"That's right."

"You know her, don't you?"

"Oh, of course. But I didn't know she was ever on television."

"She never told you?"

"No. Never."

"Don't you watch 'Gemstone'?"

"I don't have a television set, sir." Then he quickly added, "I did see, however, the launch of Alan Shepard earlier this month.

That was spectacular. I saw it with her. We saw it on television."

"Gus Grissom is next, you know. Another up and down test. But first, did you see the ceremony on the White House South Lawn for Commander Shepard and all the Mercury Seven Astronauts? May the Eighth."

"I didn't. No, sir. But I heard about it."

"The President was great. You know he gave Shepard a medal—the Distinguished Service Medal and Mrs. Kennedy called out to the President and said to 'put it on him!' So the President did. He was laughing at himself for having just *given* it to Alan. It was such a great ceremony. The President said that everyone could tell who the Astronauts were compared to the D.C. folks who were standing with them because the Astronauts were the tan and healthy ones." And Deputy Administrator Sanford laughed. "So did I!"

"You were there, Sir?"

"Yes. And tonight I'm going to be in the Capitol Building for President Kennedy's State of the Union Address."

"I thought he already did that—the State of the Union Address—just weeks ago—or am I wrong? Was that something else?"

"You're right. He did. That was on January the 31st so not weeks ago but—what—but months ago. Anyway, he is going to give another one because he believes these times call for another one. I think it will be on television. If it is, you should watch it. It's a big one. Does your hotel have a TV?"

"I think so. I'll watch it."

"If Savanah Lane has you right—you'll like it. You'll like it a lot. Now, tell me about your itinerary from here."

"Tomorrow to Bermuda and then the entire around-the-world visits to all the planned tracking sites."

"That's valuable; a very valuable trip."

"Yes, sir. It's the second time I will have done it but the first trip was before a number of the sites had been completed."

"Good. Every day those sites become more and more ready to be in shape for an orbiting Mercury Astronaut. Just last month we got the go-ahead from our friends in Great Britain to use Bermuda to track our Astronauts and whatever we want to track will look different from your past trip there. Bermuda will soon be our most important part of the network. It will pick up the track of a launch right after it blasts off from the Cape— from Cape Canaveral. What a path our network of trackers will administer around the world! Eighteen sites pending if you count—and you *should* count the two tracking ships in the Atlantic and Indian Oceans, and count the Cape and count Goddard right up the road in Maryland." Deputy Administrator Sanford opened one of the right-hand drawers of his desk and pulled out a small white celluloid-covered cardboard card, and then pushed it across his desk to Chris. "This can help you. Keep this in your shirt-pocket on the trip. It tells you the time at every place on the Agency's S.T.D.N. Just spin the dial on the bottom of it to the place—the tracking site that you want."

"Thank you." Chris played with it for a short moment. "That's very good. That can be a big help. You said the S.T.D.N.?"

"In English it's the Agency's Spaceflight Tracking and Data Network. Sorry; I'm a bureaucrat now and everyone in government speaks bureaucratese using acronyms and initials. I'm just getting used to it. Tell me, where are you staying here in D.C.?"

"The South Gate."

"What's that?"

"The South Gate? The South Gate Motor Hotel. It's in

Arlington. South Glebe Road off the Shirley Highway. AAA, y'know."

"Uh-huh. Okay. I'm not familiar with it. Just be sure they have a TV. You'll like what the President has to say. Now, let me tell you what Savannah told me about you; that you have an ambition to get into space yourself; that you have the long-range ambition of going to the moon."

"That's right, sir. It's a life ambition. Since I read Buck Rogers as a kid, I have had that—that ambition. It's a dream. I admit it's a dream. I don't think I remember life without that dream."

"Were you in the Armed Forces?"

"Yes, sir, with the U.S. Air Force."

"Well, that's good. That's very good. A pilot?"

"No, sir."

"Well, that's not good. You know our seven Astronauts have all been test pilots."

"I know, sir. I know about the qualifications and I know I'm not qualified."

"You know how many test pilots we chose to get those seven?"

"No, sir."

"Five Hundred and Eight. Then we gave them more intelligence tests than any Ivy League College would put them through. We whittled them down and down and got 32. Then we put those 32 through hell. Physical tests and psychological tests and one medical exam after another. If you thought basic training in the Air Force was tough, those weeks of your basic training were chicken-feed compared to what we did to those guys. We x-rayed every bone in their body more times than anyone ever took pictures of—of Savannah Lane's face! We finally got the Mercury 7."

"Sir, I'm a realist. I didn't know the exact figures but I did know about the test pilot requirement and that the physical requirements alone were very rigid. That means there are a lot of ways I don't qualify. I know that. But I'm hopeful that in time the requirements won't be as rigid as they are today and I'll qualify—as long as I'm not too old by then."

"You're right. We're just at the opening stages here. We have to be cautious for all the possibilities we haven't covered. You never know. No one can know when we are just starting to work on what Man has never done before. In time the requirements will go way down. It will be just like riding in the passenger section of Pan Am. Way down. They have to. Listen, when you joined the Air Force was it the U.S. Air Force or was it still part of the Army—the Army Air Corps?"

"The U.S. Air Force already, Sir," speaking in his best bureaucratese he added, "New uniforms, Sir, including the Winter Blues."

"Made a mess of the song, didn't it?"

"What?"

"The Army Air Corps Song. That ending line: 'Nothing will stop the 'Army Air Corps' last line of the song. And it rhymed with the line just before it which was, 'We live in fame or go down in flame,' then 'Nothing will stop the Army Air Corps!' The U. S. Air Force doesn't have the same rhythm with that."

Christopher nodded, not at all prepared for this trend of conversation. "Well," he said after much silence, "they—they changed it."

Deputy Administrator Sanford, realizing the man who knew Savannah Lane didn't know much about the song, nodded too, and then he said, "Yes, they changed it. Army Air Corps to U.S. Air Force. And just think: this agency used to be called NACA: The National Committee for Aeronautics. It took the Soviets— Sputnik to change President Eisenhower's priorities." There was a silence. The Deputy Administrator broke it by saying, "Well, I guess Dr. Hagen is waiting for you. I'll let him know that I kept you. Listen, just be sure that that hotel of yours has a television. I think the President's speech will be on television. Or listen to it on radio. For sure it will be on radio. You'll like the speech. You have a radio?"

"Yes, sir."

"You'll like what he has to say. That's a guarantee."

Deputy Administrator Sanford had a point about Chris liking the speech. As a chief representative of NASA, he had been involved on a particular part of the President's speech; the part that could change the exploration of space.

Sitting in the U.S. Capitol Building's chamber of the House of Representatives facing President Kennedy were members of the House and Senate, Supreme Court Justices, Cabinet officers, members of the military's Chiefs of Staff, foreign ambassadors to the United States, members of the press, and guests.

There were two men sitting behind the President with a full view of the audience but the two could only see the back of the President as he gave his speech standing at the chamber's podium. The two were Vice President Lyndon Baines Johnson and Speaker of the House Sam Rayburn seated at the permanently elevated Speaker's desk.

Combined with listeners throughout the nation, a more prestigious gathering was difficult to imagine hearing the words,

"The Constitution imposes upon me the obligation to, from time to time, give to the Congress information on the state of the union. While this has traditionally been interpreted as an annual affair, this tradition has been broken in extraordinary times. These are extraordinary times." The President went on to propose additional spending for a stronger defense beyond what he had proposed in his original State of the Union Address. And he added much more than an afterthought: "I believe this nation should commit itself to achieving the goal, before this decade is out, of landing a man on the moon and returning him safely to earth."

Even though it had only been twenty days since Commander Alan Shepard went up and down in a sub-orbital flight that lasted fifteen minutes from lift-off to splash-down, while the Soviet Union's Yuri Gagarin had already made an orbital flight, Shepherd's flight moved the President of the United States to the extent of committing this nation's effort in making the dream of thousands of years come true.

Christopher Straw heard the President's speech on the radio of the South Gate Motor Inn. He didn't bother to wipe the tears from his eyes because they were tears of exaltation that felt good. After all, he just heard the words he thought he might never hear from anyone in authority, and certainly not from the President of the United States.

Then, from his room Chris placed a person-to-person long-distance phone call to Anna. He wanted to say so many things to her. But the operator kept holding. After a couple long minutes he was told there was no answer. Chris asked the operator to keep trying and call him back when there was an answer.

Now what? That's when he had an impulse to phone his long-ago teacher Mrs. Zambroski although he didn't know how to get her phone number. All he wanted to do was repeat to her what President Kennedy said this night and then add one word of his own to Mrs. Zambroski: "Seeeeee?!"

He gave up on calling Mrs. Zambroski before even attempting to locate her, but he tried the phone number of Anna Lane four more times before quitting his series of asking one long- distance operator after another to try her number. He wanted to talk to Anna about the meeting with Deputy Administrator Sanford and what Sanford told him about her and to ask why she didn't tell him she was an actress, and he wanted to compliment her obvious success and to thank her for calling a top executive of NASA. And he was more than impatient to talk to her about President Kennedy's space-age commitment for a manned moon flight and Christopher wanted to say another goodbye before starting his trip the next morning in his second world tour of the Spaceflight Tracking and Data Network sites for Project Mercury. There was so much to say and ask Anna, but the operators insisted there was no answer.

It never occurred to Christopher Straw that Anna Lane could be having drinks at Fifth Avenue's Top of the Sixes. And even if he had imagined such a thing he would not have had a remote thought that she would be there, or anywhere, with Raj Bhavnani.

THEME THIRTEEN

THE FORTY-SECOND FLOOR

ONLY RAJ BHAVNANI COULD BE TALKING when he said: "In India we would call this place Salyaloka! In Thailand it is Nirvana! It is Cielo in Italy! Ahhh, and here in New York it is Heaven! It is the ultimate reach of all Man's hopes no matter if the Man is Hindu or Buddhist or Jain, Jew, or Christian! This, my dear Savannah, is Paradise!"

"Mister Bhavnani, you are the most enthusiastic- about-everything than any person I have ever met. This is a restaurant with a bar. Can't that be enough?"

"You don't like the Top of the Sixes? You don't like being 41 floors above the crowded streets?"

"I do. It's nice. But it isn't really all of those things you just said. Now—is it?"

"Then what do you think this magnificent place is?"

"It is between 52nd and 53rd on Fifth Avenue."

"You do not know that between 52nd and 53rd is Heaven Street?"

"My map somehow missed that street, Mister Bhavnani.

But it is nice."

Raj Bhavnani was leaning toward capitulation. "Yes. You are right. It's very nice." But he didn't carry a white flag too long. "Do you know why it is very nice?"

"No."

"Because if we danced we would step on the world! Millions of people beneath our feet! Yes, then as long as you recognize that, it is nice. It is, in fact, so nice that it is a vision of what Man has built as seen from the eyes of Gods. The Top of the Sixes is—to a degree of course"—and he whispered the remainder of his new thought—"it is the illustrated edition of what life should be for all peoples!"

"You always find a way to sway opinion no matter how outrageous—and you win, don't you?"

Raj Bhavnani shrugged his shoulders which was the peak of his ability to appear humble. "I haven't always won. I've missed a few but—even then—I just waited. Eventually what I first think I miss comes along again."

"Are you talking about me?"

"Oh, no. Not you. Why do you ask? Did I lose you once? I don't recall. Isn't that what Americans always say in court? They don't recall? I love America and now I live in America so I don't recall." And then he added a very loud, "Now! You want another Margarita? Or some other drink?"

"I never do anything that someone asks me to do if they precede the request by saying 'Now'!"

"Why does that bother you?"

"Because they say 'Now!' to change the subject as if what I said is so wrong and stupid that it isn't worthy of a response and so they say 'Now!' to emphasize their statement of intellect is just ahead—in which they simply change the subject to the one they choose."

Raj gave another shrug and quickly picked up his glass of a Cuba Libre and said, "Now!" before taking a big gulp.

Savannah shook her head, smiled, and reached for his free hand. "You don't listen, do you?"

"Of course not. Another Margarita or something else? What would you like?"

She laughed; and she released her hand from his. "Let me try what you're drinking. I hear that Cuba Libre's are good—and I'm game for that."

"Some of life should be a game! Here! For you the game is a Cuba Libre!" He passed his drink to her and he repeated, "A Cube Libre!"

She squinted her eyes while she weakly nodded and then she tested the Cuba Libre and this new nod was strong. "It's very good. I'll keep it." She put her hand back on his hand and this time she left it there.

That second touch was the interrupting reminder that was on both of their minds, but so far undiscussed. It was that he hadn't looked for her, nor would he be with her if she hadn't looked for him, although he didn't yet know if that was intended or that she somehow stumbled across him.

He watched her sip the Cuba Libre and the moment seemed right for him to ask, "How on earth did you ever find me?"

"It wasn't easy, Mister Bhavnani. You are very elusive. I tried to phone you at the Algonquin where you told me you lived and the hotel operator didn't know who you were. And—"

"A trick!" he interrupted. "My trick! I told the Algonquin's telephone operator's not to put anyone through unless I have given them the person's name in advance. It is my trick so as not to be bothered by strangers."

She passed by that highly doubtful explanation. "And so I talked to the manager. Mr. Bodne. Do you know him?"

He gave a combination of a Hindu sideways shake of his head with an American shrug of his shoulders while pursing his lips like a Frenchman.

"Among other things he told me that you went upstate to the School of Hotel Administration. It turned out it was outside of Rochester and I tried to get hold of you there but they didn't know who you were. I was told 'No Bhavnani.' How sad."

In response, Raj Bhavnani who was proving he was the master of ignoring remarks that were not complimentary about him, changed her question into his question: "But why did you want to get hold of me and how did you finally succeed?"

"I thought you were rich and influential."

"And that is why you set out to find me?"

"Yes. Because I wanted you to give me a hand in helping another person."

"Who?"

"Someone."

"Who? Are you in love with me?"

"Oh God, no! That doesn't make any sense! You're hopeless! You're not even listening to me! I wanted your money and power to help a friend but I found out I had my own ability to influence."

"But how did you find me?"

"Your Embassy."

"What Embassy?

"India! Your Embassy!"

Her temper was interrupted by two women who had been having dinner across from their side of the restaurant aisle and the two women were now standing by their table. "Are you Savannah Lane?" one of them asked.

Savannah gave a quick look at Raj and then smiled and nodded to the interrupting woman. "I am."

"See?" the interrupting woman said to her friend. "I told you!" She turned back to Savannah and laughed as though something was funny. She simply recognized Savannah and that was flattering—not funny. "Would you sign my menu?"

"Of course. But you better make sure they'll let you have the menu. It's so big! We didn't eat here. I didn't think I had the strength to hold one of their menus, so—"

"I will ask them!" the woman interrupted. "I will! I'll buy the menu from them if they insist. Here," and she placed the menu and a ball-point pen on the table near Savannah's Cuba Libre.

Savannah asked, "What's your name? I want to personalize it; not just sign it. I need your first name."

"How kind! My name is Darleen."

Savannah acted like she was writing a book in personalization. When she was done with her inscription she handed the menu and pen back to the woman.

"Now," the woman asked with some hesitation, "Would you mind, Miss Lane, would you mind if my friend takes a picture of the two of us?"

Raj was totally stunned by all this, not having any idea what prompted such adoration heaped on Savannah who was now putting her arm around the stranger's shoulder while the stranger's friend was clicking a switch on a Spartus camera that caused a brilliant flash bulb to go off and then two more repeats of new flash bulbs in slow sequence with two more successive pushes of the camera-knob to advance each frame of film with the whole procedure being an unexpected time-consumer, but a pleasant one for Savannah and a confusing one for Raj.

"There!" the posing stranger said, "One of them ought to turn out! Thank you so much, Miss Lane!"

"Thank you for asking, Marlene."

"Darleen," the woman corrected and Darleen and her friend walked toward the hallway from the restaurant.

Raj gave a forced closed-mouth smile. "What was all that about? Are you a celebrity or whatever you call important people?"

"I'm not a celebrity. But yes, I am important and that's because everybody's an important person," Savannah said in a reprise of what Christopher had told her that his father told him.

"You were saying to me that you had enough influence all by yourself. If that's true, why did you persist in finding me and arrange to meet me here?"

She was stumped. "That's my business."

"Who did you want to help?"

"Christopher Straw! That's who!" She said it as though the Salk vaccine to end polio had been nothing more than a minor story in comparison with this revelation.

Raj, with a casual nod, and without any signal of jealousy of Christopher Straw, said, "Now! How did those women know your name? Why did they want your signature and photograph?"

"'Gemstone!'" Savannah answered.

"Yes, yes, Gemstone. That's why. Gemstone."

"Do you know what 'Gemstone' is?"

"Of course. What do *you* think it is?"

"A television series."

"You are a great teacher of English! A great teacher of America! I did not know that it was a television series. Gemstone is a television series! Wonderful! Good news! It's about time!"

Savannah gave a short laugh. "I've been doing bit-player roles saying one or two lines in musicals and often singing and dancing since I was a little girl and no one ever paid attention. Then just a couple months ago I got on television in 'Gemstone' and they even give me screen-credit. It's a weekly series with some great stars. Not me, but great ones!" And her eyebrows went up as she said that. "And since I've been on, every once in a while someone recognizes me on the street or something. It's nice of people and I like it. They never recognized me from the movies. See? Movies aren't 'better than ever!' That was a slogan that was invented so people wouldn't give up movies for television!"

"Yes, yes. Television is better. Better than ever. Not movies. Television," he repeated as though she needed a clarification of some of television's basic selling virtues. "Through the wires! Through the wires it goes! Wires under the ground and in the sky and into your homes."

"How informative! I think you're right."

"Yes, yes."

His innocence and lack of knowledge combined with his assumption that he could be thought of as an expert on any and everything had great appeal to her, just as it did during some moments at Mama Leone's, and this time maybe the Cuba Libre had been given a bit-player role in supporting her as a leading player in the Top of the Sixes. "And you should know that acting is only temporary. 'Gemstone' is wonderful and depending on my schedule of shows, when I am given time off I come here to New York. I get to travel between shows some time or between seasons. But not too long. Too long can be dangerous because of what has happened to some others when they're not wanted anymore. When that happens the studio stops calling actors and actresses with a new season or a new contract—and they're out of a job. Happily that hasn't happened to me but I've learned from those who have been through it to at least be prepared! When we haven't been called we just tell people that we are 'between pictures.' That's what we say, 'between pictures.'"

"That's very good; very smart; very good! Saves embarrassment! Now, let's go," Raj said. "Let's go up to the 42nd floor."

"The 42nd floor? But I thought this was the top floor and it was the 41st one."

"But those are only the floors of a building! I am talking about the floors of longing and passion and desire reached and then contentment. Ahhh, there will then be contentment—even perhaps with American cigarettes with filters on them."

She gave a wide smile along with a heavier grasp of her hand on his hand and then she gave a nod. "Let's go!" she said. "Let's go to the 42nd floor but only to see it! And nothing more than that. And that's an order!"

"Ah, yes. Let us get up there!"

He wouldn't have known in advance but the floor of the 42nd floor was very close to the ceiling of the 42nd floor causing both Raj and Savannah to bend over just to walk to a reasonable destination up there through what seemed like fields of heavy grime and dust. And there were a lot of boxes all over the floor with the larger ones leaning against the walls. Not only all that but there was a lot of creaking when either of them walked or even moved slightly and there were large whiffs of something that probably never saw any movement of anything for years or, perhaps, decades until this night.

Since the most stimulating chapters of life, as most find out, are dependent on the vacancy of any other thoughts than the central absorption from the minds of the participants—both of the minds present on the 42nd floor of the Top of the Sixes were prevented from such total immersion by being unfortunately occupied with a crowd of unappealing and irritating thoughts that got in the way, so that the whole reason for this visit upstairs that night was a dud.

Other than all that, the 42nd floor was just fine.

THEME FOURTEEN

TRANSITIONS

IT FINALLY HIT CHRISTOPHER. Without any proof of fact or even a hint of confirmation, Chris knew that Anna was with Raj. No evidence. Just instinct and instinct supersedes evidence. Chris' only question was whether or not she would tell him. Surely her conscience would bother her and she would phone him to at least attempt to explain. But Anna Lane was not one to have done what would have been expected of her by Christopher Straw. She would always have done and would continue to do what her own unlikely thinking process dictated.

After that night at the Top of the Sixes, Raj Bhavnani disappeared again. This time the interval of his invisibility was not for a period of four months as he had chosen to vanish from the January night at the Ceylon India Inn to the May night at the Top of the Sixes. This time his interval of disappearance would be four years. When less than one week had passed Anna Lane admitted to her actress confidant, Lorna Whitley, on the set of 'Gemstone' at the television station's studios, "I was a fool!

There's not a semblance of proof that he even exists anymore and not a semblance of evidence that he cares if he sees me again. And I don't want to see Mr. Raj Bhavnani again. I was such a fool!"

Lorna Whitley shook her head. "You are not a fool, Anna; you are making such a common error: you are not using the mind that God gave you. You looked for a detour from the paved road. Do you know how you can tell in advance that you're at risk of being—of being fooled?"

It was easy to answer this one. "No."

"Ask yourself if you would advise your daughter to do what you were thinking of doing yourself."

"I don't have a daughter. I'm not married."

"Anna! I know that but just imagine it! It's a valuable hypothetical. A hypothetical. Just imagine it and think of what you would do."

Anna nodded because she knew that agreeing was probably best since she was suddenly being presented with a word of five vowels. "He is such a fool! And so am I!"

"Don't call yourself names, Anna. Did you tell your—your Christopher what you did that night?"

"I haven't even called him."

"Has he called you?"

"No."

"Oh, that's not a good sign. You should call him and tell him what you did."

"Are you crazy? And take a chance on losing him?"

"You already decided to risk that on your way to your rendezvous at the Top of the Fives."

"Sixes," she corrected.

"Anna! Pay no attention to the insignificant when it is so urgent to pay attention to the important things."

Anna wasn't listening. At this moment she was staring at Lorna's necklace. "I never noticed that before."

"Never noticed what?"

"Your necklace, Lorna. It's beautiful."

"Oh. Thank you. You never noticed it because I always wear it under my blouse so I don't forget and let it show on the Sound Stage when the camera's on. That isn't for the camera. It's for my soul. Sometimes I let it be seen at breaks in the filming when the camera's off. It's not meant for my imaginary role. It's for my living role."

"It's a Crucifix, isn't it?"

"The Christian Cross. I'm Catholic, Anna."

"Oh." She nodded. At this point, it seemed like the right response but not quite long enough and so she added to it by saying "It's beautiful" again.

That's when the loud call of Freddie, the Assistant Director was heard by everyone on Sound Stage 10: "Let's go! Page 37!" Lorna smiled and put the Christian Cross back under her blouse as the call of "Let's go. Page 37" meant it's time for Lorna's role starting, in this case, on Page 37 of the Shooting Script and not the living script between her and Anna or her and Savannah as Anna was called by everyone else on the set.

Chris had earlier told Anna that after D.C. he would be going to Bermuda that would start another of his around-the-world trips to inspect the progress of NASA's tracking posts for coming Mercury orbital flights of Astronauts. He itemized every potential stop and date and phone number of his international itinerary. "You can either phone me or send a letter to me in care of any American Express office in those cities. I'll always check with them. They do that; they hold mail for visitors."

On the second morning of his trip to Bermuda he was eating Raisin Bran in the dining room of the island's massive stone hill-top Castle Harbour Hotel when a waiter told him there was a telephone call for him "from the States."

Chris' joyful excitement from the comment caused him to let go of his spoon in the cereal bowl and that created a splash of milk over his royal blue shirt. "A girl?"

"A man."

All that remained of the delivery of the clarifying message was milk dripping down Chris' shirt in three straight paths and the directions from the waiter of where Chris could walk to and locate the off-the-hook telephone receiver with the holding caller on the other end.

Although he was angry that the phone call wasn't from Anna, he couldn't be angry that the phone call was from his boss at Western Electric, Mr. D'Agostino, who told Chris to cut his trip so as to come back home when he finished his inspection of Bermuda's tracking site because "you've been requested by the powers at NASA Headquarters for you to hurry back to the States and locate yourself in San Diego right away coordinating with General Dynamics Astronautics. You're going to be part of the rest of Project Mercury—probably including a quick trip to the Cape when John Glenn's orbital flight is launched—then back to San Diego—all on NASA's nickel—and likely the project that Kennedy talked about last Thursday night—the moon project. Sorry; you aren't going to the moon, my friend, but you'll likely be in on the rest of its history. That's not bad, you know. It's pretty close to what you always wanted, isn't it?"

"You bet."

After their short conversation, Chris returned to his table. He re-spooned some Raisin Brans that were now sagging in softness after they rested too long in milk. It didn't matter. It gave him an opportunity for his mind to go back and forth between anger and enthusiasm; between the silent Anna for his anger and most of all, the thrill of enthusiasm from the magnificent message about NASA's request for him to join General Dynamics Astronautics in San Diego including going to the Cape for the first orbital launch of U.S. Astronaut, John Glenn.

The diminishing Raisin Brans kept him company until there was no bran, no raisins, no milk, no company left. But not for long because the waiter returned and this time he pulled back the chair next to Christopher at his table.

As Christopher realized that waiters pull out chairs only for guests joining guests, everything turned gleeful. Everything. The waiter pulled back the chair so that Anna would be sitting where she requested after she had come to the entrance to the Castle Harbour Hotel's dining room and pointed to the table of the man sitting alone and playing with a spoon. "I'm a surprise," she had then said to the Maitre-d'. She held a purse and some brown file-sized envelopes. "I don't want to be announced."

The waiter accommodated all her requests.

First there was a kissing session between Chris and Anna. No words. Then Savannah stared into his eyes. "I had to see you. I was worried about you. You didn't seem interested in me anymore. I don't want to lose you, Chris. Please."

Was that meant as an apology of some sort? 'Leave it be,' he told himself. 'Why put her on the defensive? What would be gained? An argument?'

She gave a quick smile almost as though she heard what he was thinking. "I'm just a messen-juh." Her southern accent was back in full for this part of the occasion. "I have come to delivah a few pic-juhs of some of my friends that they wanted you to have." She opened one of the brown envelopes she brought with her, and took out the enclosures which were four 8" X 10" glossy photographs.

"I told them all about you," she said. The photos were all portraits of instantly recognizable motion picture celebrities and signed with only their first names below their inscriptions wishing him good luck on the moon.

Chris shook his head and asked her, "And just how did they know that—who told them about my obsessional ambition?"

"A little girl told them."

"You know them?"

"Since I was a very little girl."

"You were an actress even as a little girl?"

"In a way. I had to get a Screen Actors Guild card to work— so I did, but I didn't get any real parts."

"If you didn't get any parts, what were you doing?"

"I was just an extra in crowd scenes and a couple times I had a line so I was promoted to be a bit player but they ended up cutting out my lines fairly often. That was a while back. I won't tell you how long, long ago. Marvelous studio. RKO Studios. If you worked there you soon knew everyone on the lot. It became like a home to me. I sure met some good people and I still know them even though we don't work together now. They've stuck to movies and my real break came from television: 'Gemstone.'"

"So how did you"—and he lifted the photos from the table. "How did you get them to do this now—at this date and to write what they did on these pictures?"

"I asked them."

"You do know how to keep old friends, don't you?"

That could have been a dangerous question depending on her answer. "It was good of them; not me. They're the celebrities." Good twist for the questioner's answer.

Then he found himself doing what he didn't want to have done but he did it. He asked, "You ever hear from Raj Bhavnani?"

She was unbelievable. She raised her eyebrows and shrugged her shoulders with incredible calm as though it was a question for which she had memorized gestures and words in proof of extreme innocence. "No! Thankfully he disappeared! Poof! Gone! Thankfully!"

Christopher, with renewed self-discipline, changed the subject himself. "And Carl Sanford at NASA! You have a way to the—to the famous and the—relevant. He told me you phoned him! That was very good of you and somehow—just minutes ago I was told that NASA wants me to work on overseeing tracking sites for Project Mercury with General Dynamics Astronautics in San Diego—that's where they make the booster—the Atlas—and if things go well—maybe I'll get to work on President Kennedy's project—the voyage to the moon. Pre-flight work. Do you know what I'm talking about?"

"Yes, I do. You see? Of course I know. You can't get away from me!"

He couldn't. "I'm a Hollywoodian, you know. I hope you

know that San Diego is just 130 miles from Hollywood. See? I had it all figured out. You can drive it in three or so hours." As for now she would stay in Bermuda as long as his trip there could last even though she didn't take into consideration that she was risking being AWOL from 'Gemstone' if she didn't check with the Assistant Director. "I have one more thing for you," she said as she handed him another envelope, this one appearing to have something thick inside.

As he opened it she quickly added, "Don't get excited. It's a book, but the author personally inscribed it for you."

It was "Profiles in Courage" by John F. Kennedy. The inscription read, "To Christopher Straw whose contributions to the New Frontier will some day be material for a new chapter in a similarly titled book."

"This is incredible! Incredible! Where did you get this?"

"From a President of the United States of America."

"Anna!"

"No I didn't! I'm kidding you! He probably wrote the inscription for you when he was at his desk. I got it from Pierre Salinger."

"President Kennedy's Press Secretary?"

"Yes."

"Where did you see him?"

"Sans Souci Restaurant in D.C. Lunch. Just up the block from the White House. 17th Street. Does that make some difference?"

"How on earth did you ever work that one out? You had lunch with the President's Press Secretary? And he gave you this to give to me?"

"It's amazing that a shy girl who was bawn in Chahlston

and who now appears occasionally on television, can get to meet Pierre Salinger. He said to give these to your friend who's working on space exploration. Now you can put this book next to all your other memory books."

"I don't have any memory books. But now I do. Yes, now I do." And he read every word of the President's inscription again; this time aloud. Chris added, "That's it! Not bad! I think we can draw from this that we—us—the United States has a future in space."

"And the President of the United States has the name and dreams of Christopher Straw, as well he should!"

THEME FIFTEEN

"GOD SPEED, JOHN GLENN"

BY THIS TIME OF HIS LIFE, Christopher Straw had known and loved many women, knew and admired many men, idolized others, was fascinated by many places and cherished the mission of his life. February of 1962 held the epitomes of all those treasures up to this date: The woman was Anna Lane, the men were seven Astronauts, the idols were those who had become Presidents of the United States, the place was Pad 14 of Florida's Cape Canaveral, and the mission was the black night sky to be searched.

Ahead was the most importantly awaited rocket launch of the United States: the launch of John Glenn Jr. that he had named "Friendship 7" on a Mercury-Atlas 6 Rocket. It had arrived at Cape Canaveral on August the 27th of 1961 and scheduled for a January, 1962 launch as the first manned U.S. Astronaut's mission to orbit—not just to up and down—but to orbit the earth a number of times before landing and scheduled Glenn and the capsule to be recovered in the North Atlantic Ocean by the

Recovery Forces of 17 search aircraft, 12 helicopters, and 21 ships.

The launch had gone through what could be counted as twelve postponements of "Friendship 7" with accompanying speaker-announcements on Pad 14 that "The launch scheduled for today has been scrubbed."

It finally came on February the 20th of 1962 with a count-down of T Minus 390 Minutes, plus built-in holds—but not a scrub—to the relief and what had become the tremendous patience of John Glenn who had gone through the countless putting on and off of his spacesuit and check-outs of equip-ment—and to the anxiety of thousands of workers on the Cape who on a daily basis were running out and in and out of their offices and hangers on belief that the launch would be just minutes away, and to thousands of those who came to adjoining Florida areas to the Cape to become observers to history on the outlying sands of Cocoa Beach as they looked toward the Cape.

And there was Christopher Straw who, with others at the Cape, lived through the magic of feeling a high point of four of five senses known to Man all in one moment: the scent, the sound, the feel, and the sight:

There were the scents of the Cape and Pad 14's Blockhouse and the Pad's Ready Room and of the Pad's launching section itself, and the Cape's Central Control. All of them had a distinc-tive scent of their own.

There was the sound of the screaming noise—uncontrol-lably loud—of the liquid oxygen at a temperature of minus 297 degrees Fahrenheit flowing through the pipe lines, causing the pipes to freeze and contract and to emit the sound of a thousand high pitched screams while the rocket appeared as though it was wearing white ghost-like gowns waving in the wind.

The other towers and much of the rest of the Cape heard the screaming noise and knew it was the warning sound before launch.

There was the feel of mosquitos who likely came to bite as many strangers to Florida as they could find.

There was the totally unsuspected sight of a dog that seemed to appear out of nowhere running around the Blockhouse, then running around the Ready Room Shack, probably frightened but seeming in total control of him or herself and not going anywhere near the rocket. More predominant, there was the sight of the massive gantry; the tower as it let go of its embrace of the Atlas, then slowly and sadly moving backwards and to the east so the rocket could be free.

That was followed by the falling back of the umbilical cord that was giving the rocket its energy-juices and the moving away of the thin tower from which the umbilical cord was attached. With the cord's disconnection, any touch with the Atlas by anything other than the arms of the yellow launcher at its base were gone. The launcher arms were holding the rocket down but would lift up at the right note in the countdown, leaving the rocket free to be launched.

There was the sound of a voice from the Blockhouse. It was Astronaut Scott Carpenter as the communicator talking through the sound system to the active Astronaut Glenn as Carpenter gave one more statement heard by John Glenn prior to the launch:

"God Speed, John Glenn."

And then there was an unearthly roar that could successfully compete with any rival from thunder if there was any thunder even thinking of holding a competition. It was the roar of the Atlas leaving earth with its cargo of a manned space-craft as its capsule occupied by John Glenn Jr. who was sitting in that space-craft attached to the Atlas that was now taking off from earth in living quarters no bigger than a telephone booth.

Those observing from the Cape and from miles away in Florida were gifted with the sight of the rising Atlas now on its mission.

Four hours, fifty-five minutes and 23 seconds after launch, it was over. The third orbit and re-entry to Earth had been achieved and after recovery of the space capsule by the U.S.S. Destroyer Noa, and then after a short flight by one of the three helicopters who had been waiting, there was the sight of John Glenn emerging from one of the helicopters and walking out-side toward its pilot's cabin so as to shake hands in thanks to the last one in a series of ones who brought him to safety. And there was, to any close observer, the sight of tears of appreciation unshakably masking John Glenn's eyes.

There were also tears of joy in the eyes of the thousands or millions of those who had watched the launch and recovery on television or at least heard them on radio.

And Scott Carpenter's call of "God Speed, John Glenn" was heard by Christopher Straw on that golden day and apparently heard by so many millions around the world and particularly heard by God and by John Glenn; the two major figures for whom Scott Carpenter's message was intended.

THEME SIXTEEN

BACK TO THE SCHOOL ROOM

IT WAS SIMILAR TO THE FIRST DAY of the Fall Semester in 1939 at school but this time Christopher Straw was much older than he was when he prepared his inkwell as a recipient for one of Nancy Benford's two pig-tails. And now he was not a student but a teacher in front of those in their late teens and a few maybe in their early twenties and all of this was far away from Pennsylvania's public schools he knew so well. Instead of McConnellsburg Elementary School it was San Diego State College for his first session teaching an evening extension course on the subject of Space Exploration on assignment requested of him by his superiors at NASA and Convair Astronautics as an adjunct to his normal work at Convair Astronautics. It was scheduled for Thursday nights at 6:00 P.M. through 9:00 P.M. with pizza arriving at its conclusion.

The classroom was filled. "The 'Log-In' has 34 names on it," Chris said to his class. "And I'm glad there is that kind of attendance here. Thank you for coming. Since you don't get any credits for attending this extension course, the only reason you can be here is because you're interested enough in the subject to spend some evenings of this semester in the subject of these sessions—and that is to your credit—I mean *real* credit; not to raise your credits for a *grade* but to raise your *questions* about the new frontier of space exploration—and that says a lot about you.

"One question before anything else: How many watched the live telecast of the launch of 'Friendship 7' last week?"

Close to two-thirds of the class raised their hands.

"Wonderful. You have a real sense of the valuable moments worth watching on television. Anyone here have any questions about it?"

About six or seven hands raised and were slowly joined by six or seven more. Chris nodded. "Yes?" as he pointed to the nearest one; a boy who not only had his hand up but was nodding with fast motions. "Yes. Go ahead. First, what's your name?"

"Ned. Ned Wilson."

"Yes—go ahead, Ned."

"I want to be an Astronaut, Professor Straw. What do I do to become one? I mean I'm serious about this career and it's my ambition now—after watching John Glenn and what he did. What would you say are my chances?"

Chris nodded again. "Your chances are better than mine and I want to be an Astronaut, too," Chris said and a number of those in the class laughed. "No. I'm not kidding. I want to be an Astronaut and I wanted to be an Astronaut before there *were* any Astronauts at *all*. Your chances are pretty good considering since you, Ned, are a young guy and will have opportunities that are only going to get easier as the years go on. When this program started; the Mercury Astronauts that have now had space flights ; Shephard, Grissom and Glenn, had to go through a nightmare of requirements and, frankly, most of the requirements are still holding. You have to have been a test-pilot with a minimum of 1500 hours in flight and have a bachelor's degree and have been—or in one of the U.S. Armed Services. That's all according to Scott Carpenter and he adds that you have to be physically fit to perfection. After that basic acceptance then the real tests begin: exercising—Glenn ran five miles a day for a long while only tapering off just before flight for rest purposes prior to the flight. I'm leaving out the study of astronomy. He had to know constellations of the stars—all kinds of absorption in things. A list of those things would take the evening to itemize."

"Why do you think I could qualify?"

"Ned, I think everyone in his room will probably qualify. It's because of your ages. Hold old are you?"

"Nineteen, sir."

"You have a lot of time. Stay well, but look; Deke Slayton is one of the Mercury Seven and last year a heartbeat irregularity was discovered by the medical team that examined him. As I understand it's like a heart murmur under ordinary conditions but not known if it would be dangerous in space flight, so pretty soon the doctors will see whether or not he's able to go up. Maybe he can and maybe the Mercury Seven will have only six members while he sits it out. In addition to that kind of thing, I'm leaving out a catalogue of rigid requirements. I repeat; stay well. But keep in mind that the initial qualifications are bound to drop off. Many already will probably drop off when the Glenn flight is fully analyzed."

A young woman quickly raised her hand to be ahead of the others and she added, "Professor Straw?"

"Yes M'am."

"I'm Lauri. You said every one of us could become an Astronaut. Do you mean women, too? Can a woman ever become an Astronaut?"

"Not yet. But you can count on that in short time. It's no secret that the Soviet Union is hinting they're already training some women to go up into space. If all goes well I'm sure we'll be sending women up, too."

Another young woman, without putting up her hand but simply shouted to him said, "Professor Straw, why was John Glenn in his 'Friendship 7' capsule going *three* orbits considered to be so important when last year the Soviet Union had two launches of *their* Astronauts both going into orbit—and one of the Soviet's Astronauts went over *ten* orbits?"

Chris nodded. "Good question. Some minor corrections: first: I appreciate it but you don't need to call me professor. Call me anything you want. But I'm not a real professor—but that's kind of you. Second, the Soviet Union doesn't call space travelers Astronauts. They call them Cosmonauts and we refer to them that way out of courtesy to their work—their space programs—our appreciation of their Cosmonauts. And it was their Cosmonaut Yuri Gagarin who last year of 1961 went into orbit—one orbit. He was the first man in the world to travel in orbit. And then around four months later there was Gherman Titov who, as you indicated, was another of their Cosmonauts and he went *over ten* orbits—in fact he went *seventeen* orbits. But one great difference between their launches and ours: 'Friendship 7' was launched live on television for the entire world to see as it happened—success or failure, just like Alan Shephard and Gus Grissom. Grissom almost lost his life just before recovery of his capsule, 'Liberty Bell 7,' and that recovery was seen live in front of the world. Grissom got out safe but the capsule sunk. And you'll remember that there were four minutes and twenty seconds of Glenn's flight of 'Friendship 7' when we lost voice contact with him from an ionization blackout and those at Central Control were plenty worried that—we weren't in the know—but we were worried that maybe he was gone. Pretty rough. We had contingencies from the first time there was an Astronaut launched—from Shephard to Grissom to Glenn—including a contingency of a speech by President Kennedy all prepared and rehearsed by him just in case. Pretty rough. It would be in front of the world. You knew our fear if you were watching on television or listening to the radio. That's the way we operate when it comes to manned flight into space. Our manned launches have been and will be watched and heard by the world as they happen—or at least by those people in nations that have radio for sound or live television for both sound and sight. It's the difference between closed societies and free societies. I have no idea whether any Soviet—any of their Cosmonauts were launched before Yuri Gagarin and, if there were such launches, were they successes or failures. I don't know. Do you?"

A young man said, "Does anyone know?"

"Sure. Some people in the Kremlin and the bureaucracies that deal with such things in the Soviet Union know the answer to that."

"I'm Patricia. Patricia Hernandez. You sounded so optimistic about space exploration to Ned. How could you be that optimistic with just two men who went up and down and one who went for three orbits?"

"It's pretty easy. It is because of the incredible pace of progress we've made so far. Please remember that it was October of 1957 when the Soviet Union, using the same booster for their ICBM's, launched their Sputnik One satellite. We couldn't get off the ground. In fact, Sputnik One was the proof to us that they had an Intercontinental Ballistic Missile—an ICBM. The 4th of October is when it went up from the Soviet Union so that was around five years ago, wasn't it? We had nothing. We had tried to send up an ICBM for a test fight—an Atlas—in June of 1957 and our Range Safety Officer—Range Safety guy—the guy who just sits there and presses a button that blows up rockets whenever he has to; he had to intentionally blow it up because right after launch it was headed toward Cocoa Beach instead of just going up and then down into the ocean. Before it went way off-course he blew it up before it did any damage to Cocoa Beach. Our first successful launch of a satellite wasn't until January of 1958, and just think—not much after that we all celebrated when we got a recording of President Eisenhower's voice giving a pre-recorded Christmas Greeting from an orbiting satellite in 1958's Christmas Season. That's as far as we came just around three years ago. Then we had an Atlas-Able—a ninety foot rocket—blow up on the launching pad. That was in 1959. Then we tried another Atlas-Able on Thanksgiving of 1959 with it targeted to hit the moon. It didn't hit the moon. It got launched off the pad this time but it missed its target of the moon and kept going through space. One unexpected plus on that one was that it became the first man-made satellite to orbit the sun. It became part of our solar system. But those are all—I won't call them failures because we always learn from tests—but they didn't do what we hoped they would do. With all that behind us—and I left so much out, we now have had three successful

correctly be called a booster stage but without a mission—just sitting there I guess—or used as an exhibit someday. Originally President Eisenhower didn't want any missile used as a booster for space-flights. Instead he wanted all space missions to be launched by a new rocket called 'Vanguard' for space flights alone—and not allowed to be used as a potential war-time booster. Mixing up the two, he thought, could cause world-suspicion. Vanguard didn't work out. One after another, Vanguards kept blowing up. Missiles went through that kind of history too, but President Eisenhower hoped we could get Vanguards off the pad with the ability to launch frequent space vehicles and with the mission to launch only space vehicles. No luck."

The same young man followed up by asking, "Is the Atlas the only rocket we have for now for the flight of Astronauts?"

"No. Shephard and Grissom went up in Redstones. Those are smaller and less powerful than an Atlas. They weren't used for orbiting an Astronaut but for Astronaut flights going up and down in space. The next manned spacecraft after the Mercury 7 series is to be a series called Gemini, and Geminis will house two Astronauts at once and the Gemini series will be launched by Titans, not Atlas'. Titans have been used for simulating a warhead and Titans have been defined as a missile for those test-flights. Soon they will be designated as rockets because they will be used as spacecraft flights. Get it?"

"Who is left of the Mercury-7 Astronauts?" a young woman asked.

"Scott Carpenter, Wally Schirra and Leroy Gordon Cooper known as 'Gordo.' Then we will see about the medical decision for Deke Slayton."

"You know Shorty Powers?" a young man asked.

"The voice of Mercury! Sure! Good man!"

"Is he really short?"

"No. He's a giant. He probably knows more about the Mercury-7 program than anyone else. You know he invented the term you heard John Glenn use in his flight when he answered the Capsule Communicator's question by saying "A-Okay!"

"I mean in height—is he short?"

"I never gave it any thought. I'll pay attention the next time I see him for you. Now let me get back to the story I hoped to tell you this evening: It starts a long time ago—I mean a really long, long, long time ago. And feel free to interrupt me at any time by raising your hand. You don't need to wait until after I get done speaking and I won't wait until then to answer you. At the most I'll just complete whatever sentence I'm saying at the time."

A young woman's hand was raised already.

Chris nodded and said, "Yes?"

"I'm sorry, sir. Please go ahead."

"No. It's okay. What?"

"That statement you made about President Eisenhower's voice. I don't remember that happening. It was a recording of his voice played back from space?"

"Yes. It was called Project Score. Anyone hear of the Broadway Musical, 'Call Me Madam'?"

"Yes, sir" another of the young women said. "It was a movie, too, I think."

"I think you're right. Either way it had to be around the early 1950s so most of you were probably kids at that time. But it was a big musical by Irving Berlin: you know, he had written 'God Bless America' and 'White Christmas' and a lot of songs and he wrote the music and lyrics for 'Call Me Madam' and one of the songs he wrote was called 'They Like Ike and Ike is Good on a Mic.' That was short for microphone. Get it? Mic. That was before General Eisenhower ran for the Presidency and so a lot of people got mad because they thought this was a push for him to run against Adlai Stevenson. In short, they claimed it was a campaign song in a Broadway Show. Maybe it was; I don't know, but it was very popular. And, of course he *did* run and became President of the United States. Now, the song title was right because as we all learned he was very good on a Mic—on a microphone. Years after he won the presidency—that thought of how good he was on a mic gave the inspiration of having a space flight in 1958 while he was in his second term as President. Not that long ago—it was about four years ago. Listen to this:

"Even if you know what I'm talking about you probably don't know that there were only 88 people who knew about this particular project going on. It was held in secret. I don't mean a national security secret but just something that President Eisenhower and NASA wanted to keep secret because it was meant as a Christmas Gift or Card or something like that—to the world from the United States by the President tape-recording a Christmas greeting and we—we would get the tape to an orbiting rocket of ours in space and send the message to earth for transmission from space to the world. It was so secret that after some months 55 of the 88 were told they could go ahead to other assignments, but to retain the secret. The transition for those 55 going back to previous assignments left only 33 people who were still working on Project Score; but all original 88 still pledged to secrecy. Most people who worked on the Cape thought that this Atlas would be used for another testing of systems of the Atlas Intercontinental Ballistic Missile system—an ICBM."

Some young man confirmed its translation, "That's what they're called for short."

"Good. Good. Right," he said somewhat bothered because he already said that. "ICBM. Now, one loose word by any of those who knew its real mission meant the project would be cancelled. Not for the usual reasons of security but it was intended to be worth celebrating."

"But you said we keep nothing in secret."

"No, I didn't say that we keep nothing secret. Or if I did then I put it wrong. I surely didn't mean to say 'nothing.' We keep plenty of things secret that involve national security; now even some satellites depending on their mission. I hope I said that we don't keep launches of *manned flights* secret and, instead, if the U.S. networks want to put it on television or radio and even if *foreign* television networks send camera operators here to photograph its launch—that's fine. Get it?

"Let me go on about that unique voice message of President Eisenhower: Don't think I'm trying to be dramatic. It's the way we live. The bird—meaning the Atlas Rocket, and the red and white checkerboard tower that shelters the rocket, and the umbilical tower that keeps charging it; feeding it, and really all the elements above the yellow temporary bolted 'holder'—the launcher that unlatches—allowing the freedom of the Atlas— become our friends. We applaud when all the elements work as planned, and we blame ourselves or, candidly, maybe we even cry when they do what we don't want them to do.

"So in ten days from the rocket's arrival, it was driven to its tower and erected so as to be embraced—hugged by the tower doors that could be moved up and down either for shelter in their embrace or to stand alone prior to test or launch.

"The countdown was now Minus Fifteen Days and Counting. Added to the 8700 pounds was President Eisenhower's message, recorded by him and later to be transmitted from a tape in Atlas 10-B's communications package, then beamed down to the Earth and carried by radio to listeners anywhere on the world that could receive it.

"First, a static test, performed on every liquid fueled rocket or missile days before flight time, actuating every system needed to be rehearsed except launch itself. That is the dress rehearsal while the rocket is free from its red and white tower's hugging embrace; now parked by its side, while still held, now as captive by its yellow launching device holding tight on the rocket's thrust section."

"Were you there?" one of the young men asked.

"Some of the time."

"What did you do on it?"

"What I always do—pushed buttons on a computer and kept my mouth shut. I didn't open it until the world already heard the message and we had clearance."

"All to hear a recoding?" a young man asked.

"Keep in mind it was the President of the United States and at the time the Soviet Union didn't have the technology to broadcast their leader's voice through space, and besides, General Secretary Nikita Khrushchev wasn't known to be good on a Mic.

"For us, this forthcoming launch, our Atlas which was originally built to be an Intercontinental Ballistic Missile had its mission changed to be used as a powerful rocket booster for radio transmission throughout much of the world in—as I said—for the 1958 Christmas Season starting on December the 18th—our time; Cape Canaveral's time being the 18th at launch. Shortly after that was when millions of people around the world heard the voice of President Eisenhower; and minutes after transmission, his words were translated in many languages. It was a simple but meaningful message." Then Christopher took a folded piece of paper from his top left inside pocket of his suit-jacket and began reading:

"'This is the President of the United States speaking. Through the marvels of scientific advance, my voice is coming to you from a satellite circling in outer space. My message is a simple one: Through this unique means I convey to you and all mankind, America's wish for peace on Earth and goodwill toward men everywhere.'"

Chris added, "It was the beginning of our communications satellites." Chris looked at the young woman who had originally asked him about it since she hadn't remembered hearing about it. "Does that answer your question about what it was about?"

"Yes, Mister Straw," she said.

By the time Christopher Straw got done telling stories about the adventures of space it was close to 9:00 P.M. and the previously ordered pizza arrived. Chris held up both hands and said,"Don't get up to bring the pizza to your desks just yet. I never got around to saying what I wanted to say at the beginning of this session about something that happened a zillion years ago—and it's very short:

"I believe that God created outer space. And he painted it black and called it the heavens. That black of the heavens became a mystery for Man. Millennia passed one after another all the way into your time of births in the 20th Century with the mystery sustained. But somewhere near the beginning of your lifetimes Man started to build towers to reach the heavens. The first time ever. And he painted them red and white and called them the Towers of Canaveral."

There was a silence that overcame the schoolroom. The students were staring at him but without any audible reaction.

So Chris got up to get some pizza for himself. "All clear for pizza," he said. His '*Astronauts-to-be*' followed him to the back of the schoolroom to get slices for themselves to bring back to their desks.

"I love it!" he told Anna on the telephone about his first teaching assignment that night. "Great kids! They are great kids! I'll be doing this once a week—I hope. Every Thursday night."

"Wonderful! Where are you now?"

"Back at the Silver Spray. My apartment."

"Alone?"

"Oh, Anna. Please."

"Well, I don't know who you meet in your adventures and decide to bring home; I don't know. Maybe there's a pretty teacher there. How do I know?"

"You don't know and I want you to worry about it. Then maybe you'll hurry back home."

"It sounds like you really enjoy teaching about space."

"Of course. I love it."

"I'll go with you one of these Thursday nights."

There was silence followed by Chris saying, "I don't know if they allow guests."

"Oh, come on!"

THEME SEVENTEEN

THE UNLIKELY CELEBRITY

ALL THE TRANSITIONS CAME WITH FREQUENCY; welcome or unwelcome, breaking the sureness of yesterday. Unexpectedly, the most unscheduled transition was the one to come to Raj Bhavnani because he would not stand still, first leaving New York City, then he became a Lincoln-Mercury car salesman in Buffalo, then a bartender at the Old Town Ale House in Chicago, then he had a job changing clothes on mannequin displays at Schuster's Department Store in Milwaukee, then a waiter at Café du Monde in New Orleans then an Assistant Manager at Bullock's Wilshire in Los Angeles, then an Assistant Manager at In-N-Out Burgers in Baldwin Park. He did all that somehow remembering the advice that Chris told him his father had given to him to "travel throughout the United States" and learn. And then in early October of 1962 came the biggest change of all when he went from the United States to join the Indian Army in Kashmir that was fighting the invasion of India's two major enemies; the People's Republic of China's Liberation Army on the battlefield of India's north-east border, and the Republic of

Pakistan—or at least its proxies—on the battlefield of India's north-west border with West Pakistan.

It was a war that prompted little interest by most in the United States because at the time the United States was justifiably immersed in events taking place ninety miles from its own shores of Key West; the Cuban Missile Crisis.

Although China and its ally, Pakistan, took land from what had been territory of India, Raj became a hero for having come back to his country of birth to help India retain much of its territory from the invaders. He was promoted from his first rank of Havidar up to Second Lieutenant. "Is Field Marshal open?" he asked but was not answered. No matter; his greatest acclaim was given by civilians as he attained celebrity status in some villages, towns, and cities, with Raj known as "the Bharata who went to America and came back home to fight for his Homeland." That term, "Bharata" was significant as the Indian subcontinent was named Bharat some two thousand or more years back and still affectionately used by many as a sign of national inheritance.

When Prime Minister Jawaharlal Nehru negotiated peace-terms from the warzones, many concerned citizens of India held him responsible for having given away large hunks of India's northern territory during those negotiations. That national disenchantment with the leadership only served to give Raj greater praise for his widening role as a patriot who came home at a time of war to pick up arms.

By mid-November Raj was increasingly well known and with an honorable discharge from the Army, surprisingly he was given a free suite at the Ashoka Hotel known by its many international patrons as the best hotel in New Delhi. Just like the old days in Bombay he held free occupancy in a grand hotel but this time it was with a free suite. And this room had real air conditioning.

"Raj? Is that you?" the man's voice asked over the phone after the hotel operator connected him to their celebrity guest who was eating his room-serviced breakfast-plate of spiced biryani curry with a side dish of the Indian bread, chapatti, that was somewhat like a cross between a muffin, a pitta, and a tortilla, and by its side was a mound of rice, all of those things on a rolling tray as he sat on the edge of his bed used as a cushioned seat.

"Yes, this is Raj Bhavnani."

"Good! This is Venu Ramachandra. Do you remember me?"

"Sa'ab! Mr. Ramachandra-ji! Remember you!? I am so honored and glad to hear your voice Sa'ab! Old times! Old times!"

"Raj, I have read so much about you and I join all of India in appreciation for your helping India in its difficult moment of need!"

"No, no. I did what I so much wanted to do and anyone with our heritage would have done that." Was this the Raj Bhavnani that Venu remembered as an employee? Back in those days humility was not a word that was used by anyone to describe Raj Bhavnani.

Venu continued: "I am on a trip—I'm on a short trip here in Delhi. I would like to see you. Maybe dinner?"

"Yes, yes. Let's do that. Where are you in Delhi?"

"I'm at the Claridges Hotel. I can meet you wherever you want."

"No, no. I will have you picked up. Can you come to the Trivedi Club for dinner? I have to go there because they invited me some weeks ago for tonight. They invited me and I said 'yes'. You ever heard of it?"

"I heard of it, but I don't know anything about it. I've never been there. I believe that it's an exclusive organization. Distinguished. I don't know much else about it. Are you the guest of honor? I'm sure you are."

"Yes, yes. I've never heard of it until I was invited for tonight and I was told it was prestigious. So I'm supposed to be there at six o'clock. Can you do it tonight as a guest of mine? Maybe a 5:30 pickup?

"I'll be in front of the Claridges on Aurangzeb Road right by the traffic circle that's right off Janpath. I will be there at 5:30."

"Look for a government car. The driver will know the way to the club. Some good people have been there, you know; I mean to the Trivedi Club. They told me some good people have been there: Thomas Bata has been there—the Shoe Company owner—Bata shoes, you know. And Jawaharial Nehru has been there—He's Prime Minister, you know. And third, I'm going to be there—and I was a third-rate employee of the first-rate Taj Mahal Hotel in Bombay!"

"Three important people! Sounds good to me. Tell me, do you have a cleaned suit you can wear? Or is it still at the cleaners?" he asked in a now-cherished reminder of their first conversation years back by the Gateway of India.

"Ahhh, yes, yes; still at the cleaners, Sa'ab. Maybe they can have it ready in time."

"No matter. But I think it would be most appropriate for you to—to call me—simply call me 'Venu.' No more 'Sa'ab', no more 'Mr. Ramachandra-ji'. Your station in life; your reputation; what you have done for India reverses our positions from what they might have been when we met. You are now *Lieutenant* Bhavnani." He was acting appropriately right with the hope that Raj's old characteristics of exaggeration had permanently diminished.

Raj received a medal from the Trivedi Club that night and that was only the start of honors. He was praised by a Member of the Lower House of Parliament called the Lok Sabha, then by a member of the Upper House of Parliament called the Rajya Sabha, then a letter of congratulations for him was read aloud written and signed by Prime Minister Nehru Jawaharlal followed by a letter of congratulations and thanks from U.S. Ambassador to India, John Kenneth Galbraith, then one from the Director of the United States Information Agency, Edward R. Murrow, followed by a letter from U.S. Secretary of State, Dean Rusk. Then those attending from the American Embassy were asked to stand up so as to be introduced to the rest of the attendees. There was enthusiastic applause.

That was followed by the guest of Honor, Raj Bhavnani giving a short speech of gratitude in both Hindi and English that was, for him, remarkably unassuming.

"My friends," he said in slow pace very much like he learned from having heard the recordings of four presidents ago; the late President FDR that had been played for him at the U.S. Library in Delhi. "My friends,'" he said again even slower and more Rooseveltian than Roosevelt, "I embrace the home of my birth and blood: what was the Dominion of India and became the Republic of India; a force of good and brave people." There was much applause with many standing. "And I also embrace the second of my two homes; the home of strength, security and support to those who come to its shores and that supports us and supports other great nations in their moments of need: The United States of America." There was much applause, particularly from those representing the U.S. Embassy who did not stand at that as they were diplomatic enough not to make a competition out of this between the two countries.

"It should be known—but it isn't widely known—many are unaware that right after our border with China was attacked by China, Prime Minister Nehru received from President Kennedy a message in which President Kennedy asked, 'What can we do to translate our support into terms that are practically most useful to you as soon as possible?' Unsurprisingly the United States would not support China's Chairman Mao, but quite dramatically the U.S. did not for a moment claim neutrality between India and Pakistan's Ayub Khan. The U.S. would support India. And it supported India with American military aid and advisors, and support of the U.S. Air Force and other things including intelligence from America's Central Intelligence Agency. President Kennedy told his Ambassador John Kenneth Galbraith to let him know whatever India needed, and Ambassador Galbraith made some enormous requests of President Kennedy—and they were all granted. All granted—even as I believe you know, the U.S.'s recognition of the McMahon Line as the boundary between India and China. President Kennedy-ji's actions for India brought anger from Mao Tse-tung and anger from Ayub Khan but endorsed by those on this side of the borders. It is undisputed that tonight I can say with certainty, as all of you can say with certainty—that half the world away, the Republic of India has a friend!"

The ovation was extraordinary. No one remained seated.

Surely some probably had some physical difficulty in standing but somehow overrode anything that would limit their endorsement of Raj Bhavnani.

Other than Ambassador Galbraith, Raj Bhavnani with his unofficial but unique status representing both India and the United States, was fast becoming the symbol of U.S.—India relations.

After being made a lifetime member of the Trivedi Club someone yelled out, "Dance for us, Raj! Dance for us!"

That was not unexpected by many of the guests. It had been published and well-read in the *Times of India* that Raj Bhavnani was a master dancer as seen one night in a small club in Old Delhi, and somehow it seemed right that Raj Bhavnani would dance this night.

His innate ability to dance in Indian and U.S. concurrent dancing styles was new to this audience and most were thrilled to watch; even those who never cared much about dance. That was because there was something both magical and talented within Raj Bhavnani.

The magic and talent were applauded and cheered and soon the event of honor was done and the guests scattered in small groups of conversation while Raj Bhavnani and Venu Ramachandra were escorted by a club official taking them to the lounge for private conversation.

The two were seated among empty chairs, couches, coffee tables and big ash trays with each one of the ash-trays ornamented on its edges with cemented miniature white statues of elephants that could hold cigarettes between their tusks.

"Lieutenant," Venu started his conversation with his continued awareness of using a new salutation of honor. "They loved you—they were ready to elect you to take the Congress Party away from Nehru and make you India's Prime Minister or just venerate you in some spiritual way. Whatever it was in that room—it was something you did—or said—or danced—it was something new to India. Lieutenant, my congratulations and my respect."

"Sahib, I am Raj. No rank. That's all I am; Raj Bhavnani. As they say in America 'I yam what I yam and that's all I yam. I'm Popeye the Sailor Man!'"

Venu smiled. "Is that what they say?"

"Yes, yes. Popeye. Like an Indian he eats only vegetables; spinach. I eat other things but I eat spinach like Popeye the Sailor Man."

"Really?"

"No. I just lied. I can't stand spinach. Who can? It's grass. It's nothing."

"So you still lie?"

"Only to you. Only in fun to you. You were right, Sahib. I should not lie."

Venu stared at his friend and nodded. "I'm glad. You know, don't you, that there is expectancy in you now. People look toward you—at you as an example of something—something to cherish you know. You are what parents tell their children to emulate."

"Emu—what?"

"Emulate. Copy. Act like you. They tell them to do what you do. You do so many things. Do you want to dance as a constant? Those cheers!"

"How do you spell 'emulate'?"

Venu spelled it out for him, Raj wrote it on a small notebook he grabbed from his pocket, then Venu repeated, "Do you want to dance as a constant? As a career of sorts?"

"No. I want to be a leader."

"Good. I was hoping that."

"Dancing is fun for me. It also wears me out. Leading is fun and doesn't wear me out. When I lead, I want to lead further. No, it doesn't wear me out like dancing. What is refreshing is that leading doesn't lead me—because I lead leading."

"Now, where will you lead those who you accumulate and who will be walking behind you?"

Raj was quiet and looked around the room in what looked like a hopeless endeavor to find the answer to his friend's question. "I don't know."

"Then—then, Lieutenant—then Raj, your pursuit is aimless; used only for your own satisfaction. That is nothing. No; perhaps it is something but nothing worthwhile. To be bigger than your own satisfaction you must lead all your followers to a better place, to a better life; to make all those behind you more content than before they followed you."

Raj looked deeply at his friend's face and then Raj nodded. "You are very wise."

"No. I just want you to be what you are so capable of being."

"Yes, yes."

Venu Ramachandra smiled. "One 'yes' is enough, Lieutenant."

Raj smiled back. "Not enough. It takes two yes's. It's what I do; what I 'yam'—Popeye. I'm Popeye the sailor man."

"I know. Raj—Lieutenant—how do you earn a living here?

I know you've been given a room at the Ashoka Hotel by our government but it can't last forever and anyway how do you buy things—food—things—necessities—some savings—how do you do as well as you look like you're doing? If I may ask, how do you make money? You can't just get paid for being a celebrity—or can you?"

Raj gave something close to a shrug of his shoulders simultaneously making his head into a pendulum. "All India Radio. I do some opinion pieces they're called. And I do the same kind of things on Voice of America. Both of them are right here in Delhi and I get paid. Salaries. Payment. Rupees on All India and U.S. dollars on Voice of America."

"That's very good. Those are very reliable employers I'm sure. Can you make good salaries by doing that?"

"For India it is very good. Oh, yes, it is very good for India. And All India Radio has started television beaming. In time they say that if they use me on that; on television, then the rupees will be increased. Right now there are too few people who have television reception so radio is a much bigger audience; listeners. The Voice of America pays very well."

"That all sounds good. That is the kind of thing a leader should do: opinions—giving your opinions for big audiences on radio."

"Yes, yes."

Venu was suspicious that Raj was not telling him everything in full. No particular reason for such suspicion but it was there; perhaps just because he knew the eccentricities of Raj Bhavnani. He stared at Raj for a while without saying a word for a while and then he asked, "What else? Do you do anything else to earn money?"

Almost with despondency Raj looked at the wall and as if he was talking to the wall he answered, "The dance."

"The dance?"

"I dance."

"I know, but you said it wears you out. Just a minute ago you said you want to lead, not dance. Did I hear wrong?"

"I don't hate dancing. It's just that I don't want it to overtake my leading. Venu—Mister Ramachandra—Venu, I also earn money being in the movies. They are made in Bombay. Your home. The home of the Taj Mahal Hotel. They are made blocks away from the Taj but the first one is scheduled to be premiered here in Delhi in August. You ever see movies? I mean Indian movies?"

Venu looked startled. "Of course. What do you think? Of course."

"Then you know that India's movies are all musicals in that no matter if the film is about something historical that takes place in a 1400th Century drama or if it's a modern 1962 love story or a comedy or an anything—they all have musical numbers with dancing. It is always a musical as well as whatever else they are and the last scene is always a big, long dance of the leading man and the leading woman and there is singing with the dance. And that is how I add to be able to buy things. Not my life work but it is what is there now. Good pay. I will lead—between pictures. That's what they say in America when actors and actresses are not asked to be in a film for a while: they say 'I am between pictures.'"

Venu clamped his lips together and nodded with a slight smile. "I have no more advice or questions, Lieutenant. You know what you're doing. Just don't forget that whatever you're temporarily doing, you have great things ahead—if you remember to do them."

"I cannot forget, my good, good friend."

"Anything else? Any other surprises?"

"Yes. One more. There is a girl here that I see—often."

"Well, that is a good thing, my friend! That can give you some balance. You love each other?"

Raj shrugged. "She loves me."

"That's it?"

"Yes."

"Then there isn't balance. You don't love her?"

"She loves me."

"That comes as no surprise, Lieutenant. Just make sure she isn't in love with you as the celebrity you are—because celebrity status is not permanent. Make sure she loves you because you are you—and not because you are stature for her as an escort or that you have a wallet to draw out rupees. That should not be the criterion for her devotion. She should love you if you suddenly tell her that you have become a dhobi pounding the clothes of strangers to make their clothes clean—pounding someone's underwear on a rock to earn a naya-paisa so you can afford to buy a piece of chapatti because you are hungry."

"You mean let her believe I am an Untouchable?"

"A permanent Untouchable is better than a temporary fool. Find out why she loves you, Raj—Lieutenant."

"You sound like Gandhi."

"I want to. He was worthy of imitation. You know, Raj, that I thought you were special when you lived under the Gateway of India. Mahatma Gandhi probably would have, too. That's how your girlfriend should look at you. Now tell me about her. Make sure she is worthy of you—and would have seen your charm long before you became the famous guest of the Ashoka Hotel."

"I don't love her. I like her. That's all. British. A British girl. Her father works for B.O.A,C., the airline with the big office on Connaught Circus. It's there in one of those circles. It's a big office. What I like is every time we neck she says, 'Oh, Gawd!' 'Oh, Gawd!' It's wonderful. It's British!"

"I don't care about what she says or where her father works or how big B.O.A.C.'s office is. That's fine but just be sure that girl of yours is worthy of the man who told tall tales to tourists at Bombay's Taj Hotel—and they loved him—then she will deserve that unique man who will have continuing tremendous importance to the people of India—and to America and the world—as he now does the best of things."

"You are just like Gandhi, Sa'ab."

"You are kind in your compliments, Lieutenant."

Raj shook his head. "I wish I had your sense of what is right and wrong."

At this inappropriate time a waiter came by with a large napkin tucked within his uniformed arm-pit. He said something that was neither Hindi nor English and beyond any translation into a known language. Even worse, he almost shouted it: "Hah-Lee-Hah!"

"What?" Venu asked.

"Hah-Lee-Hah!" the waiter answered even louder than before.

Whatever it meant, the strange word stopped the conversation about the girlfriend of Raj. There then came some possibility of making sense of the waiter's strange attempt at saying something. The waiter added some words. "Cigar? Drink? Bourbon?"

Raj shook his head. "No thank you." He quickly looked over at Venu. "Do you? I'm sorry. Do you?"

Venu shook his head. "I'm fine. Thank you."

As the waiter walked away he angrily muttered something in a foreign tongue or maybe it was just a softer strange word from no country on earth but, to Raj's and Venu's relief, without yelling it out.

The limousine with CC on its rear license plate indicating it belonged to the government went directly to the Claridges Hotel to drop off Venu Ramachandra before bringing back Raj to the Ashoka.

Raj also got out of the car to shake Venu's hand and to say with respect, "Good night, boss."

"I'm not your boss. That was a while back. Things change."

"Tell me—what should I do now, Sa'ab? I mean about those things you would say are important for me to do?"

Venu nodded. "Lieutenant, leaders gravitate toward leaders. It's like any other profession. Lawyers gravitate toward lawyers; dancers gravitate toward dancers, fools gravitate toward fools, the wise gravitate toward the wise, and leaders gravitate toward leaders. Kennedy has been in office in the U.S. a short time—not even two years but by this time he knows both Nehru and Ayub Khan. Both of them. India and Pakistan. Our country—yours and mine and he even knows our enemy, Pakistan. And around the world he now knows so many leaders; de Gaulle and Ben-Gurion and Sihanouk and Nkrumah and the Shah. Around the world. He even knows Khrushchev. You—you should request a meeting with Prime Minister Nehru. He'll see you. He would be wise to let it be known he will meet with you—that you are friends. It will do him good. And it will do you good as being a leader among leaders."

"I don't like Nehru."

"You know him already?"

"No. But I don't need to know him to not like him. I don't like his hats; I don't like his jackets; and most of all I don't like the way he demanded we conduct the war nor did he seem to have a plan for India's victory. My soldier friends knew how to achieve victory; he didn't. I think he was afraid of thinking it out. And worst of all is that Nehru's peace agreement gave away parts of India's northern territory. I say none of this publicly. That is not my public business."

"That's good. That's worthy thinking. Maybe some day that will be your speaking role. But not today."

"I admire what Churchill and Roosevelt did. They were leaders. They knew how to fight a war. They knew how to win a war and achieve unconditional surrenders. And when it comes to peace rather than in war I admire Mahatma Gandhi as a moral leader—as a Hindu leader—as a Bharata."

"But the ones you admire—that at least you mentioned are—are gone—not Churchill but Gandhi and Roosevelt are gone."

"Then maybe I'll see the living Truman or Eisenhower or even the current President; President Kennedy. And you are not gone, Mr. Ramachandra. I followed you at the Taj Mahal Hotel when I knew so little about leadership. When I was so knowledge-less yet somehow you believed in me. You are worth following, Sa'ab. You are my kind of leader. And you are here walking on earth—alive—and you choose India."

"You are gracious, Lieutenant." With a modest turn in dialogue he quickly added, "Tell me, what do you think of the

Dalai Lama?"

"Fine. I don't know much about him except that his nation of Tibet is under China now and the Dalai Lama lives here in India. He was given refuge."

"By the man with the funny hats and jackets that you don't like: Nehru. And Nehru is alive and in India and you don't want to meet him. That's alright if that's the way you want it. You should then go to meet the Dalai Lama so you associate with leaders—eventually as habit. He is a leader of a great people."

"Where is he? Delhi?"

"Dharamshala. You know, the Hill Station. Way up from Delhi. Dharamshala is a real Shangri-La in the midst of the Himalayan Mountains. Right between your two disfavored places; West Pakistan and China, so don't go too far. They're dangerous—deadly for you."

"I will ask to see the Dalai Lama—but not tonight!"

Venu extended his hand. "Good night, my friend."

THEME EIGHTEEN

DESTINATIONS

HOLLYWOOD CONFIDENTIAL, the magazine that was for sale next to the cash-registers of U.S. grocery stores, devoted its cover to a full page portrait of Savannah Lane. Underneath the portrait was the quote, *"I was told my days on 'Gemstone' are through. Over. Done."* Any potential reader had to buy and read the magazine to find out that she didn't show up for work for a long time with one excuse after another, and therefore she was not called again to play her role, and her contract was not renewed. She had ignored the warnings she received when phoning from New York while attempting a lead role in one of the planned Broadway musicals in the season ahead; "The Roar of the Greasepaint—The Smell of the Crowd," "Fiddler on the Roof," "Man of La Macha," "What Makes Sammy Run?" among others, with her major excuse from being away from "Gemstone" in Los Angeles becoming more and more that she had a bad cold. "Really bad."

Once back to Los Angeles she discovered that her previously reserved parking place at the television studio didn't have her name on it anymore. Instead of her name there was a flat blue color with the insulting sign next to it saying "Wet Paint."

She knew she was wrong in what she did and she knew it was right that she was fired and so she did what any annoyed actress would do in a similar situation: she made a U-Turn from the studio parking lot and headed her car to U.S. Route 101 and drove 134 miles to San Diego and then to Narragansett Street in Ocean Beach and to the Silver Spray Hotel and Apartments that was situated on a high embankment off the Pacific Coast.

She waited for Christopher Straw in the small and uncomfortable reception room, only sharing it with the clerk near the old dark brown wooden room-key boxes; the clerk being at least twice her age and who couldn't stop staring at her. She hadn't phoned to tell Christopher Straw she was coming to see him but she never told anyone what she was going to do next. That was her style. No excuses in advance. Not a justification. Anyone had to love her in order to like her.

The locale's scenery was luxurious but the Silver Spray as a living facility at this time was starting renovation, and at least temporarily was not what would be called luxurious. Its non-luxury might have been a financial plus for its guests as Chris' apartment was an affordable $45.00 a month. Another part of the temporary minus of the Silver Spray was Melvin, the receptionist whose conversation had what he thought was a charming routine, but it was quickly a nuisance. It came about because Anna had the habit of sending Chris chocolate-chipped cookies through the mail. The first time Melvin handed him the package Chris made the mistake of offering him one or two cookies. Chris told him, "These are blues-chasers! They chase away the blues!"

It was considerate of Chris but when another box of cookies arrived Melvin held it behind his back and said, "Ehhh—one third, Mr. Straw. One third!" It was worth a slight smile to a degree at that time, but not when it happened as habit with anything received through the mail that might have looked inviting to Melvin. "Ehhh—one third, Mr. Straw. One third," was becoming a greeting of exasperating frequency.

On this late Thursday afternoon Chris returned from work in what made him look like what he was: his brown suit with an open jacket and open collared white shirt with a slightly pulled down tie hanging loose in front of the shirt told San Diego he was engaged in the New Frontier of space. He was neat enough to be a man who used his head all day but not so neat as to be a lawyer or business-man or someone else engaged in an occupation clearly held by other generations. He was a space-man. He walked into the reception room of the Silver Spray where Melvin handed Chris his apartment key and a couple pieces of mail and gave a sort nod as his glance indicated someone was sitting on the chair behind Chris. Melvin then mouthed with a near-whisper, "Savannah Lane. Savannah Lane. You won't believe me but she is sitting on one of my chairs."

Chris turned quickly around to see Anna sitting there. Had Melvin elected to have said, "Ehhh—one third, Mr. Straw— One third" about Anna, Chris probably would have slammed a fist on him in a fit of thoughtless rage.

"Hello, Mistuh Straw" Anna said in her best quickly re-stored southern accent.

"Anna!"

"Can you buy a very poo-ah girl a cup of coffee and a Bayer aspirin?"

He gave a big smile and nodded. "I think I can do that! I know a terrible place."

"Won-duh-fuhl! Let's go!"

With a quick new thought he said "No" and shook his head. "I'm so happy to see you that I won't take you to a terrible place no matter how much that's what you want!"

She gave him a startled look. "No? Not for a poo-ah girl in basic need of human necessities?"

"Not tonight. Let me take you to Sunset Cliffs. It's very close and we won't have to drive anywhere. It's a quick walk and at sunset it can be incredibly beautiful. It's almost time for sunset."

"If that's what you want with all yaw selfishness!"

"That's what I want. For a long time I have imagined you with me there."

"Don't you have a cah?"

"Yes. Yes, I do."

"What is it?"

"A Chrysler loaned to me by Astronautics. They have a fleet and let me have it unless they need it. At least temporarily, it's how I get to work and back every day."

"What yee-uh?"

"It's a Post-War. It was built after the war."

"What wah? World Wah Two or—or was it built before World Wah One?"

"Now, what war do you really think it was?"

"The Recent Unpleasantness. That's the wah you Yankees call the Wah between the States or worse yet, the Civil Wah," she said with a quick flirtation by maintaining her southern accent. "When the Yankee's came!—*That* wah! Why didn't you-all stay home? Your Yankee's General—General Sherman burned down every road he crossed in Gee-aw-ja. The Recent Unpleasantness Wah."

Christopher shook his head. "I'm not an expert on that war but I can tell you that my loaned Chrysler is a post-war car and it rides just fine."

"Oh, My God! In that case, let's walk to your sunset! I don't want to be in that cah when it explodes!" Then she talked softer. "Where was it built?"

"I don't know."

Then she appeared to answer her own question. "Detroit! By Yankees! They've timed them so they explode!"

"Not this one. The man who takes care of the loaners at Astronautics can be trusted. He was born in Mississippi."

"Thank God!"

They walked less than a block and they were suddenly overlooking the Pacific Ocean. There was a dirt pathway going down the steep hill in a reach that went even further west, closer to a wooden stairway covered with a thin surface of sand that headed to a wide cliff toward the ocean with breakers of the Pacific targeting itself to directly hit those sands, beating itself against the cliff and its grottos while a huge spectacular red setting sun was making its own calmer journey to the north-west over a calmer part of the ocean farther away from the cliff.

For the first hour there was little conversation and much of hand-holding and affection. It would be fine if it lasted forever but they couldn't do that forever and instead they started talking about how content he was working on what he called "Model 7" that started as the first U.S. Intercontinental Ballistic Missile and had now become the launch vehicle for Mercury 7

Astronauts going into orbit.

She, in turn, told him a little—very little about what was going on in her life. "I want to get out of television and back into movies. The trouble is that my favorite movie studio with my favorite movie people doesn't exist anymore. My friends in the industry are all over town ever since RKO sold its studios to Desilu—to Lucille Ball and Desi Arnaz. So I want to go back into movies at whatever studio is still in business. But right now 'I'm between pictures' and I told you before what that really means in Hollywood!" The trouble is that she didn't tell Chris about the meaning of that phrase; she told Raj while they were at the Top of the Sixes.

When she noticed a questioning expression on Chris' face she quickly remembered she had confused Chris with Raj in her memory-bank and she tried to get out of it by quickly adding, "Didn't I tell you what the line means? Well, I tell everybody! Everybody heard me because it's such a great line! I thought I told you, too. If I missed telling you it means—I'll tell you what it means. It means I'm out of a job—an acting role. But it won't last long. Things like that always happen to actors and actresses."

She tried too hard to pass over her error in who she told about that phrase. Chris knew she had probably told Raj. After all this time he still knew she had been with Raj despite no evidence. "Are you sure you'll be okay being out of work for a little while?"

"I'll be more than okay."

"They let you *go*?"

"I wanted to be with you in Bermuda and that started my short absence. Is there a law that says I can't do that?"

Chris didn't answer.

"I mean is there a law?"

"No. Not a law. It doesn't take a law."

They stayed on the Sunset Cliffs side of the Silver Spray through most of the night-time hours. After the Earth had made three-quarters of its inevitable trip around the Sun and night was done, Chris and Anna walked to Chris' apartment. Chris showered and got dressed in a blue suit so it wouldn't look by those at work that he was up all night in the brown suit he wore the day before now which was rumpled since wearing it not only the day before but obviously throughout the night. Anna was still in bed watching him put the things from the pockets of the pair of pants he wore earlier into the pockets of the pair of pants he was wearing now.

"Isn't that sound wonderful?" she asked him.

"What sound?"

"The breakers. This place is filled with romance. First, there is you—and then there is that wonderful repeated hit of the breakers against the land out there that we can even hear inside."

"Sorry, Anna. I wish you were right but that crashing has nothing to do with the ocean."

"Then what is it?"

"The flushing of the toilets in the apartments down the hall."

She laughed and rapidly changed the subject. "Where are you going, Honey? Work? Where is it? Far?" *Honey* was a good move.

"Astronautics. Not too far. I don't know the address but I sure know how to get there. My car knows the way. Can't miss the place. Big buildings. Can't miss them. No other big buildings around them."

She said, "It's 5001 Kearny Villa Road."

Chris looked confused at her reciting the address of Astronautics and he asked her, "Why did you ask me when you even already knew the address of the place?"

She suddenly exploded with tears and quivering lips and finally with loud sobs as she yelled out, "Because I wanted you to think I was smart! Do you mind?!"

He regretted he asked even though he at least controlled himself from asking, "What's that got to do with being smart?" He immediately felt sorry for her. She had taken his reaction to her knowing the address outrageously hard. There are some times in life when a man just can't help but do everything wrong, particularly when a woman is involved. At best she is the witness. At worst she is the victim. God probably has more important things to do than to continually rescue men caught in such a jam. He has a tougher job than most imagined.

Next, by 7:00am in the morning, his post-war loaned Chrysler chugged along since it was born many years ago when it claimed its post-war status. He slowly passed the Loma Theater to the parking spaces for the large ZANZ coffee shop with its interior very much alive in the early morning with the fresh aroma coming from the toasters on the counters being used with white bread leaping up after becoming golden.

After his breakfast of eggs made sunny-side up and that now self-made buttered toast with orange juice and then coffee for his near finish followed by a cigarette, he paid the bill and drove from ZANZ at Midway and Rosecrans to the magnificent giant Kearny Mesa plant of Astronautics designed by the architectural geniuses, William Pereira and Charles Luckman, consisting of two huge wide white buildings that had six thin black lines to mark the six interior floor-lines above the entrances of the two buildings. Those two buildings and a reflecting pool were hosts to a flurry of much smaller buildings within the compound that housed more secrets than any competing other structures held in San Diego, including the hotels where Soviet KGB agents stayed in quantity within the area.

By 7:50 am Christopher Straw was in the Astronautics plant with its massive and palatial presence including the reception area. Nothing like this grand entrance had existed before; certainly not in a defense plant or even a space exploration laboratory. A huge spiral ramp hovered over the welcoming area of the imposing lobby with dozens and dozens of thin metal rods looking as though they held up the spiral ramp that took forever to walk up to the floors of mystery above.

Chris was given an office that had never been occupied before and he adorned it with a map of the world that was a somewhat reduced-in-size duplicate of the map used at Cape Canaveral's Central Control with its up and down zig-zag pattern of the orbits of the solo flights of the Mercury Seven Astronauts and of upcoming two-man flights of Gemini Astronauts.

His office furniture was minimal by choice: There was his desk, two comfortable chairs and one uncomfortable chair, a small coffee table housing only a large brown government-style ash tray, and against the east wall were two iron safes with combination locks built to government standards and requirements for holding classified material of all designations; marked or unmarked.

At 10:40 this morning Chris phoned his apartment's phone number to talk to Anna. He only got to the second digit in dialing the seven numerals when a friend from two offices down the hall was standing in Chris' doorway looking heavily stunned: "Straw! The President was shot—Kennedy! Shot!"

There was noise of others talking in the hallway without their words clearly able to be separated one from another and there were sounds of people running. Chris hung up the receiver from the unfinished dialing of his phone and he said to the guest at the doorway, "Is he okay? How is he? Is he—is he alright?"

"I don't know. President Kennedy was shot. Dallas. In Dallas. In a motorcade."

"Howard, how do you know? How do you know he was shot?"

There was no answer other than a nodding of his head and then a very soft, "General Schriever." That was the confirmation from a voice of authority.

It was then that a woman's loud shaking voice was heard coming from the hallway. "What happened?" And then she pleaded: "Please! Please! Is Kennedy safe? Please!"

Within minutes the world was dark. That historical horror of November the 22nd of 1963 was one that would influence the lives of Christopher Straw, Savannah Lane, Raj Bhavnani, the United States of America, and the lives of millions of people throughout the world. For a section of time in the life of Earth there was one common thought on the minds of close to three billion people.

President John Fitzgerald Kennedy was murdered.

d r u m s

THEME NINETEEN

INTERMISSION

WITH THE SKY AS THEIR PALLET, the flags of the United States outside U.S. facilities and ships around the world hurt to be lowered to half-staff. Flags of many foreign nations also hurt as they joined the lowering of the U.S. flags in their being half-staff with empathy and to console their half-staffed friend.

Lines of people came to sign books of condolences at U.S. Embassies, U.S. Consulates, U.S. Information Services, U.S. Libraries and other United States Government facilities from Mexico to Argentina to Ireland to Great Britain to Italy to Israel to Egypt to Nigeria to Kenya to Pakistan to India to Thailand to Hong Kong to Japan and to so many more nations between and beyond.

In short time there was a massive crowd in the reception area of space exploration experts at Kearny Mesa, San Diego, and their voices spoke only in whispers if they spoke at all, and there were the frequent sounds of sobs.

"He was the head of our family," Christopher Straw said to

no one in particular but for anyone close enough who heard him. What he said brought nods and whispering of the word, "yes."

Anna was crying as were so many in the crowd. Although she cried often for so many things, this occasion was filled with genuine grief. She looked at Chris pleadingly. "How could anyone have done such a thing? What kind of monster did that?"

Chris shook his head as he, too, had tears that overtook his normal command of situations. "I don't know. I just don't know. I don't want to know."

There were people there who believed in President Kennedy and working on his pursuit for space explorations and believed in his quest of sending man to the moon. It was as though they were all his personal appointees. Outer space was the newest frontier and he put it just that way and those who accepted it and wanted it as their life-long careers were left standing and whispering and crying. The only other activity than standing and whispering and crying were the noises of some who brought in both small and large radios and even a few portable television sets.

Anna grabbed and held Chris' hand and, in view of the dark overpowering current, her celebrity was ignored by the crowd causing no more attention than that caused by strangers. On this occasion she even ignored her own celebrity and, unlike the normal Anna, had no use for it.

When television pictures were received on the monitors of the sets brought in, they were showing the exterior of Parkland Memorial Hospital in Dallas and pictures of crowds outside the hospital; mainly crowds of weeping people and those attending to them who were weeping as well.

Half the world away from Christopher Straw and Anna Lane, at the Ashoka Hotel in New Delhi where it was a little before Midnight, guests were running in the hallways and yelling in Hindi and in English, "Rashtrapati Kennedy Ko Maar Diya!" "President Kennedy was killed!" Quickly the hallways were crowded with some wearing Indian Sherwanis and Saris and others in Tuxedos and Gowns and some in Bathrobes and Pajamas. Some rushed outside for destinations unknown. In India on New Delhi's street called Shanti Path and unofficially called "Embassy Row," among the hundreds in line to enter the U.S. Embassy and record their presence was Raj Bhavnani.

Likely for the first time in his adult life others saw tears in his eyes. His celebrity status made him recognized by many as the Bharata-American. Apparently someone told an official in the Embassy that Raj Bahvnani was waiting in line and the news spread until an Indian exterior guard found him in line and told him he could go ahead of the rest and Raj untypically refused. "I will wait," he said. "I am nothing special. President Kennedy-ji is special."

The slow steps advanced in such surrounding quiet that the noise of shoes against the sidewalk were all that could be heard.

Once inside, the U.S. Embassy's Deputy Chief of Mission told Raj that U.S. Ambassador Chester Bowles expressed his appreciation for his attendance, and with obvious recognition of Raj, some of those entering the Embassy from the line almost automatically shook hands with him as though he was an official American representative of the Embassy on this day. Whether he wanted the role or not, he seemed to have it. And he handled it with humility, respect, and even with his small repeated bow as each person expressed sorrow.

The processions accompanying and guarding the flag-draped coffin went throughout the streets of D.C. intermittently for three days and the rhythmic drum-beats would be heard for three days in those streets, and millions throughout the United States and nations throughout the world would hear them on radio and television, and the sound of the sticks against the skin of the drums would, for so many, remain a life-long awareness of the mind's ease in crossing the internal border between each person's own "now" and "memory."

Paintings and photographs of President Kennedy were displayed, eulogies and epitaphs were written, memorials were built, bridges were renamed, books were published, recordings were pressed, speeches were reprinted, and his name, voice and image were permanent.

THEME TWENTY

LOOKING FOR A BEAUTIFUL MORNING

BY THE END OF 1963 events of normality should have taken hold but they didn't. Tempting his mind to be active, Christopher said to himself that it was time to dust his apartment just as usual. That, at least, was something. Not something that would fill him with glowing pride and celebration but at least it was positive. He didn't want to do it. "It doesn't have to be done today," he said in surrender. "Who's going to see it? No one will see it until Wednesday." He quickly closed the door to anything like the 30th or 31st because the 30th and 31st were cruelly holding on to 1963. They could have left early if they really wanted to be kind without leaving more fragments around.

Anna had already rented a Silver Spray apartment immediately next door to Chris' apartment since his apartment was too small for both of them to share and living in his apartment could have caused a scandal. The two apartments were separated by a connecting door that kept everything within the appearance of the straight and narrow for those who sought evidence of "funny stuff" but gave up.

Anna then planned to spend about a week's time starting with Christmas Day and into the New Year in Los Angeles as she was having appointments with those who had said they would try to help her get an acting role in something—anything. Anna had promised Chris she would be back at the Silver Spray sometime on Wednesday, January the First, giving him the phone number and room number of the Beverly Hills Hotel where she would be staying while away; that contact information meant to prove her far-away loyalty to him particularly while being away on New Year's Eve.

She minimized the time away from him, exceeding the keeping of her word by not being away on New Year's Eve but instead being back on Tuesday the 31st and being there, of all things, at 6:15am. Happily he had already showered and was already dressed although he had not dusted his apartment. She opened the connecting door between their two apartments and, in keeping with the season, but prior to when she had left D.C. for her trip to New York, she had made sure that each side of the door had its own Christmas wreath and she had left separate messages on each of the two wreaths. The one facing his apartment had the message, "It is more blessed to give rather than to receive." The wreath facing her apartment had the message, "It is more blessed to receive rather than to give."

Now back from New York, as she walked in his apartment through the connecting door at that early hour, she almost yelled, "I'm here! Yippee! I'm here! Yippee! I'm here!" She was wearing what she called her "little white dress" that she knew caught his and every man's interest.

Before he had a chance to say anything she started singing a Rogers and Hammerstein the Second song from the musical,

"Oklahoma!"

"Oh, what a beautiful mornin'!

"Oh what a beautiful day!

"I've got a beautiful feelin'!

"Everything's going my way!"

Then she sang a second verse of the Richard Rodgers melody but this time with lyrics not by Oscar Hammerstein the Second but by Anna Lane the First:

"It's a three picture deal in the mornin'!

"It's a three picture deal in the mornin'!

"My stardom is high as an elephant's eye!

"And it looks like it's climbin' clear up to the sky!"

After her new paraphrased words were sung she came very close to him, embraced him, and she gave him a long kiss.

There was certainly no harm in that, but he did not want to ignore her singing voice which she so rarely exhibited to him. "Anna—your voice! You are magnificent!"

"But that's what I have been doing since the day I was born. I sing. I love music! Music seems to love me or at least I hope so!"

"You sing so beautifully, Anna!" Beyond her ability as a singer he wanted to understand why she had sung that song and then immediately kissed him. "To what do I owe all this?"

"A Three Picture Deal!"

"Please forgive my layman's lack of understanding. I heard the words but what the devil is a three picture deal?"

"Sit down."

He did and she quickly sat on his lap. "Did you ever hear of Paramount Pictures?"

"Of course."

"Did you ever hear of A.C. Lyles?"

"No. Is he an actor?"

"No. A.C. Lyles is a wonderful man who started at Paramount as a worker in the Mail Room and he worked his way up to be one of the most respected of all those in the motion picture industry. He's produced films, has casted them, did all kinds of things and no one competes with A.C. I think he has a permanent job at Paramount."

"That's nice. Good. What about him?"

"He made a few phone calls and the girl sitting on your lap has been offered a three picture deal which means Paramount wants me to be in three pictures—not a star—probably not a star but I will be cast somewhere in three new films."

"Wonderful! Wonderful, Honey! You did it! When you want a job you get a job!"

"I have friends in high places!"

"I'm jealous—jealous of your A.C.!"

"No you're not. That's what's wrong with you; you're never jealous." She kissed him again. "A.C. thinks I'm a song and dance girl and I do love being in musicals so much and all three films are musicals and besides, A.C. loves animals—dogs and cats—and so do I and he knows that. Now, since you didn't ask I'll tell you that you have a lot to be jealous about since—listen to this! One of the three films is with Elvis Presley! It's a film to be called *Roustabout*. Then there's one called *The Girls on the Beach* with the Beach Boys! And the third is called *Harlow with Peter Lawford!* That's the story of Jean Harlow and I don't want you to think I'm going to play the Jean Harlow role because I'm not. I have small roles in all three. They're roles where I can end up hitting the cutting room floor. It could be that no one will ever see me in them—but I have a three picture deal!"

"You're being modest, Anna."

"I'm being honest, Christo-*fuh*!" (With the accent on the last syllable.)

Chris asked, "Will you still go out with me tonight—on New Year's Eve?"

"You mean instead of Elvis?"

"Yes. Instead of Elvis."

"He hasn't asked me so I should say that If the Beach Boys won't take me out tonight, then I'll go with you."

"That's fair."

"There are *five* Beach Boys, you know. Whopee!"

"No. I didn't know."

"Five. That's what I would call a Happy New Year's Eve date. Five."

THEME TWENTY-ONE

A MEETING WITH THE 14ᵀᴴ DALAI LAMA

VENU HAD TOLD RAJ that "Leaders generate toward leaders" so if Raj wanted the mantle of leadership he should "associate with leaders." By this time Raj had requested a leader's presence and was accepted not at the leader's home in the Hill Station of Dharamshala but in the crowded and loudest city of India located just above the Bay of Bengal:

Calcutta was not like the mountains of patriotic battle that Raj Bhavnani as a soldier had seen in Aksai Chin and the Karakoram Mountains and other places that he had never known were in India before he fought there.

Nor was Calcutta like Delhi with its wide avenues and government buildings and Connaught Circus of inner and outer traffic circles of shops, restaurants, and on its inner circle the Delhi headquarters of trademarked merchandise and international airlines and stores born in London.

Nor were Calcutta's streets anything like New York's 59ᵗʰ Street or 44ᵗʰ Street or Fifth Avenue.

Calcutta was cluttered somewhat like Bombay but with a

heavier dose of everything. There were processions of women carrying baskets of dung on their heads; men spitting out red Beetle-nut juice onto the sidewalk and on the sides of buildings; other residents using the gutter as a bathroom; great quantities of men and women and children with their hands outstretched pleading for anything edible or spendable; children with misshapen limbs bent by those who sent them to the streets to beg; and on a few of the corners a seated snake-charmer guaranteed to catch the eyes of foreign passerby's while ignoring residents. Between the sidewalks on streets for vehicles were taxicabs turning off the ignition at every stop supposedly saving gasoline, bullock-carts, frequent stray cows, occasional goats and other animals as no surprise even if it would be an elephant.

With all its primitiveness and odors of all kinds, there was inside of Raj, a giant affection; a love not for the terrible begging necessary for so many, but for the familiarity of his home country that many who had never lived there could not understand. It was that on each street was everything; everything; everything. He walked to Old Court House Street and passed one building after another and one beggar after another and one starving and naked person after another. He inhaled deeply and he hated it and loved it. It was a street with all senses of the passerby engaged in life and death. But in the smelling of it was the rich nostalgia of things he knew so well in youth—but never so much of all of it heaped one block after another as it was in Calcutta.

The chief attraction of Old Court House Street was the Great Eastern Hotel where, out of all context with anything in this city, foreign celebrities including Chiefs of State had second floor suites for their visits to Calcutta, and where other visitors often had large high-ceilinged single rooms on other floors. It was alright because where else could the Great Eastern have been placed in Calcutta? Was there a better place for it in this city?

At the Great Eastern's front entrance was one in a fleet of white-uniformed and helmeted doormen who respectfully called every man "Sahib" and every woman "Ma'am Sah'b." They had the welcome attitude of being able to accept a tip with appreciation and then, not so welcoming, they quickly requested a larger tip with their eyes rather than their voices. That silent talent was generally effective in receiving larger tips from Europeans and always effective in receiving them from Americans. Any American unwilling to obey the doorman's pathetic look in his eyes, would be a self-confessed scoundrel.

During the morning of Tuesday, December the First of 1964 there was a crowd around the front door of the Great Eastern Hotel waiting in hope to see the Dalai Lama of Tibet. Raj Bhavnani was already inside the hotel, having checked in the night before on the advice of the Dalai Lama's brother, Gylao (pronounced Jai-lo) Thandup and the courtesy of the hotel's management. As planned, Raj was staying in one of the tall ceilinged single rooms of the third floor. The plan was for him to do nothing at all during the entire day until he would meet a man named Rinchin at 7:00 P.M. by the lift next to Room 201 on the second floor.

Raj waited there until a man in a long purple gown appeared from the designated room and greeted Raj Bhavnani with a big smile, an extended hand and introduced himself as Rinchin. With a very soft voice he told Raj to "wait for a moment for the His Holiness" and Rinchin went back into the room leaving Raj in the hall for only a moment until Rinchin came out again and ushered Raj in the room where the 29 year old Dalai Lama stood up, smiled broadly, shook hands and he then indicated for Raj to sit down on the right side of what was an empty couch. There were three plush chairs that were arranged opposite the couch. Seated on the one to the left was Rinchin; on the chair to Rinchin's right was some other man whose name Raj did not understand; and then on the far right the Dalai Lama seated himself. The couch had been reserved for the guest, Raj Bahvnani, who by the position indicated for him would be opposite the Dalai Lama for easy conversation as they faced one another. (This was unlike China where leaders, by custom, would sit side by side with at least one straining himself while in position to see the other.) Rinchin was serving as the official translator but he rarely had to translate anything because the Dalai Lama seemed to understand and respond to Raj's English or Hindi, and the Dalai Lama always laughed at any bit of Raj's humor before the translator could even attempt to interpret what was said.

Raj cleared his throat and said, "His Holiness, I was born in India; I am an Indian, and I have recently been living in America; in New York and other cities and for the most recent two years I have been living back here in India—in the '62 War and now in Delhi."

"Yes. I was told by Gylao that you are a very important man—that you helped India in the war. Gylao tells me you have become as well-known as Prime Minister Lai Bahadur Shastri!" And he laughed very fully and loudly.

"No, His Holiness. I am no competition for Prime Ministers."

Again the Dalai Lama laughed and this time he nodded as he laughed. "Prime Ministers are a separate breed!"

"His Holiness," Raj said, "Chinese are the separate breed. I have come to hate the Chinese. They killed many Hindus in 1962. Many Hindus."

"No! No, no. Do not hate Chinese. Never. The Chinese are good people. Never confuse people with governments. Never ignore how good people may be educated badly. Education can be honorable or dishonorable; honest or dishonest."

"Since China has taken over Tibet, how are children educated there?"

"Completely by government's definition of the word 'education'. And all religion and religious practices are banned. Now I left the Potala in Lhasa with a great many Tibetans in 1959 so all I saw is what I saw before I left—and now I know more about recent times there from Tibetans who arrived in Dharamshala or Missoori or some other Indian Hill Stations here in India."

"Is religion practiced in Tibet now in secret or not at all?"

"In secret. It is against the law."

"Do the children believe the indoctrination of the government of China? Of the People's Republic of China? Or do the parents guide their children privately?"

"Their parents often tell them the truth. But the fear among the people is that within generations our religion will be terminated. It is what the government of China is striving for. It may happen."

"With 45,000 refugees in India and having freedom of religion here, how can it be exterminated?"

"I mean in Tibet itself. And besides, if Tibetans become too spread out over India their kinship and ultimately our religion can fade away. We try to keep our communities with no more than one thousand inhabitants in them. It is mandatory if we want to maintain Tibetan schools."

"Is the United States acting sufficiently?"

"Absolutely."

"In what ways? Through the U.N.? Financially? Support from private organizations? Through immigration?"

"I am very grateful to the United States. That support is very much appreciated. You know the United States has been good to Tibetans and to India. Of course we want as much assistance as possible. Of course immigration as well. But we want to stay together and in big groups."

"Is enough being done by India?"

"We are extremely grateful to India. Your two nations—this one, the nation of your birth, India, and the United States of America have done more than any other countries. Look, I am here in India. Go to India's Hill Stations or in any city close by the Himalayans and talk with all the Tibetans that live there like Dharamshala where I live now. There's Mussoorie, Chamba, Mandi, Dalhousie, Palampur. Go to Darjeeling. There are more Tibetans in Darjeeling than there are Indians there," and he laughed at what he had said. "Talk to them."

"Is Nepal helpful?"

"No. Many Tibetans have starved to death in Nepal. Many have gone back to Tibet from Nepal. I hope they can live."

"How about Bhutan? Sikkim?"

"They are better. In Asia India is the best."

"And how is the Chiang Kai-shek government on Taiwan?"

"No. Not through the government. Only through private organizations and people separate from the government there."

"What is the Panchen Lama's present feelings in Tibet?"

"He believes in living in Tibet and feels it is right to remain there. That is why he stays."

"It seems the longer the current political leaders go on in Eastern Europe, Cuba, Tibet, and so on, the harder is the possibility for revolution from within—within those countries. Is that true?"

"I do not know enough about Eastern Europe and Cuba but I do know that there are many countries in the world and Tibetans are different in that Tibet is a religion as well as a country. We are Tibetans. We want Tibet preserved in all its ways."

"Do you think your people will be able to go back within this generation?"

He laughed. "I am not a prophet. You must know more about this than I do. You are well traveled. You know the world."

"Being optimistic, assuming Chiang Kai-shek's government regains the entire mainland, do you ideally want an autonomous separate state of Tibet?"

"That is what we had. Tibet is us. It is what we want."

"Being pessimistic, if the situation remains unchanged as you and I and our generation become old and gray, I understand that eventually a search must be launched for a new Dalai Lama. Is that correct?"

"Yes."

"Must this be done within Tibet itself or could the search be held here in India—in the Hill Stations you mentioned—in Darjeeling? And will the religion end if the search, wherever it takes place, is repressed?"

"I would hope it takes place wherever the new Dali Lama may be at that time. I am 29 years old. There should be time one way or the other."

They then got into a long discussion on religion, and during much of it the Dalai Lama would speak in his native tongue and it was translated by Rinchin and often respectfully disputed as the Dalai Lama heard the translation. "Now we—you and I will talk about religion and so we can accurately discuss it I will tell you the truth that Tibetans are believing people rather than as the Chinese government wants you to think of them as their political instruments."

"Yes, I understand that."

"We believe every living thing has a soul-mind and a body. The *body* comes from seeds from the parents." He was not content with the description for the translation. "The soul-mind is *not* from the parents. Sometimes maybe but the soul-mind is usually continuous from previous lives—present life—future lives. There is no limit to the beginning. There can, however, be a permanence at the end of reincarnation. Reincarnation can be in all different forms—an ant, a horse, a human, so many forms. Now, to something else: there are two true forms of Bhudism in Tibet—Mahayan and Vinhayana—or at least there were before 1959. There are two types of reincarnation and one has no control of being reborn in a particular form but is dependent on their Karma. The other type of reincarnation has control over the form of re-birth. Among those who do have control there are stages. Again, two forms. One can be reborn into tens, hundreds, thousands, millions of forms simultaneously; the other with only one physical form. The first through the seventh Dalai Lama were the ones with High Stage—I think." This; the fourteenth Dalai Lama, kept saying 'I think.' "The eighth, I think, onward were the low stage."

"Based on what?"

"Prophets said so. One to seven were higher. So, anyway,

there could be thousands, millions of Dalai Lamas. Now the one must be selected with 'the purpose.' So in answer to your very important question I did not answer sufficiently, it could be a Chinaman, an Indian, an American. The fourth Dalai Lama was a Mongolian. Next in our belief of this mind-soul is that it is pure and good. Desire, anger, is a false self." There were translation problems. He included compassion in his discussion and it was difficult to know if this was part of a false self or a real self by his definitions. "Do you feel compassion?" he asked his guest.

"Yes," Raj answered.

"Always?"

"No."

"Do you feel anger?"

"Yes."

"Always?"

"No."

"Then what is not always, is false. Not pure. Because one person is attracted to an object, are all people attracted to it?"

"No."

"Does one person look the same to two people who look at that person?"

"No."

"You get a five percent attraction to something. Because of that five percent attraction in no time it becomes a thirty percent attraction. It is all based on ignorance. Good thoughts are not based on ignorance—so destroy bad thoughts and retain the good. Get the correct facts." He was emphatic on that dialogue. "And bad thoughts will destroy. For everything there is a cause and an effect. Bad Karma is a cause. Bad Karma is bad thoughts. That's why there is no beginning. Everything is from a succession of cause—effect—cause—effect."

"I am a Hindu and to me the hardest thing to understand is to try and comprehend a 'no beginning.'"

"I know. I know."

"In America I have learned an American phrase that everyone there knows: 'which came first? The chicken or the egg?'"

The Dalai Lama laughed uproariously. "We in Tibet have that saying, too." He looked at the coffee table. "And in this case, which came first, the cause or the effect?" He pulled the table over to exhibit his example. "This, today is a table. Ten years ago it was a piece of lumber. Eleven years ago it was a tall tree. A hundred years ago it was a seed. A thousand years ago it was atoms. And before that it was a single atom—until we go back to the formation of the world. For each there was a cause and an effect. There must have been a cause for the formation of the world. It goes on endlessly. The western religions believe in a single Creator as is often said, all good and all powerful. Did He then know suffering would exist? If He did, then is that evidence that He was not all compassionate? If He did not know suffering would exist, then was He not all powerful? Does it mean that He does not have control of the world? It is good to ask and good to answer. And if there is a God, how did God begin? How did He come into existence? From another God? Was there a series of Gods?" Raj did not know he was being given a psychological X-Ray.

While shifting in his chair, Raj asked, "Do you not believe in Gods or a God?"

"Oh, even as a Hindu you have now interpreted everything with Western fault. I am trying to make *you* think—not about me—about you."

Like most visitors with the Dalai Lama, the host strained the mind of his guest and forced his guest to think. Raj Bhavnani, as most visitors before and after him, did not leave as an unbeliever but as a more ardent believer. As provocative as the Dali Lama's statements came across to the visitor, it was not so much what he said that created the importance of what he was. There was something about him as a presence. It was different.

The two shook hands. The Dalai Lama smiled and Raj Bhavnani smiled and the Dalai Lama held Raj's arm and then the Dalai Lama laughed. Loudly and completely. Not because anything was funny but because so many things were good.

THEME TWENTY-TWO

THE DECISION

THROUGHOUT MOST OF 1964 Anna went back and forth from San Diego to Los Angeles for her acting roles in the three movies of her Three Picture Deal.

It was October of 1964 when Anna phoned Chris at work and asked him to meet her on Sunset Cliffs that they knew so well. Abnormal. Not her usual habit when she wanted to meet him somewhere when he would have been leaving work now or later and, either way, where he would more regularly see her immediately at the Silver Spray without any phone call in advance.

The Sunset Cliffs were as beautiful as usual except the meeting of the late afternoon brought some dark clouds on the far horizon coming over the ocean and maybe that was an indication of something to come that was heavy.

Anna grabbed his hand and said, "Chris—I have something to tell you."

He immediately thought—with immense fear—that she was about to tell him either she was sick or maybe that she has been with Raj and she is in love with him—of all things—from all the men in the world. There was a surge in Chris' stomach. "Are you okay?"

"Yes, I'm fine."

"Is this 'serious time'?"

Her hand left his hand slowly and a breaker came in and went back into the sea. "I suppose it's serious time, Chris. Chris, did I ever tell you about Lorna—Lorna Whitley—my best friend on *Gemstone*—Lorna. Did I ever tell you?"

He shook his head. "I don't think so. What's up?"

"She was my best friend on *Gemstone*."

"Okay. Understand. Is she okay?"

"Oh, yes. What I want to tell you is that she used to wear a Christian Cross necklace around her neck hanging beneath her blouse. Very religious. She wore it beneath her blouse because her role on TV was not someone who would be wearing that; her role didn't call for that—but she was very religious and wanted to wear it so she did when she wasn't in front of the camera pretending to be someone else."

"Sure. That makes sense. What's up? Why is that important right now?"

Anna reached under her blouse. "Look!" There was a necklace with a Christian Cross.

"She gave it to you?"

"No. It's not hers. It's a gift she sent me for this Christmas. It's mine. She's been visiting convents and now she's in the Vatican City—the Holy See. She wants to be a—a Nun—a Sister."

"Really? Wow! From 'Gemtsone' to a Nunnery? Okay!" He had no idea what all this had to do with anything of importance between the two of them. "That's quite something."

"A lot of actresses have done that. It's not that unusual. There's Dolores Hart and I'm sure you heard about her. What's unusual is that Lorna wanted to visit the Vatican and so she's in Rome now. And I'm going to visit her."

He stared at Anna. For a while he said nothing and then he murmured, "You—you're going to Rome?"

"Yes."

"Why?"

"I don't know why. But I think I may want to be a Sister."

At this point he didn't know if his stomach was ever going to feel like his stomach had generally felt in normal life. At least her subject of the day had nothing to do with her being sick or even with his unstopping suspicion of Anna and Raj having something going on. Raj, after all, was a subject of some competition. But God? Jesus Christ? The Pope?

He cleared his throat. "You aren't even a Catholic are you?"

"What do you mean? Yes, I am! On one of the most recent times I was in New York I spent almost one full day in Saint Patrick's Cathedral!"

"Did you do that?"

"Yes!"

"Was that on the trip when we met?"

"No. A visit before that trip."

"You spent the day at Saint Patrick's Cathedral?"

"Almost a day. Yes."

"Did you enjoy it?'

"Yes!"

"I mean to the point that you want to live there?"

"At Saint Patrick's? You can't live there! That is not the

objective of what I am doing!"

"So what will you do in Rome?"

"Learn. Lorna is there."

"So was Mussolini."

"Please. None of that World War II thing."

"Sorry. But what about your career? What about acting as your career? Being in the movies!"

"I'm not in *Roustabout*."

"What do you mean you're not in it?"

"I didn't tell you because I didn't want you to know—but I was cut out. That's all. It happens. I was cut out. I played in it and they cut it out. I saw the Answer Print—that's like the first print before all the release prints are made—and my scene wasn't in it. I was watching it in a screening room at the studio and it was in the scene before I was supposed to be on and there was a dissolve and the scene with me wasn't there. It was the time in the script that the scene with me was supposed to be in—and it was out. I wasn't hurt or sad, I was glad. It was a crummy part and I probably looked like a tramp so they were right in putting me on the cutting room floor. It's a relief."

"Well, you're obviously not too pleased. I'm sorry, honey— but you said that those things happen often to a lot of roles—cuts."

"And I talked to Morton, the film editor of *The Girls on the Beach*. He said I'm not cut out—I'm in it at least so far, but he said that there is no director's cut yet—that's going to be up to the director, Bill Witney. So I checked on *Harlow* and all I know about *Harlow* is that it's still being cut and that Peter Lawford said he saw the first cut and that I was terrific. But who knows? Someone else told me I look like Carroll Baker and

Carroll Baker plays Jean Harlow. So why should they want a look-alike of Carroll Baker?"

"Am I to assume that you're so scared of the fate of those two films—because of the cut of *Roustabout*—you're now worried about the two films that you haven't even seen yet—and you're so concerned that you've decided to be a Nun?"

For the first time of the meeting this late afternoon she smiled; even gave a little laugh. "Yes," she said with her smile continuing, "You can say that! Maybe anyway!"

"You're going to Rome for sure?"

"Yes."

"When are you leaving?"

"Friday."

"What Friday?"

"The coming one. This week's Friday."

"Oh, Anna!"

THEME TWENTY-THREE

"THE RIDE TO LINDBERGH FIELD"

THE BORROWED POST-WAR CHRYSLER was not at all pleased at the prescribed destination of which it was heading as driven by Chris at dusk. Like dogs can tell where they're going because of the scents of the journey, cars can tell where they're going because of the frequency and depth of the pot-holes in the streets. That Chrysler felt it was a member of the family and for some unknown reason it was now was being mistakenly steered by the heads of the family, Chris and Anna, north-east to U.S. Highway 101 toward the airport. The car was trying to figure out what was going on and if someone was going to take a plane and if so, why?

"Here's a paper I prepared for you," Anna said and took a piece of paper with her writing on it from her purse. "Address, phone numbers, all that. I'll be staying at Lorna's hotel so her main phone number and address will be mine, too. I have your phone number at work and at home, of course. It's nine hours difference. It's nine hours ahead of San Diego. So if it's 7:00 pm here in San Diego it's 4:00 am the next day in Rome."

"Okay. When I call long distance, are you using the name Savannah or Anna?"

"Savan-nauh. Only Savan-nauh. Maybe somebody has watched *Gemstone* and might treat me good because of that. Lorna said she gets noticed every once in a while from her role in *Gemstone* and probably recognized by Americans."

"This—what you're doing—changes both of our lives, doesn't it? I mean how long will it be? Before you come home will it be days, weeks, months, years, a life-time?"

"I don't know. But I know where I'll be staying. Lorna has been staying at the Excelsior Hotel and that's where I'll be. It's right up the street from the Embassy; one block, maybe one and a half streets north of the U.S. Embassy—our Embassy to Italy. It isn't far from the Vatican but it's in Rome proper—on the Via Veneto. It's where there are all the outdoor restaurants that you saw in *La Dolce Vita*. Did you see it?"

"No." He quickly dismissed that. "Anna, I'll pay for your apartment at the Silver Spray and I'll keep it clean so it's always ready for you to come home—yours—your home and your key will work—even on the connecting door. You can lock it on your side. I won't ever lock it on its other side."

Then, as Anna was inclined to do, there was a sudden sob and another one and another one and her crying took over. Then, "I don't want to lock it. Right now I want to say that this will just be days. Just days to be gone from you, that's all. Then I'll see what to do." She shook her head. "I don't know, Honey. I don't know."

Then the car passed Convair's Plant One and Plant Two where airplanes were built. Then the big stocky building without windows except for the very top floor. Chris said very softly,

"That's what we call The Rock. And across the street will be the end of this ride."

She looked at him with a sudden jerk of her head and she looked frightened. "The end of this ride?"

"See the signs? They say Lindbergh Field on the right side. That's where we're going. Lindbergh Field. That's where you're going. That's the San Diego Airport. I don't know why they named it after him. I know that he tested his plane around here somewhere before he made the first flight across the Atlantic from New York to Paris—but even if he made history as a pilot he also made history by speaking well of Hitler." Chris was struggling to bring up a subject other than their imminent separation. "Lindbergh made speeches saying the United States was getting to be an interventionist in the world and it was Europe's problem; not ours and he blamed the British and blamed the Jewish and blamed F.D.R. as forcing war on the United States."

She wasn't paying attention to one word about Charles Lindbergh. "I love you, honey," she said. "Not Charles Lindbergh."

Now he quickly wiped his eyes so as not to blur his vision while driving and because he tried to make sure she didn't know his eyes were moist. "I love you so damned much, Anna." It was the first time she ever heard him say a word that was not in his normal life-long vocabulary. "Let me park here in front of the terminal. I'll walk you to the gate."

"No. Don't. I won't be able to stand that." She then swallowed to stop herself from talking and revealing any sobs.

"Are you still allowed to be kissed?"

She swallowed again in concentration of what she wanted to say to him. "I can if I'm being kissed by you. Only by you.

Otherwise it's not allowed."

"You'll ask Pope Paul?"

"I'll tell him," and she sniffed.

"Why are you crying, honey? It's your decision; not mine. I didn't decide to join the Methodists or Protestants or Lutherans or Jewish or Buddhists or Moslems or—or Hindus—or anything."

"I'm crying because I love you." She had caught the way his tone was different when he said Raj's religion of 'Hindus'—rather than friendly as when he said the names of those other religions.

He parked and opened the door for her and took her bags from the car and while they did that a Red Cap was quickly coming over to help her with anything she wanted. "Ma'm?"

Anna and Chris were locked in another kiss with tears accompanying their kisses allowing them to taste the kisses of the other.

The Red Cap asked "What counter will you be going to, M'am?"

Chris answered for her. "She's going to Pacific Southwest Airlines; P.S.A. then her bags connect to T.W.A. in L.A. then a transfer again to London and Rome. I don't know the flight numbers. She has them and will tell you when you get in." Chris turned toward Anna. She wasn't done with her tears nor was he done with his. "God, I love you, Anna. I love you, honey."

The post-war Chrysler tried to act like a regular car but it couldn't do it. It wasn't a regular car tonight. When Chris came back in it alone, it started to cough. It couldn't help it. Anna wasn't in the car. Alone; with just Chris; not Anna, too. The car wasn't done coughing as it passed The Rock and Plant Two and Plant One and all the way to the Silver Spray where he then parked and turned off the ignition.

"Just you and me," Chris said to the car. "Don't worry. Anna will be back." At least both Chris and the Chrysler hoped for the accuracy of that statement. Chris prayed for it. Maybe the Chrysler did, too.

THEME TWENTY-FOUR

"ON THE VIA VENETO"

THE VIA VENETO was as picturesque in life as Federico Fellini made it in his 1960 film. The sidewalks were filled with restaurants that had outdoor tables for diners and drinkers and talkers, with the talkers often speaking very loud.

Anna and Lorna had met at the reception desk of the Excelsior Hotel, Lorna having been there for weeks with a room on the second floor and Anna now booking herself on the more luxurious fifth floor.

In minutes, leaving Anna's bags at the reception desk to be brought up to her room, Anna and Lorna went outside to the Via Veneto sitting opposite each other at a small table eating snacks and drinking Coca-Colas. Lorna had brought along a stack of papers, booklets, pictures and a black leather-covered book and she was back to calling Anna by her more formal birth-name of Savannah since there were public ears around, some likely attached to American heads and in accommodation, Lorna stayed conscious of Anna's public rules. "I have things for you to study, Savannah. Things like what is expected of you and prayers for you to put into memory and even a Bible for you to read."

"I read it!" Anna almost shouted. "Read it! I read it on the Twahhh."

"On the what?"

"On the Twahhh."

"Oh. I see. I understand." That was doubtful. "Savannah, tell me—is this trip to the Holy See a life-change, or is it merely an episode?"

"I don't know, Lorna."

"If you don't know, then it's an episode."

"Why do you say that?"

"Are you *considering* it as a life-change?"

"Yes."

"If it's a consideration then it won't come to be. It must be a passion and not a consideration. Do you know the difference? You can easily consider to have or not have a sandwich, you can consider to watch Ed Sullivan on television, you can consider to buy new shoes—or take another sip of that Coca-Cola. But for what you have said that you intend to become in life, you have to feel an eagerness; a spirit; a devotion to a clear destination. If it is not all that—then it is nothing other than an episode—an adventure—a trip here to Rome on airliners and an airliner taking you back home. That's fine and I don't belittle it. Such episodes bring experience. They are nothing to reject as long as they are good and meaningful. But don't confuse an easy consideration with the journey of climbing up to the high summit you told me you intend to reach and to have a platform there—where you can and will stand."

There was a long silence and then Anna asked, "You have

that passion, don't you, Lorna?"

"Oh, yes."

"Lorna, I feel it. I feel it but I don't know. There are moments when I feel I should surrender to that feeling and accept it—or reject it."

"No good. A surrender? You are misjudging the use of words. You still don't understand, sweet Savannah. If surrender is an option, surrender *now* and don't waste anyone's time; mainly your *own* time; you don't waste mine. I love being with you here. This journey ends in victory or a shrug of your shoulders. That's the choice once the journey has begun. I assure you that detours are everywhere. You'll see them because they don't go through or they are they come to a close in their own dead-ends. Decide tonight. We can then talk about other things and laugh and reminisce about *Gemstone* or, on the other hand, we can talk about your imminent victory."

Something caught Anna's eyes. "Oh, my God!" she said looking over the shoulder of Lorna.

Lorna looked confused. "What is so surprising that you call it 'Oh, my Gosh?'"

"I can't believe it. Either will you. It's unbelievable."

"What is 'it's' that is unbelievable?"

"Raj. Raj Bhavnani." Now Anna spoke with almost a whisper. "Raj Bhavnani is sitting behind you a little to your back and to the right."

At that, Lorna now finally used the phrase, "Oh, my Lord." Then she shook her head while not daring to look behind her. "Does he see you?"

"No. I don't think so. He's looking at the menu."

"What's he doing here?"

"I don't know, Lorna. How do I know?"

"This is a miracle!"

Anna gave a wide smile. "Then you can become a Saint! You can be the Saint Lorna because you are now involved in a miracle. That's a qualification! You qualify for Sainthood! Aren't I right? Don't you need a miracle to become a Saint?"

"That qualification has nothing to do with this kind of a miracle, or just being involved in a miracle, my dear."

"How do you know?"

Lorna put her hand over Anna's hand. "My dear Savannah—I know."

Then Lorna withdrew her hand as Anna said, "He sees me. He's coming over here."

"Do you want me to leave?"

"Absolutely not! You stay. You stay. You made this miracle happen and I'm telling the Vatican!"

Then it came: the all-too familiar voice: "Savannah! Savannah Lane!" And there was Raj Bahvnani moving a chair so it would be added to the two chairs at the table. Not surprisingly he sat down on the chair he had added to the table. "What on earth are you doing on the Via Veneto, Miss Lane?"

Anna, with a smile, shook her head. "That's what I was just going to ask *you*! Lorna; this is Raj Bhavnani. Raj, this is Lorna."

"No last name?" Raj asked.

"None," Lorna answered.

"Wonderful! Wonderful! No one should have to carry around a last name."

Anna shook her head again. "Why not?"

"The question is why should we have one? Now, to Savannah with a last name: Lane. What are you doing here on the Via

Veneto, Savannah Lane?"

"Studying the Bible."

"Ahhh. Very good. The Bible. The Bible. Which Testament?"

"What do you mean?"

"There are two. Are you studying the Old Testament or the New Testament?"

Anna hesitated and exchanged a look with Lorna who simply clenched her lips and shook her head and did not offer an answer to such a question.

Therefore, it became up to Anna to answer the question. "Well, they're both pretty old by now. After all, it's the mid-1960s so they're both pretty old Testaments."

Lorna whispered, "Oh, my Gosh, Honey!"

Raj gave his own answer, "Beautiful! Beautiful! And accurate! They are both very old! One is the Old Old Testament and the other one is the Old New Testament!"

Anna asked Raj, "Now, what are *you* doing here?"

"I am meeting with Prime Minister Moro."

"The Prime Minister of Italy?" Lorna asked that while squinting her eyes in suspicion.

"Moro. That's his last name like the one you don't have. Moro; Moro."

She gave a slight smile. "How did this meeting come about?"

"Leaders gravitate toward leaders."

"I see," Lorna said with both her and Anna thinking what he said was just another Rajismatic phrase originated from something in Hindi, and adding to the confusion was that neither one of them had known that in some quarters of the world Raj Bhavnani was, indeed, a leader. "I have travelled throughout South East Asia with Foreign Ministers, with Prime Ministers, and with Presidents; from Malaysia, Singapore, Thailand, South Korea, South Vietnam, Australia, New Zealand, the Philippines. Not only leaders; some with lesser titles but influential; influential. And now Europe to visit with leaders only. No lesser titles. Ask me anything you want! Then—ah, then to my second home—America again!"

Anna asked, "Don't you want to know what *I'm* doing here in Rome? All you asked me was about my being on the Via Veneto. My trip is more than the Via Veneto."

"No interest at all. None. Now, can I buy you girls a drink?"

Lorna gave the answer: "No! Thank you but we don't drink."

"What a shame! Savannah—Don't you still drink Margaritas?"

"No. I stopped."

"That's right. You gave up on them and started on Cuba Libres."

"Raj, you are still impossible!"

"Impossible; yes, yes! Very good! I can tell I am making no progress here. Please phone me, Savannah. Please do that. I am at the Cavalieri Hilton. I tried calling you months ago in the States. I was told you had moved to San Diego. I think you have a party-line. It was a man's voice that was talking on the phone when I called you. So call me here as long as we are in the same city. Or forget phone calls. Come visit me. Where I'm staying; the Cavalieri Hilton is up on one of the seven great hills of Rome. You can see down at the Vatican from there. You can see Pope Paul VI watering the plants."

Anna shook her head. "You cannot! Watering the plants!"

"So what? You can see the Vatican from up there. If he decides to water the plants while you're watching, that's good enough. But I will try to visit with the Pope before leaving Italy.

I will bring him some plants."

"You are still crazy!"

"I would never give that up! Sanity is for fools."

Raj got them both laughing which, of course, was the only clear objective left with his first objective now futile.

With even his secondary objective now accomplished, he took his chair and set it back where he found it and walked away.

After he walked down the street toward the U.S. Embassy, Lorna asked Anna, "You know what you are?"

"What?"

"A Scatter-Brain!"

"What should I do, Lorna?"

"Either phone your Raj Bhavnani tonight like he asked or become Sister Savannah in a few years. But you can't do both."

"Should I make a reservation to go home? Should I call Twahhh?"

With both Raj and Anna having said things that called for a translator, Lorna was beginning to doubt her own command of English. "Who's Twahhh?"

"The airline."

Lorna smiled and nodded at her own regained sanity. "That is T.W.A., not Twahhh. Savannah, Savannah, Savannah! T.W.A. stands for Trans World Airlines."

"I'm a scatter-brain!"

There was a long pause. "No, you're not. I'm sorry I said that without thinking. You are not a scatter-brain."

"Then what am I?"

"You're Savannah Lane. And you are—in your own wonderful way—unique Savannah. You are different than anyone I have ever known."

"I am?"

"You are marvelous. Don't forget that."

"You're not mad at me?"

Lorna, with her slight smile, shook her head slowly. "Marvelous Savannah," she said softly and with depth.

It was eight o'clock that night when Anna was alone in her Excelsior Hotel room happily whispering to herself, "Marvelous Savannah!"

In minutes the phone rang and it was Raj Bhavnani who immediately asked to see her in "half an hour from now" and let him take her on a tour of Rome "to places no American has ever seen!"

She refused, telling him, "No. I'm asleep."

Not too likely. But he asked, "You're asleep now? You answered in your sleep?"

"Yes. It's my habit. It's a medical mystery. Good night." She hung up.

He then said in his own style, "Of course! Of course!"

Minutes later her room-phone rang again.

"Yes! What now!?"

But there was no reason for anger. It was a long distance operator telling her that a man named Christopher Straw in the United States was on the line.

Anna almost screamed, "Yes! Put him on please!"

Most of the conversation was spent while she was crying with joy at the sound of his voice. When he asked how things were going in Rome she said, "Just okay. It was wonderful to see Lorna," and she went into no more detail. That "just okay" let him know that she did not seem to be as enthused about the anticipated significant change in her life as she had earlier imagined.

He let it go. "I miss you so much, honey," and "I am explosively glad just to hear your voice."

"Me, too—I mean to hear *your* voice." and then she told him, "I might—I might—no, not I might; I will come home earlier than I expected." That confirmed her hint of moments ago. And for further confirmation she added, "I want to come home."

"Soon?"

"Very soon. I am only me and I want to come home to the Silver Spray. I can't wait."

As soon as they hung up Anna picked up the telephone receiver again and asked the hotel operator on the other end, "Can you get me Twahhh?"

"Twahhh?" the operator asked.

"Yes. It's spelled T.W.A."

"Of course. I'll get that for you. You mean the airline?"

"Yes."

"In English?"

"Yes."

But it was neither in English or Italian or any other language. "All lines are busy," she was told by the hotel operator. "I'll keep trying and call you back when the line to the airline's number is free."

It wasn't free until the next morning when the operator connected her to an airline attendant who spoke perfect English: "T.W.A. Good Morning." Anna requested that the rest of her open ended round-trip ticket go into effect from Rome's Fiumicino Leonardo de Vinci International Airport to the route that would get her on connecting flights "for my—for my 'I'm going home ticket,'" leaving it up to the airline attendant at the other end of the line to work it out all the way back to San Diego. Anna added, "Fast, please."

But it wasn't fast when the phone rang again and it wasn't the airline; it was Chris again. "It must be mental telepathy all over Southern California" he told Anna. "Things are going my way and your way: Someone called here for you. Do you know a William Caruthers?"

There was a hesitant, "William Caruthers?"

"Who is he?"

"The best casting director in the whole world! He's the casting director of *Gemstone*!"

"They want you back."

"What!?"

"You had a phone call. I took it and it was some woman who said she was calling for William Caruthers and she put him on and he said he wants you to call him back. I told him you're in Rome but that I talk to you—to you every day. He got the message. He understood that we—we have something going and he said, 'We want to give it another try for Savannah. You can tell her that pretty much the same deal as before except no A.W.O.L.— No Absent Without Official Leave from her and with guarantees from her on that. Tough guarantees.' He said that 'a lot of viewers want her back'—you back and that your very popular with their viewers and so they want to give you another test if you'll be back on the 2nd of next month—January.' That's what he told me to tell you. Does it sound good to you, honey?"

"Oh! Oh, yes! It sounds like heaven!"

"I said that I was sure you would call him. You have to

gurantee to him that there will be no A.W.O.L.'s"

"I'll call him right away and guarantee him and then I'll find out fromTwah when I can get there!"

Before Anna left Rome, Lorna took her to the Trevi Fountain just blocks from the hotel. When they stood in front of the fountain Lorna asked, "Do you have three coins?"

Anna nodded. "Yes. What denomination?"

"It doesn't make any difference."

"Italian or American coins?"

"No matter. It's alright—any country. Now turn around so you don't face the fountain. And throw every one of the three coins over your shoulder into the fountain one by one—and it means you'll come back to Rome. I so much want you to be back and be able to see you here again, but I'll see you on television again before then, I'm sure!"

"I'll miss you, Lorna. You are so understanding and you aren't angry at me?"

"How could I be angry at you—Anna." She had whispered that name. And she added in the newly added whisper, "Can I say that name reserved for your closest friends? Can I call you 'Anna' here? The fountain is so noisy no one can hear."

"You can say any name you want to call me. You can scream it out and I'll never protest. And I will answer you as Sister Lorna who I know deserves that title."

Lorna smiled and answered, "If things go as I want, my name will be somewhat dependent on the Order in which I become a Sister. And, if I have my choice, my name will be Sister Mary Savannah. One name from Heaven and the second name for someone who is so good and important from my time on earth."

elegy

THEME TWENTY-FIVE

HOME

SOMETIMES OLD NAMES CHANGE their accepted meanings. Home had been the name that was given by Christopher Straw and Anna Lane to the Silver Spray in Ocean Beach of San Diego, and now Home was the name they began to describe the Bahia, a magnificent luxury hotel on a peninsula in Mission Beach of San Diego with its low and wide elevations of its exterior, and a restaurant on the Bahia's outdoor patio. Christopher made the decision for the move from one residence to another; this one up the coast from the Silver Spray, with the Bahia's own adjoining rooms as a gift to Anna and a gift for himself.

Another name that, at a minimum, was changing its definition in their lives was something that became unlocked within Anna Lane. The change started while in Rome and remained unlocked within her as she was back with Chris and living in the Bahia. That new definition was something deep and positive and important. Adding to it but less significant than the characteristic itself was that it was accompanied by a new schedule of driving back and forth each week from San Diego to Los Angeles to San Diego for the purpose of her renewed profession of acting that she loved in Los Angeles, all while she was living with whom she loved in San Diego. It all added up to new differences within her inward status of loyalty to her lover and loyalty to her employer with care not to disappoint, and confidence combined with modesty that she could feel and others could sense.

And there was a new definition of their devotion to each other and even a new definition to the job held by Christopher Straw as confirmed by the display of a round piece of metal protected by celluloid and pinned on his suit jacket. It was his badge at General Dynamics Astronautics that had changed from being a designed pattern of black and white thin stripes into being a solid red, with that solid red meaning he had achieved the rank of supervisor in the nation's pursuit of supremacy in space.

To Home and to Anna and to Chris it was a year of clean newness.

But the years closely following that washed-and-dried-year brought radical change for Christopher Straw with a jolt that rocked him as well as the dreams he had enjoyed since being a child: it was the year of 1966 after it changed through the annual loop that all years come to know and this one untied its ending loop, getting out of earth and into the surrender of 1966, allowing 1967 to enter. Within the new year's 27th day there was an explosion at the northern end of Florida's Cape just above what was known as ICBM Row.

Sitting around the desk that formed a squared hollow-centered pattern in the third floor conference room of General

Dynamics Astronautics were eighteen men with red badges. With untypical slowness and sadness, Chuck Newton, the Communications Director, among other titles and duties, stood and gave the announcement of what happened to Apollo 1 at the Cape and concluded by saying "It had to happen someday. Today was the day. From the beginning we all knew that this—this—the New Frontier—was not risk-free. On this date; today it wouldn't be direct tragedy for one of us at this table, but, still tragically, it is friends working with the same objectives in our career—at the Cape or—I don't know—but most likely one of those who were to ride the Birds. They were never without threat of horror from anything imaginable—from a bad thread on a 25-cent screw used somewhere on the Bird that was screwed in wrong—a 25-cent screw that someone missed or some other error or simply—I don't know—of the unknown. It had to happen someday. We are going to get on and we are going to the moon and into far—far deep space as originally planned and with little delay." He looked around the table and there was no comment from anyone. He walked out of the room before what he feared could quickly become an unguarded emotional display that was welling beneath his slow talk.

The room of supervisors was silent except for Christopher Straw. From his seated position he looked around the table at each one individually and he did not pick up the cue from Chuck Newton's attempt at optimism. "I can accept that none of us in this room are going to the moon. What I cannot accept is my belief today—today—that after all, no American is going there after what happened at the Cape today—from what Chuck told us just now—it's just the final—he didn't say it—but it's—come on—it's the final 'gong' over our space program. Gus Grissom is dead. Ed White is dead. Roger Chaffee is dead. Apollo 1 is dead. And of all things it was just a static test; no launch; it was only a static test on the launching pad—a rehearsal on Pad 34—without a launch scheduled! Exploded! An electrical fire! The Bird wasn't even fueled! Burned up the Capsule—the Command Module—the Cabin—Gus and Ed and Roger. Three Astronauts gone and it wlll be Cosmonauts who will be going to the moon. Not Astronauts. Space into the Heavens is not meant for our country in our times. That's all. Leave it to the Soviets; to the Gagarins, to theTitovs, to the Tereshkovas. JFK is gone and so is Gus, Ed and Roger. And just as likely, so is the moon."

He was sorry he said that as soon as he heard his own statement that came out of his mouth having originated in tough instinctive reactions.

As the sun went down that day, Chris and Anna were sitting together close to the pool of the Bahia in two beach-rests next to each other. Chris was still in the suit he wore to work including a tie, and Anna was in a bathing suit. There was an absence of conversation for a long time until Anna asked him, "Did you know them?"

"Gus. Gus Grissom. He was a friend. Good man. Great sense of humor. He was fun to be with. I knew him well because he was one of the Mercury 7. I was with Ed only a few times after Mercury was done; a kind and good man—and although I met Chaffee I didn't really know him. But I know he was a good guy. I know a number of people at the Cape who were close friends of his."

"I am so sorry, honey; sorry this happened."

"I know. I know. It just—it just shouldn't have happened. They were only as high as the capsule resting on top of the rocket that never left the launcher. That's as high as they got on this one. And even the rocket is gone. You know we get to know those—you know—those birds—attached to a umbilical cord." And then he corrected himself. "Its umbilical tower. The bird owns it."

"I know about how you all feel about those rockets. You get to know them. You told me that and I understand it."

"I don't think L.B.J. is as dedicated about space as JFK was."

"Oh, Chris! Don't! You can do it if you want but are you mad at President Johnson of all people? You know that he didn't do it and you know that Johnson has always been a big supporter of space exploration—of manned flight. That's why when Kennedy was not even President yet but when he was still President-elect, he asked Johnson as Vice President-elect to do something besides being Vice President and Kennedy made him the Chairman of the National Space Council. It is so well known that he did that. Kennedy could have chosen anyone. He did that before Shepherd even went up. You're angry, honey. I understand why. But your anger is so misdireted."

Chris nodded. "You got everything right." And he was silent for a while before adding, "Yes, I'm terribly angry."

"You're bigger than that. Anyone can be angry when bad things happen. Your anger at President Johnson is there because you're angry at the times—because you're living through a tragedy—but anger can stain, you know. Don't let that happen, Chris. Rinse it off quick before it stains on you and is permanent, unable to be washed out. That can happen, too. Don't let it."

"Look, I know you're right and I know it doesn't make sense

to level the anger at Johnson. But nothing makes sense right now. And I know you have this—analyzed right. I can't justify these times. Why did all this have to happen? Why did Apollo blow up? Tell me why that happened? I don't mean technically; I mean morally. Why did God permit that?"

She shook her head. "I don't know."

"But, Anna, you should know. You spent time thinking, even going so far as thinking in Rome and coming back with a halo. I mean it. A halo. So why do these things happen? Why are Gus and Ed and Roger dead?"

She just shook her head, not wanting to say "I don't know" again.

"Sorry, honey," Chris said. "I don't expect an answer. I'll try and be okay. I'm not going to allow myself to enter into being upset and wrathful and filled with anger because of all this—this terror. I'm not going to allow that to go on."

"There are two people who will thank you for that, Chris."

"Who?"

"Me. Right away—me. I'll thank you. And a little later, you'll thank yourself. Thanking yourself would be a God-send."

"A God-send?"

"Yes. Because that will be a wonderful treasure to put into your mind's vault of hidden secret possessions to look through some—some lonely night reserved for thanking yourself for doing the right thing." She felt as though she was surrounded by sudden goodness and that it had found a home within her. "Get some more of those possessions. They don't cost anything and I'm sure that once you get them, there is still always plenty of room up in your vault to keep them all. All they cost is just giving up some heartache."

"You have a halo, Anna."

Anna smiled at him. "No halo, honey. It is just that—that you and I are in a giant orchestra led by the conductor: God. We are members of a huge orchestra that will be here for a while. You and I are members of it and we should do something worthwhile as we play our instruments loaned to us by Him. It is up to us to play well."

"Whatever you learned in Italy, it's like something more than what you think it was. And, of all things, you were only there for hours. And you're saving me the time and effort to travel there and back. What's the way to explain it? To be guided by your trip I never took? That's very rare. I see a halo. It's new and it's a golden one."

Anna was not only listening. Maybe no one but Chris could see the halo but if others had known her for a long time they at least could now see that she had a sparkle in her eyes she hadn't had since she was a little girl. "But nothing happened in Rome. Nothing!" she said.

"Something did. It needed no time or visuals as it was an unseen instant."

"Maybe I got it on Twahhh."

"What?"

"Nothing."

THEME TWENTY-SIX

RAJ AND THE OLD POST

OFFICE BUILDING

THREE MONTHS LATER, Spring and Raj Bhavnani came back to the United States. Spring came back because of the decision of the seasons to keep on performing those rotations. Raj Bhavnani came back because of the decision of All India Radio and the Voice of America to put him in D.C. Armed with directions from a Hertz Rent-a-Car attendant at Dulles International Airport he was on his way from Virginia to the majestic, almost royal in appearance, entrance-way to the District of Columbia by crossing the Arlington Memorial Bridge.

No matter its authoritative grandeur, no one has to get dressed up nor do drivers have to get their cars washed to drive across that triumphal bridge to the District. But the splendor of the drive and the triumph of the sights on the close horizon as the drive continues gives rise to the feeling that this crossing of the Potomac River calls for a kind of formality. Ahead is the Lincoln Memorial, the Washington Monument beyond it and farther off but still in sight, the Capitol Building, while off to the closer south-west side is the Jefferson Memorial. All in eyes-view.

Even the rear view mirror gives inspiration in a visual panorama of history: there is the easily seen John F. Kennedy Eternal Flame changing its form with any breeze as it gives its signals above the grave of President Kennedy. And there is the wide expanse of Arlington Cemetery of over some four hundred thousand buried heroes from long ago all the way forward, even likely more in number today.

To the sides of the driving lanes of the bridge are the side-walks for walking or, particularly in the early morning of the day, for running as joggers give their runs through the distance between Arlington and D.C.

With all of this magnificence going on it was totally out-of-context when Raj Bhavnani, driving across this sacred bridge, would press a button on the interior of the Hertz specially rented Cadillac Fleetwood to lower the front-seat passenger window and yell to a surprised jogger also going to the District, "If you would have left earlier you wouldn't have to run!"

That sudden spurt of shouted advice would often cause a loss of stride in the jogger's rhythm who, prior to Raj's recom-mendation, had confidence in running along while thinking "Hey, you knuckle-heads who are driving, look at me! I am stronger and healthier than you, and by my running I am proving I am just a finer person than you are, you lazy lame-brained driving ignoramuses! Don't forget to shift into third if you're so proud of believing you're building up the muscles in your right arm by shifting; fatso's!"

Good for Raj to stop those self-praising thoughts of the morning joggers on the bridge. Those arrogant running exercise-nuts had it coming.

Raj Bhavnani was headed toward his assigned office on the third floor of the Old Post Office Building; a massive building that, although built in the last years of the 19th Century, looked like it could have been more appropriately been built in the early years of the 13th Century. It was topped by a clock tower and other than the Washington Monument, it was the highest structure in North West Washington D.C. towering above national memorials and the White House.

After pulling the rented Cadillac up to the building on Pennsylvania Avenue, his car was driven away by a tall, slender man in his sixties with an English accent who introduced himself as Anthony Jowett with the United States Information Agency who had been waiting for him to arrive. Mr. Jowett drove the Cadillac to the parking lot behind the building; the area unseen by Raj but shared with the parked cars of the Internal Revenue Service while Raj stood by the outdoor grand staircase of the Old Post Office Building waiting for the tall man to come back.

On Anthony Jowett's reappearance he asked, "Where are you staying, Mister Bhavnani?"

"The Hay-Adams."

"The Hay-Adams!?"

"Yes, yes. You know it?"

"I know where it is: Practically across the street from the White House. One block—one block away at most—north. It's on Lafayette Square and it's on 16th Street just like the White House! That's luxury, my man!"

"Oh, that's fine. Luxury. That's good. The hotel was booked for me by All India Radio. I didn't choose it. I never heard of the Hay-Adams."

Mr. Jowett and Raj were silent for an extended moment with the silence finally interrupted by Mr. Jowett who started nodding as he said, "All India Radio chose a treasure of luxury for you as your living quarters. They chose well. If someone phones you at the Hay-Adams and you're in the dining room or the bar, a waiter brings a phone right to you and plugs the phone in. There are plugs in every booth in the dining room and bar. After all, at the Hay-Adams it could be the White House that's calling you." And Mr. Jowett raised his eyebrows and gave a few nods to affirm what he had said. "But wait until you see your office here in this bilding! Your office is another treasure of luxury, my good man—and that wasn't chosen by your government but by my government who booked it for you to do your job here. Now, let's go see it."

Mr. Jowett led their way to the elevator and up to the third floor and then to the open doorway of the north-east corner office that was to be Raj's immediate destination.

Raj stood still in the doorway with his mouth open. "Massive! This is truly massive! Colossal—Colossal!" Raj said to Mr. Jowett. "This is a massive and colossal office!"

"Enormous. Yes, it is," Jowett agreed with a nod and they slowly walked in. "We believe that it is second in size only to the President's office—the Oval Office in the West Wing of the White House five blocks up Pennsylvania Avenue, my man! Someone over there must like you! But size is not its only virtue. Follow me to what are your corner windows and the door to your balcony."

"Yes, yes. Please."

Mr. Jowett walked behind the desk to the door from the office's interior to its balcony. They both walked out to overlook a view that was truly grand. Raj was awed. He stood transfixed on the long arm of Pennsylvania Avenue. "That's the Capitol Building, isn't it? The Capitol?"

"It is. Way down there. This is a perfect place from which to see the Inaugural Parade. You can have a party up here to watch it come straight toward us from the Capitol! Invite your friends—if the folks on the fourth floor allow it."

"Who's on the fourth floor?"

"Shhh! Some of the FBI folks!" He pointed to the ceiling. "Right above you! Fourth floor! And more of the Bureau folks across the street at the Department of Justice! Shhh!"

"Fine, fine!"

"Kennedy wanted this area of Pennsylvania Avenue cleaned up—so it will be cleaned up. Johnson is for it. You'll see the work begin. And right up that street—that's where President Lincoln was killed."

"It is?"

"You can't really see it from here but just up 10th Street over there, behind that cluster of small buildings. Ford's Theater. Then they took him across the street from the theater and he died in the house directly across from Ford's."

"You're quite an historian, Mr. Jowett."

"Please call me Anthony—and I'm not an historian. Everyone here is familiar with those buildings and that chapter of history."

"What are the hours here?"

"The hours? They are what you want them to be. You are a contactor doing work for the Voice of America. But the best kind of contractor. You make your own hours after some discussions here probably depending on the calendar for international radio and television and India's connection and your coordination here with Voice of America.

"Really?"

"Yes, Mr. Bhavnani. But I suppose Leonard Marks should know if you're going to be here for quite a while. He's really your boss. He runs the Agency for President Johnson. He's up at the Agency's Headquarters at 1776 Pennsylvania Avenue. That's up the street one block after the White House."

"He's the one who contacted me. I talked with him on the phone. I'm supposed to see him after I get adjusted here. Let's go back inside."

"You have an appointment with Mr. Marks tomorrow at 8:00 in the morning."

"I do?"

"You do. We'll have a car pick you up at the Hay-Adams."

As they walked back into the office Mr. Jowett closed the balcony door and said, "There is a lot of history here, my good man. Everywhere you look—outside and inside this building. And if that isn't enough to look at, there's your own television set. And if that still isn't enough you'll have a pretty secretary. She'll be in at Nine this morning: Tara Thompson."

"No. I don't want a pretty secretary. I want a big, fat one. Then I won't have a crowd coming up here to see her and talk with her and behave like idiots around her. And she won't entice me, either. A big, fat one is what I want."

"We can arrange that. That's not a problem. I can take all those administrative things you need or want."

"That's good. Now, what's that?" Raj was staring at a closed door in the office. "What's that door over there?"

"I never noticed. I suppose it's a closet. Go ahead and open it and we'll find out."

Raj walked over to the closed door he had noticed and he opened it. Inside the closet was a very large iron safe with the Seal of the United States painted on its white-painted door. It took only seconds before Raj opened the unlocked safe to find nothing inside. "Cleaned out!"

"Too bad!"

"Whose was it? Do you know?"

"I don't know but I wouldn't doubt that it was James Farley's safe! President Roosevelt's friend. James Farley. Roosevelt— FDR appointed him Postmaster General. A good position. That's a Cabinet Post; the President's Cabinet. This was his office when this building was the headquarters of U.S. Post Office's. Now it's the *Old* Post Office Building. He held that job for the first two terms of FDR."

"See? You *are* an historian, Mr. Jowett, just like I said—and you don't even know it! Now, what's that?" and Raj pointed to another door.

"Your private bathroom and shower. It probably was James Farley's."

"What an office!"

"Yes, Mr. Bhavnani; what an office."

"And I like that this office has been held by a leader—your Mr. James—" and he paused.

"Farley. James Farley."

"Is he still living?"

"No."

"Was he considered to be a leader?"

"I would say so. That is, if someone is a friend of the President that *makes* that person a leader. Let me put it this way—if you're a friend of the President there are a lot of people following you and asking you questions—so James Farley was a leader."

"I like to be in the company of leaders."

"Then you will be happy here, my good man. There are both hundreds of leaders living now in this city and there are the shadows of thousands of leaders who have passed into and out of D.C. for 190 years."

"That's good—even to be in in their shadows by touching—by really touching their memory. So that was James Farley's safe?"

"I think so."

"Good. That's very good. Now I inherited it. So two leaders meet between their separate times: Farley and Bhavnani!"

Mr. Jowett looked at Raj with a curious stare.

THEME TWENTY-SEVEN

LATE-NIGHT ENTERTAINMENT

AS A CONTRACTOR rather than an employee, Raj could have lasted only days or weeks but so far he lasted throughout 1967 and into 1968 and by then it had become a habit for Raj Bhavnani to eat dinner alone at the Old Ebbitt Grill; a short walk from the Old Post Office Building. His frequent nightly habit dictated that he would go back to his office to write some commentaries for Voice of America or for All India Radio or for both about subjects of particular interest to his listeners that he would schedule recording during the day ahead in the building's downstairs studio. Then, when the evening writing was close to done, for a reward to himself he would turn on his television set and click the channel indicator to Channel Four and he would lean back in his black leather-backed chair and watch a close shot of a large man who said, "And now Ladies and Gentlemen, 'Heeeeeeeaar's Our Man!'"

There would be wild applause. There had to be wild applause as everyone in the studio-audience and most people watching on television wherever they lived had no need to be told his name.

Next on the screen there was a shot of a stage with long curtains that were being opened from behind and separated by a slender man at the curtain's base which sent the applause in the studio to be even stronger and more excited. Then the picture cut back to the close shot of the large man who had introduced him and this time that large man was giving a respectful slight bow as the wild applause continued for the evening's first appearance of the prime star he had introduced.

When the applause cooled down there was the star's opening monologue that set the studio audience into uproarious laughter but Raj didn't quite get absorbed in it as he was re-writing a script of his own that he was planning to give on Voice of America the following day. Despite his concentration on his own writing he did hear and understand the introduction of the host's first guest of the evening, "What a pleasure; the lovely star of *Gemstone*, Miss Savannah Lane!" The audience cheered while Raj's jaw dropped as he quickly lost all interest in writing, jolting his stare at the screen of the television set. And there she was walking across the stage to the chair by the side of the host's desk while the studio audience kept cheering. She had that great walk of hers.

And Raj, all alone in his office, was cheering too. And Raj could swear he inhaled her fragrance coming through the glass screen of the television set. Of course not. But even though she was only appearing through the technology of current electronics, his office was filled with the magic of Savannah Lane's aura.

Then Camera-Two gave a panning sweep of the enthusiastic audience so the people at home could see their reaction in the studio, and the camera stopped its motion while it held the view of one man who had risen and was smiling broadly while clapping and cheering. It was a man who was more than identifiable to Raj.

From off-screen the host said, "That's your Space Man, isn't it, Savannah?" And the off-screen Savannah Lane said, "That's my Christopher Straw!" And also from off-screen Raj Bhavnani turned off the television-set with a push of the remote that could have broken the remote and even could have broken his thumb. No matter. The set was off. Raj walked with quick steps—almost leaps—out of the office; down the elevator; onto the ground floor; onto Pennsylvania Avenue and he hailed a taxi that took him to the Hay-Adams Hotel.

His fast-walk was revived when he walked into the hotel and straight into the bar. It was closed for business and the only other person in the barroom was its tender; Phillipe.

"You closed, Phillipe?"

"Yes, Mr. Bhavnani, but not for you. What will you have?"

"I don't know yet. Do you have a tape player?"

"No, Mr. Bhavnani. We never serve tape-players. No one drinks them."

"Wait. Just wait. I'm going to go to my room and bring my tape machine down. Just wait and then I'll have a—a scotch on the rocks. Scotch on the rocks, whatever that is."

"Yes, sir. It means on ice."

At that Raj hurried to his room. And in short time he emerged in the barroom again, this time holding on to the handle of a portable red Ampex Caprice tape player that looked like a small piece of luggage while with his free hand he held a reel of ¼" brown magnetic tape tightly wound on a clear-plastic reel. He set the machine on the bar and threaded the tape on one of the machine's two spindles with the tape being received by an adjoining empty reel. It all worked. Raj pressed the machine's red knob and then he and Philippe heard the tape's recorded music with the beautiful singing of a woman vocalist who sang in Hindi.

Raj started dancing as he did years back in front of an audience of New York City's Ceylon India Inn with Savannah Lane being part of that audience.

"Louder!" Raj yelled to Philippe and Phillipe turned it louder and Raj yelled "Louder!" again and again and one by one people came in to see what was going on and then couples knew what was going on and couples kept coming in, now not out of curiosity but to hear the music and see Raj Bhavnani dance.

And dancing he did with his legs running and jumping; his arms twisting and turning; his hips revolving; his neck going side to side and his fingers behaving wildly. This was all to cloak his missing of Savannah and receive a boost by a revival of his self-confidence. It worked. He was a celebrity again.

But he wanted it to work even better. And so Raj continued to direct Phillipe to turn the music to be "Louder!" as he danced and danced and danced and the audience got larger and larger and larger and the audience cheered and cheered and cheered as they applauded and applauded and applauded. And when the dance was done Raj almost fell onto a bar-stool, and the audience continued with their cheers and applause. Philippe shoved a Scotch on the rocks in front of Raj and Phillipe said, "You can dance, Mr. Bhavnani! And who was the singer?"

"Meena Kumari. Probably the most popular singer in all of India," he told the truth but then he lied with "We used to be—yes, we used to be in love with each other. Many nights she would sing and I would dance."

"What is the name of the song?" a woman in a miniskirt asked Raj as she came to his side at the bar.

"Ajeeb Dastan Hai Yeh," he answered. "Meena always said it was written for me—and sung for me."

"Is that a Scotch?" the Miniskirt-adorned woman asked.

"On the rocks" he said as his new encyclopedic knowledge of drinks took over. "Do you want one?"

She nodded with a smile.

"Phillipe!" he yelled over the continuing applause of the audience that was still not content without an encore. He ordered another scotch on the rocks for his new companion. He heard some other woman say, "That's Raj Bahvnani!"

"It is!" Raj confirmed.

In retrospect, Raj Bhavnani's sudden performance did not bring about what he wanted: Savannah Lane's pursuit to track him down and leave Christopher Straw for one more interlude with Raj. It didn't happen. But not all was lost: three days later something unexpectedly came from his impulsive dance at the Hay-Adams. It was a handwritten note from Bess Abel, Social Secretary of the White House, who wrote that President Johnson had heard of the acclaim Raj Bhavnani earned from an enthused audience for his dancing abilities learned in his home country of India, and at the President's request, Bess Abel would like to meet with him at his convenience in her office to discuss the possibility of providing some entertainment for the President's State Dinner of Norway's King Olav the Fifth at the White House scheduled for the evening of April the 25th.

That was when Raj's mood changed recognizing once more in his life that there are times when good things fizzle while the fizzling could bring about something else, eventually coming to the surface of life beyond and above the unfulfilled effort.

THEME TWENTY-EIGHT

THE APPOINTMENT

BESS ABEL LEFT WORD FOR HER ASSISTANT, Dora Malloy to take Raj to the Cabinet Room and to sit with him in the room's leather covered chairs at the table meant to house the members of the President and his Cabinet.

"Feel free to sit over there," Dora Malloy said as she pointed to President Johnson's old chair when he was Vice President across from his current chair as President. "That's where the boss sat when he was Vice President. Now it's Vice President Humphrey's chair that's there. The old one is going to go to the President's Library." She briefly described President Johnson's previous view from his chair when he was Vice President which was a much better view than his current one. "The view as Vice President was wonderful because from that chair he could see through the windows, and see the South Lawn and the Ellipse and Memorials and Monuments. Beautiful! Now, as President he gets a chair that has a little higher back than the other chairs but now he sits on the other side of the table with his back to that beautiful view. His new view as President is just looking at the Cabinet Members.

President Lincoln said that his cat—'Dixie'—was smarter than all the members of the Cabinet put together. Something like that. I think the boss likes that quote. He's an animal lover. Don't quote me on this but I believe he may like animals more than Cabinet Officers. He particularly likes dogs and cats."

It wasn't long until President Johnson called on the intercom. "Bess?"

"No, Mister President," Dora Malloy said. "She's still over at the State Department and she asked me to take care of the meeting between you and Mr. Bhavnani in case she was delayed."

"Yes," the President said, "I asked her to stick it out at State and not let them take over what isn't any of their business. Now, Dora, bring Mister—the fellow—the dancer from India fellow to come in here. What's his name?"

"Bhavnani. Raj Bhavnani."

"That's it!"

Dora Malloy escorted Raj into the Oval Office while the President stood and extended his hand. "Sit down, Raj. You are Raj aren't you?"

The President's question was quickly followed by Dora Malloy almost tip-toeing out of the office.

"Yes, sir." Raj could hardly take his eyes off the sights of the Oval Office near the chair that President Johnson, with a nod of his head, had indicated Raj should sit. Across from Raj was a painted portrait on the wall of Andrew Jackson who Raj didn't recognize and there were four book-shelves with books on them and there were three television sets side-by-side in one single wide case with the legs of that wide case resting on the floor.

President Johnson said, "I heard all about your showman-ship; that's what it's called—and it makes me sorry to tell you that because of the killing—the dreadfulness—the assassination of Dr. Martin Luther King we aren't going to have the kind of—of entertainment at events throughout the rest of April that we had planned."

"Yes, sir. I understand that."

"I knew you would. And we will wait for brighter times—and maybe when the Prime Minister of your country comes here. How would that be?"

"India?"

"That's your country, isn't it?"

"Yes. But are you talking about Prime Minister Indira Gandhi?"

"I am."

"Thank you, Mister President, but I don't want to entertain her. I don't like her."

That certainly cleared the air fast.

"What's wrong with her? Is there something wrong with her?"

"She isn't any good. She plays on the fact that so many foreigners think she is the daughter of Mahatma Gandhi while she isn't, you know. She's the daughter of Nehru—Jawaharial Nehru. He wasn't much good. Shastri was good. He fought the Pakistanis. I don't like Nehru or Indira Gandhi. I don't think she's good like Shastri. He died."

"I know. He died in Tashkent—away from India."

"I think they killed him in Tashkent." Raj had the rare ability to quickly make himself the equal of anyone, and President Johnson who had enough confidence in himself, liked Raj for that trait. After all, Raj was being honest.

President Johnson asked, "Who do you think killed Shastri?"

"The Pakistanis."

"Well, I don't know about that." Then the President changed the subject. "Listen, I have been told that you are a philosopher of sorts—that you do a lot of visionary work—prophetic."

"Yes, Mister President. Philosophizing is my major reward for living."

"Dr. King was a philosopher, you know. He was a visionary."

"I didn't know that." If the President could change the subject so rapidly, so could Raj. "I want you to know, Mister President, that I thought your speech to the U.S. Congress after President Kennedy's assassination was—was thrillng. The one on the 27th of November."

"That's the date alright: the 27th. Five days after that horrible day of the 22nd. You memorized the date and that is commendable."

"I did, sir. You started it by saying 'I would gladly have given everything I have not to be standing here tonight.'"

President Johnson shook his head. "Close. But it was 'All I have I would have gladly given not to be standing here today.'"

"Yes, yes," Raj nodded his head. "Yes, yes. I heard it in India so I might have gotten it wrong." (Hearing it in India was immaterial as the language spoken was English and not covered by a Hindi interpreter.)

"That happens. You got it close enough. Raj—How do you pronounce your last name?"

"Bhav-nah-nee."

"Bhav-nah-nee. I have it."

At that, Dora Malloy came to the doorway and while sticking her head beyond the framework of the door she quickly looked down at her wrist-watch, nodded and said, "Mister President, you're going to be late for that appointment."

There probably was no appointment scheduled and Raj knew it, or felt it.

"Tell them I'll be a little late, Dora." There was something about the traits of Raj that were unusual for any guest and the President simply wanted the conversation to go on longer which was not his norm with a total stranger.

"Of course," Dora Malloy said and left the entranceway.

"Tell me Raj, did you hear that I'm not going to run for President again? Do you understand my reasoning?"

"Yes, sir. I was sorry to hear that. March the 31st you announced that."

"That's right. You do, indeed, have a good memory for dates. I can't get all involved in a political campaign when the troubles in the world call for my every moment—for every moment of any President of the United States' moments during these times. I can't push aside the events of the moment."

"You mean Vietnam?"

"Vietnam, yes. And all of Southeast Asia and the Middle East and your country; India. And Pakistan and China on your border. You are right: Vietnam is central right now. You can't hear the demonstrators from here in the Oval Office but over-looking the north lawn you can hear them on the avenue and from the square across the street. I can't waste time on them or some domestic political campaign. Tell me, do you want me to give you a little tour of the office here? Of the Oval Office?"

"No, Sir because I want you to talk about leadership. It's a good office but I want you to talk about leadership. You are a leader, sir."

There was no control of Raj. Raj was as much Raj while in the Oval Office than he was anywhere else. He did, however, respect and liked President Johnson and that came through to the President.

"I'll tell you, son," Son? "This takeover of the office of the Presidency had a rough, terrible, tragic beginning. And in this office you feel it every moment. You know, when we got back from Dallas the carpet here was red. A real deep red—red. Mrs. Kennedy had it moved in and laid while we were all on that trip so by the time we got back it would have been on the Oval Office floor as a surprise for President Kennedy. But as it came to be, she asked for it to be ripped out before she ever came into the Oval Office again. Too much like blood. So I asked to have this one put in. It's a carpet pretty much like F.D.R. had."

"Roosevelt?"

"That's right. Franklin Delano Roosevelt. Not Theodore. Not Teddy. As for the carpet on this floor now," the President shrugged and gave a slight motion of adjustment in his chair behind his desk. "It's alright. It's pretty much lIke F.D.R. had," he repeated. Raj looked down at it. He wanted to compliment it but it was not begging for praise as it was a pale light gray-green carpet.

"Mister President, I want you to know I support you totally in Vietnam. It is what America always does—gives its own lives for the lives of its friends."

President Johnson stared at Raj and nodded. "Do you have Vietnamese friends?"

"No. But it's America's way. And if you don't do what you're doing for the South Vietnamese now then America won't do it for India if it's attacked by China or if it's attacked by Pakistan."

President Johnson gave a slow nod without saying anything. Instead he turned to what he often turned to in front of visitors: the fascinations of the Oval Office:

"There are some marvelous conveniences built into this office. I can see all the newscasts. Any time. Last night's newscasts, if I want to see them." Then he picked up the receiver of one of the phones on his desk and, as example of what he had just said, without dialing anything he spoke into the mouthpiece of the receiver. "Hello, Honey, this is ya' President. I need ya to call Signal or whatever they're calling themselves now. WAHKA, I think now."

"Yes, Mister President," a White House Operator answered. "I think it's just short for the White House Communications Agency. WHCA."

"That's it! Call and tell them I want to see their tape of Martin Luther King the night before he was assassinated…Has to be April the Third…That's right…at the church in Memphis. I have the television on right now and the NBC receiver is on 12…I think that's what WAHKA has been using lately… Good… Good… Thank ya.' It is WAHKA isn't it?"

"Yes, sir," she answered. It took no longer than fifteen seconds before the image came on the set. As both the President and Raj readjusted themselves in their chairs, there on the screen of the middle television set was Reverend Martin Luther King Jr. speaking to the congregation at the Mason Temple Church of God in Christ in Memphis, Tennessee. The President and Raj Bhavnani watched and listened to the entire speech in absolute attentiveness and silence.

When the speech was done the President clicked off the television set and he stared at Raj who stared back at the President. President Johnson said, "And that, my man, is a visionary. That man on that night was prophetic. He knew the future. If some yokel tells me that King couldn't have had a vision of the future the night before he was killed—then I would be talking to a yokel!"

When the President said no more but was just staring at Raj, the quiet was talking precedence, and so Raj said very softly, "Mister President I never knew that happened at church the night before he was killed. I never knew he said he wasn't worried about anything; and he said that like anybody he would like to live a long life—but he said that he wasn't concerned about that now—and that he wasn't fearing any man! Isn't that what he said?"

The President nodded. "He knew. He must have known because of what he said and then what happened." And President Johnson adjusted himself on his chair as he told his guest of the horror that came the following early evening. "Close to 6:00 pm outside Room 306 on the balcony of the Lorraine Motel at 450 Mulberry Street. Did you ever think that kids in school would be learning about the Lorraine Motel?—About what happened outside that place?

"And then horrible riots. 14th and 'U' and 'People's Drug Store.' Riots. D.C. was on fire. This House—the People's House; the White House was…this roof had to have enough amo-power to stop any of those rioters."

It was a unique visit with the importance of President Johnson enveloping Raj, and the uniqueness of Raj Bhavnani being appreciated by the President of the United States.

"How do you pronounce that last name of yers?"

"Bhav-nah-nee, sir."

"It's a tough name for a fella from Texas, y'know. But I got it: Bahv-*gah*-nee."

"Yes, sir; that's it," he lied. But a lie to be courteous is acceptable.

THEME TWENTY-NINE

CONCEDING

ONE LATE 1968 NIGHT AT THE BAHIA, when Anna had settled in bed while reading portions of the magazine, *TV Guide*, Anna told Chris how important it would be to "turn off the TV forever so we could be done with enemies." She was in the mood to give advice after absorbing some article in the magazine.

Chris admired those things that stuck with her but he wasn't in the mood for advice at the moment or any moment and so he assured her that he didn't have any enemies. "You talked me out of that when I got angry at L.B.J. So I don't have any."

"Then forgive those who *would* be your enemies if you had any."

"Oh, Anna!"

"What was that you said?"

"Oh, Susanna. A song title."

"Stephen Foster wrote it. I sang it when I tried out for some Broadway talent scouts that never even responded. They never even called. But one of them said to the other, 'too young,' or 'Jail Bait' or something like that."

"Well, don't hate them, anyway."

"I don't! I try not to ever hate anyone."

"How about Hitler? You don't hate him?"

"Oh, please. Yes, I hate Hitler. But I'm talking about people I know." And with that she broke into singing the old Stephen Foster song by singing "Oh, Susanna, don't you cry for me" all the way to Alabama and "My true love for to see!"

And that made Chris smile. The smile was so wide that he almost laughed but he didn't.

That conversation lasted in Christopher's memory and he particularly thought about it whenever he found himself angry at something or someone during the present or even a lingering negative thought of an incident in the past. He hoped that having no hatred was settling into a constant part of him, providing the guide-lines for something he would make happen the next time he went to D.C.

"You have a guest, Mr. Bahvnani," Raj's Secretary, Mrs. Erickson, said through the inter-com box on her desk.

"Who is it?"

"He says to tell you he's an old friend."

"I don't have any old friends. How old is he?"

"I don't know, Mr. Bhavnani. Do you want me to ask him?"

"No, no. Ask him his name. I need to know his name—if he has one. If he doesn't have one then ask him his Prison Number. He probably has one of those."

She was mumbling back and forth with the guest and she said through the inter-com, "His name is Christopher Straw."

"Christopher Straw!? Good Goddess Parvati! From New York! The space man! I know him alright. I know him.

Christopher Straw. He could be old; maybe middle-aged. Send him in unless he's falling apart." Raj knew that his guest could hear every word he was telling Mrs. Erickson over that intercom speaker on her desk.

Raj rose for the occasion and shook hands with his guest, Christopher Straw, and asked him to sit opposite him as Raj sat back down at his desk.

Christopher nodded. "You have quite an office, Raj. Quite an office. It's beautiful! And big!"

"It's not the biggest in D.C. It's close but the President's office; his Oval Office is bigger. That's why the President doesn't want to run again. He's self-conscious about how our two offices contrast. His office is just a little bigger than mine—but not much! And I didn't have to have an Oval Shape. Pretty good! Right? Right?"

"Right."

"What brings you here? Outer Space? Savannah Lane? I saw her on a late television show. And that's where I saw you for the first time since President Kennedy's Inauguration and Mama Leone's Restaurant where I left you to pay the check!" And Raj gave a doubled-over laugh at his own confession. "Then here I was years later doing some late work and I saw you again—this time in a television audience and you were with Savannah Lane of all people. Through that television set I wanted to shout to you that I owe you a couple dollars for that New York dinner!"

"Thirty and that's without the tip."

"Did you leave one?"

"Yes. Six dollars."

"Too much! And now that you are here in my office for

reasons unexplained, I want you to know that you owe me thousands of dollars for stealing Savannah Lane from me! Poor girl. She could have had me. Pretty girl, too. You know that this office used to be John Farmy's office?"

"Man, you drift. You go from subject to subject. Whose office?"

"Farmy's. John Farmy's office."

"Sorry. I never heard of him."

"It takes a man from India to know that Mister John Farmy was President Roosevelt's top assistant. He ran the Post Offices in this country. The whole thousands of them. All of them. Every letter posted. He took the responsibility."

"You mean Farley! James Fraley and he wasn't the President's prime assistant. He was—I don't know—the head of the Post Office's like you said; the Cabinet Secretary. I guess he was the Secretary of the Post Office Department. I think he was called Post Master General."

"That's it! Now I have his office. Want to see the safe he had? Want to see the balcony from this office? Best in D.C. Best view in D.C."

"No. Thank you, but no. I want to ask you something."

"Yes, yes. Of course. Go ahead. What can I do for you?"

"I read in Evans and Novak's column—their political report that you had a meeting with President Johnson. Did you?

"Yes, yes. You came all the way from San Diego to D.C. to ask me that?"

"No. I came to D.C. for a number of meetings at NASA. I do that occasionally."

"I, too, have been having many meetings."

"At NASA?"

"No. with the President."

"Really?"

"Oh, yes. First, he wanted to know what he should do about the assassination of Martin Lewis King, then about the assassination of Robert Kennedy, then about the invasion of the Soviet Union re-taking Czechoslovakia, then just days later about the Democrat's riots outside their convention demanding that we get out of Vietnam."

"Martin *Luther* King, not Martin *Lewis* King."

"That's right. You finally got it right. L.B.J.—that's what everyone calls him—We—the two of us meet a lot. But I don't call any man by his initials. I call him by his name: Lyndon is a smart man but he likes guidance. Lyndon calls them Matters of State that we discuss."

"Is that what he calls them?" Of course Christopher Straw was more than suspicious about everything he was being told since his host was the man who, some years back, had told him he knew Winston Churchill and was going to hire the builder of London's Heathrow Airport to renovate the Algonquin Hotel. "Okay. Matters of State. So let me ask you to ask him when—and this is not why I'm here—but you must remind him—although he has to know—tell President Johnson that he hasn't got much time to meet the objective of President Kennedy to land a man on the moon and bring him safely back to earth before the decade is done. Those are President Kennedy's words and the decade will be done pretty soon—it will be done next year."

"Yes, yes. I will remind him. He probably forgot by now. I will tell him that I know this space man who reminded me about Kennedy's setting—establishing or whatever you call it—landing a man on the moon during this decade and I want to remind him. I will tell him. Now, if that isn't why you came to see me, why are you here?"

"Savannah," he said loudly and bluntly. "I want you to know that Savannah and I live together and maybe we'll be married. No matter what we do, Raj—she's my girl. I love her."

"And you want me to get out of your picture?"

"You put it well. Good English. I simply want you to leave her alone. I want her to be safe every moment whether I'm with her or not with her."

"You don't have to warn me. Warnings mean nothing to me. What means something to me is that you came here to tell me that. And that, my good friend, has already taken place in that I have totally left her alone. My leaving her alone has already taken place."

"It has?"

"It has. Did you know she went to Rome?"

"Yes, of course I know. I live with her. How do *you* know she went to Rome?"

"I saw her at a restaurant there. Ran into each other. All by chance. Don't worry. She's a loyalist. I begged to see her later—that night. I met her at a restaurant and I begged to see her and she didn't have anything to do with me. She seems to be a serious Catholic and I suppose she doesn't want anything to do with a Hindu. Whatever it was, she didn't want to see me. I accepted that and that was all there was. Want to give her a gift?" He opened up the middle drawer of his desk and produced a bronze medal of Pope Paul. "He gave it to me."

"He did? Pope Paul gave it to you?"

"He told me to give it to Savannah."

"He did?"

And Raj shoved the medal across his desk to Christopher who examined it carefully. "Yes, yes. Please give it to her."

"Does the Pope watch *Gemstone*?"

"I didn't ask him. We discussed religion. He is Catholic, you know."

"I assumed so."

"He saw you on a late-night television show. I did, too."

"He did? He watches late-night television?"

"That's when he saw you in the audience when you were pointed out. He didn't like you when he saw you, you know."

"What do you mean? Why didn't he like me?"

"I don't think he believes you're Catholic."

"I don't know when to believe you, Raj."

"You can believe me when I say I am loyal to those whom I give my word."

"Can I? You expect me to believe that?"

"Yes, yes. I am loyal when it comes to India. I am loyal when it comes to the United States. I am loyal when it comes to getting out of the picture when it comes to Savannah. She is your girl. Not mine. I tried and failed, didn't I? Once loyal, I will not break that loyalty. You tried and succeeded. In truth, my friend, I have never in my life done anything to a girl; to a woman, ever, without the sanction of that girl; that woman. Never. So this will have nothing to do with loyalty to you, Mister Straw; it has everything to do with loyalty to myself and to strangers."

Christopher stared at his host and said nothing. And that was because he didn't know what to say.

"Do you believe me, Mister Straw?"

Cristopher was still slow to say anything. And, after a

difficult longer silence he said very softly, "I heard what you did for India during the 1962 war. I know what you have done here for the Voice of America. You have proven those loyalties. Give me the coin—the Pope's coin. I will give it to Savannah—from you—and I will tell her of our conversation."

"Good, good! But it is not a coin. It is a medal. And you should know that I was joking. The Pope didn't give it to me. I bought it at a shop in Rome. So that's the real truth and so what? I planned on giving it to her some day. This has turned out to be the day—the day to give it to her—through you. You deserve to give it to her, my friend. I not only believe in loyalty; I believe in what you Americans call 'guts.' India has guts and claimed independence; America has guts and has proved it before I was born and even many times in my lifetime. You have guts for believing in going to the moon and coming here to see me with a difficult mission to tell me to give up on Savannah. All three of you have guts; India, the U.S. and you. And so, then, I have guts too, as I am claiming, with honesty, that to my regret I have lost and you have won what you deserve to win: Savannah. There are four of us with guts now." Once again Raj stood up and once again he extended his hand as he felt the meeting had been completed.

And so did Christopher Straw. "Four of us then," Christopher said still talking softly. "Thank you for including me in. I am, then, in good company including you."

"As your father would say—As the senior Mister Straw would say, 'All important people.'"

variations on a theme

THEME THIRTY

AS IT WOULD HAVE BEEN

IT WAS THE EVENING of November the 22ⁿᵈ of 1968 and Raj's office in the Old Post Office Building was filled with members of the National Press Club who came from their headquarters on 14ᵗʰ and "F" Street in North West D.C. to ask him one question:

"Mr. Bahvnani, when you were on Barry Farber's Radio Show last week, talking about Air India and Voice of America, Farber asked you when you felt that America changed—the changes that brought about these recent massive demonstrations against our policy in Vietnam; the sudden exalting of the kids called Yipees; the proliferation of the use of drugs of kids and adults, and the questioning of our involvement in the Cold War. There were all kinds and sorts of radical shouting and massive changes that were never envisioned before. And you answered that you have studied that question more than any other question about America and that you have the answer to all of that and you would be glad to answer that at an appropriate time. This morning Farber said today—this day—the fifth anniversary of the assassination of President Kennedy you phoned Farber and told him it was an appropriate time because of the fifth anniversary and you said you would answer that question on his show. Barry is here from WOR-AM in New York. And not only is he here but so is his sound crew and so is all his equipment and technicians—and the same for many of the Washington Press Corps from right here in D.C. Will you explain what it is you have—'discovered' is the word—or 'found out'—or 'something' that you believe?"

Barry Farber with his microphone and technicians and equipment came forward through the crowd and the crowd formed an aisle-way for them to reach Raj.

"Thank you, Raj. It's up to you, Raj Bhavnani," Barry Farber said. "I wanted this on my show and I am glad to have you back on this microphone. You are a man of your word to me. You delve into all kinds of national and international issues and this is surely one of them. The great unanswered question among so many is when and why did America change?"

"Let me begin this way, Barry: On the day before the assassination of President Kennedy; on its yesterday of Thursday, November the 21st of 1963, things were different: On November the 21st of 1963, members of the Green Berets were known to be heroic. The same heroism was widely held for those in any branch of the U.S. military fighting for retaining the independence of South Vietnam and other friends under siege. No one called our military 'suckers.' The term of 'suckers' was applied after Friday, November the 22nd.

"On November the 21st of 1963, in great urban centers of the United States, although there were some vagrants who were walking the streets and there were hobos riding in freight cars of trains, there were not large districts of homeless people living in cardboard boxes or without any shelter at all. The districts of homeless in cardboard boxes came after Friday, November the 22nd.

"On November the 21st of 1963, other than signs saying 'Post No Bills' on walls and fences and only occasional personal messages, there was no graffiti on public and private property. The proliferation of such graffiti came after Friday, November the 22nd.

"On November the 21st of 1963, profanities were whispered from male to male and female to female rather than being a part of common mixed vocabularies and communications. Such public vocabulary and communications came after Friday, November the 22nd.

"On November the 21st of 1963, violent crime resulted in headlines rather than considered to be events of such frequency that they more often would make the middle pages of newspapers. That news became more frequently *non*-news after Friday, November the 22nd.

"On November the 21st of 1963, teenage pregnancies were rare rather than widespread. That truly massive increase among teen-aged girls came after Friday, November the 22nd.

"On November the 21st of 1963, public parks were marvelous refuges to be visited at any time and not forbidden at night. The practice of staying away from parks at night became justifiaby common after Friday, November the 22nd.

"On November the 21st of 1963, drive-by shootings committed by members of gangs were unknown rather than becoming an urban disease. That practice among gangs became contagious after Friday, November the 22nd.

"On November the 21st of 1963, playgrounds at schools were

not places of risk with guards, nor were there locks installed on the fences around their perimeters. Such guards and barriers on and around public schools came after Friday, November the 22nd.

"On November the 21st of 1963, the taking of illegal drugs had not become an epidemic. That wide-spreading arrived after Friday, November the 22nd.

"All of those ways of life were turned upside down from what they had been on the 21st. That was before the youngest elected President with a beautiful and talented First Lady and beautiful and talented children, and with great financial wealth, and most of all, known to be the most important political leader in the world, was dead in one unexpected instant at 12:30 in the Dallas afternoon of Friday, the 22nd. If President Kennedy, of all people, could suddenly be dead then a kind of immortality usually held by the young was upheld no more. And so the young of that time wanted to do the prohibited quickly while they were still alive because their lives could end tomorrow—even today. To many of them, their times would be spent with no moral restrictions, no religious direction, no code of ethics and so many of their elders did not know how to handle all this. To a great amount of the young the word, 'self' meant 'all that is important' with the guiding objective to do 'what feels good.' The common became to choose bad company—to choose the ignorant—to choose to listen to neighboring youth that knew and lived as the foulest of their population. In short, the common became to choose the worst as friends. And that's when the youth became accurately known as the 'Now Generation' with that phrase of self-centered living becoming a late November prevalence that would last a long time.

"But what if Oswald's bullets hit nothing other than the

white posts of the pergola structure above the grassy knoll of Dealey Plaza? So many things would then have been different than they became, and so many things would continue to be more like that week's Thursday rather than that week's Friday. Things would be as they were. That is because of something commonly known in India: every life rests heavily on its times. In India we know that we *are* our times, and our *times* are *us*. And so in your nation many lives after November the 22nd of 1963 became lives vastly different than they would have been the day before—on November's fourth Thursday.

"Countless lives changed that would have been as they were if Oswald had missed."

THEME THIRTY-ONE

"TRANQUILITY BASE HERE"

THIRTY YEARS BACK when Christopher Straw was seven years old, his teacher was critical of his belief that he had something in common with Christopher Columbus. As some incidents in early life become long-lasting unanswered questions, through the years Christopher Straw often wondered who was right and who was wrong: him or Mrs. Zambroski. He always settled on being right with Mrs. Zambroski being wrong. But he never gave up asking the question to himself over and over again when he had nothing better to do.

That, however, was rather minimal compared to the question asked without sufficient answer that human beings and probably all living things have asked through the years that life has existed on this planet. Of course living things looked upward at the night sky and wondered at its blackness that went to every horizon, acting as an infinite and unexplained roof over them with, of all things, a yellow ball or circle or some round thing that seemed to carry itself from one edge of the sky to another and with a repeating cycle of changing its position slightly from one night to another and often changing its shape all the way to complete invisibility and then, little by little on forthcoming nights, coming back into view. It was the moon, and finally having a name for it did not explain its mystery. Scientists did, however, find out some pertinent things about it and explained their observations as technology and study increased, but consistently there was the passion of Man to go to the moon and walk on its surface and come back home to tell others what it was doing all this time up there.

That curiosity lasted from the beginning of life on earth to 1969 A.D. with the Apollo 11 launch from Cape Kennedy (Canaveral) in Florida on July the 16th of 1969, with a landing on the moon on July the 20th with Commander Neil Armstrong saying the words "Houston? Tranquility base here. The Eagle has landed."

The voice from Mission Operations Control Room Two of the Manned Spacecraft Center Houston answered: "Roger, Tranquility! We copy you on the ground. You got a bunch of guys about to turn blue. We're breathing again! Thanks a lot."

Neil Armstrong responded with, "Okay, I'm going to step off the LEM now." (Originally the LEM was called the Lunar Excursion Module and then called Lunar Module). He stepped off the Lunar Excursion Module and then he said, "That's one small step for a man; one giant leap for mankind."

That was not only heard by the world but accompanied by the sight of his footprint being implanted on the surface of the moon which was being transmitted by live television and seen by an estimated 530 million people on earth.

Lunar Module Pilot Buzz Aldrin then came off the Lunar Module and became the second man on the moon. Command

Module Pilot Michael Collins was simultaneously staying in the Command and Service (CSM) Module in the Columbia craft that was launched with the Lunar Module attached and then to be docked with the Lunar Module when the period of time for Armstrong and Aldrin would be done and the ride home would begin. After all, the pledge that President Kennedy gave was: "I believe this nation should commit itself to achieving the goal, before this decade is out, of landing a man on the moon and returning him safely to earth." The decade was still not yet out and with the safe return included within that decade, the objective was achieved in full two Presidents later by President Nixon keeping President Kennedy's time-limit given some nine years earlier on May the 25th of 1961.

The plaque that boarded from the Cape and left on the moon read, "Here men from the planet Earth first set foot upon the Moon July, 1969 A.D. We came in peace for all mankind." This was followed by the engraved signatures of Neil A. Armstrong, Michael Collins, Edwin E. Aldrin Jr., and President Richard Nixon, President United States of America. [The Cape had been renamed from Cape Canaveral to Cape Kennedy by President Johnson's directive as he had misinterpreted Mrs. Kennedy's request after the assassination of President Kennedy when she wanted it to be the name of the Space Center; not trading away the approximate 400-year-old name of Cape Canaveral as a geographical entity. It was to be changed back to Cape Canaveral in 1973 and the originally intended Space Center was to be named after President Kennedy.]

Christopher Straw was among those who had "turned blue" in Houston waiting for the Lunar Module to land on the surface of the moon and, with the others he cheered and teared with joy at the words, "Houston? Tranquility base here. The Eagle has landed," and, in short time, the statement, "That's one small step for a man; one giant leap for mankind."

Anna could not be with Chris in Houston's Mission Control. Instead she watched it all on television at NBC Studios in Burbank intentionally from a vacant Green Room adjoining a shooting stage. She was all alone watching a man walk on the moon for the first time since the world began.

That vacancy of any other person in the room with Anna did not prevent her from talking out loud. With a smile she said, "I understand how God gets such good reviews!"

She did not mean for anyone on earth to hear her and she was successful at that. Like Scott Carpenter before her, she had a different audience.

THEME THIRTY-TWO

"THE INVITATION"

RAJ BHAVNANI WAS GIVEN THE TASK of going to New York periodically for his broadcasts so as to record interviews with government officials who were in New York for one event or another and also to interview those leaders from India and from currently news-making countries at the United Nations.

He did it because it was part of the radio broadcasts for which he was the host. But, as much as he liked leisurely walking in New York City, he was not fond of the time and devices to get there and back which included the taxi-ride with frequency from his office at the Old Post Office Building to Washington National Airport to the shuttle-flight from Washington, D.C. to New York's LaGuardia Airport then a taxi to Midtown Manhattan then back to LaGuardia Airport for a shuttle returning to Washington National to a taxi back to the Old Post Office Building that all became a mentally painful nuisance.

In addition, Raj had been spoiled. When he stayed overnight in Manhattan he wanted to stay at the Algonquin Hotel like old times but the Voice of America placed him at the Americana or at the City Squire when the Americana was filled. Besides that, his office in New York didn't have the luxury of his D.C. office. It did, however, have a massive view of New York City from looking north toward Central Park through one window and a lot of Midtown looking east through a narrow window, and a large south view window looking all the way far into downtown.

Happily, he was permitted to bring or send for his D.C. unfriendly secretary, Mrs. Rhonda Erickson, to New York when particular trips indicated a need for secretarial work for him to be done there.

"Erik? Erik?" he would yell out because the intercom in the RCA Building's "loaning office" was too complex for him to comprehend. "Erik?!"

"Yes, Mr. Bhavnani?"

"Where's that invitation you told me about?"

"I'll bring it right in."

And, in very little time, she came in as she quickly scanned what was written on it. She stood straight in perfect posture across from him at his desk with both her arms extended holding a large card of some sort. "It says kindly respond by March 26, 1973, Mr. Bhavnani. That's next Monday."

"What's today?"

"Friday, the 23rd, sir."

He mumbled something.

"What's that, Mr. Bhavnani?"

"I don't want to go to the dedication of those two tall boxes. Why didn't they get Frank Lloyd Wright to design something? Did he die?"

"I think so. Many years ago, sir—I think."

"Too bad."

Raj walked to the window overlooking the view to the south while holding on to the large cardboard invitation. He nodded toward the towers. "Look at them! Just look. Just look. A kid could have designed them. Two long rods in four-walled shapes. You call that creative? A kid. That's right. Where's the design? Did the designer ever hear of at least rounding something? Too creative? And why two of them? They're both the same. Why not just one—or why not three or four? No room? Is that what would have been done if there was room? Twenty boxes?"

"Yes, sir. Should I say 'no' to the invitation for you? The dedication is for April the 4th at 3 o'clock and your calendar is blank that afternoon, Mr. Bhavnani. And Governor Rockefeller's secretary called to find out if you'll be at the dedication and the reception. He's going to be there and maybe Mayor Lindsay will be there, too. Apparently the Mayor doesn't know for sure yet if he can attend. Governor Rockefeller is going to speak in the North Tower Lobby and his secretary said that he would like to see you there."

"I don't care about Rockefeller. He calls me 'fella'! See if *he* likes it."

"Yes sir."

"From where does he get that kind of greeting? Tell him that I said to tell the fella I won't be there. And John Lindsay probably doesn't know if he'll be there because he doesn't know anything; not even if he's a Republican or a Democrat and he certainly has no idea what his political party will be by April the 4th or whatever the date is supposed to be."

"I'll just respond that you're sorry but that you can't be there, Mr. Bhavnani."

"No! No! No!" He grabbed the invitation from her hands.

"Respond that I can be there but I don't want to be there and I'm not sorry I won't be there but I am delighted to refuse! Erik, honesty is the best policy. I never lie. Never have. Look at this invitation. It's on stiff cardboard; see? That's to show it's expensive. That's supposed to look royal or something." And he looked down directly at the invitation in his hands. "And the whole thing—see? A silver invitation with the designs of those metal stripes they have all over those two buildings. And the invitation says that the Commissioners of the Port Authority of New York and New Jersey have the honor and pleasure of inviting me; not Rockefeller inviting me, as though I should be honored that the Commissioners of the Port Authority want me there. They probably want some money. You know who they are? Do you know any of their names?—If they even have names."

"No sir."

"I know one of their names. One of them. He's Bozo the Clown; that's who he is."

"Yes, sir."

"Get a big silver cardboard and write 'Dear Bozo the Clown. My boss won't be there. Don't forget to feed the elephants.' And send it to him."

"I will."

"You sure Frank Lloyd Wright's dead?

"Yes, sir."

"He probably died when he saw those two buildings."

"I don't think he could have seen them. I think he was probably gone by the time they were really visible."

"For his sake that would probably be best."

"Perhaps, sir." She walked out of his office.

The moment Venu arrived in her outer office she pressed

the proper button on the intercom and said, "Your guest, Mr. Venu Ramachandra has arrived. He's early."

Raj Bhavnani stood up behind his desk when Venu walked in. His standing automatically put his back to the large picture window looking south over the city. "Sa'ab! Good to see you! Venu Ramachandra! Venu Ramachandra!"

"Raj Bhavnani! Do you mind if I only say it once?"

"That means you are not as glad to see Raj Bhavnani as I am glad to see Venu Ramachandra; that's what it means! I am twice as glad to see you as you are when you see me!"

"That's good of you to say, Lieutenant Raj. Thank you. May I sit down? That's some view you have here."

"Sit down! My rudeness in not offering that immediately. My rudeness; that's what it is. Sit down!"

Venu nodded. "No problem," and he sat facing Raj as he too, sat down.

"No problem? That's U.S. Astronaut talk, isn't it?"

"Yes, it is. I heard every moment of Friendship Seven!"

"Through All India Radio, I am sure. Now, what can I do for my first real employer? I mean my employer at the Taj!"

"What you can do for me is easy—just to let me see you and find out if your importance is increasing. It should be."

"I had a rough time during the whole Bangladesh crisis a few years back. I wasn't going to go to India and risk my life again and this time having to support Indira Gandhi—and at the same time, of course I was opposed to Pakistan's Yahya Khan. Unlike 1962 I didn't go home to India to fight a war because this one was a war I didn't support, and I didn't talk much about it on either All India Radio or the Voice of America. I'm glad to say neither one fired me, but it was uncomfortable to avoid talking about the war. I think that many of the people in both places secretly felt as I did: both Pakistan's leadership and India's leadership were not worthy of support and if Bangladesh would become an independent nation it would become what much of the world would call 'a basket case.' Do you know what that means?"

"Yes. I understand."

"So now it's the People's Republic of Bangladesh and it *is* a basket case. I have learned a long time ago to beware of any country that calls itself the People's Republic of anything because those countries are neither for the people nor are they republics. Sa'ab, notice that our country doesn't call itself the People's Republic of India, nor does the country in which we are sitting call itself the People's Republic of the United States."

"You're good, Lieutenant. You're very good. You think well and talk well. You don't have to argue with me about the subject of Pakistan nor the inabilities of the People's Republic of Bangladesh, particularly with Indira Gandhi's handouts of India's funds. If it was a different Prime Minister I would think differently. And, I suspect, so would you."

Raj nodded.

"How do you think you survived your jobs with All India Radio and Voice of America during that war?"

"I changed my own format. No commentaries. Instead, a lot of guests. Willis Conover was a frequent guest with his great talking and playing of American music—jazz—on my All India Radio programs, and I played a lot of repeats from my Voice of America programs that I got from the Voice of America itself— ones that he recorded for the Soviet Union and their satellite nations. Mainly jazz. The kind of shows that Conover made so many Soviet citizens secretly listen to the V.O.A.—The Voice of America."

"I suspect you made no enemies nor friends in Bangladesh, nor by Pakistan nor by Indira Gandhi."

"I recovered since then. No one brings it up. What is new with you, Sa'ab?"

"Talking with the Hyatt people. They have big plans for hotels. Big plans for hotels in Delhi. I might go with them."

"Good! Good for you! You never hesitate to investigate what's worth knowing. That sounds like something good."

"I'll see. I love the Taj Hotel. It's a wonderful place—as you well know. But I'll see. My interest right now is finding out *your* next step, Lieutenant."

"I have one but I don't want to tell you."

"You don't trust me?"

"It's because I *do* trust you and I trust you more than anyone else in the world."

"Then why the secret?"

"I can embarrass myself for a failure in front of anyone except you. I want to be sure I will succeed before going ahead with what I plan to do when I know I will tell you. Besides, you're the only one on this side of the ocean—any ocean—that still calls me Lieutenant. I like it. I think it sounds good. Don't you think so? I think it sounds very good. It gives me prestige. I mean more prestige than I already have."

It was difficult to ever leave a meeting with Raj Bhavnani with total satisfaction of his resolve.

THEME THIRTY-THREE

"THE WAY IT MIGHT BE"

WHEN CHRIS CAME HOME to the Bahia suite during one late afternoon in 1973, the walk down the hallway passing other people's living quarters was markedly different than usual in that behind every doorway could be heard the distinct voice of Senator Sam Ervin. That meant all the television sets had been turned to watch hearings in Washington D.C. as Senator Ervin was the Chairman of the Senate Select Committee to Investigate Campaign Practices more often known throughout the country as the "Watergate Committee."

But when Chris opened the door to his and Anna's suite it was happily silent inside except for some unknown song coming from the humming of Anna. He literally grabbed her and they kissed much more passionately than when he normally came home early. It was all because Senator Ervin's voice was not in their suite.

"Is he under the bed?"

"Who?"

"Ervin! Senator Ervin! For sure I am not complaining but

how come you are the one person in the United States who is home and not watching the 'Watergate Hearings?'"

"Because I can't stand them! Because they make me sick! One man—and unfortunately he's from a southern state—North Carolina—is leading this travesty!"

"You're not kidding, are you?"

"Honey, he's ruining the country; him and that 'Johnny Gonna- get-the-President Special Prosecutor! Where's that in the Constitution?"

"Cox. You're talking about Archibald Cox."

"If he's the Special Prosecutor."

"He is."

"Did you elect him? Somehow I missed that election."

"You have a point. There wasn't any election for Special Prosecutor."

"See what I mean?"

"I totally agree with you; you know that, but why so avid about the subject today?"

"Because I voted for and like the President and I don't like some outside force trying to bring him down without my vote requested."

"You didn't ever tell me you knew him!"

"I don't but I know a lot of his appointees."

"You do? How did that happen?"

"Pierre Salinger introduced me to some Nixon people when I met Mr. Salinger at the San Souci Restaurant when—you know. They eat there too, and we all got along great! I went back a number of times. We all just became good friends!"

"You never cease to amaze me, honey!"

"Why?"

"I just don't get it. Or maybe I do. There's a song, 'A Pretty Girl is Like a Melody.' You're their melody."

"They just think I'm smart!"

"You are! But I'm not an illiterate and I don't know anyone at the White House—not one person. Not ever. Never have known anyone at the White House and I've been around since F.D.R."

"Have you not even met one of the White House Ushers?"

"I didn't know they had ushers. With flashlights to find someone's seat?"

Anna shook her head. "No! I'll tell you when you get a little smarter!" And she winked as she took her usual very close-to-him position and gave him a loving and long kiss.

"Not bad! I'm smart enough to know that isn't bad."

"Thank you. I'll tell you something else—and this *is* bad—*real* bad."

"What?"

"They're going to get him. The President. They're going to get him. They have the script just like a shooting script at Warner Brothers. They're going to get the ones no one ever heard of first. Keep going up and up the ladder. After that, get Chapin then Haldeman and then the President and poof: it will work—and it will work because the people don't know what's coming off. It will be the new instruction book on how to get rid of a President. A new precedent and elected Presidents will become game for a cerebral assassination—not a killing—just a torturous fate for elected presidents by a circuitous road to a president's removal from office by the actions of a Special Prosecutor; a position started this year—but you can be sure, not to be ended this year."

"You're good, honey. You're really good—and where did you pick up that vocabulary?"

"My D.C. friends at the San Souci—and a Thezerus."

"Thesaurus."

"That's what I said. And all that's needed is a Special Prosecutor. That's how to start it. There isn't one thing that President Nixon or even his staff did that hasn't been done in previous administrations in my lifetime and even in your longer lifetime—very much longer than me. The only difference between the others and President Nixon is that no one ever thought of getting away with an unelected Special Prosecutor who would have more power than the President. You know the tapes?"

"I know *of* them."

"Everyone in the country has been led to believe he was the only president to record conversations with people who didn't know they were being recorded. Every President since your F.D.R. did that on a wire recorder. But not one former President is alive to tell that to the public and I believe they would all tell the public. But those who were on their staffs who *are alive* and who knew their president had a system of recording, won't reveal it to the people. President Johnson advised President Nixon to have a recording system like his installed for both legal and historical reasons. I think he was right. I'll bet you if any of those presidents were alive they would support him no matter their political party."

He nodded. "I don't doubt that at all. I just can't get too involved because it isn't my sphere and I can't do anything about it. What I can do something about is my craft, the world in which I live: space and its exploration. That's what I do. I so much admire how you think and I totally agree with every word but my mind is admittedly filled with things not around me but above me. That's all. It's inborn. I crave for the day when humans visit the planets and the whole solar system we live in and eventually to other solar systems and knocking down the barrier of distance and time so that some not too distant generation can be the first generation without those barriers. I concentrate mainly on whatever exists somewhere—every-where—in and beyond the sky."

"Oh, my heavens!"

"Is that not what you expected? Or are you disappointed?"

"No, no. Never. I didn't expect anything less—but I guess I didn't expect the way you put it. Tell me; you said you want to break down the barrier of distance and time. Can they be broken down? Haven't they been invented by God?"

"It sure wasn't anyone else. But God also invented Man. And hasn't He allowed and probably encouraged Man to invent all kinds of things to exceed what He initially created? I believe He will allow me to succeed and if He would rather I fail then I'll fail. I can take it. Maybe He will do it later without me."

"You sound like you are the one who went to Rome. Not me."

"Anna, in truth I never talk this way. I cool it—but you've probably rubbed off on me. Something inside of you came into light when you went to Rome, maybe, and ignited a beam into me that was broken off some time ago. You told me that life is like being a part of a giant orchestra and God is the conductor."

"I did? I said that?"

"You did."

"Did I put it that way?"

"Close. Yes. I don't know. Maybe you put it better; I don't

know. But you put it some way and maybe some time in the future He will allow me to stand on the pedestal at His podium and loan me His baton for one piece. Not long. Just one piece. That's all. That's good enough. I'll give His baton right back to Him as soon as the piece is done. Does that seem right? Does that seem possible?"

She gave a short assuring nod above her now trembling lips. "Not just possible, Christopher Straw! Do it! Just do it!"

THEME THIRTY-FOUR

THE SECOND TIME SINCE JESUS

CHRIST: A NEW MILLENNIUM

FOR MUCH OF THE WORLD, every thousand years there is a celebration of a new millennium. Admittedly there was only one anniversary of a new millennium before this one, but even with such little precedent its celebration was not exactly as expected for an anniversary of the beginning of Christianity. This one was widely known as Y2K. That's because there was such concern over what computers planned on doing when they had been so used to a change in year meaning only advancing the last two digits of the new year, never mind the change of a century or, of all things, a new millennium and identify it in digital language.

There were some—admittedly not many—who wondered if the last time this happened on January the First of the Year 1,000 (One Thousand) the change of millennium was called Y1K. Nor was there any discovered evidence of any earlier people using the designation of Y1 for the entrance of the very first year of all time. If there was any such evidence it has been lost.

This year the fast-living people of the coming new century wanted the designation to save time by making it one syllable shorter than having to say "Year Two Thousand." Instead they would use the initials of Y2K whose shorthand name gave a more digital presence in recognition of modern times. That one syllable that was tossed out must have saved an immeasurable amount of moments—perhaps millions of such moments—for painting pictures or writing poetry or creating sculptures or for quick tap-dancing or blinking.

There were any number of theories predicting what would happen at the dreaded midnight when computers would start messing up records of daily logs to diaries, to purchases, to tax records, to perhaps some computers ending their own lack of self-confidence by exploding in desperation.

What happened was totally unexpected: somehow most computers knew exactly what to do by simply ignoring the first two digits of the new year altogether just the way they always did while using the last two digits of the new year all the way from January the First. There were some reported difficulties but not many and not beyond fixing and certainly not worth the horror that was expected worldwide.

During the arrival of the year 2000 there was little more than a computer's yawn.

Nothing to do with Y2K but along with the new century's events of what was predictable as well as some surprises, it did not take long to bring about a day that was to be known as an important date in the biography of life on earth with that date being filled with both the torment of hell performed by human's evil, and the heroism performed by human Gods and Goddesses.

THEME THIRTY-FIVE

"LET'S ROLL"

RAJ HAD BEEN STAYING in his New York office for over three successive nights in September of 2001 and now his fourth day, all since Tuesday, with continued standing and pacing and standing again and again by its southern-most window overlooking what was now known as Ground Zero of 9-11.

It started moments after 8:46 A.M. of Tuesday, September the 11th when he was writing a radio commentary about the L.A. Dodgers when his secretary, Mrs. Rhonda Erickson, shouted into his intercom box to turn on his television set. "Any channel, I think! I think it's on everything! An airplane crashed into the North Tower of the World Trade Center! Maybe you can even see it through your window!"

"Come in! Come in!" Raj shouted back. "Get it for me!"

As she fiddled with the television he said to her, "The same thing happened years ago to the Empire State Building. I read about it. This is probably another accident like that one when that small plane crashed into the Empire State Building."

She didn't answer. It wasn't worth answering. The image

of the World Trade Center's North Tower came on the screen with smoke pouring from upper stories and there was no question that this was not like what had happened to the Empire State Building years back.

At 9:03 A.M. there came another airliner, this one crashing into the South Tower of the World Trade Center. "Oh, My God!" Mrs. Erickson almost screamed. "Another plane! Oh, my God! This is no accident! This is something else! These are airlines! This is what the pilots want! This is intentional!"

Raj was silent. The realization of the grim unthinkable importance was coming to both of them and to all of New York and to the entire United States and to most of the world. It was as though there was a contagion of disbelief and fear from the recognition of the horror that had happened and dread of what might happen next.

On the lower New York streets people ran away from the scene as they were covered with soot and some were screaming and people from within the two buildings ran down stairs if they could while there were those who jumped out of windows, their lives ending on the streets below.

Both of the two towers collapsed.

At 9:37 A.M. a third airliner crashed; this one into the west side of the Pentagon Building in Virginia.

At 10:03 A.M. a fourth airliner, UAL Flight 93, that veered off course from its intended target of hitting Washington, D.C. but it crashed into a desolate and unoccupied field in Somerset County of Shanksville, Pennsylvania, with its passengers having rescued the targeted objective of either the United States Capitol Building or the White House from the destruction of the hijackers.

9-11 ended with casualties greater than Pearl Harbor of some sixty years ago.

All those four flights of 9-11 had been hijacked by al Qaeda Islamist terrorists hosted and supported by the Taliban Government of Afghanistan.

On this year's 9-11 President George W. Bush had said in a speech to the nation, "Today our nation saw evil; the very worst of human nature and we responded with the best of America; with the daring of our Rescue Workers, with the caring for strangers and neighbors...Tonight I ask for your prayers for all those who grieve, for the children whose worlds have been shattered, for all those whose sense of safety and security has been threatened...And I pray they will be comforted by a power greater than any of us, spoken through the ages in Pslam 23: 'Even though I walk through the valley of the shadow of death, I fear no evil, for You are with me.'

"America has stood down enemies before, and we will do so this time. None of us will ever forget this day, yet we go forward to defend freedom and all that is good and just in our world. Thank You. Good night and God Bless America."

And so, like an FDR echo, this was a day of infamy.

Then on Friday, September the 14th, the third day since the recent hell started, the President stood amidst Rescue Workers and piles of smoldering rubble on Ground Zero and with his left arm around the shoulder of a Rescue Worker and his right arm holding a bullhorn, the President said: "Thank you all. I want you all to know—" and some man yelled from the crowd that he couldn't hear the President.

President Bush answered that it (meaning the bullhorn) "can't go any louder. I want you all to know that America today, America today is on bended knee, in prayer for the people whose lives were lost here; for the workers who work here; for the families who mourn. The nation stands with the good people of New York City and New Jersey and Connecticut as we mourn the loss of thousands of our citizens."

Again, a Rescue Worker shouting: "I can't *hear* you!"

President Bush answered, "I can hear *you*! I can hear *you*! The rest of the *world* hears you! And the people—and the *people* who knocked these buildings *down* will hear *all* of us *soon*!"

The Rescue workers started chanting: "*U.S.A.! U.S.A.! U.S.A.! U.S.A.! U.S.A.! U.S.A.! U.S.A.! U.S.A.!*"

President Bush responded: The nation—The nation sends its love and compassion—"

A Rescue Worker interrupted with: "God Bless America!"

President Bush continued, "—to everybody who is here. Thank you for your hard work. Thank you for making the nation proud, and may God bless America!"

Again there was the chant of Rescue Workers: "*U.S.A.! U.S.A.! U.S.A.! U.S.A.! U.S.A.! U.S.A.! U.S.A.! U.S.A.!*"

On Friday Mrs. Rhonda Erickson was becoming scared that her boss, Raj Bahvnani was in psychological ruin. "I'm sorry," he said to her. "I'm sorry I said anything bad about the architecture of those two towers. They were the most beautiful towers I ever saw. I apologize, Eric."

To her relief a message came that she believed might be a

comfort to hear. "Mr. Christopher Straw is on Number Three. Do you want his call?"

Raj grabbed the phone. "Get him on, Eric! Get him on!"

The voice of Chris said, "Raj? Raj Bhavnani?"

"Yes, yes! Christopher Straw?"

"Are you okay, Raj? That's all I want to know. Are you okay?"

"Thank you for caring. No, no one is okay. But I am not physically hurt. I was not down there. But no one is okay. Our hearts; our souls are all critically hurt. Everyone. Can't shake it."

"I understand."

Raj asked, "Where are you?"

"I'm home. San Diego. You're alright then?"

"Do you know that it smells in here? At this distance from where the Towers were downtown, this midtown office without open windows and after three days it still smells of the fire and smoke and ruin and death and all that and it doesn't go away. I'm not sure it will go away—ever."

"It will go away."

"No. There are some things that never go away. Did you hear what the passengers did on that Flight—UAL Flight 93? Some passenger said to fellow passengers, 'Let's roll'! Can you imagine? And they all agreed and they all knew they would crash into somewhere a—crash and be killed so as to avoid the Islamist terrorists crashing into the lives of our government in D.C."

"Todd Beamer."

"What?"

"Todd Beamer. He's the man that said, 'Are you ready? Okay—Let's roll.' And there were all those passengers in that airliner whose lives were lost insuring that the target of the murderers would be denied. The actions of those passengers were meant to save the leadership and shrines of our nation. And they did save them. The idols of 9-11 proved the United States really *is* the home of the brave, not just a lyric. And there are new stories told of other American heroes, too. You probably heard of them: the fire fighters running in when others were running out—and then after Tuesday was done there were others on Wednesday and yesterday and today by the Armed Forces and those in intelligence agencies. Absolute heroes emerged from absolute anonymity. They have become idols with good reason. They went to fight the fires and police the towers, knowing they could lose their lives— lose their lives in their attempt to rescue strangers. And many did. That's the ultimate morality—risking life to rescue a stranger."

"Chris?"

"Yes?"

"It's like everything lives in the shadow of what happened last Tuesday. There is nothing else. Do you know what I mean?"

"Yes."

"I have a window view and I can see—I can see that hor- rible vacancy. That's what's there. And still the smoldering. And everything that happened before 9-11 was like a different and better life—the way I saw it before Tuesday. And I want to confess—I had been privately—I was critical of the World Trade Towers. I was. I was. I thought—and even said that the World Trade Towers were terrible examples of architecture. But since Tuesday, when I saw and know what happened, those two towers were magnificent; like religious shrines. I miss them beyond any of my words can express. If I could exchange my entire bank account and things—things—possessions—to bring them back into view, I would do so in an instant. In an instant. No—that is not enough. My entire fortune is irrelevant compared to those towers. Although only one person, Eric; Mrs. Erickson heard my criticism of the towers, that criticism was petty; so petty. I apologized to Mrs. Erickson after all this. But in addition to being critical of the towers to Eric, I heard myself criticizing the towers too, and that hurts indelibly."

"Raj, don't do that to yourself. Enough hurting yourself. The terrorists have done it to us. We didn't do it to ourselves. But we have to live with it. This is a world war. It's another world war. It has to be. World War Four."

"Three."

Chris didn't say anything. Nor did Raj. Neither one surely didn't want to argue numbers of wars. Since the silence went on too long Chris offered, "Raj, we are going to win this war. Come and visit Savannah and me when you can."

There was silence.

"Raj, will you do that?"

"Do you mean it?"

"I mean it."

"That would be such a contrast. That would be so good."

"The Bahia Hotel in Mission Beach; part of San Diego. That's where we live. When you get tired of Washington, D.C. and New York just let me know when you'll be able to come out."

"You're kind. I'll be there. I'll let you know and I'll be there sooner than you think. I'll do it when I can get myself together. It gives me another reason to get myself together."

"Raj, in the meantime please do me a favor. Close the blinds or shades or whatever can cover that window. Close them and leave them closed."

"I will."

"Don't look at the vacancy anymore. There's nothing to see."

THEME THIRTY-SIX

ON SHELTER ISLAND

IT IS CUSTOMARY TO THINK that old age comes slowly; one symptom after another with wide spaces between those indicators of time-passage to body and maybe to mind. But there should be little surprise to some if it comes not slowly, but with something that makes the changes come almost all at once, like snapping the fingers. Somehow, the push of one millennium off the calendar substituted by a new unlived millennium caused many to be pushed into the category of the quick-aged for no better or worse reason than that a huge chunk of time-designation had passed with a new entance in its place. Not even two years after the year 2000 started, 9-11 changed the belief that this new millennium was going to be better than the previous one. In addition, other than personal joys and tragedies, the old date of the Kennedy assassination marking a world-known change of time seemed to have faded with the age of generations and the date of November the 22nd changing into more and more of a regular date to the young and then as that generation grew older, to some there came September the 11th taking precedence as the new memorized date.

As was true for all generations, those who had been national leaders or entertainers or tremendously wealthy found they were not exempt from the aging process, with the only thing different for them from others was that they were foolishly surprised that just like other people, they too were immersed by the duties and doctor-visits that older age demanded, or from the things that brought its once-heard-of-displeasures into reality.

Christopher Straw and Anna Lane and Raj Bhavnani were to different degrees, of course, creatures of the 20ᵗʰ Century, appearing by the new kids on the block to be relics of those older folk who probably remember dinosaurs roaming the planet and maybe have some dinosaur-skins hanging in their trophy rooms.

To other diners, it was a unique threesome at diner at the Bali Hai Restaurant on San Diego's Shelter Island where Raj Bhavnani conceded to an unmentioned fact noticed by his hosts: "I have aged into being older than before. Everyone ages but I'm afraid I am too rapidly ageing into an old man. I have a cane. See?" And he lifted the cane he had hidden by his side of the table.

Savannah immediately asked him, "How long will you need to have it? I mean can you still dance?"

"Dance!? I can barely walk."

"Will that last?"

"It's just for a while. Maybe a couple weeks. I fell. Maybe I'll need this cane for another two weeks or so. Maybe more. I'm okay. I really am. I named it, you know. I named it."

"Named what?" Chris didn't know what he meant.

"The cane."

"Oh. You named the cane? What's its name?"

"I named it 'Citizen.' Citizen Cane. I think they're going to make a movie about it."

Chris and Anna exchanged smiles and nods. "He's the same, honey," Anna said. "And you, Raj, are you really okay?"

"Fine, fine. Good, good. And you, Christopher Straw, has aged only one year for ten years of mine. While you, Savannah, you avoided it altogether as I suppose you found and drank from the Fountain of Youth in Rome. Was it in Rome? If so, I missed it."

Anna smiled, "Ponce de Leon is said to have found that fountain somewhere on Florida's east coast as 'fah nowth' as Jacksonville—but probably right *below* Jacksonville in Saint Augustine and maybe it was as 'fah' south as Port Saint Lucie."

Raj nodded. "I knew you'd know! That's where it is! You drank from it! I knew it!"

Chris nodded. "She's right; it's Florida," and he nodded at Anna. "But that's a lot of territory you just outlined, honey, and some years back I knew it was supposed to be in Florida but I thought the Fountain of Youth was in the Cape: Cape Canaveral. That's because I was told it was there and someone I trusted pointed to what appeared to be a natural small falls there so I drank from it and it didn't do me one bit of good and it tasted funny. I think it made me older. It sure made me sick for a while."

"Do you still go down there?" Raj asked. "Do you still go back and forth to Cape Canaveral for space launches?"

Chris shook his head. "No. I kicked myself out before the government would retire me from NASA. They staged a tribute to me. Filled with my friends. But sometimes tributes aren't as good as the name 'tribute' implies. I know that all too often they are like a thoughtful, kind, caring and sympathetic firing squad. Your working years have become an organizational liability."

"Well said," Raj nodded. "So what are you doing? No more going to the moon?"

"Lately private-enterprise is getting into space exploration and maybe I'll try to be working with one of them—one in the private sector of space so that I won't leave the field and I won't let space exploration leave me. I'll see if that works out. At least for my well-being." He then looked down, pretending to be interested in the menu, and he turned to Raj with a forced smile. "Now, how about you, Raj? The governments of India and the U.S. leaving you be?"

"Same things."

"Still comfortable in the Old Post Office Building in D.C. and going back and forth to New York?"

"Yes on D.C. No on New York. I took your advice and never looked through that window again—the window that overlooks the south end of Manhattan. I told the powers behind my work that I wanted to stay in D.C. and maybe some trips to India. I miss India. No more New York. They agreed. They understood. That window in New York was too much of a reminder of what it once framed in glass. In retrospect, it used to be a glorious view I never appreciated."

Chris nodded. "Good that you'll be doing what you want. You're going to stay with the Voice of America and Air India Radio, then?"

"They're keeping me. It's just because of my voice. That's what the audience knows. Age hasn't changed my voice. It's the only thing about my physical presence that's just the way it used to be," and he laughed loudly.

"Raj," Anna said softly with a smile, "You look exactly as you always looked and you act the way you always acted—sassy and mean and frightening and ornery," and she couldn't help but laugh at her own remark.

"Thank you!" he said. "That's the nicest thing that anyone said about me in a long time!"

Savannah didn't fight that. "I think it's time that either Chris or I gave you a compliment! Raj, you do a wonderful radio broadcast!"

Raj said, "Radio has been kind to me. You know what they say about children? They say that children should be seen and not heard. I agree with that and I believe that those who have become old enough to be called elderly, by and large, should be content with themselves by being the opposite of children and be heard and not seen. So that makes radio wonderful for someone like me. I am thankful I haven't been on television. If I had been I would have been kicked out of work years ago."

"I doubt it," Anna said.

"I'm sure of it," Raj said. "Now for you—I'm sure that you're still working, Savanah. TV or movies?"

"I'm between pictures."

"Oh, oh!"

She shook her head. "It's a bad season for actresses over the age of 18. You know; it's like I have been cast in roles for 18 year olds for the last number of decades. So I need some scripts to read that have a good role for a motherly type and maybe I'll find one or someone will find one for me—a new script—a good one in 2002."

Chris changed the subject away from the individual and

away from the subject of age with Chris favoring the subject of the world. "Let me bring this dismal outpouring to a valid celebration. We have all weathered the storm—the biggest storm being what we lived through during September the 11th. In less than it took for even one month to pass—by October the 7th Bush—President Bush sent U.S. troops including our Special Forces to Afghanistan and along with us, our coalition of the Northern Alliance of Afghanistan and a number of allies— Afghanistan was ridded of the Taliban Government. Not bad. They ran away. They're out of their capital city; Kabul. They're hiding in caves. Isn't that worthy of a toast? No question; they're still around but they're out of territory."

The dinner table became three people nodding. Raj and Chris raised their wine glasses. Anna half-way raised her glass of orange juice and carefully transferred its contents into the empty wine glass that had rested near her plate. The three of them clinked their glasses and Chris softly said, "To our ultimate and total victory."

"Here! Here!" Raj said loudly. "Isn't that what you folks say? That's what the Brits always said in India! Here! Here!"

Anna nodded. "It's what we say not as often as the Brits, but we say it too. Here, here!"

When they finished with their wine and orange juice toasting, Christopher said, "Not even two years ago, in 1999 there was an event in D.C. It was a dinner with the event marking the end of the 20th Century hosted by a number of prominent speakers who were asked to give predictions of what lay ahead for the nation in the coming century. That was common practice in 1999 at a lot of events. Almost every magazine, every newspaper, in every public discussion there were those predicting what would happen in the century ahead. Ambassador Frank Shakespeare was there. You know who he is?"

Raj nodded. "Yes. Reagan appointed him to be Ambassador to the Vatican. I know who he is."

At the mention of the Vatican Anna perked up and paid avid attention.

Chris continued. "Ambassador Frank Shakespeare was asked what lay ahead. I'm paraphrasing but he shook his head and said, 'I have no prediction. I have no prediction because if the most brilliant minds in the world were gathered together in *1899* to predict what would happen in the coming *20ᵗʰ* Century, none of them would have predicted—not one—that in the century ahead the British Empire of some 62 colonies would be willingly reduced to nothing but a few islands, and the most powerful nation in the world would become the United States of America. And there would be three world wars, the third lasting over four decades stemming from communism during which the United States would land men on the moon.' And so Ambassador Frank Shakespeare said 'None of the 1899 speakers would have predicted correctly.' Ambassador Frank Shakespeare ended his speech, 'No. I will make no predictions.'"

Chris continued to Anna and Raj, "And now not even two years have passed in this century and I can safely say that Ambassador Shakespeare gave the most intelligent comment of all. None of those who gave predictions said a word about the coming horror of 9-11 or anything like it, and what will come from it, and there are still some 98 years to go in this century."

There was a long silence and then Raj said to Chris, "You called the war against communism World War Three again."

"That is attentive of you to notice, Raj. Yes. I did because it is misnamed the Cold War, a title given to it very early in its initial phases written between 1945 and 1947 prior to knowing what history of that war lay ahead in the forty-some years. It was named the 'Cold War' by the author, George Orwell and by an Advisor to U.S. Presidents, Bernard Baruch and by Walter Lippman who was a well-known newspaper columnist. As that war went on and on it was not very 'cold' for all those to be killed in it in military engagements: Europeans, Asians, Africans, South Americans, Central Americans, and North Americans including some 92,000 members of the U.S. military being killed through engagements in the Korean and the Vietnam theaters which were two major chapters in what was surely the Third World War. Add to that the 65 million Chinese estimated to have been killed by their own leader, Mao Tse-tung in the People's Republic of China and some estimated 60 million Russians by *their* own leader, Joseph Stalin of the Soviet Union. Not very cold for all those during decades of what is still mistakenly called the Cold War."

Savannah and Raj who knew him so well were impressed with Chris' emotional history that poured out of him. Not to be outdone, Raj made a major addition. "And another part of it was the Kashmir war waged against India by the People's Republic of China with its ally, Pakistan."

Chris nodded. "Good point."

"My friend," Raj said, "I see what you mean about this current war—this war against terrorists being World War IV."

Savannah nodded to Chris. "Honey, you're generally so quiet and that was rather unexpected."

Chris bit his lip and then offered, "I know. I am generally a lot more like Ashley Wilkes: a quiet cool guy."

"Who?" Raj asked.

Rather than giving the floor to Chris, movies were Savannah's education and partial career and she preferred to answer with "Ashley Wilkes was a fictional character in the book, *Gone with the Wind*, and then in the movie that character was played by Leslie Howard who you probably never heard of him, unless the movie played in India."

Raj nodded. "I saw it." Of course, as always it was still not easy to be able to tell if Raj was telling the truth or telling a lie because he was so well known as generally preferring to lie without any reason.

"Look," Chris was almost apologetic. "The reason I know all this business about the Cold War being World War Three is because Sputnik One was a baby in that war—the Soviet's baby and that was the first satellite made by any nation, and it was launched by the Soviet's ICBM as a booster, and so the whole space exploration pursuit became a large part of that war."

When his sentence was finished a middle-aged man came over to the table and stood there looking tremendously interested in those sitting there. It certainly appeared as though he wanted to meet either Savannah or Raj since both had been such well known figures. Not at all. His interest was Chris. "Professor Straw?"

Chris perked up his head and his interest. "Yes, sir. I'm not a full-blown professor. An adjunct professor. Not a real one."

"Doug Morrison here. You were my professor in the class of Summer '63! I enlisted into the Air Force because of you! I wanted to be a part of winning in Vietnam and at the same time get the experience to be able to become involved in space exploration! You did that for me!"

"My Heavens! Of course, Doug. Good to see you, Man!"

Savannah gave a wide smile. "God Speed, Christopher Straw and God Speed to you, Doug Morrison!"

Chris again had to do it: "You know who these two people are, Doug?"

The stranger squinted as he studied their faces. "No, Professor. I'm sorry M'am—and Sir! Should I know you?"

Chris nodded. "She's Savannah Lane—a movie star and a TV star and a Broadway star and he's Raj Bhavnani from India who is on radio world-wide and he is a world-famous dancer and soldier."

The man looked amazed. "That's wonderful! I'm sorry. Of course I knew right away who both of you are. Just wonderful! What a stroke of luck this is! I'm sorry I was so rude. I was so struck by my old Professor who influenced me as much as he did," and he looked from side to side and stopped his gaze at Raj. "You were that guy from India who became so big in this country" and he shifted his eyes from Raj to Savannah; "and you Miss Lane—television!" Then he looked directly at Chris again. "Professor, do you still work for NASA and Astronautics?"

Chris shook his head, "No. I hope to still be involved in space—the New Frontier as it was called when I joined the ranks. I'm not going to let them get rid of me from space exploration."

"Missiles, too? ICBM's? Defense? And the college? For S.D.S.U.?"

"No. The demonstrators; the Anti-Vietnam protestors kicked out a lot of courses from campus."

"That's our loss. I'm sorry. I'm sorry for so many things these days. Professor, I ask that about missiles and defense because I believe that 9-11 changed our country forever and the threat of jihadists will never go away."

"Doug, I'm not with you on that. We should never accept the belief that '9-11 has changed America forever.' It better not. If 9-11 changes our nation forever by Americans learning to live for all time with caution; with metal detectors at entrances and concrete blockades in front of buildings and the search of pockets and purses and being patted down and explosive sniffing dogs and other anti-terrorist measures, then we'll be living *with* terrorism rather than *defeating* it. Then the war will not have been won but at best, a status quo will have been accepted. To *win*, which is what we *have* to do—we mustn't change America forever. The next generation must feel invited into federal buildings—welcomed into them—not having to go through an anguish of entrance. The next generation should know the joy of travel by air, not an ordeal of airports. The next generation should have a future even better than our past, when the towers were still there. That, I believe, *has* to be our objective: not accepting temporary measures and rejecting permanent ones. It has to be permanent or our lust for liberty won't be permanent. It must be permanent."

Raj felt obliged to enter the conversation and asked Chris, "You think it will really happen? That we'll win—really win— win over the terrorists that we have today?"

"Yes. I do. And you will see that and so will I. We *will* see the day—we better see the day—when there will be a September 11 when school children will be in their classrooms, stumbling over the words 'Al Qaeda' and 'Islamic Jihad' and 'Hezbollah' and 'Hamas' and 'al Aqsa Martyrs Brigades' and "Boko Haram" and 'Al Shabaab' and the children will likely spell them wrong, and that's okay—that's just fine because those names won't have relevance for them. Just history. Just history that bores them because we will have long-since won, having attained total and absolute and unconditional victory. Let the kids be bored—please!"

"Brav-o!" someone yelled from a near-by table while all the others at near-by tables seemed to be silent as they, too, were listening in. "And I salute your guests, Savannah Lane and Raj Bhavanani! What a table to be near ours!"

There were smiles and "thank you's," but then there was someone else, a very young man at a more distant but still fairly near-by table directing a remark at Chris: "You're nuts, goof-ball!" He was with a very young woman who laughed.

Chris couldn't resist. "My friend," he said to that stranger who obviously was not a friend, "Listen to this: Just months ago, a movie actress made a television spot against our military intervention in Iraq and she looked at the camera—you know—she looked at the audience and asked, 'What did Saddam Hussein ever do to us?'"

"Good for her!" the young non-friend answered. "She's right!"

"Let me finish. Really? Do you think she has a valid point? If you and a number of your friends were walking on a night-street and saw some stranger being accosted, you would have three options, and which one would you take? You and your friends could try to save the victim. Or if you felt you didn't have the physical capabilities to enter the fight, you could call the police for help. Or you could take the actress' option—walk away and say 'What did the assailant ever do to us?' Good luck, my friend, if someone attacks your wife or mother or girlfriend—by anyone at all who has your philosophy."

There was another yell from the first person who had inter-
vened on the conversation. "Bravo again! You are right! And I
salute your guests for being with you! So Bravo tis-i-mo', Mr.
Straw!"

Raj looked confused and with a soft whisper so Chris would
not hear, he asked Savannah, "What does that mean?"

"Bravo tis-i-mo'?" she asked back in a whisper.

"Yes," he said continuing the whispering session.

"It means a lot of Bravos!" she nodded as she whispered.

Raj leaned toward Chris and ended the whispering session
entirely by talking noticeably loud, "Chris?"

"Yes, Raj."

"You have tis-i-mo'. You know what I mean?"

"I think I do."

"That is a Hindi expression meaning courage!" Raj lied as
normal.

"I know," Chris abnormally lied back.

Raj was turned on and said to Chris and Anna, "The three
of us have been made for the 20th Century. I am not pleased
with this new century and this new millennium in which we
find ourselves without our permission."

Anna nodded. "You won't find any argument here."

Raj couldn't stop. "I know what could have been a remedy:
Almost everyone now living does not know how to address a
century like this one because we are used to saying '19' before
any other numerals in the name of a century. It is not in our
nature to say '20.' Therefore I believe we should have done
the following when the year changed from 1999 to 2000: We
should have called the new year 1999-A. And then the next year,

which we so foolishly went along with most people by calling it 2001—we should have called it 1999-B. And so on. Yes, yes. It is what we should have done."

Both Chris and Anna were laughing and attempting to put on serious expressions. Anna said, "I think you have gone nuts, Mr. Bhavnani. Are you serious?"

"Yes, yes. I have gone nuts. You guessed right. What do you think, Chris?"

"What do we do when we get all the way to 1999-Z?" Chris asked. "*Then* do we go to 2000?"

"No! My entire plan is to retain the '19' preface to the number. After the year 1999-Z we go to 1999-Z2. Understand? We can now go on forever that way with 1999-Z3, then 4 then 5, and forever! None of the unborn ever need to learn anything other than that saying '19' when starting to talk about a year refers to either the last century or the current century or any next century—always. That's the end of my explanation. Now let's put this behind us and let's talk about kids and men and women and what the new millennium is doing to them. And it's not very good.

"The new generation has no bad words saved for an emergency. The kids use all the bad words during good times for any purpose at all. They should have saved some. They don't know what words they'll be missing when they really need them.

"In addition to the words used by the Millennials, there are the beliefs of the Millennium's young women. They have joined the ranks of popularity by demanding that men treat women with equality. And the Millennial women will continue to demand being treated with equality until they *are* treated with equality. The nation was so much better when they were treated with superiority."

Now there appeared to be a near-riot from a number of tables, some in total "booing" coming from those who did not find him funny and those who yelled "Bravo tis-i-mo'!" from those who supported him.

Anna laughed the loudest of all and she repeated "Bravo tis-i-mo'!"

The most argumentative of all close-by strangers yelled back, "You're all tis-ee-nuts, Goof-balls!" And he suddenly turned on his brand new i-Phone to something that sounded like garbage can lids being clanked.

He probably didn't recognize Anna's and Raj's once publically well-known talents, although that was a factor of no importance by that table of opposition. It was a factor of tremendous importance to Raj who was already figuring out what he could do about the scene that had developed. Of course calling the management would have been the right thing to do but that was not in Raj's quickly developing list of things that could be done. Instead of calling the management, he would *be* the management.

Raj, after all his thinking, had no hesitancy to become Raj. He stood up and walked to their table and talked in a threatening tone as he was freshly inspired by Chris' remarks to some of the restaurant's younger guests: "Hey, Dumbo's! Turn that noise off! I am Raj Bhavnani, born in India and now the owner of Shelter Island and frequent writer for the San Diego Union-Tribune and also Honorary Chief of Police of San Diego." It was an unusual combination of careers and talents and honors that he gathered in just a few seconds. "I am not going to try and get down to the level of your mold-caked feet. Instead, listen to me, Dumb-o's! Turn that deafening noise off! You idiots who don't care about nobility or romance, turn it off for good or I'll take it away and *throw* it out! And turn your mouths off while you're at it and get your corrupted brains out of here! You call that tin-banging clatter 'music'? Don't you know what a love song is? You ever heard one? You jerks have become a generation without a melody! Where are your composers? Where are your Gershwins and Kerns and Cole Porters and Richard Rogers that can compose? That's music! Don't call that junk that *you* play 'music'. It isn't. In fact, did any of what you call 'songs' have composers? And where's your singers; not screamers? Where's your Frank Sinatra and Perry Como and Frances Langford and Theresa Brewer? Can you sing that stuff you call 'music'? Whistle it? Hum it? I guess it doesn't take much to remember the lyrics. Were any of those who are writing words to songs think they're lyricists? Does any of that junk have lyricists at all? Or do those who call themselves lyricists just find two words that rhyme and repeat them enough times to drive any sane person crazy? That pile of smell has no resemblance to music from any culture or time around the world—least of all from America! Or India! You Fools! Now, knock it off or I'll phone Sergeant Big Bart Bigelow and ask him—no, not *ask* him but I'll *tell* him to come here and to arrest you and your rancid foul brains for disturbing the peace! Get it?"

There was applause and cheering from a number of tables and booing and hissing at other tables at the Bali Hai restaurant, with both sets of occupants having found themselves at an unexpected dinner-show featuring the not necessarily cool and calm Raj Bhavnani who was surprisingly accompanied with his supporting cast who at least were still known by some of the older diners as Christopher Straw and Savannah Lane.

THEME THIRTY-SEVEN

IN MUMBAI

THE LAST TIME RAJ WENT BACK to India he landed in Calcutta at Dum Dum Airport. Now, back again, he found the city's name was spelled Kolkata and pronounced that way and Dum Dum Airport was called Nataji Subhas Chandra Bose International Airport. Makes sense. Moreover, It used to be that from Dum Dum he would fly to Palam Ngurah Rai Airport in New Delhi but now the airport had been renamed Indira Gandhi International Airport and that was enough for Raj. He wouldn't want to set foot inside the terminal of Indira Gandhi International Airport but instead he would take a flight from Kolkata directly to Bombay which was now called Mumbai where he planned landing at Santacruz International Airport but it was now called Chhatrapati Shivaji International Airport. Of course.

Great name. Easy to remember. Nothing stays the same. Nothing at all.

Not even a particular woman could stay the same who had been standing in a long line of those who wanted to get into the plane that was boarding but now surrendered that place in line so as to greet Raj. "Raj Bhavnani!"

"Thank you!" Raj responded with some glee. When under ordinary circumstances he would have instinctively said, "Yes?" This time he was giving away his pleasure at still being recognized by, at least, someone.

"Raj! Do you remember me? I'm Margaret Merriman! It was in the early 1960's! Remember? My father worked at B.O.A.C. in Dehi!"

"Of course! Of course I remember! Margaret!" He had absolutely no idea what she was talking about so he improvised: "Margaret or as I sometimes called you, Marg or Peggy or—"

She interrupted, "You called me Margaret!"

"Yes! Yes! I remember."

"Raj, you look the same. I don't."

Suddenly it came back to him. This was the very pretty young woman he knew in 1962 after the war in Kashmir. She was still pretty no matter the added years in, of all times, the year 2008. It was November the 26th.

He asked, 'How is your father?"

She shook her head. "No. He passed in 1970." She quickly asked, "Where are you coming from? Where are you going?"

"I'm sorry about your father." He cleared his throat and answered her questions. "I'm coming from the U.S. and I'm going to the Taj—the Taj Hotel. I used to work there a million years ago," he said in attempt to give a thought of lightness.

Her expression changed to one of fear and realization that he didn't know what was going on in Mumbai. "No!" she said with her voice sounding hysterical. "No, you're not going there! You can't! Don't you know? Look around! This terminal is filled with people leaving Mumbai for good reason! Mumbai is being killed! We are at war in Mumbai and the hotel where you are planning on staying is one of those under heaviest attack!"

He didn't know of such news as he had slept the latter part of the journey from his previous stops in Rangoon, Burma and then Kolkata. "What happened?"

"Everything! Everything! Get in line with me and I'll tell you. So that you are safe you have to leave this city. Leave with me. I'm going to Delhi!"

The wait in the airport took hours with him standing in line with her while she told him in detail what she knew about the current horror or Mumbai: "It was somewhere around 9:30 tonight. It was the Lachkar-e-Taiba—they're all Islamist Jihadist terrorists and they attacked the Taj Mahal Palace Hotel—your hotel—and the Oberoi Trident Hotel, too, and there have been terrible explosions and fires and killings of guests and workers and all kinds of things happening at both places and Mumbai is very dangerous now. They seem to want to kill tourists; Brits, Americans, and of course Hindus staying in vacation. Please! We are at war! You must come with me to Delhi if this plane ever takes off! I'll tell you everything I know and that I've heard from others in this line!" And she said that someone told her there was an attack on the railroad terminal; Chhatrpati Shivaji Terminus. "A lot of fires and explosions!" she said. "The sky-line is horrible. More fires than lights! The streets are empty of people unless they are running. The stadiums are empty. The theaters are empty. The hotels are empty. The fires and explosions are many. People are hiding!"

He went with her to Delhi after receiving the promise of an airport worker that his baggage would be taken from luggage in Mumbai and put on the plane to Delhi. It was of little comfort when lives themselves rather than possessions were in such jeopardy.

Margaret Merriman's head was on his left shoulder the entire distance from Mumbai to Delhi and he remembered the aroma of her perfume from over forty years ago and he remembered her "Gawd! Oh, Gawd!" that she said anytime during their necking sessions those forty-some years ago. Not now. No "Oh,Gawd's."

Her apartment in Delhi was big and had many rooms. B.O.A.C. had apparently been good to her father or to her or to both of them. Raj was invited to stay there in a room she gave to him and would be his until he would know what he wanted to do. He said in the meantime all he wanted was chapatti; the bread-like food easily available in India but unavailable in most places of the world.

And what he wanted to do was written on the plane to Delhi while Martha's head was resting on his shoulder: Call the Hyatt Hotel headquarters to insure that Venu was alright and still working in Delhi and not back to Mumbai; to call the office of the Minister of Defence A.K. Antony to offer help to the Armed Services either in Delhi or back in Mumbai in any way he could as a former Lieutenant with an Honorable Discharge and in continued good standing.

Raj called Venu and although Venu was not in the Delhi office at the moment he was still working there; not back in Mumbai, and he would be given the message of Raj's number at Margaret's apartment.

Raj then placed a phone call to the office of Minister

of Defence A.K. Antony leaving Margaret's phone number. The secretary at Minister Antony's office knew all about Raj Bhavnani's history and seemed delighted for Raj's call. Within minutes Raj was called back. He was told that he should contact the Ashoka Hotel to be a guest of the government just as he was a guest of the government during the most recent time he was in Delhi. In addition, although his volunteerism to serve again in uniform was much appreciated, he was told there was nothing he could do in the Indian Armed Forces at this time. That message did not miss Raj's understanding that "at this time" probably meant because of his age. He was also told that the proper radio transmission and playback equipment would be installed in his room at the Ashoka from which his radio programs for All India Radio and the Voice of America would be handled. Moreover, he was given a news report that the main entrance and the dome of the Taj Mahal Palace Hotel had been detonated and so was the pool area and many guests and hotel staff were killed with the terrorists going from one guest-room to another of both the Taj and the Oberoi Trident.

Raj had known that Minister Antony, although not a member of the the Bharatiya Janata Party favored by Raj, was a unique member of the Indian National Congress Party who bravely and happily for Raj, had been in opposition to Madame Indira Gandhi.

When Raj told Margaret that he will be staying at the Ashoka and he would be broadcasting from there, she was not glad. She wanted him and all of that broadcasting ability to be located in *her* apartment. He shook his head saying he would like that too, but this was what the government wanted him to do.

"Will I still see you, Raj?"

"Of course. I have to be grateful to the military for all they are doing, putting me up there again, giving me the material for radio transmission and I am so grateful to you because you rescued me from Mumbai and made some marvelous food for me as well as just being you. I am so grateful to you—" and he stumbled over her name and that set her laughing.

"Margaret," she re-informed him.

"Margaret" he repeated. "And I know you are glad you will have your privacy back in this majestic apartment building."

She gave a wide smile accenting her femininity. "Oh, no!" she said almost as she used to say, "Oh, Gawd!"

THEME THIRTY-EIGHT
EMPTY STADIUMS

ONCE BACK AT THE ASHOKA Raj received a call-back message first received on Margaret's phone from Venu Ramachandra with that message transferred to Raj at the Ashoka. Venu's message told Raj he was safe and in Delhi and would work out a meeting with him. Raj also received another call from the Minister of Defence's Office giving him a report that he should know that Nariman House; a Jewish synagogue had been attacked in Mumbai with many killed and the building torn apart.

Then Raj became involved in a new kind of life that he never had before. He became a recluse. Other than his radio broadcasts that were done by radio and telephone lines in which he saw no one, he had nothing scheduled. He did not want to see anyone other than Venu but even for that Raj had no desire to travel anywhere; not even to Venu's office at the Hyatt headquarters, leaving Venu to say that he would come to see Raj in one of the Ashoka's dining rooms for a lunch soon and he would let him know when. There, too, were periodic and, in this case, welcome interferences of Raj's isolation with telephone-calls from the Office of the Defence Minister. Best of all was the report from the Defence Minister's Office on Saturday, November the 29th that the Mumbai attacks were done and most of the Lachkar-e-Taiba Moslem terrorists had been captured. Both All India Radio and Voice of America asked him to make a commentary for both Air India Radio and Voice of America highlighting excerpts from the speech of U.S. President George W. Bush that was given that Saturday:

"We pledge the full support of the United States as India investigates these attacks, brings the guilty to justice, and sustained its democratic way of life...On Thursday morning I spoke to Prime Minister Singh...Throughout the process we have kept President-Elect Obama informed...The killers who struck this week are brutal and violent but terror will not have the final word. People of India are resilient. People of India are strong. They have built a vibrant, multiethnic democracy that can withstand this trial...The leaders of India know that nations around the world support them in the face of this assault on human dignity. And as the people of the world's largest democracy recover from these attacks, they can count on the world's oldest democracy to stand by their side...May God bless the people of India."

Just as Raj had insured, other than calls from Venu and government offices, no one called Raj or saw him before Tuesday, December the 16th that was finally when both Raj and Venu agreed to meet for their lunch at the Ashoka's main luncheon dining room. For the remainder of the days leading up to that meeting, Raj's calendar was intentionally still kept clean and empty even intermittently going on and off radio. In a sense he wanted his calendar stuffed with important decisions made by him. But in no sense at all, he *did* want his calendar *kept* clean and empty and he couldn't figure out why he willingly *retained* its emptiness without current or future appointments or notations.

At last came the turn of the calendar page to December the 16th in the main luncheon dining room of the Ashoka Hotel with its prescribed involvement with civilization. He met the challenge well as though there had been no period of acting so factually as a hermit.

"Venu!"

"Lieutenant!"

"Oh no, Sa'ab. Haven't you heard? That rank has been taken away from me by the Military."

"What!?"

"Sorry, Sa-ab! There is no need to call me Lieutenant anymore. I know you liked doing that and I liked hearing it. But the Military has the right to take away those things they had given. The Military has that right."

There was a short silence and then Venu shook his head and made a correction of Raj's statement by saying, "The Military doesn't have that right. The Military has that wrong!"

"Well, that's kind of you. But I'm not concerned. What they did is fine." Raj then dug in his inside jacket pocket. "Here. Take a look at what they gave me in return," and he took three of the Military service's five-pointed stars that were vertically assembled on cloth as symbols to be sewed onto the shoulders of a uniform. "These are for Captains. If you want, you may now call me 'Captain.'"

Venu shook his head slowly as a wide smile emerged on his face. "At first you had to make me believe something that was not true and that would infuriate me. You couldn't just say that the Military gave you a promotion. That's what happened. You had to say they took away your rank of Lieutenant."

"The Military gave me a promotion."

"Why not just tell me that right off? Oh, God!"

"No. They cannot promote me to a God but maybe—I don't know—maybe in the future."

Venu nodded. "Not maybe. They will for you. Just give them enough time."

"Time," Raj repeated the word. "That's what is important these days. I hate to sound morbid, Venu, but I concern myself with the matter of time a great deal lately because I don't know how much of it is left on earth for me."

"No one knows how much time is left for anyone."

"I don't mean just time before death. I mean the possible time of old age with its likely reward being survival itself and guessing and knowing what survival could entail; possibly not much *more* than survival. That could be a difficult course, couldn't it?"

"Enjoy it, my friend. It's life. The only alternative is to be frightened by the prospect of having little more than survival. Is that what you want to do? Fear? Don't."

"I'm with you, Venu. You are the smartest man I know. It's what I told you before. You remind me of Gandhi—Mahatma Gandhi."

"But it's you who says you philosophize. You say that you are a philosopher."

"I am. But I have run out of philosophizing."

"No, you haven't. You have one great, mammoth, tremendously large asset that creates your philosophizing."

"What is it?"

"The gift of thinking. You reserve time for it, don't you?"

"Yes. About two hours a day. I have done that for years now. Did I tell you that?"

"You didn't have to. I can always tell the few people who reserve time to think. They are different. You are different. And you have time to take on fear and clobber it. Don't run from it. Clobber it. Take it on. Turn away your fears by grabbing their ears and turning them upside down and clobbering your fears until *they* are frightened by *you*. They'll run away. Once that starts you won't have to keep clobbering them because they will be far over the horizon and scared to return."

"I know that you are right but it isn't just that. Other than you, today, I see no one now. I don't want to. I want to stay alone."

"Why?"

"Because I used to see everyone and that was because it seemed that everyone wanted to see me. Now no one wants to see me. If I went outside it would be like a soccer player or a baseball player going to a stadium to play in a game but the team isn't there and the fans aren't there. The stadium is empty except for him. No. I don't want to be in an empty stadium. That would be terrible. So these days I don't go outside."

"I'm glad you told me. Let's go, Raj. Let's go outside. Remember that medal that you received and the other honors and reception given for you at the Trivedi Club after you returned from the war up north?"

"Yes, of course. I have them all. I'll' never forget."

"Let's go to the Trevedi Club. And say that you have come by their place again because you are back in Delhi and you can't help but go there to tell how much their kindness has meant to you and to the U.S. Government and you just want to thank them again for what they mean. No one does that years later. You do it. And from there we will go to the U.S. Embassy and thank them for all they have done for you, including your position with the Voice of America for all these years. Thank everyone; anyone. I'll go with you as *your* Lieutenant since you aren't one anymore." Then, with a nod and smile he added, "You spoiled Captains are all the same in that you always need someone to make sure you are taken care of at all moments. It's time I was lackey for a Captain. I know when God gives me an assignment."

Raj just stared at his friend and allowed the silence to be his instant speaker.

Venu filled the gap: "And tomorrow, rather than spending the day alone and feeling sorry for yourself, go out and grab your world importance back and this is how you do it: Go talk to your producers at All India Radio and Voice of America in person or if you have to, by phone to the Voice of America in D.C., but do it, and tell them you are feeling much better and you want to get back to work. Do this, Raj. And thank the Ashoka or whoever is the decision maker on your accommodations and equipment for radio transmission. And most important of all, Captain—most important of all—hold on to what you can grasp. Recognize that you have a great reputation built in the past and you have a great podium for your future. If you feel you need a vacation first, then ask for one—but no longer than two weeks."

And then in a more formal tone he added, "Captain Bhavnani,

your podium is the power of radio: Air India Radio and Voice of America. Use your podium. You speak to millions. You can't see them but they can hear you. That is power. Years back I told you that leaders associate with leaders. I still believe that but let me add to remember that leaders also associate with the people—the average persons of their times—and, with hope, if they are right, those leaders have influence even *after* their times."

"Venu-ji, I will do everything you just said. Everything, everything. I am so grateful for your wisdom, Venu-ji. It is part of you. My wisdom is simpler. I wish it were deeper than I may sound to someone like you but mine is that, as Popeye always said, and I paraphrase for you, Venu-ji 'I yam what I yam and that's all I yam, I'm Raj Bhavnani, India's man.' But Venu-ji, I do feel I need a vacation."

"Alright," he said with some dismissal as well as a smile. "Take a week or two and rest and then then go back on the air, my friend, and talk to your constituents."

After a while Raj cleared his throat and extended his hand and said, "You are the definition of a friend, Venu. You always have been. You even allowed me to go to New York City and arranged my free room at the Algonquin and you knew—you knew I would never go to Rochester to be in Cornell University's Hotel Administration School or whatever it was. Yes, I will go to the Trivedi Club and to the American Embassy with you. And I will go back on the air after no more than a two-week vacation. Thank you. Thank you, Venu-ji. And thank you, Mahatma Gandhi-ji for giving me Venu-ji as an eternal friend who is real."

"Get on the air, my friend, and when we get back from the Trevedi Club and the Embassy, you can start preparing for those coming talks to and for the millions of those who appreciate you."

THEME THIRTY-NINE

ON AIR

IN THEIR SUITE AT THE BAHIA, Anna turned the television to mute. That caused Chris to look up from a wrapped package he had received in the mail. He knew it was a book he requested from NASA about its projected future events. The wrapping of the package was so heavily double-taped that he was having difficulty opening it while he balanced it on his lap. He was at one end of their couch and she was at the other end with her feet on his lap. Chris looked over at Anna and in a disgruntled voice said, "I used to be able to open packages like these with my bare hands. Now I always have to use a scissors because they wrap things with a different kind of tape. You can't rip it—or anything. You can't open things anymore without a pair of scissors or some other device or something. I bought a Snickers candy-bar yesterday and I couldn't even open that without using my teeth. By the time I bit into it I didn't even want it anymore."

Anna was not overridden with interest in his observations of modern times. She looked over at him from her comfortable position on their couch and said, "Huh!" and that response was most likely to be her unabridged thought on the crisis of new packaging techniques over which Chris had no control.

Nodding at the muted television set Chris said, "What's up, honey? I thought you were listening to that. Wasn't that the show you like with all the women talking at the same time?"

"Yes, but then you started talking," she said in attempted explanation beyond any solid reporting of what had happened. No matter as she rushed to a change in subject to something that was on her mind: "Honey, I have a premonition."

"Oh? A premonition? What is it? Is it about that show or my package?"

"Neither."

"What is it?"

"It's about Raj. Have you heard from him lately?"

"No. I haven't but I think he's still in India. Why?"

"I don't think we will ever see him again."

At that Chris closed his eyes and slowly opened them with his lips tight together. "Anna, he's not a member of the family. He can do what he wants and he doesn't have to let us know those things that are his business. He's in India."

"You're right. But I'm bothered. At times he just disappears and sometimes I am relieved by his disappearances but lately he's been a friend to both of us and honorable to both of us— even to me—and I got to thinking that now he seemed like something was wrong—deeply wrong."

"Really? I didn't catch that. Raj seemed normal for being Raj."

"It was because he wasn't his usual happy self. As much as I could get disturbed by him, his happiness was always welcome and fun. He makes you laugh, doesn't he?"

"Or cry." And then the non-jealous Christopher Straw practiced his trait of never exhibiting public jealousy. "Then I'll call Voice of America and find out if he's okay."

"Really? When?"

"Right now."

"Do that, Chris. I want to get this off my mind. Do you know where he's staying in India? Could he have gotten in trouble there?"

"I don't know where he's staying. And I'm sure he's in trouble. He always is. If he isn't, then he's really in *deep* trouble." He picked up the phone and dialed NASA in D.C. and whoever he talked to at NASA gave him the phone number of the Voice of America. He then dialed it and it was a very brief call because the operator at Voice of America was a robot. "Your phone call is important to us and will be answered in the order of calls received." Then there was a piece of music and, with relief it was interrupted by a live woman human being. She said, "Good Afternoon; Voice of America." He asked if Raj was there. She had no difficulty at all in telling him that "we don't give information on our hosts or other talent but I *can* tell you that he has no scheduled return to the Voice at the *moment*. Call us back at any time."

He hung up and told Anna what the operator said to him. Anna nodded slowly as if to say, "I *told* you."

"Anna, are you fond of him? What's your interest?"

"No! I'm not fond of him in the way it sounds to you. Are you finally jealous or something?"

"No. I'm not jealous at all. I'm just asking because, unlike you, you're the one who's asking."

"Chris, he has come in and out of our lives back and forth

and he's given me some problems but he always accepted the slightest shake of my head. He accepts that I *like* him but that I *love you* and I do appreciate that he doesn't insist on anything at all and that he has an inborn courtesy. Maybe that's an Indian characteristic; I don't know, but he has manners. He never puts me on the defensive."

"Well, who does? Do I ever put you on the defensive, Anna?"

"Never. Never in all these years except for just now!" And she smiled and quickly added, "No! You don't!"

"I'll call the Embassy of India in D.C. Let's tackle this strange premonition of yours right now. Let's find out if he's alright so you can be sure you don't need to have premonitions of something terrible." He picked up the phone's receiver again and repeated, "Let's tackle it."

It was not tackled since he did not find out as the Public Affairs Officer at the Embassy of India told him that, "at least for the present, Raj Bhavnani is not doing his usual radio broadcasts" and "we have had a lot of calls of those listeners who are trying to find out if Captain Bhavnani will be back on air. As of now, we don't know. You might call us back as time goes on and see if we know more. We can call you if you prefer, Mister Straw, as long as you leave a number." Chris gave an unseen nod and gave the Public Affairs Officer the telephone number of the Bahia.

The weather in Delhi was marvelous as most winters are generally the most comfortable of seasons there, and Raj Bhavnani was back to what had become his longtime habit of doing nothing. Raj was going back to radio as both stations agreed to revive the schedule he once held. The great difficulty was that Raj had little to talk about when his radio schedule was to begin. He didn't know much of anything that was going on in the world around him and that included his absolutely total blank of political events in both the United States and India. In fact, he didn't even know who had run for President of the United States. He knew so little about what was going on in world events that he knew he had no business to host a talk-show anywhere. He decided to put on radio those philosophizing subjects that were simply on his mind while being aware that some may think he had gone berserk and he had his own recognition that he had brought on his own berserkness.

Finally, like an unlocked and opened door of a prison cell along with a few bars of "The William Tell Overture" being played by an invisible orchestra, the two weeks of vacation were done. He would start with "The Voice of America."

ANNOUNCER: "And coming in just one minute is Raj Bhavnani back from vacation! And if you want to phone in to talk with him and, as always if you also live in a place where you hear this program live rather than a recording, we will give you the phone numbers for your phone-in."

Then interrupting in Raj's earphones he heard the far-away director saying to him, "Ten seconds to 'Go', Raj! We are at—Ten—Nine—Eight—Seven—Six—Five—Four—Three—Two—One—'Go!'" It wasn't exactly a rocket going into liftoff, but it had its share of drama.

With inspiration still coming from listening to Chris during the Shelter Island evening, and later guidance from Venu, Raj had his subjects itemized. "This is Raj Bhavnani back with you after I have had a wonderful time on vacation!" For good luck he felt *obligated* to start off with a lie by saying he had a wonderful time on what he called his vacation as though it filled that requirement perfectly. "And I thank you all for being back at your radios, my friends. And I want to devote this session with you to thoughts that I believe are important—thoughts that are under the broad umbrella of what I call philosophizing.

"After thousands of years, there is the proposition that no longer should there be a word used to define a union solely between a man and a woman. The word 'marriage' is on the 'gallows for old words' to be exchanged for a union between persons. No substitute word has been proposed. The generation with that objective also believes in the acceptance of the smoking of marijuana with no smoking of cigarettes. Third, there has also started the adherence to cowardice and selfishness devoid of fighting for the liberty of others.

"Let's change the subject because I do not want to hear your hostile telephone calls. Let's turn to the topic of my current awareness; ageing. I have talked about political topics for many decades, and during that time I was often threatened by others. For those who have not had my occupation or do not currently share my age, it's not fun knowing that no one wants to kill me anymore.

"For any person, regardless of background or career, if you are getting older you will likely find that the trouble with talking with young Millennials is that everything they say makes you think of something else that you believe is amazingly fitting and appropriate for what the Millennials just said. But after you say your statement, you realize that what you said has nothing at all to do with what they said. They are mystified and there is nothing you can do about it.

"When told by a doctor to take a pill in the morning and also at night before going to bed, the new patient is inclined to accept that directive easily not realizing as little by little they will be given those directives for other medicines until the duties of medication at morning and night begin to expand and to merge with one another and in time the patient has little if any time for anything else. With enough of those directives, there is no clear space between the bookends guarding your time.

"To some, the phrase 'Merry Christmas' goes unsaid but I don't understand why. Just because it may not be part of a person's religion, can't a Merry Christmas be wished by anyone or everyone? What's the risk? January the First has nothing to do with one religion but that doesn't prevent anyone from wishing people a Happy New Year and no one seems to get angry at receiving that greeting. How about 'Happy Labor Day?' Let's get Labor Day stopped immediately unless the recipient of such a greeting is a proven laborer.

"Some warnings: Don't ever place any object where you do not normally place it—even for what you think will be for a moment. That moment can last beyond the day.

"What you say to others in these years may not any longer be tempered by thoughtful common sense as in earlier days. Common sense can too easily be traded for a new common stupidity where anger is king and queen.

"And don't ever retire if you can prevent it. Unless, of course, you enjoy absorbing yourself in the petty."

Through the earphones Raj heard the Director: "A News Alert, Raj. We have to interrupt your show. You remember—we always have to interrupt you for a live speech by the President of the United States. I turned off your mic and volumed up the reception of the President."

"Did you tell him I was on and he's going to get my audience angry by his interruption!?"

"Yeah, yeah, yeah. You're back alright! And in seriousness, it's good to have you back, Raj."

"Who's President?"

"Are you kidding me?"

"Yes, of course I'm kidding you! Thank you, Alex. I thought it might be Adams or Jefferson. I knew that Hoover didn't have a chance this time. Alex, it is so very good to be back! You know that I enjoy kidding you."

"I always enjoy your gags! I turned up your earphone volume, too, if you want to listen to the President."

"Of course I do."

"You should know that the entire switchboard is lit up to talk to you. All lights are red and blinking. It seems like you hit some subjects your listeners are aching to talk about."

"I'm glad we've been interrupted and I know that it's just the President helping me out so I don't have to answer those screaming listeners right now."

THEME FORTY

DANCING IN DARJEELING

CHRIS ANSWERED THE TELEPHONE and instead of saying his usual "hello" he gave a sudden and unexpected answer to the telephone's ring by saying what he used to say many, many years back when he was in the Armed Forces picking up a telephone receiver while sitting-in at headquarters—and it was even unexpected to hear *himself* say it again—"Christopher Straw here, Sir."

"Sir? I'm no sir, Mr. *Christopher Straw!*" a woman's voice said.

"Excuse me; Ma'm, I'm sorry. For some unknown reason I picked up the receiver without even thinking and I suppose the rewind button quickly found some old times in my brain."

"Well, I'm flattered!"

"Who's this?"

"A voice from your past! Does the name Nancy Benford mean anything to you?"

Chris said nothing until his brain reacted with a giant spurt, "My God! Nancy Benford! School! McConnellsburg!! Mrs. Zambroski's class! My God! How *are* you, Nancy?"

"Then you *do* remember me."

"How could I forget you? You hated me!"

"I did not!"

"You said so!"

"Oh, Christopher! I never hated you. In fact I had a terrible crush on you! My crush wasn't even destroyed when you put my pigtail in your inkwell! Remember?"

"I apologize. A little belatedly but I apologize. How the devil did you get my number?"

"A long and tedious procedure which started with Google."

"Who's that?"

"Google?"

"Yes. I don't know who he is."

"Where have you been!?"

"What do you mean?"

"Google is a search engine on the internet."

"Oh, I don't know those things. I worked in our space effort. I haven't talked about goo-goo in decades!"

"Oh, I know you work in our space effort. Google answered my query by telling me all about you being in NASA and they gave me your work number and from there I went through a procedure too long to go into now. But I found you tonight! Since finding out your number—finally—after dialing a lot of C. Straw's and names similar to that—I found you! And I couldn't help but phone you to finally find out if you are going to drive that green Chevrolet to get to the moon!"

"You *do* have a good memory—but it wasn't a green Chevrolet."

"It was too!"

"No, it wasn't. I ought to know."

"Then what was it if it wasn't a green Chevrolet?"

"It was a yellow Plymouth. That's what I wanted to drive to the moon, and that's what I told Mrs. Zambroski and you laughed!"

"I'm sorry I laughed at you in class but it was a green Chevrolet! And you are still as stubborn as you were when we were in school. Now can you see why I hated you?"

"You just said you didn't hate me! Women have memories that drive me nuts! They get everything all mixed up from the way they were when they happened."

"Christopher Straw! And, of all things, you did pretty well—you married Savannah Lane, didn't you?"

"Not really married but—it works between us—it's everything *but* marriage."

"I better not comment on that as I'm on my third."

"Third what? Goo-goo?"

"Two divorces is what I mean. I'm now married again and this one is number three and it's forever."

"Well, what do I say, congratulations three times?"

"You are really terrible. I'll bet if I saw you, you would stick my hair in ink again."

"Probably."

"It was just my bad luck that they didn't have ball-point pens back then. You would have stabbed me."

"Where do you live now? In Pennsylvania as you started out when you were a little girl?"

"Alaska. Juneau, Alaska."

"Wow! Like it?"

"Love it!"

"Nancy! I really am so glad to be talking to you. This is so unexpected and I'm thrilled."

"It's a dream to talk to you again, Chris. And will you tell Savannah Lane that I'm a big fan of hers? Not a *real* big fan under the conditions that she got *you* and I *didn't*—but I'm just a woman who—when I was a girl—who turned old blank scrapbooks into something wonderful by pasting pictures of movie stars in them—filling them up: Gable and Lombard; Bogart and Bacall; Tracy and was it Katherine Hepburn? And just think a real movie star turned out to be my competition; Savannah Lane of all people. Well, she's beautiful and such a talented singer and dancer and actress and all that and I should never have told you I hated you! I was crazy about you. It was a real girl's crush—and they can be pretty difficult."

"I'm glad you didn't hate me. What a great feeling to know you had a—a crush. I wish I knew it at the time."

"But don't get the idea that it was a yellow Plymouth you were going to drive to the moon. It was a green Chevrolet. I thought about it a thousand times. My heavens! I never even heard of a yellow Plymouth. No one did."

"I did."

No sooner did they hang up with her throwing a fast kiss, when the phone rang again.

"Christopher Straw, Sir."

"Is this the *real* Christopher Straw?"

"Yes, sir. Is this the real—the real—the real Raj Bhavnani?"

"Yes, sir. Yes,sir."

"It's like a miracle requested and answered! Raj! Raj! Raj! We have been going frantic for so long looking for you! Savannah and I have called everyone we could think of calling. We called Voice of America and Air India Radio and asked all kinds of leads we found on Savannah's internet thing and couldn't get hold of you. Not just here in the United States but any number of places in Delhi and you weren't there; that's all. Then we tried almost every big city in India. Where *are* you? *How* are you? Are you okay?"

"Yes, yes. I'm fine. I'm in India and for a while—just a little while—I didn't feel well. A lot of travelling in India. It's like America. A big country. You know; the change of climate, food, all kinds of things that are fine but different. I'm fine now."

"Where are you now?"

"I wish I called but I didn't want to bother you and Savannah. I am not in a big city. I am in Darjeeling—and Christopher, first, do you have an extension phone?"

"Sure. Of course."

"Is Savannah listening?"

"No. She doesn't do that. We don't spy on each other."

"Good, good. I just ask because I want to tell you something in confidence because this is just man-talk."

"What's up? You in trouble?"

"No, no! I'm in heaven! A girl. The most striking, beautiful, gorgeous, exotic, romantic Tibetan girl—beyond any man's imagination. She would make Hugh Hefner go crazy."

"Really?"

"Oh, so very really."

"Raj, you are saying a Tibetan 'girl' not 'woman'. Is this—is she—I mean could she be your—your granddaughter or something?"

"No, no. To me every woman is a girl. When someone calls me a boy I'm not insulted. I have been called 'boy' throughout my life. Why is everyone offended these days? Tara is a girl in everything except years. In years I suppose she's a woman but who cares about technicalities? Anyway, we danced and danced and danced in the shadow of the Himalayan Mountains. It made 'romance' seem like a minor word because this was so much bigger and better.

"Wow! Not bad, Raj. It sounds like you are having a marvelous time."

"This is what life *should* be! And it *is!*"

"Her name is Tara?"

"I thought of your interest in names from *Gone with the Wind*, but I asked her if she was named Tara after seeing *Gone with the Wind* and this Tara is named after the Tibetan Goddess whose name is Tara. She is every man's dream. Not just her looks—but her passion, her entire style. And her dance is beyond words."

"It sounds like you like her."

"That is too minor a word."

"Good for you Raj."

"Something else—"

"Yes?"

"You ever hear of Aldridge Killbrite?"

"Sure. He runs or is the C.E.O. or President or something of Nova Industries in London or right outside of London making all kinds of rockets and boosters, some of them for NASA sending up supplies to the Space Shuttle and I think they make reusable boosters; first stages for missiles as well. They're big. Why do you ask?"

"We played golf together."

"You did? Aldridge Killbrite?"

"Yes, yes!"

"In India?"

"Of course. In Bengaluru. South. Way south. I didn't even know who he was until we started talking. He knew of what I did during the 1962 War here in India and he's in all kinds of businesses and I thought you might have heard of what he's doing in space. When I heard what he did I let him know I knew you. He knew only that you and Savannah Lane were together and he thought you were married. I said that wasn't true but that you and Savannah have been living together for years and I was a friend. He said the next time you were in London to look him up."

"That's very nice but I don't travel overseas much anymore. Those are the old days. But that was good of you, Raj. I think they're going to be doing some work for government, too; some rockets to bring supplies up to the Space Shuttle. Raj, would it be alright if I put Savannah on the line, too? She will be so glad that you're alright. She has been tremendously concerned about you for such a long time. She knows you go your own way but she was truly worried. It has been a long, long time and no one could give us a clue that worked out. Okay if I put her on?"

"I would like that."

When Anna joined the conversation she was breathlessly excited and joyful that Raj seemed to be fine and was calling to tell them he was fine. "Where *are* you and what are you *doing*?"

"Dancing in Darjeeling. I have friends here."

"That's way up there, isn't it?"

"It is. Way up north by the base of the Himalayans."

"That sounds wonderful! You're dancing alright? No need for a cane anymore?"

"No, no. That's done. I put Citizen Cane away and I'm

doing what I used to do on any dance floor I can find. And they have a wonderful one here in Darjeeling! Luxurious! Heavenly!"

"I'm so glad!"

"So am I."

Christopher asked if he would be coming back to the United States soon. He said, "I'll see. I met a girl—a woman up here and I'll just see how things go between us." He cloaked his original enthusiasm since Savannah was now listening to him.

"Good for you, Raj. Bring her here—both of you! There's plenty of space here at the Bahia whenever you can."

When the phone call ended, Chris was somewhat silent.

"Are you okay, honey?" And she quickly added, "Did something he said bother you?"

"Yes."

"What?" Anna asked.

"Remember when you had a premonition?"

"Of course."

"Now I have a premonition."

"You do? What is it?"

"Raj is an artist at telling stories that are not true. I don't think he's in Darjeeling and I don't think he met a woman that has his interest. With all his talents, one of those talents—a major one—is telling tall tales."

Anna nodded slowly while he went on. "I hate to say it but I think you're right. Where do you think he is?"

"I think I know. Not Darjeeling. I just don't believe him. I believe that he's still in India but not Darjeeling. For one thing he gave not one detail about the place. Nothing of detail about one of the most magnificent places in the world at the base of the Himalayan Mountains. The base of Mount Kanchenjunga. No detail about the place. In addition, his voice was sort of gravelly. At least—I don't know—different. My belief, Honey, without any evidence at all is that he is not well. Just a premonition."

"Where do you think he is?"

"Near the Ganges. The river. Raj takes care of himself. It's sacred to be near the Ganges."

Three months later Aldridge Killbrite, the President of Nova Industries in London, sent a letter from one of his offices; this one in Titusville, Florida. He requested that Christopher work for him by teaching a course in his west coast offices near Orange County, California. The course would be under his employ; the officers and staff in a course of study regarding the early days of space from the first ICBM to the first U.S. satellites to the Mercury 7 Astronauts to the entire history of Cape Canaveral's Pad 14 before it became inactive. Most of his officers and staff were too young or even unborn to know those days. Then he added an additional request; that he wants Chris and Savannah to be two of the first passengers of his corporation's non-governmental space vehicle that goes into deep space. There will be no fee as two tickets will be provided by Raj Bhavnani's written request made days before he passed in Varanasi, India.

the curtains close